EVERY

Missing

THING

EVERY

Missing

THING

MARTYN FORD

Text copyright © 2020 by Martyn Ford
All rights reserved.

Published by Thomas & Mercer, Seattle

www.apub.com

Amazon, the Amazon logo, and Thomas & Mercer are trademarks of Amazon.com, Inc., or its affiliates.

ISBN-13: 9781542023788
ISBN-10: 1542023785

Cover design by Ghost Design

Printed in the United States of America

EVERY

Missing

THING

PART ONE
ROBIN CLARKE

Chapter 1

She woke to the sound of crickets and movement in the trees. Something snapped out there, made her flinch. A twig, some leaves. Stepping out of her bedroom, she pulled her dressing gown on and went downstairs. Cool tiles on the kitchen floor, the faint white oven timer, flashing slowly on, then off, on, then off – a power cut, all clocks set to midnight zero. Nothing ticks in this house.

Anna Clarke began her ridiculous late-night rituals. These compulsive things that simply had to be done. She made sure the back door was closed, locked, double locked. Made sure Button had enough water – *he's getting old and sometimes spills it*. Made sure the TV was off, not hissing on standby. She checked these things three times and, when stressed, three times more – just in case.

Finally, she went to check on Robin, sleeping upstairs in the orange glow of her night light. Anna arrived back on the second floor, stepped across the thick new carpet, along the staircase railing and towards the dim warmth from her daughter's bedroom. The door was ajar, as it always is, and she pressed it open with a finger, as she always did. Silent, expensive hinges – wood brushing wool. The art box. The closed curtains. The row of stuffed toys on the shelf – all their eyes glistening.

And an empty bed.

Calm and nodding to herself, Anna stood in silence. There was no cause for panic, no sense in searching the house and calling the police. No reason to run into the garden, desperately screaming her daughter's name, and fall to her knees in the grass and ask an empty sky why, why, why. There was no need for any of that drama. After all, she'd had this nightmare before.

Chapter 2

We see a man walking along the pavement, holding a mobile to his ear. At his side seagulls hop along taut ropes, frayed at the knots, dripping and furred with ocean moss. Boats bob in the dark water, bumping hulls and moving as far as they can from the harbour wall. Men haul crates of fish as they laugh and smoke rolled cigarettes that stay between their lips until they're finished, only to be flicked into the sea for keen-eyed birds to swoop on, inspect and disregard. They squawk. Zooming out, a cafe's window and awning comes into view.

The man is a mosaic of shifting squares – tiny pixels making fractured pictures. Even in this digital form, it's obvious he's slowing down.

This camera, mounted on the corner, pans over the entire scene, zooms in on faces and scans delivery vans coming and going from the old port. It films the gulls, the fishermen, the wet harbour wall. A cyclist bouncing over cobblestones.

And there, the man stops. He's standing still in the middle of the pavement, fellow pedestrians weaving paths around him like water around a rock. With a slow breath, he lowers the phone and looks down into the screen. For almost a minute he holds this exact pose. It's as though he's a statue – a bronze tribute to someone who, years ago, might have been important.

◆   ◆   ◆

There were no cameras in the bathroom where Sam Maguire, unseen and alone, splashed his face and stared at himself in the mirror. He rubbed his eyes and checked his watch – 2.30 p.m. It was strange being back here. Not because of all the changes, but the precision of his memories. Almost photographic. The little details – the chip on the corner of the sink, coarse and dirty now, the bent lock on the cubicle door, the shined tiles at his feet, the moving water in the walls, clunking old pipes to fill a cistern or squirt down the face of the steel urinal. These noises, these smells, these familiar things.

He stepped back out into the main office and towards the interview rooms. Number three was occupied. Inside, Francis Clarke sat at the table with his mouth pressed into his palm, his elbow supporting the weight of his heavy head. It seemed insufficient a word, but Sam, watching him through the glass, would have said he looked unhappy.

'What do you think?' Sam said.

'I think blood on the passenger seat.' Phil passed over a piece of paper. Sam didn't even glance at it.

'Robin's blood?'

Phil Webber – Sam's replacement – was nodding with tired eyes and a mind made up. Behind him the office was busy, phones and printers and warm lamps on every active desk. The overcast sky outside just wasn't cutting it. Felt like night.

'Possibly. Freshly wiped. Right there on the front seat of his shiny new Volvo.'

'Anywhere else?'

'Maybe, they're still swabbing.'

'So why am I here?' Sam asked.

'Are we keeping you from something? Retirement's meant to be relaxing.'

'I was looking at a boat.'

'Really?' Phil frowned. 'I'd have you down as more of a midlife-crisis biker.'

'Oh, I doubt this is the middle of my life.'

'Is that optimism?'

'No.'

'You and Francis . . . you . . . He asked for you.'

'What were his exact words?'

'He said, "I want to talk to Sam."'

'And you said yes? Why?'

'We're bordering on a charge and he's saying nothing to us. What's the harm in giving him what he wants?'

Sam sighed. 'You're bordering on what?'

There was a pause.

'I'm glad you're here.' Phil turned, took a step backwards. 'Do *you* think I look fat?'

Sam had already noticed, so didn't make a show of inspecting him. 'You appear to have gained some weight, yes,' he said. 'It'd benefit your health if you lost a few pounds.'

Laughing, Phil clapped once. 'Oh, Sam, I've missed you so much . . . and in there? Tempting, isn't it? Just a quick one. A white lie. Hell of a lever.'

Sam nodded. 'Does he know you've found blood?'

'No.'

'Can he know?'

'Sure, why not. Tried everything else. He's glued to his story – he wakes up, Robin's gone, that's all he knows.'

'How old is she now?'

'Eight.'

'So, you're thinking what? He'll confess to me?'

Leaning close, Phil whispered, 'What if she's still alive? Shit. What if we find Ethan too?'

Sam felt a surge of something else familiar – anxiety, excitement: pure cortisol, which needed some meaning. *Ethan.* He found plenty for that name – more than most.

'Look, do your best,' Phil said. 'If nothing else, you've always had a keen eye for a lie.'

Then, with a breath, Sam approached the Interview room and opened the door.

◆ ◆ ◆

The film starts with a blank screen – a choir humming in the background. Words fade in over the black. A name. Ethan Clarke. No further prompts are needed – we know Ethan Clarke. We can already see these pictures, hear these words. The documentary could end right here, just three seconds in. Ten-year-old Ethan Clarke, a name synonymous with whatever happened to him. Just as dates soon inhabit their most noted tragedies. Things we see again, on screens, on calendars, real and imagined.

Cut to a TV studio – the voices continue haunting the footage, though their tune is buried now by the thump, thump, thump *of the ten o'clock news.*

'Police are tonight appealing for information following the disappearance of ten-year-old Ethan Clarke, who hasn't been seen—'

The image jumps and flashes to another newsreader.

'. . . in an emotional press conference earlier today, the parents of Ethan Clarke—'

Another – the picture fragments to double vision, jarring colours and fast zooms. The drums continue.

'. . . acres of woodland in the search for any evidence that might—'
More.

'Assisting officers in their search for Ethan Clarke—'
'—a community effort—'

'*Ten-year-old Ethan Clarke*—'

A fast, flickering montage – the name drummed out with beats, on the right side of cheap, but only just. News, papers, hashtags snowing down the screen. The name read in different accents, in different places, at different times. It's all here now, edited and crafted and streamlined in the name of entertainment.

'*A week on, and a reward for information on the whereabouts of*—'

'*Ethan Clarke*—'

'*The disappearance of Ethan Clarke*—'

'*. . . a photo of Ethan Clarke*—'

'*. . . six months down the line, but family and friends remain*—'

'*—hopeful that Ethan Clarke*—'

'*—could still be found alive, despite vanishing a year ago today*—'

'*Asking again, have you seen*—'

'*—Ethan Clarke - a renewed appeal on the five-year anniversary*—'

'*—in a now dwindling search for Ethan Clarke*—'

'*Ethan Clarke*—'

'*Ethan Clarke*—'

The montage moves now to a quiet street at night – the background pulse of the news jingle falls as the choir comes into shot. Hundreds of people, holding candles at their chests, swaying and singing hymns over a glowing shrine of framed photographs and flowers. Fading transitions. Tears. Strangers cry in firelight for a child they've never met. Now about three minutes of previews – snippets of talking heads, detectives, members of the public, the Clarkes on a stage, speaking to the camera, speaking to us – and then a final, single beat thuds, echoing through a long silence as the screen turns black again.

The voiceover is stern. Direct. Serious.

'*On August the twelfth, two thousand and ten, a ten-year-old boy disappeared from his family home. To this day, his whereabouts remain a mystery. In this film, I will explore how the investigation unfolded,*

9

showing unseen footage and shedding light on the question we've spent almost a decade asking: whatever happened to Ethan Clarke?'

Renowned journalist and filmmaker Daniel Aiden is of Welsh descent, but speaks the Queen's English – his amiable voice carries authority, conviction. He stands in front of a house on a quiet street with nothing but leaves and parked cars for company. This award-winning, feature-length documentary leaps through time, it drifts forwards and backwards to show us everything we've seen before. Everything we already know.

But Sam tried to put the sensationalism out of his mind. The urge to blame Francis Clarke had been difficult for the world's media to resist. Tomorrow, when they hear it's happened again – when they know the Clarkes have been struck by familiar tragedy once more, what sort of conclusions will the papers splash? The past eight years had seen accusations of culpability swatted with swift, expensive legal action and the voice of reason. What would that voice say now? He was not looking forward to the coverage.

As he stepped inside the interview room and made eye contact with Francis, Sam hid his adrenaline behind calm movement – beneath the steady weight and heavy gait of feigned routine. Was he about to learn the truth? Was this the day he'd been imagining?

'Sam.' Francis, half standing, returned to his seat when shown a hand and a nod.

'It's been a while,' Sam said, sitting opposite.

The room had a substantial recording device on the table against the wall, and a CCTV camera in the top-right corner at the back. It smelled like stationery, school-desk wood, dust. Years ago, when this was Sam's place of work, he would have had a pen, a notepad, a sense of duty anchored to the law – instead of the quiet mania that drove him here today.

'They told me you'd retired,' Francis said. 'I just . . . the other detective. He's speaking as though . . . as though I've done something.' There was fear in his eyes. It was real.

'Have you?' Sam asked.

Leaning forwards in his chair, Francis whispered, 'Look at me, look.' He turned his hands, showed his palms. His slight Canadian accent had survived – certain words lured it out.

Sam stayed silent.

'What exactly are you asking here?'

Still, Sam just blinked.

'No,' Francis said, his voice teetering on a precipice, tears there, waiting below. 'I haven't done anything. I haven't hurt Robin. I have no idea where she is . . .'

'You know what they're going to say,' Sam said. 'You know what this looks like.'

'I do, yes.'

'You and Anna, you are now the common denominator.'

'But I haven't . . . I promise you . . . I swear . . .'

Wincing, Francis touched his cheek with shaking fingers. He seemed older than he was – grey hairs above his ears, crow's feet and a broader face than Sam remembered. Age had filled him out, tanned his skin like leather. But those pale canine eyes, that husky-blue stare – it hadn't changed at all.

'They found blood,' Sam said.

'What?'

'In the boot of your car.' He watched him closely.

Pupils darted, searching the room for an explanation – for an answer, a word, a sound, anything. 'I . . . please. Just, for a moment, think what this is like for me. Can you imagine the pain we're going through? Can you imagine what it feels like to lose Robin as well?

For this to happen to us *again*? Just . . . please . . . even if you don't believe me, please just *imagine* the horror if I am telling the truth.'

Sam stared at him for a long, long time. In any other scenario, such sustained eye contact could only end in conflict or love. And then he sighed. 'That was a lie,' Sam added. 'I said they'd found blood in the boot of your car, but it was on the passenger seat. You know how I feel about lying. I am sorry.'

Rolling his head back, Francis let out a single, desperate whimper. 'You're testing me, fine. Good. Did I pass?'

'Let's move to the other option. Whoever took Ethan has come back for Robin. And they want it to look like you're to blame.'

'Well . . .' Francis shrugged – hopeless jitters. 'Yeah, I mean . . . I guess?'

'Listen to me, I think they want to charge you with murder.'

Francis covered his mouth and tears finally trickled down his cheeks, as though he'd been holding them back for the sharpest cut. 'Does that mean they're going to stop looking for her?'

'No, of course not. But they will push you for a confession. They will try and make the Ethan case fit too. Plenty who want that to be true.'

'You *know* I didn't kill Ethan.'

Nodding, Sam echoed those words. 'I know.'

There was no one on earth who knew more about the disappearance of Ethan Clarke than Sam Maguire. The tabloids, the comment sections, the supermarket queues – they all had their theories, ranging from plausible to downright supernatural. But they were all wrong. Sam didn't know what had happened to Ethan Clarke, but he had a long list of things that *didn't* happen to him. Murdered by his parents was one of them.

But the list for Robin was short – options constrained by physics and little else.

'Tell me everything you can remember about the last week,' he said. 'Every interaction with her. Tell me where she has been, what she has done, every single banal question she has asked you.'

This account took another thirty minutes or so – he did his best to furnish Sam with an enormous amount of information. When it was over, Francis gestured around the interview room and said, 'And now I'm childless, and I'm here.'

'I'd advise you not to watch the news or read any papers,' Sam said. 'They won't be kind.'

For a while, Francis couldn't do anything but look at the floor. He held his fist to his lips – maybe vomit was the next port of call for his body. It was, after all, dealing with a calibre of psychological trauma you only find in textbooks, in test cases you'd scarcely believe.

Then he glanced back up. 'Please,' he whispered. 'Please help me. Please find Robin.'

Outside in the corridor, Sam filled a plastic cup with chilled water, which bubbled and glugged out of the cooler. He went to Phil's office.

'Well, you buy that?' Phil said, sitting on the edge of his desk, reading something on his phone. 'He pass your little test?'

It was inconvenient for Sam to admit that, yes, he had scored high. Francis Clarke, contrary to the evidence, contrary to the vehement certainty riding over the horizon towards them like cavalry at full charge, was telling the truth.

With a single, tired nod, Sam confirmed it.

'You know what I think?' Phil said, in that uniquely confrontational tone of his. 'I think you've been searching for an answer all these years, and you simply don't like the one you've found.'

'Francis is not—'

'You know what we know. This guy ticks every box.'

Weary, calm and honest, always honest, Sam blinked. 'I'm not saying he's a saint. I'm not saying he's a nice man. I'm just stating a fact. Francis Clarke hasn't killed either of his children.'

'Then tell me.' Phil placed his mobile on his desk, folded his arms and shrugged. 'Where are they?'

Chapter 3

Across town, comfortably covered by thousands of CCTV cameras, there's a disused bus stop with a smashed roof and an empty billboard box. Here, a boy, maybe twelve, thirteen years old, drenched and alone, is sitting on the slanted plastic seats. Cars pass, but none of them stop.

After ten minutes, he steps out into the rain, looks to the sky, back down, flicks his hood up on to his head, and begins to walk. A pair of football boots, tied at the laces, dangle, bump and spin from the rear of his rucksack. The lens tracks him almost entirely without a blind spot, right up until Kendell Street, where he unknowingly enjoys almost two minutes out of sight as he travels through the underpass. Rare nowadays. He arrives in the viewfinder of a council CCTV camera erected at the edge of the estate's play equipment. Now he's soaked to the skin, the frustration washed away, replaced with bog-standard sadness. At the end of the road, no more than three pixels tall, he pushes open a front-garden gate and steps out of the frame.

Sam pulled up at the house, groaning and weighing options. He had driven slowly along Kendell Street, checking the face of every pedestrian he passed. As he suspected, he was too late.

'Fuck,' he whispered to himself, squeezing the steering wheel, pulling at it. Squeaking leather, strong metal. A sigh. He wondered if he should just drive off – but that would look even worse. Calming down and nodding, he decided to face the music.

The rain had stopped now, which seemed somehow unjust – if anyone should get wet, it should be him. He strode over a fresh puddle, black on the tarmac, and clicked the gate open, wiping his damp hand on his jeans as he approached the front step.

Two knocks on the door – the door he himself chose all those years ago. He owned the first key, he planted this flourishing rose bush, he laid the slabs at his feet, *he*—

A shadow behind the glass. The door swung open and rolled eyes then a turned back greeted him. Marilyn walked away, up the narrow hall – it seemed like apathy, but Sam knew better. This was good old-fashioned anger.

Following her inside, he pushed the door closed and took off his shoes.

'Is he here?' Sam asked, arriving in the kitchen. There she was, still with her back to him. The smell of her cooking, just heat, no flavour yet. That smell. Not quite home, but doing the same things to his mind. Like the false tang of aspartame. Empty. Lying on your tongue.

'Yes, about half an hour ago.'

That too was a lie. The times didn't tally, but Sam decided not to bite. 'I'll go and apologise.'

'He doesn't want to see you,' she said, opening a packet of pasta and checking the hob dial. *Normality, look, look at the normality. Look how no one gives a shit about you any more.*

Before Sam could call this assumption out, before he could say that Freddie can speak for himself, that he doesn't need his mother to tell him what to think, a small voice from the doorway repeated the words.

'She's right. I don't want to see you.'

And, with that, tired teenage footsteps in the hall, on the stairs – a door above not quite slammed, but most definitely closed.

Sam sighed and blinked. 'I got called to the station,' he explained. 'You see the news?'

'Yes, I have,' she said, still cooking, never looking at him. 'I wasn't at all shocked to hear it. If anything, I'm surprised it took them this long to do it again.'

'Marilyn.'

'Guess that wraps things up then? Case closed?'

Sam shook his head, but she didn't see it. 'Sadly, no.'

Something clinked on the kitchen worktop and, for the first time, she turned to face him. 'Then maybe we'll drop this little arrangement? David can pick Freddie up from football next week. You don't need to worry about it any more.'

'Marilyn, please.'

'Look at you,' she said. 'You're still not getting it. You chose your favourite years ago. You know what hurts most? You know what stings? The one who's actually *alive*, the boy crying upstairs right now, he understands that he comes second.'

'They called me in to speak to Francis. Webber and co. think Robin might be—'

'Ohhh. Sorry, sorry, I spoke too soon,' Marilyn said, tilting her head – a dramatic *of course*. 'Freddie is in *third* place now, got it.'

Sam blinked. He looked over her shoulder, out the window. Above the still shrubs, the top of the fence, then more leaves and finally a wide strip of sky. A thin, slow covering of clouds passing behind black telegraph wires – maybe ten, fifteen cables, sprawling out from a main mast across the street, every line slack and birdless. Always birdless here.

'It's not that simple.'

'But it is, Sam. You either forgot because you don't care enough, or you remembered and felt something else was more important. Which one do you think would upset him least?'

He'd become the cliché of a disappointing father – it was just, as she might say, so typical. Would Freddie recall these memories in years to come on the pillow of a girl who says she loves him? Or, more likely, would he shrug and whisper, 'Not much to tell really . . .'? Is that worse? To fall away into a void so absolute that not even memories can find you?

'Look,' Sam sighed. 'I'm not playing this game. Please can you just tell him I'm sorry and I'll see him on Friday.'

Marilyn shook her head – it was authentic this time. There was real pity on her face. It wasn't meant to insult him. This was just how she felt.

'Oh, Sam,' she said. 'What are you going to do when they find out what happened to those Clarke kids? You'll have nothing left.'

Through the webcam on his desk, we see his entire open-plan apartment. An old TV, a scruffy kitchen and a sofa that'd be better suited outside. This place is sacred, secret and, peering into the rear of the flat, we can see why. The back wall hosts photographs, newspaper clippings, even X-rays and receipts. Photocopied evidence – much of which the man has no business possessing. Another desk filled with folders and files and junk. The hoardings of obsession.

There are just two framed photographs of his son, of young Freddie, taking pride of place on the breakfast bar, behind a pile of unopened mail. One in his football gear, holding up a trophy. The second picture taken when he was younger, maybe three, sitting on the man's shoulders in a foreign country.

And yet, if we were to count, we would see twenty-six photographs of Ethan Clarke visible from here. How many more he has tucked away in boxes and on hard drives is anyone's guess.

The man is home now, microwaving some food and searching under his desk for something. Paper spills out as he pulls documents from a container. When the dinner drone stops, with a triumphant beep-beep, he stands and turns. He's drinking white rum from a tumbler and, having finished eating an indiscernible dish from a flimsy plastic bowl, he drinks two more.

For a while he is out of sight, only to return ten minutes later, wearing just a damp towel. He approaches the laptop and leans into it. For the first time, we get a close-up of his face – his hair slicked back, his skull and jawbone visible under worn, stubbled skin. Beneath wet eyelashes, his irises are dark brown, maybe even black. But perhaps it's the lighting, as the room barely exists behind him, faint blue and white from the glowing screen. He presses a couple of keys, almost looking directly at the camera, and it's clear that, years ago, many would have considered him handsome. Two tiny squares of light in the centre of his pupils. He blinks. It's a strange blink, more of a twitch. His arms and chest have that taut sinew which comes from a once-muscular physique left to wither and shrink. He blinks. Standing up straight, exposing his torso. A slight beer belly is beginning to form – visible when he turns side on and checks his phone. Then he walks away. The man's frame looks most neglected from behind.

Ethan Clarke has cost him many things – a marriage, a career, his relationship with his son. It'd be quite fair to add his body to the bill.

'Yeah?' he says, his mobile against his cheek. 'I'm getting it now . . . I know . . . all of it . . . I'm not . . . No, Phil, listen . . . I know . . . yes . . . yes, that too. I'll bring it all . . .' He looks back into his laptop. 'Probably about five.'

◆ ◆ ◆

The news was outrageous. Sam had seen some hype in his time, but this was something else. It was a parody of itself – the theme of the radio report was how widespread the coverage had become – a house of mirrors, like the media turning inside out. He listened as he drove and, more than once, reached out to switch stations, or even turn it off. But each attempt saw his hand stop at the dial and then return to the steering wheel.

Ethan Clarke's disappearance was said, again and again, to be the most-reported missing-child case in history – virtually all others, past and present, were set against this benchmark. The idea that, in almost identical circumstances, the *same* family had suffered the *same* domestic calamity nearly a decade on seemed too good to be true. It didn't even occur to the presenter to dwell on the possibility, and the sheer implicit dread, that the Clarkes were in no way to blame. They even pulled some young statistician on to ponder the odds of a child going missing – unlikely was the answer. He said peanut allergies posed a bigger risk. When asked about the chances of losing *two children*, he sighed and added, 'We're in the realms of absolute . . . well . . . other factors are clearly at play.'

Other factors are clearly at play. Sam repeated those words in his shaking head. Despite being meaningless, this guy's mathematical sound bite did the rounds for most of the day, before suddenly disappearing later that evening – perhaps a qualified statistician phoned in and ruined the fun.

The Hallowfield Criminal Investigation Department operated out of a building called Parkside Heights, which sat at the end of a long straight road – the third exit off a roundabout with signs that prominently said the route went nowhere. And yet, at peak times, a steady stream of cars came down that stretch of pitted tarmac, until the drivers realised they'd made a mistake, turned around and disappeared off into the world again. Sam used to joke that he did something similar, but took twenty years to escape.

He pulled to a stop in the underground car park, climbed out and popped the boot. It hissed open and he lifted a heavy plastic box. His keys slid on the lid as he shuffled inside and up the narrow stairwell to the main room, where he set it down on an empty desk near the doorway to Phil's office. He was on his feet and stepping forwards – a radio whispered the news behind him. Jutting a thumb over his shoulder, Phil parroted the statistician's absurd comments.

'What the fuck are you even saying?' Sam asked.

'I'm *saying* it's not likely.'

A slow blink gave him time to calm down. 'It's happened. You throw a hundred darts at a wall, draw a circle around one and yell bullseye,' he said. 'Don't get lost, Phil, don't see what you already believe.'

'Believe what you see.'

A young voice was approaching. Sam turned. 'Isabelle, Sam, Sam, Isabelle.'

She was maybe thirty, with slender hands and broad shoulders – feminine, but obviously a fan of the gym. Strong and small. Low body fat. Her hair was straight, neat and all the same colour – a dark, dyed brunette. It was tied back in a loose ponytail.

'This all of it?' she asked, dragging the plastic container across the desk. Side on, her nose had a slight bump in the bone – perhaps it had been broken in the past. Thick eyebrows, shaded skin around the lashes, Caucasian parents – but possibly some Mediterranean from a prior generation.

Sam took his keys off the lid, then unclipped it. 'Everything tangible,' he said. 'Things that matter most weigh the least.'

'*Things that matter most weigh the least,*' Phil echoed. 'You'll hear a lot of that sort of stuff from this one.' He patted Sam's biceps. Sam slowly turned, looked at him, then returned to the box.

'Can you run me through it?' Isabelle picked up a folder. On her left wrist she wore a thin, weathered leather bracelet.

'You?'

Laughing, she creased her chin and frowned – as though she'd have been justified to take offence.

'I mean,' Sam added, '*just* you?'

'Remember how tight things were?' Phil said. 'Remember how there's no money? Well, imagine that but twice as bad.'

'What else are all these people working on?' Sam gestured into the main office.

'You can't see the twenty officers out there combing the woods,' he said. 'Or the thermal cameras flying overhead. We have divers at the bottom of the fucking quarry, Sam.'

'What are you hoping to find down there?'

Phil took a long breath. 'If you were me, would you do it all again? I know it's an inconvenience, but if you can step outside of your little bubble for just five minutes and at least *consider* reality.'

Sam almost smiled.

'We'll go over everything,' Isabelle said, in a gentle voice – as though he was in need of comforting. Like a child who's convinced there's a monster in the room. 'We're not just ticking boxes.'

'You *are* just ticking boxes. You're literally looking for a corpse.'

'Sam.'

'Just say it. What do you think has happened to Robin?'

Phil stepped closer. 'Honestly? Francis killed her and hid the body,' he whispered. 'Is that direct enough? Maybe he did the same to Ethan. Or maybe the stress of the last eight years pushed him over the edge. Maybe not. I don't know. But we're not wasting another decade pissing about with your theories – this is coming to an end soon.'

'Francis called it in,' Sam said. 'He reported Ethan and he reported Robin. He kickstarted the coverage – the whole campaign was because of *him*. If I'd just killed my kid, you know who I wouldn't welcome on board? The world's media.'

'Because someone who kills their children *wouldn't* do something irrational?'

'Again, why am I here?' Sam said. 'What do you want with all this shit if you're sure?'

'Contingency. Hard to build a case without a body.'

Looking out of the window, Sam let this image settle. But it wouldn't.

Eight years old, curly blonde hair, as photogenic as her brother. Somewhere now, somewhere scared or dead, but somewhere. Although wary of certainty, Sam felt sure their fates were aligned – that whatever had happened to Ethan had now happened to her. It had been years since he imagined finding him alive – but *Robin*'s survival was still on this side of plausible. And if their fates *were* aligned . . . a strange optimism. It lasted less than a second but, in his mind, young Robin Clarke raised her brother from the dead. Would he be that ten-year-old from all the pictures – the child he'd never met, yet thought about more than any other? Or would he be . . . what . . . still a teenager? For all his thinking on the topic, it struck Sam that, despite the easy sum, he had lost track of Ethan's precise age. Reason had stripped him of all the early fantasies that he was more than charred bones. Even the digital artist's impressions hadn't ventured beyond fourteen years old. Ethan Clarke would be eighteen. Eighteen or dust.

'I'm going to swing by the house,' Isabelle said. 'Have you got a number I can get you on, if I've got any questions?'

All of Sam's attention seemed to be on the window – his eyes wide, staring, staring and—

He blinked. 'Yeah, sure.'

'Fuck it, go with her.' Phil flicked his arm again. 'It might even do you good.'

The house. That large detached property – visible from above, from below, even from an opposite window in a neighbour's bedroom, commandeered by an affable photographer who charmed his way into possibly the best vantage point on the street. It's a mansion. The shallow, zoomed picture he takes of it is good – the entire building is in the frame, set perfectly between trees with a backdrop of clear afternoon sky and a media circus hazed out in the foreground. The Clarke residence will become a familiar sight once again. We should get used to seeing it.

Chapter 4

That underground car park, camera A, camera B, camera A, camera B – switching feeds every five seconds. The man strides next to Isabelle and follows her round to an unmarked vehicle. He tries to open the passenger door, but can't. Then two yellow flashes from the indicator lights, and the clunk of the lock, silent for us.

'Better safe than sorry, hey,' Sam said, climbing in.

'You never know – some of these PCs.' Isabelle started the engine and lowered the handbrake. 'My headphones went missing last year. And the milk situation in the office is a pint away from all-out war.'

As they drove up the ramp and out into the light, Sam clicked in his seat belt and glanced through the window, instinctively checking the road was clear. When he turned back to his right, he looked down at Isabelle's lap. 'You lock the car in a police station but you don't wear a seat belt? You know what a dead stop does to a human body? Want to run through some physics before we talk about Ethan?'

Smiling, Isabelle tugged her seat belt with one hand and pressed it home. She seemed as though she was about to say something, but Sam spoke first.

'You're tempted to make a joke – maybe "thanks, Dad"? You don't need to.'

'I was actually going to tell you that it's always on before I leave the car park – this is private land.' Isabelle was well spoken – Sam reckoned her education cost a fair bit more than he could afford.

'Legality aside, plenty of bad things can happen in that time.'

'You sound more like my mother – she was the cautious one.'

Sam noticed the use of past tense as he reached inside his jacket and pulled out a packet of cigarettes. 'I'm going to smoke in here, will that upset you?'

'Would you stop if I said yes?'

'I don't know, try.'

'It's fine.'

Cupping his mouth out of rekindled habit, Sam sparked his lighter. He tapped the window switch with his middle finger, opening it an inch. Then he held the packet out for Isabelle, who just glanced back at him in silence. Sam shrugged, and put them in his jacket pocket.

'Maybe we should talk biology first?' she said, opening the passenger window another inch. 'If calculating risk is your cup of tea.'

The car came on to the roundabout, away from that dead end behind them.

'Oh, I can handle a steady decline – that's part of the game. It's the sudden catastrophic damage I worry about. The quick stuff, you know, out of the blue. Can't be left helpless.'

'A stroke tends to come on fast.'

Sam blew out a huge drag, then held the cigarette between his thumb and forefinger. He looked at the ember and thought of that blackened strip of dead lung plastered across the packet. The ragged

26

piece of zombie heaving precious oxygen inside him, every second of every day. 'True,' he said. 'As long as one hand still works.'

'I think you'd feel differently if you'd seen one of these steady declines in action.'

'Your cautious mother?'

'Aptly, throat cancer, long bout of treatment – something to avoid.'

'I've seen plenty of final years. My brother was a doctor. I know exactly what to take, and exactly how much.'

'To cure cancer?'

'In a sense. Fistful of pentobarbital, eased in with some weapon-grade morphine, topped off with your drink of choice.' He blew out some more smoke. 'Just fall asleep smiling like a lazy cat on a lazy Sunday. Risk of vomiting them up if you're prone to such things, but do it in a long bath and that's no issue. Just make sure you haven't got visitors for the next few hours. Post a letter to the authorities, if you've got close friends or family who might get curious. Hanging is the most common, particularly for men. Can't say that appeals though. In the States, obviously it's guns.' Sam put two fingers against his temple, then pointed them at Isabelle. 'How about you?'

Frowning, she cast an eye his way. 'I . . . I don't spend time thinking about how I'd kill myself.'

'You should.' Sam lifted the cigarette against the whistling glass and the ash flew clean off. 'The alternative is checking out like your dear mother. Doubt that was a festival of smiles.'

'Fuck, man. Jesus.'

'You're what – thirty?'

'Yeah. On the money, birthday's next week.'

'Well, you're done growing, terminal decline now. Your body's treading water. Might as well go under on your terms.'

'Shit,' Isabelle said. 'You *are* fun. I can't say they didn't warn me about you.'

Sam took a final drag, then poked the butt out of the window – the embers exploded in the wind and bounced, sparking orange on the fast road behind them. 'You think, one day, honesty won't be taboo?'

The next five minutes or so were spent in total silence, bar the engine and the rhythmic *thrum, thrum, thrum* of passing motorway lights – still too early for them. Isabelle just drove, Sam just looked out of the window at the cars, at the trees, at the rolling fields and slow dusk clouds – wide sheets of pink and red and colours he couldn't name. A Malibu sunset, the kind he'd seen on horizons over still water, carved by the wide hull of the *Coriolis*. The kind you see in memories, on postcards. Alive and familiar. Incongruous here, above Hallowfield's concrete and agriculture. Sam put his hands on his lap and pulled his mind from the past. He should think about Robin Clarke. Pink. Pink like the pyjamas she was wearing when she was . . . what? Taken? Picked up? Killed in her bed?

'You want to know what else they say about you?' Isabelle asked, as she checked her mirrors and pulled off the motorway.

'Not really,' Sam said. 'But if you'd feel more comfortable speaking than not, I'm happy for that to be the topic.'

'They say you're obsessed with Ethan Clarke. Deranged.'

Sam blinked and tilted his head – it was a fair comment. 'I can see how someone might think that.'

He noticed Isabelle's posture as she drove – it was perfect. Stately. Immovably calm. Such composure can't be feigned. Sam knew all the things we cannot hide. This girl really was the embodiment of balance.

'Why this one? Plenty of missing kids out there. If you're trying to make the world a better place . . .'

'Is that what we're doing?' Sam glanced out of the window again.

'If not that, then what? What could matter more?'

'The truth.'

Isabelle thought for a moment. 'So . . . we're . . . we're pursuing knowledge.'

Blinking, Sam turned and faced straight ahead. 'Exactly. That's exactly what we're doing.'

The car came to a T-junction, halted at a red light.

'And once we know everything, then what?'

'Well, then we'd be gods,' Sam said.

There was a long pause.

'Have you been drinking?' Isabelle asked.

Sam felt his eyes smile, his ears might have lifted slightly, but his mouth stayed still.

And now for the pain – the full-frontal, close up agony of Anna Clarke. Mid-forties, pretty – lucky with genes as well as lifestyle. That healthy, wealthy skin. We've seen her countless times before, but we've never seen her happy. Today she's tearful, fleeting, stepping across a driveway, shielding her blotched face from camera flashes. An older man is helping her into a car. He doesn't look at us – as though we're not even here. He holds a bag to his chest and pushes a photographer away. Someone is shouting a question, but we only hear the tail end of it. The last word is 'Robin'. Anna adjusts her sunglasses and pulls the car door shut. We move closer, trying to make her out through the tinted window, now just a metre away from the older man. He doesn't like this intrusion. We've crossed a line. He shoves us – we hear gasps. The camera is lurching up and showing us the pink sky, then quickly

*left to a bush and a wall and, when the shaking stops, when we look
back, we see the older man is inside the car and it's moving down the
driveway and it's gone.*

◆　◆　◆

Text glowed on Isabelle's phone, held on the dashboard. 'Can you
read that to me,' she said.

Sam frowned. 'Why?'

'The law. I'm driving.'

'Right . . .' He took the mobile. 'Says they've . . . they've moved
Mrs Clarke. She's not at the house any more.'

'Good.' Isabelle nodded. 'Why not do it sooner?'

'New blood. Cordoned off the whole place now.'

There must have been more than a hundred people at Orchard
Court, mostly TV crews, gathered at the police barriers. Uniformed
officers, like fluorescent sculptures, stood on guard, hands clasped
together at their waists, keeping the throng on the road. Occasionally
the figures came alive – pointing, or leaning to speak into their
shoulder radios, turning away from the press as they did so.

Isabelle pulled into the property's side drive, opened her window
and exchanged pleasantries with one of the men. They laughed at an
inside joke as he waved them into the busy scene. A space had been
set aside for vehicles on a patch of concrete which ran across the
front of the garden, hidden by the tall walls and well-kept hedges.

Climbing from the car, Sam surveyed the grounds. He hadn't
been to the house for a long time, had only seen its changes in
photos. It was significantly larger than it used to be, with two exten-
sions that almost doubled its footprint. He agreed it was odd they
hadn't relocated – instead they chose to live here, the last place
they saw their son, for the eight years following his disappearance.
Perhaps moving on physically also seemed impossible without the

truth – their ticket both into and out of grief. Here though, in this house of fresh horror, it was clear they were well-off. Rich in all the ways that didn't matter. They could afford a gardener, an automatic gate, a place to hide from all the cameras that, before today, had just started to lose interest in them.

But by some vital measure, they could not afford to leave.

Forensic officers in white overalls, dust masks and purple gloves were preparing equipment at the side of the building, setting up lights, a tent over the front of the garage. Sam followed Isabelle through a designated path towards the rear entrance. As he went, he glanced to his right and into the garage – a 4 x 4 receiving meticulous attention. And, closer, there were two yellow evidence markers on the tarmac. An officer crouched over one of them, held out a camera and took a photograph with a powerful flash.

We see a tiny plastic eye. Stark and vivid and cast hot white with the kind of clarity that nature only achieves in storms. The eye of a teddy, torn from its body a pale brown thread instead of an optic nerve. A wider shot reveals its location. Dead centre in the otherwise empty driveway.

Placed there, Sam thought, stepping inside. *Not dropped*. He relived it all. The initial optimism, the steady beat of logic and finally the dull inevitability of unknowable things. After a cursory tour around the house, which was being swabbed, photographed, preened with tweezers and suspicion, Isabelle and Sam arrived at Robin's bedroom. They weren't allowed inside – as with an exhibit in a museum, they could look as long as they wanted, but they must never touch. Never step beyond the velvet ropes. Or, here, through the invisible screen built by the glare of two busy forensic officers crouched behind a chest of drawers.

Her duvet cover was twisted, her pillow upright against the wall. Plain in style – no Disney motif, no princesses, just floral stitching at the seams. Whoever chose the decor cared about aesthetics – this room had been designed. Some childhood shone through though. Plastic stars and a half moon on the ceiling were, thanks to the closed curtains, starting to glow green above the bed. There was a box of pastels, pencils and paints – *creative being*, Sam thought, *the default setting for all children*. And a standalone chalkboard hosted doodles and the words 'I can fly' in young, unjoined handwriting. Sam looked across the carpet, up to the wall. A window. No breeze. Closed. The door, then. He passed his eyes along the frame and back down to the skirting board. Nothing visible.

'Anna turned in at about midnight,' Isabelle said. 'Robin sound asleep. Come three a.m., she wakes up and finds an empty bed. Exact same situation as Ethan.'

'Almost,' Sam added. 'Ethan's bed was made.'

They checked a few more rooms then went back downstairs. In the kitchen, Sam pointed at the oven – the timer was flashing slowly, on, then off, on, then off. A row of zeros.

'Power cut,' she said. 'Something tripped the switch.'

'Alarm on the back door . . .' He turned to the electric control panel.

'Not triggered.'

Outside, Isabelle and Sam wandered down the back garden, which ended with a wide hedge and a tasteful wrought-iron gate. Without touching, he peered over, left, right, up and down a long footpath. A rural alleyway, just for the four houses on this street. Beyond it were fields and trees. The very finest edge of suburbia. It was quiet here, away from the house, away from the whispering radios and massing crowds. Just evening birds and moving leaves.

'Feel familiar?' Isabelle asked.

Sam nodded. *Terribly so.* 'Why do we remember the past?'

Her attention was on the house. 'I don't know, but I'm sure you're going to tell me.'

'We remember the past so we can handle the future. That's it. Our subconscious does all the work – memories have no place in waking hours. Every second we spend reliving a memory without choosing to is a form of psychosis. If you live in the past, you're lost, trapped in yourself.'

'Sure, OK.'

'That's what consciousness is. Observing the chaos and finding order.' Sam stared up the fields, thinking aloud. 'We don't even see most of what we look at. We're just redrafting an internal model. We're just logging anomalies.'

'Yeah, pretty good, but it's going to need some work if you're putting it on a bumper sticker . . .'

'The past is order; the future is chaos. We're on the front line. The truth is our only weapon.'

'Better.'

'You asked, in the car, why I didn't focus on other cases.'

Isabelle turned now, keen, interested. That solid balanced posture, all lined up to listen.

'When Ethan went missing, I was first to interview Anna. She was upset, as you can imagine. I remember, standing in their kitchen, maybe trying to offer comfort, I don't know. But she made me promise. And I'm still there, at that breakfast bar, telling Anna Clarke I will find her son.'

'Why did you say it?'

Sam frowned and looked Isabelle in the eyes. 'Because it's true.'

The gate squealed for half a second as he pushed it open with the end of a biro. 'Where are they all?' he asked. 'Why is no one down here?'

'They're thinking whatever happened it happened in the house and the garage.'

'If you were an intruder, where would you come from?'

'I don't think they're looking for an intruder.'

Sam walked carefully down the narrow footpath, stepping through the grass and avoiding the dusty track. Not far along he was at the rear of their next-door neighbour's property, where—

We fade in with a high-pitched whir and see a shadow, passing right to left, along the path. Movement behind the hedgerow. We record it.

Arriving at another gate, Sam paused. This one was open, and he peered up towards the neighbour's house. Smaller than the others on the street, but still a mansion by anyone's standards. Their garden was cluttered though, with rusting machines sitting in beds of long grass, old tools and a dried pond guarded by gnomes, two of which were broken. Tiny insects, like living dust, buzzed in the remaining patches of sunlight. A washing line connected the house to a shed – white sheets shimmered, breathing in the breeze.

Sam sighed, turned and started walking back the way he'd come. But, blinking, he stopped. Something there, on that tree, in that garden – it glistened at him. A small box. He leaned sideways and, again, the light caught a tiny orb of glass reflecting the evening sun. A lens, like a rifle scope, like the last thing you ever see.

It was a camera. And it was looking right at him.

Chapter 5

Like a child with no concept of trespassing, Sam walked into the garden, straight up to the tree. He crouched and inspected the item. A plastic cube, small and flat, tied to the trunk with orange baling twine. It was painted green and grey – a camouflage design.

'Can I help you?' A voice at his side. He had noticed the light changing, but didn't bother to look up.

'What is this?' Sam asked.

'Excuse me?'

'This thing, what is it?' Standing again, he finally took his attention away from the object.

The old man had a thin head of white hair, tied back in a ponytail. A slim, clean-shaven Father Christmas, with none of the festive cheer.

'It's a wildlife camera,' he said, somewhere between angry and confused.

'Just films down your garden?'

'Well, no, it's motion sensitive. Something moves, it records it. Who are you?'

'It's filming now.'

'Yes, you're moving.'

'How does it work? Where's the footage?'

'It's . . . it's connected to our Wi-Fi. It's all on my computer.' The man seemed to take pride in this – at least enough to distract him from his previous concern. 'Mostly foxes, sometimes deer. I even get a notification on my phone in the mornings – tells me if there was any activity.' He took his mobile from his pocket, holding it in his frail fingers like it was his most prized possession.

Sam gestured for him to hand it over. Frowning, the man looked over his shoulder, back towards his house, as though he was saying, *Can you believe this guy?* to an audience that wasn't there.

'*Who are you?*'

'Sam. Check your notifications – see if there was anything on Wednesday night.' A long pause. 'Please,' he added. Not in frustration, but total absence of mind. He just hadn't thought to say that word.

'What exactly is . . . is this about the Clarkes?' the man asked, as he laboriously unlocked his phone with his index finger. Freddie was right, it was irritating to watch old people use technology. Was this how he saw Sam? 'Yeah, three pieces of film. First at 10.04, second at 2.30, third at 2.49.'

'Show me.'

Wildlife footage. First, a video gathered at 10.04 p.m. The frame suddenly alive with grey night vision – bright unseen light illuminating the end of the garden. Moonlit in tone, invisible to anything moving out here. The film features a fox, which slides low under the hedge, then creeps across the grass to the waterless pond. Marble eyes reflect back at us – absurdly bright, almost demonic. The fox sniffs the broken gnomes and scratches itself with a hind leg. On fast-forward now, the blasé creature zips right to left, sits for a few seconds, left then right

again – it loiters, twitching in the quick footage, then disappears. We fade to black.

The second piece of film is much shorter – it starts with nothing more than a shadow triggering the motion sensor at 2.30 a.m. Recording now – the slight movement of something passing left to right along the path at the bottom of the garden. Something tall behind that thick hedge. A person. Sixty seconds of nothing and then, again, it fades out.

The third, captured nineteen minutes later, is the same but in reverse. The shadow passes right to left and, as before, there's a minute of nocturnal tranquillity before the camera stops recording.

'And no one's spoken to you about this?' Sam asked, watching and rewatching the videos.

'Nope,' the man said in his spacious kitchen – open-plan and visible from the living room. 'I see all the commotion though. Just steered clear. Didn't think to check the camera.'

They've not even knocked on doors yet, Sam thought, shaking his head. But his eyes, as wide as they'd ever been, stayed locked on the screen as he clicked the footage back for perhaps the tenth time. Again, the shadow, left to right, nineteen minutes later, right to left. Steady speed. Walking pace. 'That's you, isn't it,' Sam whispered to himself. 'You're carrying her.'

'Huh?' A *clink-clink-clink* of a spoon on a mug, then a bin lid opening.

'Can you email this to me?'

'Sure.'

Once Sam had explained he was assisting the police, the white-haired man had invited him in to look at the wildlife footage on his laptop. It was perched on a low coffee table, atop a stack of magazines – mostly women's interest. These, plus the size-five boots by the back door and noises upstairs, and Sam assumed a wife was present. However, the man wasn't wearing a ring and everything else about this place said single, maybe even lonely.

'And if they do come, I'm more than happy to answer any questions,' he added, quieter now as he entered the living room and set down two mugs. He sat on the chair to Sam's right and took a hard, green sweet from a bowl on the cluttered table. The wrapper crinkled open like a flower on the armrest.

'And your wife?'

He threw the sweet into his mouth as though it was a pill. 'My . . . well . . .' It clattered around his teeth when he spoke.

Sam turned his gaze to the ceiling.

'Mmm.' He wiped his lips. 'Mmm, no, that's my daughter. Middle of a divorce. Very involved, I won't bore you with it. But, of course, yes, she will assist however she can.'

They sat for a while in silence – the man watching Sam watching the screen.

'Little Robin's a gem.' He sighed, holding his tea now. 'Always waves. So polite.' He took a sip and Sam heard his old tongue working. 'Can't say the same about her mother.'

'Do you know the Clarkes well?'

He tilted his head one way then the other. 'Francis says hello in the mornings and, as I say, Robin's a sweetheart, but we're not particularly close, no.' With some effort, he removed a handkerchief from his pocket. 'Not much community spirit round here.' He dabbed his mouth. 'Mmm. Tall gates, you know. Mostly stuffy old millionaires.'

'Are you a stuffy old millionaire?'

'What do you think?' The man gestured around his messy property. Big, but yeah, Sam agreed, hardly any sign of wealth.

'Back to the wife – it's her house, God rest her soul. Or, really, her father's. Now *he* was a stuffy old millionaire.' He laughed.

'Mr Shanley?' Sam remembered the previous owner he'd interviewed all those years ago.

'That's the one.'

'What's your name?' Sam asked, still focused on the screen. He'd opened two windows, both pertinent videos displayed at the same time. On the sofa, leaning forwards, he blinked, paused them and looked at each in turn.

'Sorry, Jasper. Jasper Parker.'

'Well, Jasper Parker,' Sam said. 'I would be grateful if you could—'

He stopped, lifted the laptop and held it near his face. Blinking again, he rubbed an eye, then squinted at the second piece of footage.

'You found something?' Jasper placed his tea on the table.

Sam moved the cursor and zoomed into the top right-hand corner. A tiny shape nestled, tucked neatly on a tree branch right by the edge of the path. Not visible in the first film, but definitely visible in the second. Spot the difference. In the second film, the leaves had been parted.

'What do you suppose *that* is?' he said, rotating the screen and pointing.

Jasper turned his mouth down, held a pair of bifocals to his face and peered closer. 'Bird maybe? Small. Probably a sparrow, that.'

'In the middle of the night?'

Back outside, across the grass and past the broken gnomes, Sam's eyes took a moment to adjust in the hazy dusk. The sun was behind the horizon now, just beyond the long barley field that rose up gradually into the sky at the foot of the garden. He identified the branch in question.

'There you are,' Isabelle said from the path that ran behind all four properties.

Ignoring her, Sam walked through the gate and stood behind the tree. A section of old metal fence was wedged in the bush, brambles had grown out and claimed it, but he reckoned he could climb on top and reach round to that nook. But he stopped himself. The camera couldn't see him here. He was not the first person to stand in this spot.

'Didn't activate the motion sensor,' Sam whispered to himself. It could tolerate twigs and leaves in the wind, or the hand of a hidden shadow. 'Jasper,' he said, rolling up his sleeves, heading back into the garden. 'Got a stepladder?'

Isabelle watched as Jasper, bumbling and slow, cursed the mess in his shed, then produced a small steel ladder, which he wrestled out and handed to Sam.

The tree was in the corner of the yard by the side fence, and the tall canopy, like the upper half of Jasper's wide house, was still catching the last of the day's light. The highest leaves glowed like embers, a spent torch, fluttering out in the cold air. Sam set the ladder next to the trunk, then climbed and stood on the second-to-last step. It wobbled when he held the handle – Isabelle grabbed either side to keep it steady.

'You all right?'

With an elbow on the knotted limb, Sam manoeuvred himself to the right-hand side of the tree and used his phone's torch to illuminate the area. A freshly snapped branch near his wrist. Someone had cleared the way to the object.

'What is it?' Isabelle said.

Some kind of wooden toy – *or, or cloth maybe?* Sam blinked and leaned in closer. The small figure was scruffy, home-made, like a voodoo doll? *But no, different.* Hand-carved from burned wood – the face was black – a fractured protrusion of what might have once been charcoal. It had no legs, but this was hard to gauge as the object had been half swallowed by the tree. Like hot metal on wax, it had sunk into the knot, its back pressed into the curved bark. Thinner twigs had crept out and caged it further. Time had done this. Lots and lots of time.

However, jutting from its wooden cocoon, it did have arms – one of which was lifted, pointing away from Sam. Pointing over his right shoulder. Pointing, he saw, directly at the Clarkes' house. He left it in place and took three photographs.

Not bad, he thought, coming down the ladder.

'What is it?' Isabelle repeated, this time quieter.

As Sam arrived back on the grass, he brushed bark from his sleeve and said, 'Significant.'

They returned to the house and Isabelle – much more equipped to deal with this officially – reported the find. Two forensic officers, anonymous in dust masks and white overalls, went to check. Then names were called on the radio – 'Uh, you'll want to see this' – and three more faceless hoods disappeared down the Clarkes' long garden.

'Any ideas?' Isabelle asked on the driveway, zooming in on the photo on Sam's phone. 'Looks like some recent damage around the head. How long you think it's been there?'

'Hard to say . . .' Sam sighed. 'Years.'

Her eyebrows lifted. 'Eight?'

'About that,' he said. 'It's wedged there, it's stuck. The tree . . . has absorbed it.'

'Why would someone interfere? What were they doing?'

Blinking, he crouched over the tarmac and inspected the plastic teddy eye. 'They were trying to take the figure from the tree.'

'But why?'

'Because . . .' he turned towards the garage, looked into Francis Clarke's bloodstained car, lit now by flood bulbs so bright they stained his vision with two green, orange, flashing blue spots and rendered the evening a starless night. Standing, he took his mobile back and held the photo in the palm of his hand. 'Because *this is* something we weren't meant to find.'

◆ ◆ ◆

We see the Hallowfield Criminal Investigation Department in full swing. The room is busy. Men and women at computers, on phones, one looking at a map on the wall with his hand on his hip – another by his side, pointing something out with a pen. Then, with sudden purpose, one of the younger female officers pushes her swivel chair away from her desk and stands. All this is visible from a webcam on her monitor. However, she strides out of view and steps towards Phil Webber's office. The camera can't see in there, only the doorway and the female officer's shoulder. She's wearing a white, pinstriped blouse – her watch comes into shot as she places a hand on the wooden frame.

'Got the data back from Virgin Media,' she says.

'Yeah?'

'God bless the internet.' *Paper rustles.* 'Last week, late-night searches. Listen to this: "modern forensics",' she reads. '"Decomposition" and, my personal favourite, "how to dispose of a human body". All on the Clarkes' secured Wi-Fi.'

'Fuck off,' Phil says, in a high-pitched, jubilant tone.

'Yep. Social media, news, some stuff about insurance, loads of streamed cartoons – Robin likes the classics, Tom and Jerry's a winner – and then that, bam.'

'Is . . . I mean, who . . . Are they Francis's searches?'

'Can't confirm for sure yet,' she says. 'But it's Anna, Francis or Robin. Guessing we can rule out an eight-year-old. And the dog doesn't have fingers. Weirdly though, there is VPN use – private browsing.'

'What does that mean?'

'Well, someone in the household is security conscious and covers their tracks. Someone is going online and looking at stuff they want to keep secret.'

'Is that common?'

'Nowadays, yeah, nothing incriminating with that alone.'

'Any info on which device uses the VPNs?'

'You're good at this, Phil, you should turn pro. Yes, Francis. Private networks for a lot of browsing – not all of it, mind. The guy used to work in IT, remember.'

'So, this shit is what, a slip-up?'

'Looks that way. Just forgot maybe?'

'Unbelievable,' Phil says. But, from his voice, it's clear he does in fact believe what he's just heard. 'It'll be a late one – let's get all this written up.'

'What do you reckon they'll say?'

'I don't give a fuck – I just want to see Blinky's face.'

Chapter 6

Sam had never seen inside Hallowfield University. Besides fleeting visits to friends back in the day, he had never seen inside *any* university. The *Coriolis* was the closest he had ever come to academia – oh, what would his father say about that? Despite his efforts, Sam's contribution to man's bank of knowledge remained relatively pedestrian.

Once Isabelle had parked the car, they walked up some narrow stone stairs and along a path lined with shrubs so neat Sam had thought they were fake. But when he leaned down, plucked a leaf and folded it twice between his thumb and finger, a residue, sticky and real, was left on his skin. Hallowfield University, bold and big, sprawled out ahead of them. A new build – still clean, still modern, like a perfectly conceived life-size model of itself.

Nowadays, upon entering an open-plan space, particularly a campus, Sam found himself thinking about the dynamics of a mass shooting. Maybe an overexposure to American culture, or maybe knowing that, when it comes to weapons, 'difficult to get' isn't the same as 'impossible to get' – either way, he considered funnel exits and imagined newsreel footage of crowds screaming, running from the dull *clack-thud* of semi-automatic gunfire. No sparks, no blazing muzzle flash, just dust and noise – nothing romantic at all in reality. He assessed large public spaces from an attacker's and victim's perspective. Often, when hearing news of a spree killer's body count, he would shake his head and roll his eyes, both at the senseless violence and at the typical ineptitude rife in men who carry it out. Their cause – be it God or lesser – would be similarly unimpressed.

They were heading towards Professor Adriana Moretti's office, which, Sam learned from a theme-park-style map on an outside wall, was on the second floor of Red Block. *You are here*, it told him – a grand, philosophical claim for an arrow to make.

'How do you know her?' he asked, as they turned a corner into an ideal choke point, wondering if these thoughts said more about him or more about the world he called home.

'I was a student of hers,' Isabelle said. 'She used to teach at the old site.' Anticipating the next question, she added, 'History and politics.'

'Quite a diversion. How's the debt?'

Isabelle slowed and looked at him – she would pause before each response, processing everything she heard – the disarming stare from those dark eyes almost bringing an apology to the table. But no. Initially, Sam thought these micro beats in conversation were shock, naivety, even disapproval – however, he soon realised Isabelle wasn't taking offence, she was just paying attention. She was simply listening. A rare trait indeed.

'Well, you know what I earn,' she said. 'You do the maths. And, no, not a diversion – making sense of what happened years ago is an adaptable skill.'

With half-shut eyes and a tilt of his head, Sam gave her that one.

They walked for a few seconds in silence, passing a couple of evening classes but otherwise seeing no people. After a while, Isabelle added, 'And you're wrong, by the way – plenty of chaos in the past, not nearly as orderly as you'd like to think. The future is the only place with any guarantees.'

Arriving at the university's Red Block just before 8.30 p.m., they crossed limestone slabs dappled in fresh rain which filled the air with a damp warmth that reminded Sam of greenhouse strawberries and the humid metal underbelly of the *Coriolis*. Back there again with the slightest prompt – the bounce of a speed bump, the disparity between an escalator and the relatively still earth or, today, the ground steam from a summer shower.

He couldn't say why he was being so candid but, when the topic of first memories had arisen in the car on the way here, Sam told Isabelle about those years aboard the ship. About how he still looked for birds overhead, and still associated the sight with the token tasks given to him at sea. You can tell a lot about a place by the type of things that fly above it. An abundance of feathers meant land, safety, a chance of survival, should you find yourself stranded and alone.

On and off, the *Coriolis* was his home for the first eight years of his life – a wide, maroon research vessel captained by his father and run with a crew of twenty or so men and women. Academics prepared to leave the grass behind for months at a time. As its name implied, the boat, a former cargo ship, sailed in long curves around the globe, taking samples of water and sea air. Other researchers, from countries he couldn't recall, came for the ride and studied everything from avian migration to ocean litter. It was ahead of its time in that sense – well before the days of landfill islands, well before great swathes of plastic bottles and bags drifted without direction, tricking gulls, killing turtles, posing for viral videos. Even now, as environmentally culpable as the next man, Sam felt the sea should be somehow exempt from all this. A mysterious supermodel at the edge of a pub brawl, far too beautiful for such casual injury.

Those days, homeschooled on a home away from home, were among his happiest. Although his brother, older by six years, recalled the time less favourably, so perhaps this nostalgia, like all nostalgia, had more to do with youth than it did with reality.

'We used to hang off the stern railings.'

'Why?' Isabelle had asked.

Sam just shrugged.

It involved him and his brother sneaking up to the top deck when it was dark. At night, the two spotlights that jutted from the bridge like a pair of glowing horns sent white beams into the sky above them – long, fading triangles filled with mist. Everywhere else would seem almost as black as the water below. But, of course, as his brother used to say, nothing is darker than the ocean at night. The game went like this: they would head to the rear of the ship, clamber over the railings, lower themselves down on to a narrow shelf, shuffle around the bulbous outcrop of metal at the base of a flagpole, then climb up the other side.

Sometimes, they would hang by their fingers and do clumsy pull ups. Worse still, Sam would occasionally creep out of bed and play this game alone. Certain death awaited anyone who slipped. A thirty-foot drop into pitch-black water, flowing away at invisible speed. It wouldn't be instant. It might even take hours, or days, depending on the temperature and injuries sustained from the fall. He would have watched the ship sail away into darkness, lights turning to fireflies, a fog, and finally becoming any one of a thousand unreachable stars arching up and over him from every nearby horizon. At the time, Sam didn't imagine this horror. He scarcely even thought of it as water – those nights the ocean looked as though it wasn't there, looked like a void, so his childish mind treated it as such. Just nothing. A boat balanced, suspended impossibly in the vacuum of space.

Thinking about the absurd, unnecessary risks involved used to make Sam feel ill – a cringe, a pang of *what if*. Nowadays, he found the idea uniquely comforting. The *Coriolis* was a solid, shifting home that felt as secure as land itself, so to fall off, unwitnessed and sudden, would be the antithesis. Young Sam didn't know what the opposite of safety and life was – but he enjoyed dangling his body above it when everyone else was asleep.

At Hallowfield University the hall doors were swinging open.

Professor Adriana Moretti greeted Isabelle like a mother greets a daughter – warmth and pride beaming from her smile. Speaking in a faint accent Sam couldn't place – somewhere near Italian, but with an odd American twist – she offered them both a drink.

'Water's fine for me,' Isabelle said.

They hadn't made it to her office, instead they met at the front of an empty, modern lecture hall. The three of them stood at the lectern, fixed auditorium chairs rising like a staircase at Sam's side. Once they'd dealt with formalities, he placed his phone on top of the wooden stand – Professor Moretti stepped closer, curious and keen to be of service. Glasses on, she leaned over to inspect the photo. She zoomed in with two fingers and frowned.

'Huh,' she whispered.

'Know what it is?'

'Well, it *looks* like a crying Hecate,' she said. 'Or what's left of one at least.'

Sam and Isabelle made brief eye contact. A bit of Adriana's pride had rubbed off – this visit had been Isabelle's idea. He gave her nothing.

'It's, uh, well, it's strange.' Adriana rubbed her earlobe. 'Of course, Hecate is the Greek goddess of magic, necromancy, the dark arts, among other things. Polytheism at its most malleable – she can be all sorts. Warden between the realm of gods and mortals. We see her in *Macbeth*, with the witches. Lots of these things popped up in the Nineties. Mostly in the States. Satanic ritual abuse – remember all that? A real culture mash to find her creeping into fringe Christianity. Often depicted holding a torch, sometimes two.'

'And this one?'

'It's . . . The point is, it's all fake.'

'Yes,' Sam said.

'No, I mean, fake, a hoax. Conspiracy theory peddled by people for, I don't know, fun. They planted them at day-care centres, politicians' houses, stuff like that. Also, usually the face is painted white – and has spikes. This one's been . . . I guess burned? Hard to tell.'

'So, what, left as a joke?' Isabelle wondered. 'A distraction?'

'Hmmm. Not necessarily. These artefacts, these icons – they might start as a prank, but they tend to take on a life of their own.'

She moved to a table on her left. Two clicks and her laptop woke from standby. She tapped on a keyboard, drawing up a couple of websites. Sam watched as she dismissed a few tabs, then landed on a strange, amateurish page with a border of pixelated GIFs, little burning pentagrams running down each side of the text. Garish backgrounds, an awful cyan font – the kind of cheap internet aesthetic you rarely see nowadays. However, dead centre, right at the top, there was a photo of a similar wooden doll, with its white face intact. In one hand it held a torch, the other was raised and pointing.

'So, the crying Hecate is said to lure the Devil himself to earth – to recall his demons.' Professor Moretti then read from the website in an ominous voice. 'But, be warned, wherever the finger points, the hands of fire shall rise, be that in the forest of men or the kingdom of heaven. The light of her torch exposes all truths, all evils. Even God – I guess we're talking Abrahamic God now – fears Hecate's hellful – that's not a word – gaze.' Still reading, now silently, she said over her shoulder, 'Where was the finger pointing?'

'At the Clarkes' house.'

'Well,' she said, standing straight again, 'then someone is either having a laugh, or Satan has dragged poor Robin Clarke into the depths of hell.' She seemed to realise that the fun she'd been having with all this fiction had just collided with reality. Her face was immediately serious, and then sad.

'No, it was put there a long time ago,' Sam said. 'I don't think it's for Robin.'

'I can send you some literature on all this, if it would help.'

'It would.'

We see him again, in his flat, working away. He trawls through everything, emptying folders, searching his laptop, scanning reports, witness statements, anything he can lay his hands on. This doesn't stop, or even slow down, until morning is coming through the curtains. Now, after a long night drinking and reading, the first signs of fatigue arrive. He sits cross-legged on the floor in his living room with paper fanned out across the carpet in front of him. His back against his old sofa, holes in the cushions, stitching frayed, padding exposed.

And finally, at dawn, he rests. His head bows slowly as he closes his eyes. But, instead of dreams, a harsh, loud buzz on the floor at his thigh snatches him from any fleeting peace – real or imagined.

'Yeah.' Sam was wide awake now, still seated like Buddha on his living-room floor.

'The blood.' Isabelle's voice was quiet, tired. 'Hospital mucked around, but it's definitely Robin's.'

'Fuck . . . It's all the same,' he said. 'Just . . . faster.'

It had taken three years before they found anything of value with Ethan. But there it was, his coat, thirty-eight months after his disappearance. Torn and worn and stripped to threads on a rock on a beach. The endless sea beyond. Sam remembered that night. Glossed sand still and black. And it had scared him more than anything to think that Ethan might be in the water. The darkest place there is.

Standing right there on that beach, next to that rust-touched fishing boat, he saw how quickly a discovery like this changes everything.

'With Ethan it was the blood, traces of blood on the fabric,' he said. 'That's when they stopped looking for a missing child. And started looking for blame.'

'Well, they've certainly found that.'

'Any update from them?'

'Last night Francis refused to answer questions, asked to leave.'

'And?'

She sighed. 'They talked him round Phil's on the cusp of an arrest. They're buying time. I think they're going to go with murder.'

Sam's eyes closed all by themselves. He grabbed the bridge of his nose.

'You there?'

'Yeah.' He took a breath. Eyes open again. Back to it.

'It's inevitable. It's the best we've got.'

'What about the—'

'Phil said he could have planted that doll himself.'

'Left it there for almost a decade, then decided to try and move it on Wednesday evening?'

'The wind could have broken that branch. You found it because you were looking.'

'Francis is not—'

51

'I know, I know what you believe,' Isabelle said. 'But it's possible you're wrong.'

Sam shook his head, but didn't actually say, 'No it isn't.'

'Any luck your end?' she asked.

'Nothing.'

He had found no mention of Satanism, the occult, Christianity or sensible permutations on those themes. It was as though Ethan and Robin Clarke were, aside from blood, fame and absence, totally unrelated.

'You read the full search history?'

'Yes,' Sam said. He had thought, if anything, that data helped his theory, despite Phil's glee. When Isabelle had handed him the paper listing the sites visited, she remarked that it was almost too good to be true. Sam had no qualms scratching the word 'almost' from the record.

Yesterday, Phil had spoken deliberately, as though to a child, when Sam suggested again that Francis was innocent.

'So, the alternative is that he's being set up?'

'That is the implication, yes,' Sam had murmured.

'You're suggesting someone managed to break silently into their house, take Robin, leave without a trace *and* have the foresight to visit a week prior, hack into their Wi-Fi and plant false evidence? Which is to say nothing of the blood. Have you any idea how insane you sound? Do you honestly, in your heart, believe that's more likely?'

Sam had nodded.

'Why, Sam, *why* would someone do that?'

'I don't know.'

He replayed the conversation all night. It did sound farfetched, but so did every other explanation. Every single scenario, even those coloured in his most outlandish bouts of imagination, seemed implausible. And so they should. The things that *could* have happened to the children were almost infinite. The truth was a solitary creature, small and alone in the chaotic haze, hiding out there, isolated in the wilderness. He would know when he found it. But now, startled, it knew it was being hunted. And it was getting away. There wouldn't be another chance. Not for Sam.

'Look,' Isabelle said, 'I'm on my way to see Anna now. A few things to go over in her statement. She's at a hotel just out of town.'

There was a familiar, hopeless futility in the centre of Sam's chest. A bleak sense of detachment he'd felt before. He'd delivered everything they wanted. His job, as far as they were concerned, was done.

'Phil said you are, or used to be, pretty close with Anna,' Isabelle added.

He knew what was coming next. But Sam couldn't decide whether it was out of pity or a legitimate desire to have him there. Either way, he agreed. What else could he do?

Drunk and exhausted, he got dressed and waited on the street outside his flat. Staring nowhere with blurred vision and a cold headache – blinking helped as much as it hurt. But he blinked. And blinked.

Phil was right, he thought. After all these years, he'd arrived at an answer. And it was, put simply, one he did not like. As Sam listened to the silence above, heard the birdless day plough on around him, swift logic appeared in his mind and almost knocked him from his feet.

They're both dead. They're both dead and you'll never know why.

His total inability to picture an answer he *did* like made him feel utterly lost – the kind of desperation reserved only for the nightmares of the terminally ill. Doctors rarely mentioned this symptom – perhaps because it has no name.

Marilyn was right as well. This irrational, maddening obsession couldn't save him. As she said: when it was over, he really would have nothing left. So eloquent, so succinct, so fucking true.

He lit a cigarette and drew as much smoke into his lungs as he could, wishing they'd burn, wishing that sudden catastrophe *would* cut through his mind and fix it. End it. Drop him into whatever oblivion awaits. Wishing he was back there, overlooking the invisible sea. Wishing he had slipped.

Chapter 7

We hear rustling. A microphone struggles against the sound of cloth and movement. Muffled distortion in absolute darkness. A bump. But then, light. We see a grey ceiling, a narrow room. The camera pans down and a shelf comes into view – bottles of cleaning products, a broom, two mops and, to the left, a pile of folded bed linen on top of drawers. A shadow moves past and a woman, a hotel chambermaid, steps into frame. She's holding an object in her hands – something plastic. An alarm clock, or the bottom half of one at least. Exposed circuit board and a dangling plug. She walks over and crouches. Up close now: blonde hair and a gaunt face – we can tell, even from here, that she is tall. Perhaps six feet or more. She's working fast, frantic. Wiping her hair away and checking things – darting eyes. The dissected alarm clock is placed next to us and the woman's thin hands block the lens. More muffled interference and darkness and then a strange clicking sound. We see again, from a different angle.

The chambermaid's uniform, a brown tunic with a white apron tied at her waist, fills the entire picture. Some motion and then another noise, this time above. Translucence covers our narrow world. Clunk. A glaring red light on the right-hand side of the frame, close and electronic. Again, we're lifted and the chambermaid is looking at us, inspecting us. She seems satisfied, but nervous. Another clunk and the red light is gone. A bang startles her and we're dropped, a wire and a white object fall quickly and we're in the dark again.

'Yeah, two secs,' she says.

Movement. A door. Wheels below, one is squeaking. We hear inane conversation, small talk, two colleagues chatting about television, their boss, ordering more pillowcases following an incident that occurred over the weekend.

'Are you all right?' one of the female voices asks. 'You seem . . . distracted?'

'Just tired.'

'Well, an hour left and you're out of here. By the way, what's happening with you and— where are you going? Room twenty-one's done.'

'Alarm clock is busted.'

'So? You do know who's in there, right?'

'They're outside.'

'Quick then.'

That squeaky trolley wheel and the towel is lifted away. The lens strains as it adjusts to the new light. Her apron and a hip, then the side of her face. A familiar clunk and the electronic red glare is back. We slide away from her and see the bed, a chair in the corner and the long blue curtains.

We hear a door close. And we wait, watching and listening.

Chapter 8

A three-star hotel at the edge of town. Squared-off Georgian windows with black iron grilles across the front – each metal upright ending in an arrowhead. Faded brickwork, sandy and fawn, broken at random intervals by dark slate blocks.

Upstairs, in room twenty-one, Sam sat on the bed in silence and watched Anna Clarke cry. He breathed it in like smoke – poisonous but necessary. *Let Robin join Ethan in your mind*, he thought. Sam hadn't committed much imagination to the family's domestic intimacy in recent years. His approximations were getting dated now, all of them featuring Ethan and the old version of their house.

Listening to Anna recalibrated this. Images arrived all at once – a montage of unfilmed home movies, memories he didn't have, but sketched as best he could. The bedtime story. Amber night light glowing at the plug. The polite eight-year-old at the foot of the stairs, wearing her school uniform, holding her book bag. Patient. The child humming made-up songs in the garden, in the evening, in the lens-flare sunshine. Catching a beetle and asking for his name. Naming him. Losing him. Rehearsing grief. Using her fork to stab peas instead of scooping. Drawing with her tongue out, tilting her head, holding the pencil at an awkward angle. Asking to stay up later than usual. A hug. A quick kiss on the cheek when Mummy is sleeping. Sshhh. I love you, Mummy. A smile and a squeeze. Hysterical laughter coming from the bath. Dancing. That split second of realisation after a fall. The calm before the storm. The decision to cry or not to cry no longer a choice at all. And peace. Sleeping on the sofa, rosy cheeks and shallow breathing. No story tonight. Carried to bed. The empty bed. Now silent. Gone. Simply gone. Gone for too long now to be unharmed. Scared. Alone. Alone in the birdless void, wishing the low white dots were boats on the horizon. Old enough to realise they're just stars.

All fables for Sam. But as real as anything could ever be for Anna. You are here. You are *here*.

You are here again.

Her room was neat, chambermaid fresh. Anna's suitcase was on the floor, unopened, and she was sitting on the chair in the corner, elbows leaning on her knees, clutching a well-used tissue. It looked as though she couldn't settle, couldn't even take her coat off.

'Can you think of anyone he might have upset?' Isabelle was asking. 'Anyone who could might have a . . . a reason to dislike Francis?'

Anna sniffed and glanced around the sparse hotel room, swaying her head and opening her mouth to speak, but no words came out. The gesture clearly meant: I don't know.

'Were there any visitors to your house *last week*, Wednesday evening in particular?'

Sam let Isabelle handle these obvious lines of questioning. After all, it wasn't his job to ask.

This time, she managed sound. 'No. No one. We're . . . we're very private.'

'How about your neighbours? What's Jasper like?'

'Who?'

'Mr Parker.'

Hesitating again, Anna sighed. 'I don't think I've ever had a conversation with him. His daughter seems friendly though . . .'

The one piece of mess she had allowed herself was her phone, face down on the carpet, against the skirting board. It seemed like she'd thrown it.

Anna's natural, curly hair was tied back in a messy bunch. It was thick and, from time to time, she grabbed strands at the front and pulled on them – three tugs. The signs of physical discomfort, of nausea. Acute withdrawal from a substance that warns you about such side effects. Seek immediate medical attention if you experience any of the following . . .

Prescription. Anna was on drugs, Sam remembered.

'You've been prescribed anti-anxiety medication in the past,' he said. 'Had you taken anything on Wednesday evening?'

She nodded. 'But I would have . . . I would have heard if . . .'

'Who else knows you're here?' Isabelle asked.

'My father. Francis. And Daniel. No one else.'

'Aiden?'

'Yes.'

Daniel Aiden was an acquaintance of Anna's from university – a journalist and filmmaker whose career had benefited from all this in a big way, proving that it really isn't what you know. He had been instrumental in turning Ethan's disappearance into the extraordinary global story it had become. Without his influence, it would have been a mere statistic – the media usually preferring its missing children younger. However, considering there wasn't a press mob outside yet, it seemed he was a friend first and a reporter second. Still, Sam found Daniel a strange somewhat risky person to confide in now. Anna must trust him.

'They'll find me soon enough,' she said. 'The things they're saying . . . about Francis . . . They've been doing it for years. Accusing him, accusing me. For what? For attention? Publicity? Money? What the fuck do these people think?'

'It's comforting to assume someone is in control,' Sam said. 'People prefer to believe there's a conspiracy. The alternative is chaos, and it's terrifying.'

'They say . . . they say I burned Robin's body.' Anna looked at the floor, at her phone. 'There's a fucking forum, Sam, where they speculate. They say I killed my own daughter.'

'Did you?' he said, with a blank face.

Anna closed her eyes. 'No. I didn't.'

They left this in the air for a few seconds. It was the truth.

'The appeal website, the emails . . . I . . . I have an open inbox – anyone can contact me. It's anonymous,' Anna said.

'Why?' Isabelle wondered.

'In case there's any information – in case someone sees . . . or hears something. I will be the first to know. This morning, there was a message. From a person called JJ.'

'What did it say?'

'"Robin is safe, please don't cry."' She tried a smile. 'Occasionally the crackpots are quite sweet.'

'Can we read these?'

'Sure. I'll give you the login. But it's not a nice place to be.'

She scribbled on a loose piece of paper from her bedside cabinet.

'How has your relationship with Francis been recently?' Isabelle asked, pocketing the details.

Lifting her eyebrows, Anna shrugged, as if this line of questioning couldn't possibly matter. But, still, she played along. 'Well . . . fine, I guess. Normal, for us.'

'What is normal for you?'

'Are you asking how often we have sex?'

There was no response.

'Rarely,' she said. 'Happy? Believe it or not, the past few years have put a bit of a strain on things.'

'I didn't mean . . .'

'I know. . . I'm . . . I'm sorry.'

Isabelle held her notebook and moved back a couple of pages. 'In your first statement, after Ethan was declared missing, you said he'd been "unsettled" for many months. You thought there was, maybe, trouble at school? Had you noticed any similar behaviour from Robin?'

'She . . . no. She was fine. Perfect. Herself. We . . . we kept her sheltered. We kept her away from it all. We kept her . . . safe.' Anna cried that last word.

After a few moments, she composed herself, then looked up and breathed. *Remarkable recovery*, Sam thought – she was well-versed in this. Her eyes were still glassy, but her body had stabilised. Staring out of the window, she took another breath, which juddered once.

'There was a story online about me not crying enough at a press conference. Another about me crying too much. Do *you* count your tears?'

'Best to avoid the news,' Isabelle suggested. 'If you can.'

'The truth is, I'm numb. I remember thinking they'd find Ethan's body. I pictured police at my door, asking to come in, holding their hats. Back then, I thought it'd be the worst thing that could happen. I never even considered how much more it would hurt to not know. How can that be possible? How can there be something worse than a dead child?'

'It must—'

'I had an awful dream, last night. I dreamed that . . .' Anna covered her mouth and paused, then placed her hands on her knees and took another unsteady breath. 'I imagined that Robin was dead. And I felt better. Lighter. If I had to pick, between a coffin or another eight years of silence? Another decade of *this*? A cold-hearted monster – that's what they say I am. I think I've spent it all – I just have no more pain left.'

Sam and Isabelle listened. She spoke for another five minutes about Robin, about the normality they had almost perfected. Things had finally been getting better. After a while, a bolt of hope arrived from somewhere, and Anna turned to Sam. 'You said, years ago, do you remember, do you remember what you said? You said you'd find Ethan. You said it. In my kitchen. Do you remember that?'

He nodded. 'Yes. I remember.'

'You were the only person to say it.'

'We're doing everything—'

'Will you find her? Sam. Sam, look at me. Will you find Robin?'

Still standing in the corner by the television, Isabelle folded her arms and gave him that uncomfortable stare. She didn't shake her head as such, but moved it in a way that warned, *No, don't.*

Sam never lied. He couldn't lie. He believed every lie, even a small one, would pollute the water, corrupt it. Push us a millimetre in the wrong direction. As far as he knew, unless for humour, the deception of an agreed game, or some unlikely life-or-death scenario (is Anne Frank in your attic?), he could only speak the truth. Even a momentary lapse during an interrogation irked him and he'd always straighten the record before it was over – as he'd done with Francis. In all his years on earth he was yet to encounter, first-hand, a situation in which deception yielded a moral net gain over honesty, no matter how raw, no matter how much it might hurt.

So, then, what must he believe, he wondered, as he nodded, looked Anna in the eye and said: 'Yes. I will find Robin.'

A slow blink from Isabelle. He could have stayed within the realms of truth. He could have answered, 'I would rather not say.'

But he didn't. Instead, he promised a desperate mother that he would find her lost child for the second time in a decade.

Isabelle turned her hands over and mouthed the word, 'Why?'

But Anna, whose eyes were fixed on the floor between her feet, didn't even flicker. What he'd said hadn't comforted her. Not in any detectable way at least. Of course, he had a pretty poor track score – maybe these pledges had lost their edge.

Still, Isabelle's question was an interesting one. Why had he said that? Did he think he was the author, commander of the future? Could an affirmation really pave the way? Could he say something, believe it, and watch as the universe unfolds and grants him the reality he so wishes to be waiting over the hazy horizon? No. He did not believe that. Stuck, then, he knew, on this path.

'Maybe we should go.' Isabelle gestured for Sam to stand up.

'I also dream about what I'd do to the person responsible,' Anna whispered. 'If I ever got the chance . . .'

'What would you do?'

'*Sam.*'

This topic *did* offer comfort. 'It involves a sharp knife and would take about five seconds. I have almost fifteen years' experience in spinal surgery, I know exactly which bits to cut.' Anna closed her eyes. 'Pop, pop, pop,' she said. 'They would survive.' Then she held her hand out in front of her face and tilted her gaze to look at it. 'See, it's always steady.'

A professional photograph of them at the front of the hotel, with a uniformed officer, then another of them on the pavement, the man holding his phone. In the next they're mid-stride on the way to the car park.

Sam noticed photographers and an unmarked van. The press were here. Lots of them. Another two vehicles pulled in and parked beneath the swaying elm trees that lined the turf along the car park's borders. They opened fire on arrival.

As he approached, a few questions were yelled out, but Sam and Isabelle blanked them. A photographer stepped close, took a picture, checked it, then crouched lower and took three more. He didn't make eye contact.

'This is our fault,' Sam said.

Isabelle ignored their new company. 'What was all that about?' she asked.

They arrived at the car and stood for a moment, talking over the roof as a nearby camera crew prepared itself.

'Oh, I think we can grant her some violence. Don't you ever fantasise, Isabelle?'

'No, not that. Look. Let's go.' She struck the metal with her palm. 'Grown-up time. What do you, in all your professional wisdom, think is most likely? Just on maths, what do you think would get the best odds?'

Sam sighed. 'Lower your voice.'

'Come on. What's happened to those kids? Say it.'

A long breath. 'Ethan probably died within twenty-four hours of disappearing. Whoever killed him did so quickly and disposed of his body. I would imagine a similar thing has happened to Robin. *That* would get the best odds. I'm hard-working Isabelle, but I'm not delusional.'

'Then why do you keep promising to find them?'

Silence.

She gave him one of those vacant pauses. This wasn't thinking time – this was disapproval. 'Fucking hell, Sam.' For the briefest of moments, she seemed almost unbalanced. But it was all back now.

Her perfect posture, her calm, calculated mannerisms. 'You need to think about other people before you speak,' she said, opening the driver's door. 'If you want to be honest, that's fine. But understand you are causing harm.'

A van door slammed nearby. Isabelle looked down and pulled her vibrating phone from her pocket. As she spoke, she kept her eyes locked on him.

'OK . . . yeah . . .'

The crowd of men and women filling the car park and pavement were all on the move, cameras lifted on to shoulders, boom mics carried quickly into place. Turning, blinking, full circle, Sam saw a man in a suit, also talking on his mobile, holding a finger up to a colleague – excitement on both their faces.

Isabelle was hanging up when Sam looked back at her. 'They've found a screwdriver, hidden in the garage – blood and prints.'

He waited.

'Formally arrested on suspicion of murder.'

Word spreads fast, Sam thought, as he lowered himself to the ground and sat on the kerb. He listened to the traffic, the bustle and all the silence in the sky.

'That's it then,' he said.

Sam felt his doubt seeping in, filling him, drowning him. It happened almost immediately and he was quick to identify the sensation. His mind was changing. An arrest, a weapon, they brought validity to Phil's suspicions – they cemented what everyone already believed. A final piece of the puzzle, fitting in place to finish an ugly picture – a picture that was, no matter where Sam stood, somehow wrong. All these people, heads and shoulders, microphones held to their chests, they were now free to stand in front of the house, in front of the hotel, and say it – announce to the world that, yes, yes it *was* Francis Clarke.

Just look. Why else would they arrest him? What possible explanation could there be? If not him then who – who had done this? This. This being what?

One thing felt almost impossible to deny.

The officers traipsing methodically through woodland, in rows, through fields, the soil probes pressed into the earth, the divers out there in the deep quarry water – they had all been implicit. Subtext. Tacit whispers. But now? Now it was definitive. Now it was true.

Now, Robin Clarke was dead.

Chapter 9

Francis Clarke was exhausted – as tired as he'd ever been. When the metal door made that awful noise, which clattered off the cell walls like steel on teeth, he flinched as though waking from a nightmare, to no avail.

This officer's name was Darrel. A large, middle-aged man with a thick grey moustache and a beer belly. Generally, he was stationed at the front desk, and Francis guessed he was well beyond passing any physical exam. But he was kind. Strange how comforting a smile can be at a time like this. Earlier, when bringing in a bowl of microwaved porridge, Darrel asked how he was doing. Francis had said he was scared – and the words sounded all wrong. For a few seconds, standing there in his dingy cell, he felt tempted to hug the large officer. It wouldn't have been appropriate, so he stopped himself. Darrel. Kind Darrel.

'Mr Payne is here,' he said, walking the metal door open until it was against the wall.

It hurt to stand, but Francis placed his hands on his knees and drove himself upright. He rubbed his eyes and pushed a fist into his cheek, moving the flesh around his back teeth.

'You OK?'

'It's a . . . uh,' Francis said, pointing to his face, rolling his chin. 'Ongoing thing.'

The tooth ached every second of the day, apart from when he clenched his jaw. However, like scratching a mosquito bite, the pain that blossomed right after was, without fail, far worse. A dull, constant throb may have been tolerable, but momentary relief was impossible to resist. He bit down as he followed Darrel the full length of the custody corridor and didn't let go until he was shown the open interview-room door. Unbearable, dizzy agony as he relaxed his jaw and stepped inside.

Sweating, wincing, Francis nodded at Jeremy, who stood and thanked Darrel. They remained on their feet until the door closed.

'Tooth again?' Jeremy said.

He sat at the empty table, and Francis took the seat opposite.

'Among other things.'

Jeremy's clothes were always tailored and elegant – today he was wearing a navy blazer and slim-fit trousers, with thick rimmed glasses and a staunch professionalism that made him all the more handsome. It was an undeniable fact that his lawyer was an attractive man. He'd heard a female officer comment to this effect and was relieved Jeremy hadn't been in earshot – he already thought plenty of himself.

Unclipping a leather briefcase, he leaned down and pulled out two brown folders. He opened one of them, removed a sheet of A4 paper from a clip and slid it over the wood towards Francis. Then, back down to his briefcase.

'Take these,' Jeremy said, thumbing a couple of strong painkillers from a blister pack.

Francis threw them into his mouth and took a sip of water.

'Don't focus too much on the clock – they'll extend as long as they can.' Jeremy liked to cover all the formalities first – it sounded like he was reading straight from legal text but, occasionally, he would slip into human mode.

But Francis didn't even listen to the majority of this precision. He spent most of this time holding his back teeth together, pressing them down into the sweet spot – just light enough to cut the pain by about 50 per cent, without aggravating it further. Really, there was only one thing he wanted to hear.

'You need to read that,' Jeremy said, pointing to another piece of paper on the desk. Although he'd paid enough to fool a cursory audience, his tan was sprayed on. Pale palms tell tales. 'We need to start thinking long term, start framing these transcripts as sound bites read out in open court.'

Clutching his hair, Francis was becoming impatient. He was past crying now. Just a hopeless passenger, accepting his fate – whatever it may be. This feeling of being a prisoner – it scared him more than anything else. Life without control was, by quite a margin, worse than death. The tooth only added to it. In his cell, alone at the razor edge of anxiety, he sometimes kicked his legs out and slapped himself on the cheek. But he was resilient and forced himself to stay strong. Strong Francis.

'Look, listen.' Jeremy set his pen on the table. 'Can I speak openly . . . ?'

'Please do.'

'The number of people *convicted* of murder without a body? It's rare.'

'Jeremy.' Francis's eyes closed – saw Robin's face, sweet Robin's smile. 'Don't . . .'

'I know, I'm sorry. But it's positive.' His lawyer lowered his head, and his voice. 'They want nothing more than to find Robin dead – they are searching for a body. And they're searching hard. The timing – it's no accident. They think they're on course to find her soon. They probably expected to have it wrapped up by now.'

'This isn't making me feel better.'

'The reality is they *haven't* found a body.' Jeremy stared at the door. 'They will lay it on thick. These people believe you're to blame.' He looked back. 'What you've told them already, it's all   '

'The truth,' Francis said.

'Yes, but now ease off the gas. We don't want to do their job for them. They will pick your story apart. You'll tie yourself in knots. You just will.'

'Sam said I should be honest.'

'And whose side is he on?'

'I have no idea.'

'It's up to you. I'm here to advise. When these sails are up, you point them wherever you want.'

'And when time runs out . . . if they haven't found her?'

Jeremy exhaled. 'As I say, a charge without a body is difficult . . . but it's not impossible.'

'What does that mean?'

'It means I can't see them releasing you. Put yourself in their shoes . . . There's blood, Francis. Blood . . .'

'They're asking about Ethan too. Retreading everything.'

'Good. Honestly, I think that helps us. A lot of room for doubt.'

There was a quiet moment and Francis looked at his lap. 'When I was a kid, at school, I used to get picked on.' He didn't know why he was saying this – just thinking out loud. 'Didn't have many friends. Used to sit alone, every day. I'd have my lunchbox on my lap and the moment I started eating my sandwich, someone would snatch it. Or kick it out of my hands. Every day. And it wasn't just the bullies – that's the point. It seemed everyone would have a go. Like I was just . . . fair game. Social proof at my expense. And now, this morning, one of the officers – she looked at me like I'm a piece of shit. It's a look I've seen before. From strangers. People who don't even know me. It's strange, isn't it. You can keep doing the right thing, and still end up in the wrong place.'

'Yeah, life's fucking . . .' Jeremy opened his hands – what could he say?

'If everyone believes something, does it make it true?'

'No.'

'Deny something once. Twice? Hmm? A thousand times? What then? Sorry . . . I . . . I'm tired.'

'You had any further ideas – anyone who . . . ?'

Francis shrugged, shook his head.

'They will be trawling through everything. Including the Clarke Foundation.'

'Why?'

'The money. They'll use anything they can to chip away at you. Your reputation might be what swings it, if it goes all the way.'

'But that . . . that money has nothing to do with me.'

'Yes, but who knows what'll come crawling out of the woodwork. I just think we need to plan for all eventualities. Get one step ahead.' Jeremy pressed his glasses higher with two fingers. This was a habit Francis had noticed. One he didn't like. Every time Jeremy did it, he touched not just the frame but the lens too. Francis imagined the fingerprints, greasy little spiral smears in the right hand side of his vision. The urge to snatch those glasses from Jeremy's face and wipe them with his sleeve was like a sudden abstract itch – the kind that appears on your scalp or somewhere around your ear. Instead, he just treated himself to a brief bite. He grimaced as the pain shot through his skull, fading out behind his eye.

However, it changed as the drugs began to work their magic. The ache was still there, but it was fuzzy. Like a thick covering of snow at night – the world hasn't disappeared per se, but it sounds different, it feels soft. By the time Jeremy had finished his spiel, everywhere was white with fresh powder. Not a single footprint,

71

nor any echo. Just like those Canadian winters he remembered so fondly.

Inverted now, the tooth hurt only when he bit down. Francis was in control of the pain – he could feel it whenever he wanted. That, plus the gentle opiate embrace, had half soothed the sting of this ordeal.

He realised he hadn't been listening to Jeremy for a while now.

'You should be careful not to touch the lenses,' Francis said, interrupting him. 'Sorry . . . it's . . . ignore me.'

Jeremy didn't like criticism, but he removed the dirty glasses and placed them across his notepad. His client's requests mattered more than 20/20 vision.

Finally, he shuffled in his seat and took a long breath. *Finally*, he was moving towards what Francis really wanted to know. He could tell that the subject, the elephant in the room, was the last thing left to discuss. Jeremy seemed agitated – a couple of false starts before he spoke.

'I . . . liaised with the private investigator you recommended, and he's working on something,' he said, closing a folder and screwing the lid on his pen.

'Yeah, what?' Francis asked. 'What's he working on?'

Leaning forwards, hand on the table, Jeremy whispered, 'Listen, it's . . .' He groaned. 'It's difficult to shadow as he normally would, because she doesn't go anywhere without a police escort. They're keeping her location quiet, for obvious reasons. Hasn't worked, mind. You know what the press are like.'

'I told you where she's staying.'

'And, as I said, he's made arrangements.'

'Tell me. Please.'

Jeremy closed his eyes and rested his head in his hand. 'Anything we discover can't come . . . My role in this is strictly—'

'Yes, of course. By all means, deny it. I don't care. Just tell me what he's actually done.'

A nervous tap with his pen sounded like a modest drumroll. 'He paid a chambermaid to install a camera and a microphone in the hotel room – he gave her a modified alarm clock. All she had to do was plug it in and, hey presto, hours of footage.'

This was a better answer than Francis was expecting. 'Well . . . I . . . How much did that cost?'

'Enough for the chambermaid to risk her job and even prison, put it that way. You'll get the bill, don't worry. Quite a tab.'

'Has he . . . has he seen or heard anything?'

'I imagine he's seen your wife in varying states of dress, and her most intimate moments – does that bother you?'

Francis looked down.

'And Sam and . . .' Jeremy checked his phone '. . . a detective called Isabelle Lewin visited Anna at the hotel. He says he can copy me in with raw video.'

'Thank you, Jeremy. Really.'

'What are you hoping to find?'

Biting down, once, twice, three times – three expansions of pain in his jaw, in his neck, melting the snow. In truth, Francis did feel uneasy about the arrangement. Should this breach of privacy ever come to light, as he suspected it inevitably would, it might be the final nail in their coffin. And this was regrettable. Despite their differences, the strain and de facto separation of late, he did still love her. Anna. Her thick vanilla hair, her perfect skin. Those kind eyes she'd given both the children. Beautiful Anna. Clasping her hands at her chest and crying real tears on that bus as she said, 'Yes, yes of course I'll marry you,' beneath that falling Montreal sky. Her lips and nose cold and red. A baby face almost too pure for lust.

Anna. Beautiful Anna.

The only witness on earth who could attest his innocence. Anna, who slept, zonked off her head on those benzodiazepines she swallowed like Skittles.

He doubted any revelations would restore his liberty – he didn't for a moment think Anna was capable of anything on a par with the accusations thrown at him. She'd give her life a thousand times to bring Ethan and Robin back.

However, the brutal, aching, irrefutable fact was: Francis Clarke did not trust his wife.

Chapter 10

We see a dark room. A bed. A window boarded up with wooden planks and metal bars. The only light in here is from a small reading lamp, on its side, on the floor – a short tear of warmth on the plain carpet. In the centre of the room, lying perfectly still, we see a shape. It could be an eight-year-old girl, facing away, looking towards the bed.

As we watch, it seems this might be a photograph – or possibly a piece of looping footage, less than a second long.

The figure on the ground, lying with an arm stretched straight, is cast in modest resolution. Such quality makes it impossible to detect subtle movements, like the slow breaths found in deep sleep. All we see is the faint shift of pixels, gradients, light levels fluctuating ever so slightly.

But we hear a noise, a clunk. A door. And yet, still no motion.

Again, another sound. Now a vivid change in colour – the floor hosts a triangle of white glare that strains the lens and darkens the walls.

Finally, with a long yawn, the girl pushes herself upright and shuffles to a seated position. She turns, leans over and takes a bowl from the carpet by the door, now closed. Pink pyjamas, curly blonde hair, the iconic face we've seen a thousand times this week.

And then, as though she's felt something, as though the camera's gaze has activated a sixth sense, Robin Clarke lifts her head and looks directly at us.

Chapter 11

Hallowfield's high street offers haircuts from fizzing neon signs, alive even in the day. We see its boarded shops, its shuttered doorways, its parade of stores selling coffee, fast food, the last few things you cannot buy online. Some familiar chains hold on – commercial reminders that, to survive, you must look like everywhere else.

Local people know it for its history, its former affluence, its weekly farmers' market. We know it only because we hear its name every day. We know it because at the furthest edges of this place, where sparse streets widen and grey things turn green, there is a row of houses called Orchard Court. And this is where they live. This is where it happened.

But now we look across the pavements, from camera to camera, and see a man and his son stepping across a grass verge and towards the path that leads to the city's old football ground. Disused, but kept in reasonable condition for the general public. At the side of the grandstand the late-afternoon sun streams across the open playing fields – each tree dotted throughout the acres of land hosts a shadow, twice the length of its looming height. A sprawling park disappears out of view – it's quiet, just a few children near the play equipment, and a few more walking along the path in their school uniforms. Suburbia at 4 p.m. We really could be anywhere.

The man is carrying a plastic bag and his son bounces a football on the tarmac as they go. The boy's dressed in what looks like a PE kit. And he's happy.

◆　◆　◆

'Mr Thomson wouldn't even listen,' he was saying.

'Did you explain?' Sam asked. He had decided to give him the gift when they arrived at Kendell Street, but Freddie's eyes kept drifting to the bag.

'Yeah, I told him everything.'

'Believe it or not, teachers are only human. They make mistakes.'

'I have no idea what species Mr Thomson is but, trust me, it's not human.'

As they entered the open park, warm now off the shaded path, Freddie dropped the ball and kicked it as hard as he could. It flew over the play equipment, curling into the next field, where it bounced through the stretched shadow of a tree.

'Gone.'

'I'm not getting that,' Sam said.

'It's not mine. Found it on the path.'

'You stole it?'

'No, I *found* it. On the path. And now I've donated it to the park.' Freddie turned and walked backwards. 'So, what's in the bag?'

'It's . . .' They slowed down. Stopped. 'It's actually for you.'

There was cautious excitement as Sam slid the plain shoebox from the plastic bag – it was the right size, right logo, but it couldn't possibly be . . . and yet, it was. Freddie held it, kept it horizontal like a delicate cake, as he lifted the lid.

He'd had to liaise with Marilyn for the specifics of this brand. She warned him they'd be expensive, but he still double-checked the receipt in the shop, to make sure it wasn't some kind of error. The clerk also offered some advice and bombarded Sam with phrases he did not understand.

'Great boots though, no question,' he had concluded.

Freddie wasn't one for big leaps of joy – it had been years since he hugged an object to his chest and declared it the best thing to grace this universe. Nor, thankfully, was he 'too cool' to show any gratitude. One foot still in childhood, the other stepping tentatively into a strange new place.

'Thank you,' Freddie said, pulling one of the boots out of the box, taking some of the glossy paper with it. He placed the cardboard on the ground and stroked the leather – sturdy, thick stitches, expensive – oh, so fucking expensive. Freddie turned the boot and looked at the studs, inspected them like this was a career-defining archaeological discovery, a lost treasure assumed by most to be mere myth. 'Really, Dad . . . thank you.' He checked the label. 'Oh. But I'm . . . I'm actually size seven.'

'What?'

'Ha ha, your face.'

They repackaged them, and carried on across the playing field. It was hot today and Freddie's hair was still damp at his ears from PE – a few strands making a sideburn. He'd also caught the sun on his cheeks and the grass on his knees.

'You can wear them on Sunday.'

'Mum told you.'

'It's a big deal, Freddie.'

'I . . . I feel bad about it.'

'What do you mean? The academy is . . . It'll be brilliant. Think of all those names in the hall of fame. Yours will be on that wall one day.'

'It's just . . . no one else got in, no one from school, no one from the team. I'll be on my own.'

'You're saying that's a bad thing? That you're literally the best player you know?'

Freddie smiled. This wasn't just parental flattery – this was an objective fact. Sam's commitment to honesty wasn't exempt here. His son had been under no illusion about the coins under the pillow, or the presents under the tree. This isn't to say that Sam, with Marilyn's insistence, didn't play along. Of course he did. He played his part right up until Freddie asked him outright. And yet, even when exposed as fabrication, the stories retained their magic – it was a small price to pay for trust. The truth always, *always* gave more than it took.

So, Sam's praise would invariably mean something. Freddie was, by any measure, very good at football – there was no need to encourage him with considered language. Reality sufficed. Sam had no idea where this athleticism came from – if it wasn't for his eyes and that dry humour, it'd be quite reasonable to demand a DNA test.

'I guess.'

'Look, Freddie, I'll level with you. The boots, they're an investment. Those feet are little money-makers. I need you to pay for my retirement.'

'You could always get a job?'

'Sore back. Tired knees.'

'And an undying love for *Countdown*.'

Sam laughed. This kid was definitely his. They passed through the wide opening in the hedgerow at the edge of the grounds, and came into the alleyway just off Kendell Street.

'Sorry, about the other day,' Freddie said. 'I was just cold and wet.'

'No.' Sam could have cried. 'Don't apologise. I was in the wrong. I should have let you know I'd be late. It won't happen again.'

'David said I should give you some slack.'

He shot Freddie a fake scowl. 'That guy . . .'

'He said you're only human – bit like a teacher, I guess. And that you're helping the police again and it's important.'

'Aw for God's sake.'

'What?'

'It's just . . . I really try and hate David but I can't do it. Why is he so reasonable?'

Freddie laughed. 'Sometimes he doesn't use a coaster, if that helps.'

'Scum. Maybe I should arrest him.'

That wry smile again. 'If only you could.'

The truth was that David, despite Sam's primal, caveman hostility, was a good person. Kind, smart, honest and, crucially, there in all the ways he wasn't. In all the ways that mattered.

'You let me know how you get on,' he said, holding the gate open when they arrived.

'If we argue, we should always make up before you leave.' Freddie looked up at him. 'I don't want our last conversation to ever be a sad one.'

A nerve here. Sam opened his mouth to speak. To tell him. But couldn't do it. He half wished Freddie would just ask – say something like, 'Are you ill?'

And then, cornered, he'd have to share what only he and two doctors knew.

A grey flurry on a scan – the headaches, and the blinking, both explained with a straight-faced diagnosis. The consultant called it a 'malignant' growth, no larger than a penny, swelling inside his skull. That adjective seemed somewhat unnecessary. Sam would have assumed his well-being wasn't at the top of its agenda.

There was a strange pride in the grading – the scale goes up to four. He had the worst one on the market. Top shelf. Absolute state-of-the-art death. They threw a load of jargon at him, but the headline was – you, sir, are fucked. Timings were difficult to forecast but, long and short, don't bother buying a whole calendar for next year. Sam had joked that he might as well take up smoking again. It was an unusually intimate moment – both doctors had been relaxed enough to drop their medical facades and smile. 'Sure,' one of them had said. 'Why not?'

If there was any misery to be found, it was here, standing in front of him.

'Deal,' Sam agreed. They shook hands.

Freddie disappeared up the path, past the rose bush and into a place that still, on days like this, when the light was just right, looked like home.

Chapter 12

We remember the man. We have seen him before, on TV, in the newspapers, quoted in reports about Ethan Clarke. But he looks quite different now, out of his white shirt, away from blue press-conference banners emblazoned with the constabulary crest – cameras, cameras, cameras flashing. Today, in his one-bedroom flat, he looks lost, sitting on his sofa, smoking a cigarette, watching a film on mute. Colours flash and paint him blue, then green and back to blue again. He sips a drink and checks his phone at regular intervals. When it does ring, he's frowning. Clearly, he does not recognise this number.

◆　◆　◆

'Hello?'

'Hi, is that Sam?'

'Speaking.' He cleared his throat and stubbed his cigarette out in the ashtray.

'Not sure if you remember me. I worked in intelligence for a couple of months, just before you left the force. Kelly Howells.'

'Hello, Kelly.'

She was young. A redhead. Her husband's name was Neil. She had a tiny hole below her bottom lip – a piercing he'd never seen filled with metal. Other than that, he couldn't remember her – he couldn't recall a single conversation. She was just a picture – a static hologram, her features disappearing if he looked too hard.

'I . . . I don't know why I'm telling you this and, you should know, I've already gone down the official channels. But, something Isabelle said. And I . . . I remember you were honest, and kind to me after the whole dispute.'

The whole dispute. Something there, but vague. An internal issue. One of any number of staffing matters he'd dealt with – something relevant to her and not even worthy of long-term memory to him.

'What is it?'

'A friend of my father's, he works down at Bronzegate. The prison.'

'I know it well.'

'So, he works on one of the open wings, not totally open but it's quite relaxed – where they did all those exercise schemes last year.' Sam heard a pen click and saw her sitting at her desk, leaning back in her chair. Maybe glancing around the office. But he knew his imagination was flawed, tainted by memory, as it had cast an old CRT computer monitor in front of her, instead of the flat screens they used now.

'Right?'

'Anyway, they do woodwork, in the shop – spice racks for the girlfriend, wooden spoons, sanding tables, whatever. I showed him the picture of that thing, that doll. It's been doing the rounds here.' She moved – he heard some paper turn. 'The crying Hecate.'

Sam's gaze lifted a bit higher – he looked at the wall but didn't see it.

'Well, everyone else I've shown it to just shrugged. But he recognised it straight away. He says there's an inmate on his wing called Joe, I think. The guy's got crazy tattoos, heavily into the Bible. This bloke, he loves woodwork, goes every chance he gets.

A while back, they're turning over his cell and they find a box, a whopping cardboard box full of these things. He'd made *fifty* dolls.'

Standing, Sam stepped over to the window, pleased that honesty, or if you could stretch as far as Kelly, kindness, really did pay dividends. He was curious, but nothing more than that. Adriana did say these Hecate figures crop up from time to time. Only thing unique about the one they'd found was the charcoaled face.

'What were their heads like?'

'Well, that's the thing, it must have taken a fair while with a cigarette lighter.'

'Thank you, Kelly.'

The nostalgic tingle of progress. A little glimpse into what satisfaction might feel like, if it was ever even possible.

Chapter 13

Bronzegate Prison. Razor wire wrapped around high walls, CCTV cameras posted on anything vertical. Squared spires and concrete and windows shrouded in steel painted blue years ago, now flaking and weatherworn. Seagulls circled above – confused and lost and squawking about it.

Inside, that echoing sports hall brickwork, those shiny rubber scuffed floors, and the claustrophobia you surely never get used to. The room set aside for them was just off the main quad, next to offices and well away from the other prisoners.

Their contact was a guard called Peter, the friend of Kelly's father, who wore smart trousers, a white shirt and a heavy leather belt that jingled with metal as he walked. He met them at reception and escorted them along a warren of corridors, beneath suicide nets and through three locked checkpoints. Everything was clad in thin steel grids, many of which seemed to serve no purpose beyond a reminder that this place was, first and foremost, a cage.

'Sorry we have to do it in here,' Peter said, holding open the office door and inviting them inside. 'The family area is quite spacious and, well, visiting times and all that. I know you're here too,' he added, nodding at Isabelle, 'it's just that without the proper call, the paperwork, it's a bit . . .'

'This is fine,' Sam said, peering around the small room.

'How long has he been here?' Isabelle asked.

'Here, six years – but inside, about double that.'

'Does he get many visitors?' she added.

'His mother comes once a week – and he calls her every single day, four p.m., like clockwork. In case you were wondering why he has "Mary" scribbled on his face. These bruisers, they always have a soft spot for their ma.'

Sam helped himself to a seat and Isabelle stood against the wall, waiting while Peter went and fetched Joey Osbourne.

Wearing baggy jogging bottoms and a navy fleece zipped right up to his chin, the inmate entered a few minutes later carrying a curious contempt that filled Sam with a blip of fear. Those wild, violent eyes he recognised from a hundred places. Men who can hide behind charm and smile for decades, only to erupt when given half a chance. And yet, unrestrained and well behaved, the bald man strolled slowly past Isabelle to the foldable chair held out for him. He sat directly opposite Sam, the corner of a desk between them.

'You all right, Pete?' Joey said.

'All good. Joey, this is Detective Isabelle Lewin and her colleague . . .'

'Sam's fine,' he said.

The tattoos were as billed – outrageous and pervasive. The kind of brazen artwork that advertises you have no interest in employment, no interest in normal exchanges with normal people in normal places. A crucifix on his left cheek, spreading diagonally across his temple and down to the top of his ear. Latin scripture spiralling around his thick neck like a noose. Just behind his fleece collar, the top two legs of a swastika. Although, Sam noted, the symbol was almost hidden – perhaps regret, maybe even tolerance, had seeped in through these bars over the years. But that was unlikely.

Extended periods of time with hostile men of all colours and creeds tends to make such tribal prejudice worse before it makes it better. Maybe he was just feeling cold.

The tattoo that interested Sam the most, however, was on the right-hand side of his bald head – a busy pentagram hosting weaving snakes and two naked women. Predictably crude, their poses were as pornographic as they were gratuitous. One had a slit throat, though thankfully no colour besides swamp green had been used. The other poor lady was missing her hands, her feet and the flesh and skin from her skull. Despite this, the women seemed happy and horny, wrapped around the frame of the tilted star, stretched over a bulging vein on Joey's temple.

And there, on his chin, calligraphy. 'Mary'. The mother he still spoke to every day, without exception.

Peter placed a fire extinguisher on the floor to keep the door open, and then left the room. Sam wondered now just how well behaved a convicted murderer has to be for such a blasé lack of security. Twelve years of peaceful, polite civility wasn't enough for him. Despite Peter's confidence that he posed no risk, Sam made sure his feet were planted firmly on the floor. His body was drip-feeding him adrenaline – his intuition detecting things everyone else seemed able to ignore.

'How can I help you?' Joey said, getting himself comfortable. He slouched with his legs spread wide and his arms folded across his chest.

Isabelle stood by the door, hands clasped behind her – like an exam adjudicator, here to keep this visit somewhat official. She breathed through her nose and surveyed the room with her calm, almost docile eyes.

'Have you any idea what this is?' Sam asked, holding his phone out with the picture of their crying Hecate on the screen.

Joey leaned forwards and pretended to strain his vision, glanced to Isabelle, then back to Sam. 'That, my friend, is a mobile telephone.'

'Of course.' Sam tutted. 'Obvious now you say it.'

'Pleased to assist.'

'How about the photo, seen one of them before?'

'I've seen many photos.'

'Joey.' Peter's voice came through the corridor from the office next door. 'Be nice.'

Smiling, Joey waved his hand. 'It's a . . . a religious thing, called a crying Hecate.'

'I understand you enjoy making them?' Sam said, sliding his mobile back into the pocket of his jeans.

'Yeah, but they told me to stop. Ironic, as it's remarkably hellish in here, wouldn't you say?'

'Oh, I've seen worse.'

'As have I, friend, as have I.'

'Why did you make them?'

'To curse my enemies,' Joey said, laughing with wide eyes, waving spooky, childish fingers.

There was a loud buzzing sound, a rumble above them and then a lock clanking nearby. The electronic ligaments of this metal beast were on the move. Bronzegate Prison was old – it required more than a lick of paint – what it really needed was a bulldozer and dynamite on its load-bearing walls. Sam was then aware of a fan on the ceiling, which twitched on its axis – it had been left on but something inside stopped it from turning.

'The hand of the dark lord shall rise from below and snatch whomever she chooses,' Sam said.

'That's right. The light of her torch exposes everything.'

'Do you believe they work, the dolls? They drag demons back down into hell?'

'What do you believe?'

'I believe you got the idea to burn their heads from someone else.'

Joey stopped in his tracks, narrowed his eyes.

'That, or you carved this one too.' Sam tapped his pocket.

'Mine are neater. That one looks like shit.'

'As I understand, charring the face is not conventional.'

Joey seemed reluctant to go down this road. *So, go down it we must*, Sam thought.

Looking at his tattooed knuckles, Joey picked at a nail. 'I'm guessing this has something to do with the Clarke kids?'

With the slightest turn of her head, Isabelle exhaled. It had been a while since he'd been stopped in the street but, to this day, people still looked at Sam and frowned in recognition, or something close to it. He had the lowest celebrity status one could attain, rivalled only by first-week rejects on obscure reality TV shows. Joey was simply joining dots.

'Where was it?' he asked.

Hesitating, Isabelle opened her mouth to speak, but decided instead to stay silent. It probably was too late anyway. They could move on, but he would piece it together himself. Was this the kind of man who would talk to the press? Isabelle was leaving it up to Sam to decide.

If in doubt, be honest. 'In a tree near the Clarkes' house,' he said.

'Well, fuck me. Was it pointing?'

Sam nodded.

'Going by your photo, looks like it's been there a fair while too.'

'Yes.'

'Do you believe in God?' Joey asked, tilting his head.

'I believe God is just a word for things we don't know yet.'

'And you think *I* have some of that precious information? What does that make me?'

Sam's eyes went briefly to the ceiling, to that crippled fan, and he sighed. 'An angel.'

More laughter.

Last try. 'Do you know anyone else who might make a doll like this, with a burned head?'

'I'm afraid not,' Joey whispered. This was a lie, the first one of the day. The tone of the conversation had changed. A door had closed – silent and without ceremony, but they could go no further.

Sam sat back in his chair. 'I don't work for the police any more, you know that, right?'

'And her?' Joey nodded towards Isabelle.

'You can tell from a mile, can't you?' Sam turned, looking up. 'Think it's her posture. Like a bouncer.'

Total serenity from young Isabelle – bulletproof, immune to the outside world. He wondered if she could even blush.

'I was on a job back in the Nineties.' Sam shuffled round to face forwards again. 'There was an officer, a colleague of mine, they called him Wiggie – his old nickname at school.'

'Here we go.'

'Wiggie was trying to build a case, tracking this heavyweight drug dealer. And we knew, I mean, we *knew* what he was up to. But he was almost supernatural – we just couldn't tie him to anything. Frustrating, to know something you can't prove.'

Joey looked bored.

'Anyway, eventually, when everything else had failed, when he walked free from court, when he'd bribed, wrestled, wriggled out of the system, he finally slipped up. Routine stop and he's got a kilo of heroin in the boot of his car. Hurray. Dead to rights. Down he goes, they throw the book at him. Later, Wiggie told me over a drink or two that he'd planted the drugs. It was seen as ticking boxes – a formality. After all, it's the kind of thing this guy did anyway – true enough, right?'

'Has this story got a point?'

'The point is, Joey, that the police can cause an enormous amount of harm when they want to.'

'Good job you're retired, then.'

The interview fizzled out after this – a few more attempts to pry some information, but, as Sam suspected, Joey wasn't willing to disclose specifics. He'd taken the Wiggie story as a lazy, idle threat. And what else could Joey lose? Sam gave him his personal number and told him to call if he changed his mind. They left just after 11 a.m.

On the way back to the car, beneath those tall wired walls and bewildered seagulls, Isabelle seemed dejected, as though they'd wasted time.

'That anecdote true?' she asked.

'Certainly is.'

'How does that square with your honesty?'

'Perfectly.' Craving poison, Sam began to smoke. 'I reported Wiggie – that shitty bastard. He lost his job, his pension, everything. The dealer in question was released, I think even compensated. I wasn't a popular man. And I'm not sorry.'

Isabelle appeared, in an odd way, to like this answer. She would not, however, like the rest of his plan.

Back home, in his flat, Sam took out his phone, scrolled through his contacts and pressed a number saved as Lei R.

'Is that Mr Maguire?'

'It is indeed. How's the uniform treating you?'

'Itchy, smells like plastic.'

'Sorry to hear that. Listen, this isn't a social call.' Sam twirled a biro in his fingers, leaning on his kitchen counter.

'Thought not.'

What he was about to do was at the very edge of his moral borders – misleading, unpleasant, but not – and he was careful here lying. When it was over, when the ends had justified these means, he would rectify any deception. But first, like a conductor, he had to make certain things happen.

'Remember that morning, ages ago, at the estate? The fire?'

Lei sighed. 'I know I owe you a favour,' he said. 'Just tell me what it is.'

'I need you to arrest someone.'

'OK, that shouldn't be a problem. Who?'

'A woman, Mary Osbourne.'

'What's she done?'

'Nothing, as far as I know.'

'So . . . why would I arrest her?'

'Well, Lei, that's why it's a favour – if she'd broken the law it'd be, you know, your job.'

'OK, fine. We generally need a reason though.'

'Of course – arrest her on suspicion of possession with intent to supply. Class A. Heroin.'

'Jesus Christ. Then what?'

'Go through the motions, swab her, grill her, whatever. Then release her without charge, before three thirty p.m.'

'Can I ask what this is about?'

'You can.' There was a short silence, then another sigh. 'Good choice,' Sam said. 'Look, it's theatre, all right? Break a door if you can, shout a bit. Just make sure it's an experience she remembers.'

'Fucking hell, Sam.'

'Half past three. And, Lei, there's a good reason for this, I promise.'

He gave him the address and then rested his phone face down on the arm of his sofa, next to the ashtray. Then he read through the statements taken from the Clarkes' neighbours. Jasper Parker was among them but not, Sam noticed, his lodging daughter. He made a note to change that.

From a small camera mounted on a stab vest, we see a narrow, shaded corridor. A radio crackles, electronic voices whispering. Boots on the floor – the footage shaky, fish-eyed. Close. We see a door with a brass number five at the top, in the centre of the wood, next to a peephole. To the left, three officers wearing full riot gear are ready to go – the closest one gives us a single nod. Below, a pair of gloved hands hold a metal battering ram. It swings back, out of view. And bang. It begins.

At exactly 4.10 p.m., Sam picked up his mobile and placed it on his thigh. He stared down into the screen, waiting, waiting, waiting. Two minutes later, vibrations from an unknown number.

'Joey,' Sam said, with win-win optimism.

'You sleep well at night?'

'Not particularly.'

'These calls are recorded . . .'

'So?'

'You've crossed a line, my friend. You really do not want to fuck with me, Sam.'

'I know. I just want you to answer my *fucking question.*'

The grand bluff – a nuclear warhead loses all power the moment it's unleashed. But we must pretend. Helpless, locked away, unable

93

to protect his dear mother from an atrocious weapon Sam wouldn't even dream of using, Joey finally opened that door.

'I'll tell you what I know, and then it's over. Deal?'

'Of course.'

'This . . . this is a hornets' nest. These guys, they're cold, heart-loos, eye for an eye killers. Literal interpretation of the worst Bible passages. Fire and fury.'

'Names.'

'There's a group, a fringe Christian sect,' Joey whispered. Sam pictured him huddled into the prison phone mounted on the wall, checking left and right. 'It's called North Serpent.'

'*North Serpent?*'

'Yeah, ha ha, get your laughs in now. The church was estab-lished by the Marston family. Bunch of horror-show nutjobs.'

'Friends of yours?'

'No.'

'These dolls – they make similar?'

'Yes.'

'I thought it was a satanic thing?'

'It is. The church is all about using their own weapons against them.'

'Them?' Sam furrowed his brow at the absurdity. 'Demons?'

'Yeah, witches, Jews, blacks, gays, you name it.'

'And you were part of all this?'

'I was a member for years. You want to know why I left? Because they're fucking maniacs.'

'Quite an endorsement from someone like yourself.'

Joey gave him a tired laugh. 'Thanks.'

'OK, so who do I need to know about?'

'Right, so there's three brothers. Henry, Gregory and Max – those last two are twins. Then there's Diane, the oldest. The sister. She founded it. Max is the worst one, he's just . . .'

'You sound like you're scared of them.'

'You will be too. I've seen first-hand what those brothers are capable of. And I've heard plenty of rumours.'

'Give me an example.'

'These occult rituals get a bit nasty when the sun goes down. At that old house, in that garage . . . Let's just say a few missing people have died screaming their safe word.'

'North Serpent still up and running?' Sam asked. 'Where are they?'

'Church itself has folded. They never meet. Got a lot of bad press in recent years. It's toxic. Last I heard they're all in hiding. You won't be able to find the Marstons, let alone Diane.'

'You'd be surprised what I can do, Joey.'

Chapter 14

Robin ate her cereal on the bed. She held the bowl between her crossed legs and, when she finished, drank the last of the chocolatey milk. As the voice had told her to, she left the empty bowl by the door, then sat back on the mattress.

Her arm was less sore now. She picked at the tiny scab in the crease of her elbow joint, which tickled more than it hurt. It was a bit like the bruise she had after a blood test at the hospital when she was poorly. She thought, when she first woke up here, in this room, that the voice might be a doctor. Maybe he had wanted to test her blood for something. But she was confused and sleepy. Now she knew he wasn't a doctor and this wasn't a hospital. Hospitals are white and they don't have bars on the windows.

But her plan had worked. The door opened and the hand came into the dark room, took the empty bowl away but didn't ask about the *other* spoon. When the cereal had arrived, she'd said quietly, through the opening, that she would rather have a little spoon. She only liked big spoons for soup. The voice had returned a few seconds later and passed one through. Now she had that big spoon hidden under her pillow.

She could hardly remember the first day – it was all a strange dream. This was another reason she thought he might be a doctor, because she felt woozy like she'd been sent to sleep. She'd had anaesthetic once before, for her appendix operation, and remembered waking up and thinking she was on holiday in Canada, at Grandma's house. It took ages for Mum to explain they were in the hospital – it just happened to be snowing in England that day.

Robin had only cried once, on the first night, when she couldn't sleep. She'd wondered if she had been put in prison. Maybe the police had found out about the supermarket. Her heart raced at that thought – it had been such a stupid thing to do. She was at the self-service checkout with Emma and Emma's big brother, Carl. They bought fruit for the smoothies they were going to make at the barbecue – but Emma and Robin had each picked up a packet of wine gums. While Carl beeped all the fruit through the till, Robin put her sweets on the metal counter, to pay for them properly. But Emma passed them back to her and smiled. They both held on to their wine gums and left the shop. Robin felt her cheeks turning red in the car. When they arrived back home, she was too worried to even eat them. Instead, she put them in the kitchen bin and pushed them right to the bottom. She covered them with greasy tinfoil and old flowers Mum had thrown away. There was always the issue of fingerprints, but Robin decided the police probably wouldn't look in the bin.

She thought that, as soon as she saw Mum, she would tell her what she'd done and apologise and promise never to steal again. *Never*. It would be the first thing she'd say. The reason she had cried was because, if this *was* punishment for something, then maybe her parents knew she was here. And that meant no one was coming to get her.

But Robin knew that real prisons let you go outside, sometimes only for a little bit of time, but they do allow it. You need vitamin D from the sun so, even if someone is really bad, they don't keep them inside forever. It was possible that children's prisons were different, but why would they have stricter rules for young people?

And why would they arrest you in the middle of the night? It was like she went to sleep at home, then woke up here. She hadn't seen any policemen or a judge, not even in her weird dreams.

And the voice wasn't mean. It didn't speak much but, when it did, it was always friendly. On the second morning – or maybe the third, she wasn't entirely sure how long she had been here – he gave her some porridge, and asked if she wanted anything else. She said no thank you. Then he asked what her favourite cereal was and she replied, without thinking, Coco Pops. She panicked and thought maybe she should have said porridge instead – she didn't want to seem ungrateful. But he obviously wasn't upset because, today, he gave her Coco Pops. With a little spoon.

So, she decided this wasn't a proper prison. Which meant she didn't have to feel sorry about escaping.

The room was quite small, with a bed, a TV and another door that led to a bathroom. The TV couldn't get proper channels, but it was connected to a DVD player, which she worked out how to use. There were a few brand-new films for her – all still wrapped in see-through plastic. Some she'd seen before, but a couple she hadn't – including an old movie with music. At first, she stubbornly refused to watch them but, fairly soon, she was just so bored. That was the hardest thing about this place, there was nothing to do besides watch DVDs. And, of course, plan her escape.

The only window had bars, and also wooden boards over the glass. She had tugged on the metal, but it didn't budge. Besides, she couldn't climb through here because there was a camera on the wall, near the ceiling – like a little black eye. Which meant someone was watching. But there were no cameras in the bathroom. So that would have to be her way out.

She lay on the bed and pretended to relax for a few minutes, while the old black-and-white film with songs played on the TV. This would make enough noise. Then she rolled over, slid her arm under the soft pillow and grabbed the spoon. She held it up her sleeve, just like a packet of stolen wine gums, then stood and went into the bathroom.

For a couple of minutes, she waited there, standing still on the tiles. She had butterflies in her stomach and her cheeks were hot. Maybe she should do it later. But if this wasn't a hospital and it wasn't a prison, then the voice was a bad man. At school Mrs Pickford did a special assembly about not getting lifts from people you don't know. Even if they act like your best friend. Even if, she said, they *seem* nice. The voice seemed really nice. This made her want to escape right then, but also made the idea much scarier. She had to at least try.

Above the toilet, in the top corner of the wall, there was a white fan. Robin put the seat down, stood on top and placed her knee on the cistern. The plastic flapping parts were closed but, when she pulled a dusty switch on the side, they tilted and let cool air in. She pushed the spoon under the frame of the fan. It took some wiggling. When it was in place, she grabbed the handle and lifted it up, expecting the plastic to snap. But it didn't. Instead the metal spoon just bent, almost completely in half. It was stuck. She panicked and tugged. On the third yank, it came free and she slipped off the toilet and fell, landing awkwardly in the corner with her legs twisted above her.

'Ouch,' she whispered to herself.

Another idea arrived. She could use the spoon as a screwdriver, to get rid of the screws in each corner of the fan. Again, back on top of the toilet, she bent the spoon straight. But it wouldn't grip – it kept sliding off. Each time it did, the metal bent again and she had to pull it back in line. She noticed the spoon getting warm at the neck and, eventually, it snapped – her knuckle slipped hard into the plastic, leaving a graze so bad there was a little bit of white skin sticking out.

'Stupid, stupid, stupid,' she said, stabbing the wall with the useless spike, the top part clattering to the tiles below.

She sat down on the toilet seat, held her stinging finger and, when blood appeared, she rinsed it under cold water. It was a bad plan anyway. Even with the fan gone, the hole in the wall wouldn't be big enough to poke her head through, let alone her body.

There was a noise.

Robin hid the spoon handle behind the sink, but panicked when she couldn't find the top part. She fell to her knees and patted around on the cold floor. Another sound from the room. She had to leave it.

She went to the bathroom door, then stopped, turned back to the toilet, lifted the seat and pressed the flush button, even though she hadn't been.

In the bedroom now and the main door was opening. As always, it stopped on a small latch attached to the wall on the other side. It only ever opened a few centimetres, or sometimes wide enough for a bowl of food.

'Are you OK?' the voice asked.

'Yes, thank you.'

'Is there anything you need?'

It seemed silly to say, but Robin, now sitting on the bed, holding her sore graze, figured that he'd given her everything else she wanted, so why not try.

'Please may I . . . please may I go home?'

'You are home,' he said.

What a strange reply, she thought. Could that be true? Was this a secret room somewhere in the house? Where would it even be? She decided he was lying.

'I don't think I am,' she whispered. 'Can I go outside?' she asked.

'Maybe one day. Is there anything else you need? Books, games, more DVDs?'

'Um, yes please.'

'Lessons start soon, OK. You won't be so bored.'

'Lessons in what?'

'Maths, science, English . . . everything.'

'Please may I see my parents?'

He didn't respond, instead he just slid something in through the opening. 'Here,' he said. 'This is my favourite book.'

And then the door closed and he was gone.

Robin knelt on the carpet, picked up the book and tilted it towards her small lamp. It was called *The All-Seeing Eye*.

She stepped back to the bed and sat down. It was a bit like a comic book, because it had drawings with speech bubbles. But it was the longest comic book she had ever seen. The back said it was a 'graphic novel'. Near the barcode, she read it had cost £12.99. Which was quite expensive for a book.

A quick thought. *Her* favourite book was *Ruby and the Giants*.

There was a chapter when Ruby was in the castle dungeon. All *she* needed to escape was a metal candlestick. She spent all night dragging it across the floor until it had a flat end, then used it as a chisel to break the cobblestones.

Robin began to do the same thing with her spoon, scraping it again and again down the bathroom wall, leaving long grooves in white paint. Soon she found the metal was too strong, so she moved to the shower, which had very hard tiles and seemed to work much better.

It was evening – she'd been working on her chisel for hours. So long her hand had gone numb. She went back into the bedroom for a rest, and sat for a while on her bed. Strangely peaceful in the house. Sometimes she would hear a radio, or footsteps. But now, it was silent.

Robin stood by the door, looked up at the camera and listened. He wasn't home. Of course, it would be locked, but she still pulled the handle down to test—

The door opened, stopping on the small latch.

She put her feet on the wall and tugged as hard as she could, but wasn't strong enough to break it. The gap was about half the width of her head so, unless she became a snake, or an octopus, she couldn't squeeze through.

But then she heard a noise. He *was* home.

She closed the door as quietly as possible, then rushed to the bed. She grabbed the book from the carpet, laid flat and pretended to read, in case he was watching.

After around five minutes, he arrived. Her heart was beating fast, like a mouse's, as the door moved. Maybe he had seen. Maybe he was angry.

But a small bundle of clothes came in through the opening.

'Here,' he said. 'You can't wear pyjamas forever. Are you hungry?'

Earlier, he'd told her she could have *anything* she wanted to eat.

'Anything?' she'd asked.

'Anything.'

So, now, a new plan. 'I want marshmallows,' she announced.

'Pardon?'

'Please may I have some marshmallows?'

'I . . . I don't have any.'

'Oh . . . OK,' she whispered. 'Never mind.'

And then he was gone.

She sat still – as still as a statue – and listened. Just as she'd hoped, she heard the front door clunk shut. He must be going to the shop.

As quickly as she could, she swooped to her door and pulled it open as far as it would go. Then she poked the spoon handle through. The latch was a bit like one of those metal hooks she had sometimes seen on garden gates and, with a lift and a wiggle, she felt it slide up out of its hole and dangle on the other side of the wood.

For the very first time, the room was open.

Robin stood for a moment, looking into a short hallway. She thought this had been quite easy – she could have done it with a DVD case. In fact, it seemed *too easy*. And now she realised why.

At the end of the landing was another window, also covered in bars. It wasn't just her cell. The entire house was a prison.

Swallowing, she felt her throat gulp as she took her first step.

She peered round into a bathroom, then crept inside and to the window. More thick metal. Back on the landing, she noticed a few crosses, like at a church. One on every wall. Another door to her right was open. This was a study – it had a wide desk with three computer screens. The one in the middle showed her room – she leaned closer and saw the bed, the TV, the book she'd left on the floor. And the one on the left—

Robin flinched, hand to her heart – there was someone on the screen. But, when she discovered the person was her, she sighed. Looking into the hall, she found a small black camera near the ceiling. Then, turning back, she waved her hand and saw it move in the live feed. There were cameras in every room. She could see the whole house from here. And it was empty. But not for long.

Robin went to the stairs. Holding the bannister, she stepped quickly down, stopping only once when a floorboard creaked. There were tiles on the ground floor. She walked across them, feeling the cold on her feet, even through her socks. The front door had a round window. She tried the handle. It didn't budge. He'd locked it from the other side.

Turning round, she rushed down the hallway, through a messy kitchen and to the back door. Also locked. She searched for a key, lifting up the bristly mat and moving an empty flower pot. Nothing. A bin at her side smelled terrible. Tiny flies, as small as dust, flew silently around the lid. Maybe he had a phone?

Robin went back up the hall and, when she stepped into the living room, stopped dead in her tracks. It was full of *horrid* paintings. Scary faces. Nasty men with animal legs and horns. They were everywhere. Her lips shivered, her eyes stung and a single tear trickled down her cheek. She wiped it away and sniffed. She would be brave, she decided. Like Ruby.

On the shelf above the fireplace there was a stuffed goat's head. It was lying on its side, its glassy eye staring up, looking nowhere. Either side of it were huge candles, the wax had melted and hung like icicles from the wood. There were more crosses too, lots of them. Big ones, small ones – some on the wall, some on the floor. The man who lived here wasn't a doctor, he wasn't a prison guard. He was, she thought, mad. And this made her more frightened than she had ever been.

Robin put her hand over her eyes, like she was shielding them from the sun, so she didn't have to see any of these awful things. Then she went into the living room. She clambered up on to the sofa and, leaning left then right, tried to catch a glimpse through the window, through the bars. But she could only see green leaves and a thin strip of blue sky. Carefully, she climbed back on to the carpet.

Still hiding her eyes, she turned and faced the other end of the room. She kept her head down, pointing at the ground, at her feet, and swallowed. If she was going to find a phone, then she *had* to look. No matter how scary it would be. She took a big, slow breath in through her nose.

And, when Robin lifted her head, she froze again, standing utterly still. She clamped her hand over her mouth, felt her chin quiver beneath it, and finally burst into tears.

There were hundreds of photographs, maybe thousands, all over the wall. Photos of her. Photos of her parents. Photos of their house. Some were framed, some were pinned, some were spread loose over a table.

She scrunched her eyes shut, as hard as she could, covered her face with both hands and cried and cried and cried. Whimpering, sniffing, she felt her shoulders bounce up and down. Her stomach ached, her head hurt, she could hardly take a breath. All she wanted was to go home, to see her mum, to say sorry, sorry, *sorry* for anything she might have done—

But, with a sharp gasp to silence, she stopped. Her eyes were wide open now, looking through her wet fingers.

A noise. The unmistakable sound of a key turning in the front door.

Chapter 15

We see that living room through one of the fifteen cameras in this house. The crucifixes. The rubbish. Demonic prints pinned on every surface. Inverted pentagrams and dark art. Spent candles and symbols scrawled on scruffy sheets of paper. Crazed scribbles, endless spirals in endless notepads. Drawings of the Devil himself, rising up from fire sketched in biro. Claws and horns and carved dolls with burned heads. Windows clad in steel. A shrine to the Clarkes – framed pictures of Anna, Francis, Ethan and Robin, arranged in a rough family tree. Anna's and Francis's photographs dominate the upper half of the wall, then hundreds of home-printed renditions of their children below. Newspapers piled high – this sad story told on every front page. And there, tiny in the frame, we see Robin crouched by the end of the sofa with her knees pulled up against her chest. Her eyes wide and ready, at the centre of it all.

The only noise she made was her heartbeat. Robin pressed herself forwards, trying to keep it quiet, in case he heard it too. With a slight tilt of her head, she listened as he locked the front door behind him. Then the sound of keys dropped on a table in the hallway. And now footsteps on the tiles.

When she realised he wasn't coming into the living room, she crept on all fours, past the front of the sofa. He was in the kitchen. She heard a plastic bag, and the fridge door – clinking jars, bottles. Then a cupboard and a plate on the worktop.

Crawling, Robin placed her hand on an empty drink can. She winced at the sound and carefully moved it aside. A bit further on, she rose and stood by the living-room doorway. Leaning as slowly as possible, she moved her head until she could see up the hall. A shadow, a flash, and she shot back round again, her hand resting on the frame. She'd seen the voice. For the first time, she'd seen him. She'd seen his back and shoulder and the side of his head. He was wearing a black jumper and smart trousers. Although he wasn't that tall, his bony body made him seem long. He had grey hair. It was messy. In his hand, he was holding a plate with pale-blue-and-pink marshmallows, which he'd arranged in a small pyramid.

Robin held her breath and felt warm tears on her cheeks as he stepped right past the doorway and to the stairs. She listened – one, two, three, four, creak on five, six, seven, eight then she had another peek. The side table, by the front door. A set of silver keys. She crossed the tiles and used a thumb and finger to pick them up. They jingled so she squeezed the rings together to keep them still. Crouching to check up the stairs, she walked backwards, slowly, slowly to the door.

Then fast. She tried one. It didn't fit. Her fingers scrabbled, the keys clinking loudly as she tried another. She slid it in – the lock didn't move. The final key in her hand, in the lock, turning and working and a terrible noise upstairs.

He knew. He knew she was gone. Thudding, loud footsteps above. A slammed door. On the stairs now, coming down. Hard and loud behind her. She shielded her face and fell to the floor.

'I'm sorry, I'm sorry, I'm sorry,' she was saying, huddled in the corner.

But he was shouting. She couldn't hear exactly what he said – she was holding her ears and apologising and crying and apologising and he loomed over her, yelling that she had done a very bad thing and she would get hurt if she ever did anything like this again.

'I won't, I won't, I promise I won't.'

And when he grabbed her shoulder, turned her round and she saw his face for the very first time, Robin heard a shriek echo through the house. It sounded like a girl screaming.

When Robin had stopped crying, she decided once more to be brave. If there was any chance of getting out of this place, she would need to overcome her fear. Like she did on holiday when she jumped off that high diving board and into the sea. She was so worried but, once she walked to the end and looked down into the clear ocean, she ignored all her doubts and just stepped forwards. Her eyes opened at the last moment and saw blue, and then splash – she was cold and deep underwater, her legs kicking her back up to the surface for a breath. And she was laughing – rising bubbles tickling her body.

'See?' Mum had yelled. 'Fun, right?'

'I want to do it again,' Robin said, turning and swimming back to that slippery green ladder.

The second time she wasn't scared. And it would be the same when she escaped.

She felt her foot twitch, waking her up – she must have drifted off to sleep. Somehow, she could tell a long time had passed since he'd brought her back to the room. Her stomach felt empty, so she got out of bed and crouched by the door, where a small pile of marshmallows was waiting for her on the plate. She sat there chewing the squishy sweets, staring at the bathroom door, wondering what her next plan would be. Again, like always, she found boredom overtook the fear. After a while, she lay on the bed and picked up the book.

Usually, at school, it took her ages to read a whole book, even one with pictures like *The All-Seeing Eye*. But, later that afternoon, she'd finished it.

And it was quite good. Her favourite character was called Julius Jacob – a mega-intelligent man with spiky black hair and sunglasses. He was a sort of spy who could hack into any system. In the story, Julius said the human mind is like a computer. A brain is just an 'information processor'. Sometimes, in school assembly, Mrs Pickford did a breathing exercise to calm everyone down. She said to close your eyes and concentrate on your nose and mouth as you inhale and exhale. The idea, she said, is to notice what thoughts arrive. That was really the only time Robin paid much attention to what was going on in her head. But Julius Jacob knew so much about brains that he invented a gadget that could hack into them, just like with computers. He built a device called a neuro wire, which, the book said, 'bridged the gap' between mind and machine.

It was called *The All-Seeing Eye* because, once Julius had connected his brain to the internet, he could see through any camera on earth. And, incredibly, he could remember anything a 'digital eye' had ever seen, like with his real eyes. So, he had all the knowledge on the internet in his memory, which made him even more clever. The book was set in the future and, by the end, everyone had a neuro-wire, which meant Julius could see through other people's eyes as well. If you could really see everything, then you wouldn't be you any more. The book said your human body would be just one tiny part of yourself, like your little toe.

The ending was strange though. Julius was fighting an organisation that wanted to take over the neuro-wire and use it to make people love the president, who was a baddie – a kind of demon, with red eyes and hair that looked a bit like horns. It confused Robin because Julius died. But he was still living on all the computer networks and in people's minds, like a sort of virus. And, in the last chapter, he saved the world by giving everyone his power. Which meant they could see everything and know everything too.

She read the last paragraph aloud a couple of times, stumbling over some of the unfamiliar words. 'And so, on the cusp of the grand transition, they saw the world in all its hidden glory. There were no shadows left. An om . . . omnipotent collective descended from the digital sky, a blanket upon a planet that belongs now not to any one soul, but to all. They see. Like Julius. They see.'

Robin wasn't sure if it was a happy ending or a sad ending. It was weird, but she kind of liked it. By far her favourite part was the pictures – they made her want to draw and paint. She missed her pencils.

However, the second she'd finished, she looked up at the camera by the ceiling and felt scared again.

Later, he came to the door. When she heard it open, she turned on to her side and pretended to be asleep. He told her he was sorry for yelling and sorry if he frightened her. But Robin had to understand, he insisted, that something very bad would happen to her if she tried to escape. Soon, if she behaved herself, she would be able to come out of her room. Maybe, one day, he would even take her into the garden. She was allowed anything. *Anything*. But she could never, ever, ever leave. All these wishes, besides the only one she actually wanted to come true.

Robin could tell from the light that the door was now completely open. Maybe she could make a dash, slam it shut, trap him inside and then run away. But she was just too scared to move.

'Did my face upset you?' he asked. Robin pretended she hadn't heard. 'What's your favourite subject at school?'

The mattress springs creaked and she felt him near her legs. When he touched her foot, she flinched away and bundled herself near the pillow. There was a long silence.

'Thank you for the marshmallows,' she whispered. 'I'm sorry.'

'It's fine.'

She blinked and fiddled with the corner of her duvet cover, brushing it over her fingers. 'Art,' she said.

'I'll get you some paints and sketchbooks . . . Do you like clay?'

'I like plasticine.'

'I'll buy one of everything in the craft shop, OK? But, Robin, if I leave, you have to promise to stay indoors.'

'I . . .' She thought for a few seconds. 'I promise,' she lied.

'I know this must be scary for you, but it's really a good thing you're here.'

She didn't respond.

'Soon, you'll be able to have the run of the whole house. I'll clean everything up downstairs, you weren't meant to see that.'

'What's your name?' she asked.

'Julius.'

'Like Julius from the book.'

'Yes, just like Julius from the book. Remember that. I see everything.'

'You like cameras.'

'I do.'

'How . . . how old are you?'

'How old do you think I am?'

'I . . . I don't know. Maybe forty?'

He laughed through his nose. 'Well, that's good to hear. I'm fifty-one. How old are you?'

'Eight.'

A gentle pressure on top of the covers, his hand on her knee. This time she didn't move. 'Please don't be frightened, Robin,' he said. 'I swear, I *swear* that as long as you do what I say, you won't get hurt.'

'OK.'

'Do you believe me?'

She looked at the wall. '*Yes.*' Frowning, she felt her bottom lip tremble and turned her head into the pillow so he couldn't see her face. Because, if he did, he would notice her tears. He would realise that, once again, Robin was lying.

Chapter 16

Hallowfield Criminal Investigation Department is quiet. We see just three officers in here, two at the window, drinking coffee. The third is at her desk. She's sitting up straight, typing on her keyboard.

'Isabelle, can I have a word?' Phil asks, off camera.

Turning her head, she rises from her swivel chair and enters his office. The door closes. Only they hear what is said inside.

Diane Marston, as Joey warned, was proving difficult to track down. There still exists, in the modern world, a certain type of person who makes a concerted effort to cast no digital shadow, to leave as small a mark as possible on the humming servers that document our lives.

At a pedestrian level, this might be a reluctance to engage in social media, an inbuilt aversion to store cards, a belief that abstinence from online banking somehow protects those gold bars your bank doesn't even have or – and this was Sam's favourite – that turning location data off makes a difference.

But he soon discovered the Marstons were well beyond this banal child's play. These were individuals without bank accounts, passports, addresses. People who were, in the starkest way possible, not taking part in society. And, on the rare occasions they did, they seemed to trade only in concrete things like cash and harm.

'I've got it down to one,' Isabelle said, passing Sam a printed sheet of paper in her car. 'Henry Marston. Works for Green-Mac.'

'As in the road company?'

'That's them. Diane Marston, former Anglican priest, property developer – apparently lots of family money. She established North Serpent about fifteen years ago – there's a couple of old videos of her sermons online. Troubling stuff. She thinks our culture is infected with impure blood, says homosexuals are demons, the government is run by paedophiles – judgement day is looming. And so on. Since then it seems she's distanced herself from it all and gone into hiding. The group is now essentially a prison gang. Still Christian Identity, they call themselves knights, lots of crusades imagery on the literature, but the religious side of things has taken a back seat. There's a petition to get it banned under the Terrorism Act, for promoting hatred.'

They were parked outside Sam's flat. He'd clocked her car from his bedroom window, and rushed down the stairs to meet her before she even had time to undo her seat belt. Better she didn't see inside.

'Not much else on the system,' she said. 'Saying that, an arrest warrant was issued for Max Marston in relation to the disappearance of a Swedish student, Luke Johansson. A Scottish case, which was later dropped.'

'How come?'

'I don't know – it's strange,' she said, half turning her key so the ignition came on. Cool air hissed from the plastic slats. 'If I didn't know better, I'd say someone made a conscious decision to stop investigating him. He's also wanted for a number of other misdemeanours, but, like his siblings, he seems quite adept at laying low. As I say, Henry's the only real lead. I'm guessing, at twenty, he's the youngest.'

'Let's go.'

'No, Sam. We're bringing him in properly.'

Inevitable that this was going to happen. Phil had no doubt caught wind of their impromptu visit to Bronzegate. The look on Isabelle's face was familiar – that disapproval he would get at school, from the smart girls, the good girls, the prefects. *You know smoking kills you. You know assembly has started. What* exactly *is wrong with you, Sam?*

'Why?' he asked.

'What do you mean *why*? What's the alternative? We go and rough him up? There's a process for a reason. I'm sorry you can't be a part of this, but it isn't . . .'

'My job any more?'

'Yes, exactly.'

'It's your job.'

She nodded.

'Do you know what the Coriolis effect is?' Sam said, holding his hand out to the cold breeze coming from the air conditioner.

A near-silent groan from Isabelle. 'Yes, I do.' She watched him like he was crazy, although her face stayed perfectly still.

'Why do you do it?' he said. 'Your job.'

'Look, Sam, I'm tired, all right.'

There was conflict here – he could see it. For the first time Isabelle seemed unsettled. Still cool, still collected, still peaceful. But now he was asking her to do something she'd been explicitly told not to do. Just entertain the guy. Occupy that blinking wreck who, years ago, may have been a colleague. But no more than that. She'd already taken this too far.

Isabelle was compelled to do the right thing, maybe at any cost. Even if that cost was bringing Henry Marston in, sitting him on a chair, posing the vaguest questions imaginable and learning nothing. Do you recognise this doll? No comment. What do you know about North Serpent? No comment. Where's your sister? No comment. Their suspicion was tenuous. It'd be futile and, above all, a slow process. But it was the *right thing to do.*

'I see that.' He looked at her like her fatigue was irrelevant.

She turned in her seat. 'You want to analyse me,' she said. 'OK. Growing up, I always wanted to be an actor, a movie star.'

'So, what was the degree for?'

'I know the history factory isn't employing – education is not all about getting a job.'

'Good answer. Why ditch acting?'

Isabelle, spine straight, formal mannerisms, calculated body language, seemed to take even longer than usual to formulate an answer.

'I had . . . a negative experience in my early twenties, and it made me value the rule of law more than the arts.'

'What could *possibly* do that to a young mind?'

Another moment of hesitation. Isabelle glanced at the steering wheel, then seemed to consider her options.

'I know why you lost your job, Sam,' she said. 'I know what you did. I've been to countries where laws mean nothing. Where you dial nine-nine-nine and no one comes. These are not good places.'

She knew about George Hinds. He wondered then if her account had come from a report or from Phil, with all his poetic licence. True, it wasn't a pleasant story, but Sam had heard plenty of embellishments that made it sound much worse.

George Hinds owned the strip of beach. He was loitering around the day after they found Ethan's coat. Sam had been on his knees scouring through the sharp grass on high mounds near the scene, the dry sand stinging his face in the blasting gusts of sudden wind. Upright fence poles stood like driftwood at odd angles, all the wire long since gone. The waves were small, each capped with whipped mist lost in the white glare of sun on the ocean beyond. A shadow of a man, and Sam looked up.

'The sea is cold today,' the man had said. 'You can tell because the water is dark. You should never go into the water on days like this. You might not come out.'

He asked what the police were looking for and then offered to help. By that evening, he was in custody, telling lies for all the wrong reasons.

'Hinds was a publicity-hungry madman,' Sam explained. 'He pretended to know where Ethan was – and I believed he was telling the truth. So, when he refused to cooperate, I hurt him. And I regret it. I didn't know the extent of his mental illness at the time.'

'Maybe you were angry, because of what you'd found? Because of what it meant?'

'Maybe.'

'Sam. Look.' She spoke so softly, so quietly. The way you talk to someone young, someone young who's just shared their most intimate fear from a pillow, late at night. 'Ethan's dead. He's dead. You know that. You know it.' She lowered her face for eye contact and made sure he saw her nodding. 'You've known that since the coat. It was washed up on a beach. He's gone. But . . . Robin . . .'

'It wasn't washed up.'

'What?'

'It was too high on the rocks, above the tideline. It was left there. Put there.'

She took a deep breath. 'And what does that justify?'

'Nothing at all.'

'We'll do it properly, OK. The lawless path leads only to trouble.'

'Is that Shakespeare?'

'No,' she said, 'that's me.'

We see the man in his flat, drinking again, alone and with nothing to do. For a long while he just sits on his sofa, his quiet TV flooding him with flickering colours. He stares at a spot on the wall, just above the screen. Fading slowly, the apartment moves from dusk to dark as the earth turns away from the sun.

And then, with sudden urgency, he downs his drink, stands and grabs a hooded jumper from the kitchen counter. When he presses the button on his remote, the room disappears completely. A glimmer of yellow from the door as he leaves and, again, black silence prevails.

A quiet pavement, damp grey and glowing under street lights. Sam, dressed in a brown hoodie and jeans, walking to the edge of town. Too drunk to drive. Not merely over the limit, but swaying so much he believed he would crash if he tried.

A dog grumbled somewhere nearby, a chain clinking as it tugged on its restraints. Sam passed a long parade of front gardens, one of which looked abandoned – a caravan sat on broken, shingled concrete, with thick tufts of grass protruding where they could. A truck was still attached to the tow bar and moss had rendered its windows opaque.

Down an alleyway and towards a track that would take him—

The dog lurched hard against its tied leash, behind a metal fence, roaring into the alley – deep, rhythmic barks. Sam didn't flinch. The animal was furious, enraged that he wasn't scared – its idle threats echoed out behind him. At the end, the path split in two with a route on the left opening up to a wide cul-de-sac.

The night was hot and humid, the streets long and empty. These industrial outskirts of Hallowfield, hidden between the graffiti bins and derelict factories, had a sense of menace that no statistic can temper. He stepped along the narrow footway, his shoes crunching on rocks and glass. Through dark lands made of concrete, corrugated iron potted with rust holes and pipes that seem to lead nowhere. Among the brown rats that scurry from every gap, every hole, every lightless place. Only poverty can build neighbourhoods like this.

Or maybe Sam was being melodramatic again. Grand, drunk thoughts. Vodka writing bleak poems about an impending apocalypse, about how there was no need to fear any of this because, no matter how far he strayed, he would never find something worse than himself.

On the right, he saw the dual carriageway, running behind these homes and industrial parks. Partially closed, as he knew it would be. He clambered up a steep bank and out on to the open tarmac.

About a quarter of a mile ahead it was cordoned off – rows of traffic cones intermittently crowned with flashing orange lights. A curved runway. Huge machines, beeping metal juggernauts were busy down there.

They were carving an exit ramp, connecting the road to a sprawling building site at the bottom of a slope – the bare skeleton of a half-finished shopping mall. The ground was dried mud, gravel, lined trenches with steel foundation rods spiking up from cement beds, like exposed vertebrae. Diggers and trailers, all dark and hidden behind temporary fences clad in glossy boards which promised consumer nirvana by the end of next year. Brand logos. Expensive smiles.

But Sam wasn't interested in that – instead he needed to speak to this small team of nocturnal roadworkers, who were yet to notice his approach. Two of them were shovelling sand, both with high-visibility trousers, boots, and nothing covering their chests. Another was reversing a large roller, holding the steering handle, looking over his shoulder through the yellow siren light above his head.

'You lost, chief?' someone said.

The engine cut out and there was a lack of sound, so quiet it seemed lower, if it was possible, than silence.

Now all the men were staring. Sam imagined what they saw – a hooded figure, standing there in the middle of the empty road.

'I'm looking for Henry Marston,' he said.

'Oi, Hen Do,' the guy sitting high on the roller yelled.

A younger man carrying a broom emerged from a pile of earth to Sam's left. 'What?' he said.

'Think you've been rumbled, boy,' one of the men shouted, triggering some laughter.

Henry seemed embarrassed, then scared – a startled white to his eyes that Sam recognised as someone who was about to flee. On that thought, he dropped his broom and ran – his heavy boots thumping down the dirt path towards the dormant building site.

Something had taken over and Sam was, without thinking, chasing him. Younger and faster, Henry was up and over the tall fence with ease. Sam, close behind, smashed into it shoulder first, bouncing off and thudding to his back on the gravel. But he'd hit it hard enough to dislodge a panel and, denim ripping at his knee, he was through and scanning the area. Henry was jogging now, past a cement mixer, heading for an exit on the far side. But when

Henry checked back, he picked up the pace and took a quick right, disappearing into the gloom of what would be a multistorey car park when this project was complete.

Inside, Sam found him at a dead end, heaving and resting his hands on his knees. But, once again, Henry took flight and ran towards the spiralling ramp. With a sigh, Sam followed, catching odd glimpses of fluorescent trousers half a floor above as they mirrored each other, round and round, up and up the fresh tarmac.

Three tall storeys later, Henry stopped and turned. He'd clearly realised that altitude was no advantage for prey.

'Why are you chasing me?' he said, out of breath.

'Because you're running.'

'That doesn't make sense . . . I didn't tell them anything.'

'Where's your sister?' Sam asked.

'My . . . what?'

'Your sister, where is she?'

'I . . . I haven't got a sister.'

'Don't lie. Diane.'

'She's not . . . I . . . I have no idea.'

Behind Henry, there was no crash barrier, no railing. All that stood between them and the edge was a thin strip of plastic tape – red and white and rippling in the breeze.

'Why did you run?'

'I thought you worked for . . . I thought you were someone else.'

'What do you know about North Serpent?'

'What?'

'The church, your sister's cult.'

'I—'

'It's connected to them.'

'What? Who?'

'The Clarkes. *The Clarkes*. Just fucking—'

Sam moved closer and, as though he'd hit a tripwire, Henry swung a punch – it connected, rattling Sam's vision. He tried to block and, somehow, they were gripped in a clumsy grapple. A handful of T-shirt and flesh, arms locked straight – teeth and eyes – until another strike seemed to come from above. Sam's jumper pulled up, his face falling, a strong arm squeezing him in a headlock. All he could see were his feet, stepping, stumbling. He couldn't breathe. Something struck his back, his ribs. His face hot, swelling with blood. And then, at the mercy of instinct, Sam felt his legs drive forwards. Adrenaline granted new strength to his arms. And he pushed.

Slapping, knees first, on to the tarmac, he looked straight down over the edge. For a strange, eerie moment, Sam was all alone, three storeys up that spiralling ramp. As though Henry Marston had been nothing more than a vivid hallucination he'd simply stopped believing.

But, below, he saw that this was not the case.

The upper half of Henry's falling body had clipped a horizontal scaffold pole, which sent him spinning. He landed backwards, sideways. A savage thud as the torso hit the packed earth, bouncing flat and sending out a perfect shockwave of dust.

Now a ragdoll, helpless, injured in the way you are in nightmares, Henry wheezed as he tried to roll over. Tried to move. Tried, perhaps, to wake up. But he couldn't. So he screamed.

PART TWO
FRANCIS CLARKE

Chapter 17

This was not the first time Sam had watched dawn rise through a prison-cell window. But he decided it would probably be the last. He rolled over on to his side, then swung his legs off the plastic crash-mat bed. Piss-proof. Blood-proof. Apparently sleep-proof too.

Now sober enough for a statement, he stood and put his belt-less trousers on. Something juvenile, oddly domestic about walking around this place with nothing but socks on his feet. It took Sam a while to realise who the custody officer was – the years had done some work on him.

'Morning, Darrel,' he said.

Professional as ever, Darrel kept it strictly business as he escorted Sam for his questioning. He felt nervous as he sat down – like he was about to be grilled for a job. A job he didn't want. Sam sipped water and, the moment he swallowed, discovered just how dehydrated he was – with three more gulps he finished the cup.

About a minute later, the door opened and Isabelle – of all people – entered. Before he could remark on the odds, he realised it wasn't a coincidence.

'Hello, Sam,' she whispered, sitting opposite him, her shoulders square to his.

Situations like this are significantly less stressful for honest people. Sam had watched countless men and women tie themselves in wild knots – lies can take you anywhere you need to go, anywhere but backwards. He told her everything.

'Henry Marston has a broken spine, spiral femur fracture and his pelvis was described to me as a "bag of bones",' Isabelle said. 'He won't walk again.'

'I assure you, that was not my intention.'

'He says it was an accident – a misunderstanding.'

'That's true. I didn't mean for him to go over the edge.'

'You put yourself in that situation.'

'He attacked first – I defended myself. But, yes, I shouldn't have been there. I shouldn't have chased him.'

'Are you even sorry?'

'Yes. It is unfortunate.'

'He's twenty years old. He's going to be in a wheelchair. It's more than unfortunate, Sam.'

He didn't respond. Because she was right. This was so many things alongside unfortunate.

'I'm suggesting a charge of perverting the course of justice,' Isabelle said.

'Fair.'

'As for possession, that's being overlooked.'

Sam frowned.

'The cocaine they found on you.'

And he remembered. While waiting for the ambulance, he'd pulled three bags from Henry's pocket – all weighed up and ready to sell. There was also a folded packet of prescription SSRI antidepressants, with all but two pills gone. An extra touch of guilt at this memory – poor Henry Marston was struggling to endure reality at the best of times. What kind of doom was he navigating now?

Sam pictured him lying in a hospital bed, broken, machines beeping. A glimpse of anger at the punch. *Stupid kid.* But there was no mitigation here. Literally none of this would have happened if Sam had just stayed at home.

'Henry thinks you should face no charges,' Isabelle said.

'I imagine his brothers have something else in mind. Every cloud.'

'Do you want to go somewhere safe?'

He shook his head.

'Eye for an eye . . .'

'If it really was an eye for an eye, they'd go after *my* brother,' Sam said. 'And he's already dead.'

Upon his release, Sam took back his mobile, laced up his shoes and checked all his personal effects were in place. Then he stepped outside, out into the warm morning, and scrolled through his contacts. Lei R. He would help.

'I'm in the alley by the station, you about?'

A few minutes passed before Lei arrived with a disappointed face — *this was all such a shame.* 'What's going on Sam?'

'I need you to do something else for me.'

'No. We're square.' Lei moved closer. 'There's already a complaint lodged against me for yesterday's antics. Don't know what I was thinking. We're looking at very serious ramifications here. What the hell am I supposed to say?'

'Tell the truth,' Sam said, shrugging.

An outrageous suggestion. '*What?*'

'You arrested her after a former colleague gave you a tip-off. Say I told you there was a good reason to bring Mary Osbourne in.'

'You want me to blame it all on you?'

'It was my idea.'

'And what about last night?'

Joey's warnings echoed in his thoughts. *A hornets' nest. Fire and fury. The most literal interpretation of the worst Bible passages.*

'I think I've upset some . . . bad people.' *Bad people.* He sounded like a scared child.

'You want me to protect you? I'm not your big brother, Sam. Report it.'

'I don't trust the police to keep me safe.' This was true, but not the whole reason. If he'd baited the Marstons, it made little sense to hide. Sam had their attention now – he couldn't find them, but he would bet big money they could find him. 'Listen, you're often out with armed response. Maybe you can send something for repair or . . .'

Lei regarded him with actual disgust. 'Sam, I respect you – I would do anything I can to help with any problems you might have. But I am *not* doing that. And if you ask again . . .' He glared.

'I understand,' Sam said. 'It's a tall order.'

'I've got to say, I'm surprised. What is it about Francis that makes you so sure he's innocent? You always struck me as a rational person, and a good judge of character.'

Contrary to all this speculation, Sam had no special attachment to Francis and, should he die, should he serve the rest of his life behind bars for a crime he didn't commit, Sam would feel no more sorrow than he would for the next man.

'It's not his character I'm reacting to.'

'You can see why people think he's guilty, yes? At least tell me that.'

'Of course,' Sam said. 'He's eccentric. His mannerisms are off. I get the impression he's not a nice person to live with. Bookies' favourite, no question. But there is a lot of ground between being mildly unlikeable and murdering children. Francis is telling the truth. It really is that simple.'

'You're willing to do all this for a man you don't even like?'

Sam shook his head. 'I'm not doing *anything* for him.'

'Blind faith, then.'

'No, I can see clearly. Who's working Operation Clove nowadays?'

'We are . . . We all are.'

'Then you must know someone who knows someone. Just give me a name, that's all I ask.'

Sam drove north, to a dairy farm, and parked by a broken wooden fence. The estate shop was at the far end of a concrete track lined with open barns. Most were empty, besides one that housed a few cows. A smell of straw, dry ground dust and, when the wind blew, faint manure. Sam stopped and leaned on a steel gate – it wasn't bolted in place and instead rested against the enclosure, which was made from wooden pallets tied together with wire. Deep scratches traced the dragged metal – a trench in the concrete – the kind of damage that takes years.

Sam watched one of the cows – its dark eyes stared back, its rubbery nose wet and glistening. A yellow plastic tag on its left ear, the ink faded to a smudge. It stepped forwards into the light, hooves brushed through matted hay. He touched its head, felt its strength as it turned its neck and showed him its broad side. Short hair, warm and thick, black and white – he patted its haunch. It shivered flies away. Now uninterested, the cow wandered off into the barn, back to the cool shade.

Turning, Sam left the slumped gate and went towards the farm shop, rubbing his lightly greased fingertips together. Just as he arrived, the white wooden door jingled open, a brass bell ringing twice. A woman holding a bucket strode out across the flat concrete, wearing wellies and a summer dress.

'Afternoon,' she said. 'Can I help you?'

'I'm looking for Hannah.'

'You've found her.' She was thin and her youthful clothes were at odds with her face – Sam guessed she was maybe sixty years old.

Hannah took him inside the shop, where tall freezers hummed, their glass fronts clouded in frost and condensation. He had to squint to see the products on display. All the white tubs were marked with a green ribbon, on which the words 'Dairy Day's Ice Cream' were written.

This was not at all what he was expecting.

'So, are you after something in particular?'

'I would like to buy a gun,' he said.

'We sell mostly ice cream here. Lamb in the spring. Eggs. Lemon cake.'

Sam reached inside his pocket and pulled out a brown envelope, held it low and lifted the flap. It was bulging with fresh notes. Confidently, he placed it on the counter.

Glancing down at the money, Hannah said, 'What makes you think I provide such a service?'

Cue that unique feeling Sam was able to ignore like no one else – the temptation to lie. Most people experience it daily, most people barely even notice, most people simply comply with its demands.

But no.

'A man called Lei Rin told me – he's a police officer working on Operation Clove,' Sam said. 'It's a long-running initiative to stamp out the sale of illegal firearms. He described you as relatively small-time, although with relevant contacts to larger importing groups. I would suggest, if you want to continue trading, you do not expand.

And cut ties with your current suppliers from mainland Europe – their days are numbered. I would also recommend that you do not inform them of this, as it might impact the investigation and, in turn, your livelihood.'

Hannah was frowning – trying to process what possible reason there could be for such a candid explanation. What grand scheme was at play here? What could this man want from her?

Sam lifted his shirt, then he showed her his phone was not recording, and slid the large brown envelope of cash across the counter.

Here was her answer – the man wanted exactly what he said he wanted. There could be no simpler transaction than this.

'Which flavour are you looking for?' she said, taking the money.

We see a living room. The back wall hosts a wide, panoramic TV. The news is on. A large man sits in the middle of a sofa in the foreground. Flanking him either side are two other men. Both are bald, although one has a long, plaited rat-tail at the base of his skull and a pointed beard. His moustache is twisted at the ends, curling up his face like bull horns. He is visibly underweight.

Easy-listening jazz plays in the background, gentle drums, low bass, the piano waltzing up and down – sounds better suited to a hotel lobby. Elevator music. Somewhere gold.

We can see World War II memorabilia on a shelf to the left, including a German helmet, stamped with the imperial eagle, a faded swastika carried in its talons. There's a red flag, various medals and crests pinned to a noticeboard and a pair of well-worn Luftwaffe goggles. Somewhere within this shrine – the outline shape of a crucifix, buried amid the eclectic icons. Aside from this collection, the decor is new and expensive – this place is home to a wealthy person.

The music continues.

'What did she do?' the man on the right asks.

'She just laughed,' the bearded one says. 'She thought I was joking.'

These two are animated, chatting, both swigging from bottles of beer — the one on the left, the slimmer of the pair, is wearing camouflage trousers and a scruffy vest. His counterpart dons a shirt and a loosened tie. It looks like he might have just come from a white-collar job. Despite the disparity of their body fat, and the long plait on the slim man, these two are identical. They are twins.

The living room is arranged in a square — three sides are taken up by equal-sized sofas and the television covers much of the fourth wall. We are at the back, looking out through a webcam on a laptop.

The man in the centre of the frame, facing away, has short, thick hair, although it is thinning on the top. He wears a pale blazer — his broad shoulders are square and still. Unlike the other two, he's neither talking nor moving. He just sits there, a silhouette watching TV.

And the jazz is close, whispering from small speakers somewhere below.

'What time we leaving?' The man with the rat-tail checks his watch.

'Soon,' his twin brother says.

'You getting changed?'

'Of course.'

'I'm pretty much ready.' The slimmer man stands and puts on a cargo jacket — it's khaki green, scuffed and frayed.

'You can't wear that.'

'Why not? It's my favourite.'

'It's got an Iron Cross on the arm.'

'So?'

'Are you going to leave a business card as well?'

'Max,' the man in the centre says, his hand on his own throat. His voice is deep, croaky. Electronic. The gravel left behind after a laryngectomy. 'You are burning your clothes when you get back.'

The bearded twin – Max – sighs, then takes his jacket off.

On the TV, the news displays a photograph of Robin Clarke, as it so often does – curly blonde hair, sweet and smiling. Then it cuts to a reporter, standing at Orchard Court. 'That's right,' he says – slightly drowned in the chords and rhythm of our piano-bar music. 'Police confirmed today they have been granted more time to question Francis Clarke in relation to his missing daughter . . .'

Ignoring the television, Max leaves the room, and returns with two crowbars and a wooden baseball bat, which clatter down on to the coffee table. He then brandishes a large hunting knife – it glimmers, catching the TV's blue glow when he slides it from its leather sheath.

'Why are you bringing that?' his twin says. 'We're not breaking skin.'

'Protection.'

'Pro— I think we can handle it.' The television plays stock footage of Francis and Anna Clarke, sitting on a stage at a press conference. 'I haven't seen Henry for years. Poor guy. What was it all about anyway?'

'Was about this, apparently.' Max points his thumb at the TV. 'What did I say, all those years ago, what did I fucking say? It's the dad.' Now Francis Clarke's photograph fills the screen. 'Look at him. Look at his eyes. Looks like a vampire. Fucking dead-eyed zombie. The mum's probably in on it too.'

'I've always quite liked Anna Clarke.'

'Yeah, I mean, yes, I would, but she's still dodgy.' The screen cuts to an earlier interview with filmmaker Daniel Aiden. 'And then there's this fucker, cashing in again.'

'You see his one about the slums?' The completely bald twin pulls his tie from his neck, then unbuttons his shirt.

'Yeah, that was good. In some shithole? Indonesia?'

133

'That's it. Imagine living like that.'

'Might do you some good, Greg, few days' starvation.'

'Fuck you.'

Max puts his brand-new leather boot on the corner of the coffee table and laces it up tight – then he tucks his baggy camo trousers inside. Finally, he zips up an old bomber jacket.

His now topless brother – Gregory – steps towards the laptop. 'So, we'll park here – there's a little underground lot below these flats.' He points at the screen.

Behind him, Max leans down into a rucksack and removes a small bag of pills. He carefully picks one out.

'No,' Gregory says. 'You need to be straight. Come look at this map.'

Rolling his eyes, Max puts the bag away again. 'Why? You're driving.'

However, as Max walks over, we see, when no one else is looking, that he slips one of the white pills into his mouth and swallows it without water. 'This music – can I put something else on?'

'Leave it alone,' the croaking voice says – still facing away.

'You sorted the number plates out?'

'Yes.'

'So, once we're in, it's masks on, down the stairs, out across the corner of the park and to the underpass – we do it there, quick and hard, no fucking around. And, Max, don't kill him, all right. Do not fucking kill him.'

'Who do you think I am?'

'That's the problem,' Gregory says. 'I know exactly who you are. Then we double back on ourselves, exit through the other side of the tunnel, up the alley and to the car. If there's any trouble, we run our separate ways. Remember, no speaking.'

'We sure it's secluded?'

'Yes . . . There are no cameras in the underpass. Now, clean up, let's get going.'

Max and Gregory return to the coffee table and use wet wipes on their hands, forearms, necks and faces. Then they both put on medical gloves and repeat the process with the tools. Gregory picks up the two crowbars and clangs them together. 'You pay cash for this – how far did you go?'

'Two-hour round trip, same for these.' Max seems proud as he lifts a rubber horse mask from his duffel bag, then a chicken mask of similar style.

'What the fuck are they?'

'Scary, is what they are.'

Checking his watch, Max leaves the room again and returns with a plate. Then he takes a small object, a brown rat's corpse, from a rolled sandwich bag.

'Do you have to do that in here?' The croaky robot voice is quiet but stern.

Ignoring him, Max puts the rat on the plate and, sticking his tongue out to concentrate, cuts a hole in its neck. He holds it by the tail and lets blood drain on to the white china, milking the last of it out with a squeeze. He's careful not to make a mess. When there's a dark shallow pool, he holds the plate up and Gregory dips his little finger in the liquid, then puts it in his mouth. The third man, the quiet, still man, does the same.

Max returns to his seat and uses two fingers to swill the blood around, before rubbing them into his gums. He repeats the process, this time with both hands, and massages the liquid into his eyes. Painting his sockets, he leaves smears of red down his cheeks.

'You little fucking weirdo,' Gregory whispers.

'Well, boys, I am ready.' Max is holding the wooden bat.

'I can't help but think . . .' the gurgle, the electronic gasps for air '. . . there is a simpler way.'

The twins turn.

'It's not about what's simple, it's about what's right,' Gregory says, crouching down in front of him.

Max lifts up his jacket, showing a tattoo across his flat stomach. 'Eye for an eye,' he says, pointing at the text. 'Eye for a fucking eye. He has to feel exactly the same pain.'

Now, suited and booted, the men pick up their masks and remaining weapons. Gregory puts some keys in his pocket and then mutes the TV.

They stand together, hands on each other's shoulders, and all three bow their heads. Through the piano, the tish-tish-tish *of a high-hat, through this warm, golden music, they begin to pray.*

The words are mumbled, whispered in a chorus. Max – evidently lacking the piety of the other two – rolls his hand, gesturing for them to get on with it.

'Amen.'

'Amen,' Gregory repeats.

And the twins head for the door.

'Laptop,' the third man croaks, as he sits on the sofa once again.

Max returns and clicks the mouse twice. The last thing the camera sees is his face, his cheekbones and his rat-red eyes.

Chapter 18

Sam walked along Orchard Court, checking faces as he went. Public places felt safe, but still he let his biceps rest on the heavy, loaded Glock 17 holstered beneath his jacket. He'd told Isabelle he planned to go door to door, interviewing the Clarkes' neighbours. Of course, this had been done before but, as Sam observed, all attention was centred on the most recent Wednesday.

'No one's asking about the week before that,' he'd said.

'Why would they?'

'The browsing history.'

'Phil won't even entertain the idea that data came from outside the house.' She'd sighed down the phone. 'Sam, look, please, just stop.'

'Last time I checked, talking to people wasn't illegal . . . The choice is simple, Isabelle.'

'I could arrest you.'

'Easily. You know where I'll be.'

Isabelle, wearing jeans and a plain black T-shirt, approached him on the pavement. When she arrived, he held his hands out, wrists turned up. She looked at him with those patient eyes – that passive reluctant stare, like a mother who's resigned to the fact that some things, some misbehaviour, will always defy her protest. Better she did not know about the gun. Withholding information was not the same as lying, but Sam still hoped she wouldn't ask him directly what he had hidden there, warming at his chest.

They walked the length of the affluent road, lined on both sides with evenly placed trees, cylindrical iron cages protecting each trunk. The wide canopies put cars in shifting shade and rained leaves, twigs, sap and seeds whenever the wind would shake them. One of these trees, a horse chestnut, was already filling the pavement with its spiked shells and precious, early conkers. A stark image – Robin, in her school uniform, crouching and finding the perfect one, running home and showing it off. Orchard Court, summer smells – warm grass, flower beds, the colour green. Somewhere, beyond these trimmed hedges and clean mansions, a motorway was rumbling and an ice-cream van hummed a distant tune about a long-dead queen.

They spent the afternoon talking to the street's residents. Sam could tell Isabelle was profoundly uncomfortable with this. But what was the alternative? Leave him to his own devices? Henry Marston lay still in a hospital bed, proving *that* was a bad idea. Or maybe she actually wanted a share of anything valuable he might find. Maybe she believed he was right. Maybe she thought those incriminating searches were nothing to do with Francis Clarke.

At any rate, they'd swapped places – she now shadowed him. As though his misadventures, his collateral violence, had reclaimed the wheel. Still, his hangover-guilt throbbed from time to time. And shame came, as shame does, in waves, but he could not bring himself to regret his actions. Because that would imply he could have done otherwise. It helped that Isabelle believed him, it helped that it was an accident but, most of all, it helped that Sam was making progress.

The last stop on their clockwise tour was Jasper Parker's relatively modest house. They went through his gate, past a tall shrub and down a path that cut his front garden into two strips of land left to nature. Long grass and weeds brushed Sam's trousers, and petals of every hue shone within the undergrowth. Compared to the sterile street behind them, this space was shimmering, literally buzzing with life. Patio furniture slumped amid this wild garden, bleached in the afternoon sun and, as they arrived on the doorstep, Sam had a strange sense of being abroad. Large, loose egg stones around the side paving and dried leaves rustling – he half expected to see lizards scurry at the edge of his vision.

Jasper's front door was painted dark blue and had a stained-glass window embedded in the upper half – an abstract chess-board made of pink and yellow squares. Sam used the chunky metal knocker and, a few seconds later, the hallway inside lit up. A female, yellow and pink and peering curiously through the glass. She opened the door.

Halfway through their introductions, Jasper emerged behind her.

'Hi there,' he said, coming forwards to greet Sam. This, he explained, was his daughter, Iris.

Today, Jasper's long white hair wasn't tied up and hung in thin wisps from the sides of his head – he curled these strands over his ears as he spoke. After pleasantries, he welcomed them inside, through his cluttered hall. Each of his wooden stairs hosted a pile of dusty magazines and newspapers. It was cool in here – the stone tiles on the floor radiated a chill, like the smoothed slabs of a church.

The doorway to the living room was blocked by a rusting bicycle, which Jasper wheeled out of the way and propped up in the kitchen.

Isabelle entered first and stood at his shelves, next to the empty fireplace. She scanned the rows of books. Sometimes she looked almost cybernetic, filling herself with information – logging every detail.

'I spoke to the other detectives at length,' Jasper said, returning from the kitchen. 'I hear that wacky thing up the tree was some kind of religious whatnot?'

Sam confirmed this with a nod.

Iris was a short, overweight woman with a large mole on the left of her mouth. Like Jasper, she had thin hair, which, Sam noticed, had been dyed blonde, although her ashy roots were coming through by a clear inch. She also seemed, somehow, as frail as her father, and held a walking stick at her chest like a sword, but didn't once use it. Despite this, Sam put her at no older than forty.

'We wanted to talk to you about last week,' he said. 'Wednesday night in particular.'

Iris and Jasper sat side by side on the sofa – Sam and Isabelle were directly opposite one another on two armchairs. Between them the table was, again, bulging with magazines and, on top, a broken oil lantern. Leaning forwards, Jasper picked up a bowl of sweets and offered it to each of them. Isabelle showed a hand but Sam simply ploughed on with the conversation.

'Were you both here that evening?'

'W-w-we were,' Iris said. 'I . . .' There was a long pause – an awkward moment where she kept their attention, kept the focus on her, until she managed the next words. 'I arrived late on T-Tuesday – we had pizza the . . . the following day.'

'Oh, yes, yes that's right,' Jasper said, pointing. 'We were tired after carrying all your things in. Too tired to cook you said. I had a coupon from the newspaper.'

'Iris, you've recently moved in?' Isabelle asked.

'Yes, yes,' Jasper said, turning to his daughter. 'Blame the mess on her.' He held his hands up, as though innocent of hoarding. This was done in jest, but clearly still struck a nerve for him. 'She's staying temporarily. Divorce. Complicated. *Don't ask.*'

Sam cast an eye towards Jasper and the old man simmered down with an apologetic nod.

'Of course, she can speak for herself,' he said, as he sucked on his sweet.

Like a child to a surface warned too hot to touch, Sam felt drawn to any subject deemed off-limits. This wasn't part of an interview technique, but more a general glitch in his programming. To him, the words 'don't ask' always meant the precise opposite.

Invasive enquiries were, by far, his favourite kind.

'Why are you getting a divorce?' he asked.

Jasper tensed up.

'My, my, my hus— Andrew and I, we've had a . . . a . . . rocky time lately. We were trying for a b-baby. I've just had a second, unsuccessful, bout of I . . . I . . . IVF.' The stammer then eased, as though anger oiled her gears. 'I said, if he wants someone who can give him what he wants, he should . . .'

Iris began to cry. Sudden, jarring tears. Isabelle took a tissue from the box on the table and handed it over, looking at Sam as though this was his fault.

'He's fine . . . but me?' She sniffed, and gestured down at herself. 'It . . . it just doesn't do what it's m-m-meant to. He thinks I don't care. He . . . he blames me.' She was talking now to the wall. 'But I would love that child . . . I would love that child more than he would. I would love her m-m-more than anything. I've bought the toys. I-I-I've painted the cot.'

They left this in the air for a few seconds.

'I'm sorry, Iris. Is . . . is there anything you can remember from that night?' Isabelle asked.

Jasper pointed to his daughter. 'You said – about that bloke. The man you saw. That was Wednesday last week, wasn't it?'

Iris frowned, like this was an obscure thing to mention. She sniffed again and searched her memories.

'The man, in the car,' Jasper added.

'I'm not . . . it's . . . well . . . I saw an old m-m-m-man who had scars on his face, but I'm not even sure what night it was.'

'*Wednesday*,' Jasper declared. 'You told me about him – I . . .' He seemed embarrassed. 'I made a joke about the pizza.'

'Where was this man?' Sam asked.

'Parked on the street, in a car,' he said. 'Right outside the Clarkes'.'

Again, even though it took longer, Sam wanted Iris to speak – and he let Jasper know. 'How old was he?' he asked her.

'H-hard to say . . . he had, he had very bad b-b-burns on his face. Like acid burns m-maybe. I'd guess middle-aged – grey . . . grey hair. Definitely old. I suppose he seemed, I don't know, d-d-disabled?'

'Type of car?'

She winced. 'I'm sorry, I . . . I think dark, blue maybe, but, I don't know.'

'Roughly what time?'

'M-maybe nine p.m., or just after.'

Without a prompt, Isabelle took her phone from her pocket, checked it and gave Sam an approving nod. It tallied with the searches.

They left through the wild garden and arrived back on the street, where the media presence was still significant at the Clarkes' house. Annoyingly, Sam would have to stand right next to them. But, then again, he felt safe in front of thirty TV cameras – their watchful eyes protected him like no gun ever could.

As they approached, a few clicks and flashes, a few hasty questions – but Sam and Isabelle made it crystal clear they would not be talking to the press. Message received, the crowd retreated.

Now being largely ignored, Sam held his mobile as he walked to the road. He scrolled to settings, then refreshed his Wi-Fi connections and waited. There was nothing.

'Out of range,' Isabelle said in a low voice.

Still on the tarmac, Sam moved sideways through the shadow of one of the picturesque trees.

'Could have been using a laptop,' he said, tilting his mobile. 'Or something with a better connection, maybe a tablet or—'

But then, right there, right at the top, it appeared. One bar of signal, all the way out here – 'Clarke333'. He showed Isabelle the screen.

'So, what, this old man parks up and logs in to their Wi-Fi? Is that even possible, without the password?'

'We've been to the moon, Isabelle. A person could hack into a router. Reckon we can get an artist out here to mock up her description of this guy?'

With a single call, Isabelle made it happen. The power she wielded as an active officer far exceeded Sam's – even counting his unclaimed favours and relative disregard for the law.

'What are you thinking about Iris?' she asked.

'The same thing you are.'

'Oddball, worth checking out.'

'Almost verbatim.'

'I'll have a little look,' she said. 'It's a family home, the Parkers have had access to that garden for years. They could have hidden something in a tree at any point.'

'And then filmed it?'

'Does *Iris* strike you as a wildlife photographer?'

'Not particularly. But she doesn't strike me as especially capable either.'

'I agree.'

'We should ask Anna about the scarred man too.'

143

'Burned faces.'

Sam nodded, recalling the dolls, remembering the rarity of scorched heads.

He stared over at the Clarkes' house – a wide mansion behind the gate, behind the hedges – and thought of all the ways Robin could have left it.

'They're still teaching kids not to talk to strangers,' he said. 'But parents hurt children, or it's the uncle, the bus driver, the caretaker, the family friend, the neighbour, the vicar, that milkman who loves to chat. Strangers are the ones who come and save you.'

'You believe whoever took Robin knew her personally?'

'Anna said she woke up around three a.m. – she listed all the things she noticed. Her daughter's night light, the oven timer, the back door, the thick carpet . . . the dog that wasn't barking. Yes. I'd bet my life on it.'

Chapter 19

Hallowfield, like any city of this culture, size, day and age, is home to untold numbers of CCTV cameras. Digital eyes watching, recording, witnessing a thousand silences, the day-to-day interactions of countless, nameless souls. Most of whom are oblivious to any audience. And on the path that leads from the park, behind the tall fences, we see Freddie walking this route again. As before, a pair of trainers, tied at the laces, dangle and spin from the rear of his rucksack. His earphones are in – his hands tucked into the pockets of his tracksuit top. His gait is steady, perhaps stepping to the beat of the tune he can hear.

He comes down a curved tarmac slope, heads to the right of the frame, towards a tunnel that burrows beneath the dual carriageway and splits off to Kendell Street. The bare grey concrete around the opening hosts water stains, old graffiti and the speckled black print of exhaust fumes. Brambles at the sides, filled with litter, faded packaging, shopping bags thinned in the weather, catching the wind. Suspended. Fluttering.

Freddie turns into the walkway, into the tunnel, and out of sight. Here is that blind spot again – around two minutes at his pace. One hundred and twenty seconds go by unseen.

Because it's true. There are no cameras in the underpass.

❖ ❖ ❖

Sam had made provisions in his flat, taping a knife to the underside of his coffee table and hiding another beneath the sofa cushions. In his bedroom, he had a small hammer in his top drawer and a baseball bat perched against the wall, behind the door. Of course, he couldn't account for every eventuality. Besides, he suspected revenge, in whatever form it took, would be served outside, somewhere cold – as is customary. But still, he'd feel foolish to come home, find an intruder and be more than a few paces from a deadly weapon. The Glock 17 he'd purchased was, day and night, holstered beneath his hooded, zip-up jumper, no matter the weather. He'd practised loading, reloading, racking the slide, clearing the chamber. For this he'd driven out to the woods – to a place where you might expect to hear the crack of distant shotguns turning pheasants into feathers and dust and continue about your rural business.

There was something ridiculous about following a YouTube tutorial on how to handle this pistol. But the reality was Sam had minimal experience, especially with small arms. He rehearsed the motion again and again, reaching down, pulling it clear, having both hands in place within a second – one on the grip, another cupped beneath.

The final test of the day saw him twenty feet from a tree. Shoulders firm and leaning into it, he fired a pair of rounds into the bark, which spat splinters back at him and sent startled birds flapping from every treetop in sight. He blinked and stood there alone as the last of the sparrows faded out, dissolving in the late summer haze above. Twigs snapped underfoot as he walked back to his car – another happy customer. If he could, he'd give that eccentric dairy-farming arms dealer a glowing review. The ice cream wasn't bad either. Five stars.

After this, Sam drove to Hallowfield General Hospital and sat in the cafe. He ordered a cappuccino and bought a newspaper. They were props more than anything, but he sipped the coffee and read the front page nonetheless. Still yesterday's news – no mention of the custody extension, just hours old at this point. The hunt for Robin Clarke intensifying – a quote from Daniel Aiden about 'offering his support to the family'.

'All they ask,' the BAFTA-award-winning documentary filmmaker added, 'is that their privacy is respected during this difficult time.'

And, dead centre on the front page, the school portrait photograph of Robin – cute and blonde, curly hair just like her mother. Rotting somewhere now, if the arrest held water. Sam didn't know what to think. Perhaps Francis Clarke was a masterful liar – a stone-cold professional. Perhaps he was a monster. Perhaps he had killed his own daughter.

But he had not, and Sam believed this as much as he believed in gravity, killed Ethan. The papers weren't afraid to plant that suspicion though – picturing Francis on page three, above photos of both his missing children, looming over them with those steely blue eyes. Eyes like a winter dog.

Back then, when the days were barely weeks and the coverage was just a seed of the mammoth it would become, Sam had tried to spur himself on by thinking about Freddie, five years old at the time. He imagined how hard he would work should his own son suffer a similar fate. There was no excuse to treat Anna's and Francis's child with anything less than that obsession. And it didn't take long to flourish. There had been no comfort with Ethan – nothing plausible enough to believe provisionally in lieu of an answer. It was total darkness – pitch-black, the kind of thick night that tricks your eyes into doubting they were ever even capable of detecting light in the first place.

So when they found that coat on that beach, it was given far more weight than it deserved. And those looking took every bit of undue solace from the only glimmer there'd been. For Sam, the idea that Ethan was in the ocean, that he'd fallen into that void, offered little but horror.

However, as time went on, he created a divide and never allowed himself to imagine Freddie entering the same blind space in his mind. It hurt too much. Plus, it wasn't necessary. Within six short months Sam thought about little else but the case and, when he noticed the other cornerstones of his life beginning to wither from such wanton neglect, it was already too late.

This was also when his commitment to honesty stopped being merely an ideal. If he treated the truth with the respect he always knew it deserved, then maybe, just maybe, it'd grow to trust him. Maybe it'd lower its guard and unfurl, expose every shade of its elusive beauty as though seducing a mate. He was, after all, a compatible species.

He spent a long time thinking about Francis and realised that, despite the tide, despite the current pulling everything in this direction, nothing had changed. Sam would need far more before he believed Francis Clarke was a murderer.

Surveying the scene in the hospital cafe, he closed and folded the paper. From here he could see the foyer – a large open space with two sets of wide automatic doors. Then a semicircle of grey carpet and a long reception, staffed by a busy woman with a couple of nurses behind her – desk-bound but dressed in uniform. Phones rang. Beds carrying elderly people rolling past from time to time, back trolley wheels wobbling and squeaking on old metal swivels. Blank eyes looking nowhere.

A doctor pressed an alcohol gel dispenser on the wall across from Sam and, when she strode close, rubbing her hands, he smelled the sterile liquid in the air. Clean. In the same way the faint sweet smoke out the front made him want a cigarette, this made him want a drink.

Sam could also see the corridor to the trauma centre, where men and women in shirts and scrubs would intermittently gather, disappear inside and respond to an ambulance arriving. Like a factory arrangement but, instead of produce, the conveyer carried critically injured humans for an urgent dose of medical intervention. Earlier, Henry Marston had been treated in there, heavily sedated, strapped to a bed, head held in place with a plastic neck brace. Sam had managed to wander in and overhear talk about an upcoming scan – he'd caught a glimpse of Henry and the empty chair by his bed. No visitors. He had hoped to catch sight of a face or follow up a number plate – something to bring him closer to the remaining Marston brothers, to Diane, to North Serpent. And yet, he had found no such thing.

He left just before 7 p.m. and returned home for the smoke and drink the hospital had suggested. Perhaps he could orchestrate something from here. With a cold vodka and Coke, he sat at his laptop and removed the small white cardboard box from his top drawer. Henry Marston's prescription was for citalopram – an SSRI antidepressant which Sam familiarised himself with online. Crucially, on the packet, he found a label with Henry's GP practice printed in bold letters.

Acorn Wood Surgery had a cheap-looking website, with nothing flashy besides a repeat-prescription form which didn't work. Sam clicked through to 'About Us'. Three doctors. Two female and one male. Smiling headshots.

Doctor Roland Patel – a Bangladeshi man. Sam googled him and found an academic profile. Although he had studied medicine in Germany, the doctor appeared to have worked in the UK for over twenty years. There it was again – the temptation to lie. To phone the hospital and feign a diluted accent which, however hard he tried, would invariably sound comedic. No. He would play it straight.

There were two missed calls from Marilyn, notifications he ignored for now. He'd text her later.

He found the number for Hallowfield General Hospital and called the switchboard – 'If you know the extension you need, dial now. If not, press two.' Beep and it rang again.

'Hallowfield General.'

'Hi there.' Sam stubbed his cigarette out and spoke through the smoke. 'I'm wondering if you can help me – I just wanted to check on the status of a patient who checked in last night, Henry Marston.'

'Which unit?'

His phone buzzed in his hand, he looked down at the screen – incoming call, Marilyn. He dismissed it.

'Intensive care.'

The tone changed and he was put on hold – three seconds of crackled, hissing music and the ice clinking in his glass as he swirled the liquid. Another voice. 'ICU.'

'Hello.' He sat up. 'I wanted to check the status of a patient, Henry Marston—'

'We can't give out details to members of—'

'No, no, of course. I am a . . . I was there when he was injured. All I want to know is that he's being cared for and that he's not alone.'

'He'll be receiving the best care, sir.'

'Has he had any visitors, can you at least tell me that?'

There was a sigh, 'Please hold.'

Around thirty seconds later she was back. 'Yes, sir, Henry Marston Junior has had two visitors.'

'He's . . . sorry, Henry Marston *Junior*?'

'Yes, Henry Senior was here earlier today.'

His son.

With a plummeting dread, a nightmare sense of falling, Sam felt his heart throb in his chest. He recalled Joey's warnings again and again – the words eye-for-an-eye rattling, screaming in his ears. A literal interpretation.

His hands were shaking as he went to missed calls and pressed Marilyn's name. She answered after a single ring – tears clear in her jittering voice.

'Sam,' she said. 'Sam . . . God . . . it's . . . it's Freddie, he's . . . It's bad, Sam.'

Dizzy and sick, his pulse drumming, he stood and listened to her cry down the phone. She was still saying unthinkable things when he leaned over his desk and vomited on the floor. Brown, bitter coffee and froth, stinging vodka and shit he couldn't remember eating poured out of him. It stank.

The world tapered in – the walls tilted down towards his head as he swayed and left his flat, past the spectacularly misplaced weapons he'd hidden throughout. Outside. Into his car. Into the night. And back to that hospital, where invisible borders mean nothing. A place where sharp things hurt you, all in the name of healing. A place that makes you better, or kills you trying.

Chapter 20

There was just one place left in the house that Robin hadn't seen yet. But today, that would change. Although she knew whatever was in that room was forbidden, and would most likely scare her, as so many things here did, she still wanted to know. And it wasn't only curiosity. It might even be that, inside, there was a window, or a door, or some other way out of the building. Maybe that's why she wasn't allowed to go in there.

Actually, she thought, he hadn't *exactly* said she couldn't go into that room. But he *had* said she must never, ever touch any locks. And that tall door in the kitchen was bolted shut with two of them – one at the top, one at the bottom.

Over the past few days, Robin had been allowed out of her room. They now ate meals together at the kitchen dining table, mostly in silence. And, yesterday, she'd even had a bath. This was good because she preferred baths, especially compared to the cramped, trickling shower in her bedroom.

It also gave her time to think. To plan. Because, whenever she was alone, even for a second, she would begin examining the house for weaknesses. He would turn away and suddenly her eyes would dart to look for keys, or inspect the screws on a door's hinges, or she'd come up with crazy ideas like starting a fire and slipping out under all the smoke and panic. She often had ideas in the bath.

During these sly searches for chinks in the house's armour, she had confirmed that *every single window* leading to the outside world was covered with bars, apart from a small one in the downstairs toilet. But, like the fan in her bathroom, it was way too narrow to get through, even if she was bold enough to break the glass.

The problem with her plan was that whenever he left the building, which was rarely, he never gave her any clues about how long he would be gone. He probably did this deliberately. On one afternoon, he was out for almost an hour and, as time ticked away, Robin grew annoyed that she hadn't tried to escape again. But, with every second that passed, it became more and more dangerous because it was more and more likely he would return. So, in the end, she just sat on her bed and waited. Just like she'd been told to do.

But *this time*, today, when he left, she wouldn't hesitate. She would stand up and go straight to that secret room. She knew, from counting the boxes on the monitors, that there were no cameras inside. And there was only a single camera in the kitchen that could not see the door or the right-hand side of the dining table.

Still, even with that blind spot, she would need to be quick. She had never seen him reviewing footage, but what were the cameras for if not to keep an eye on her?

'I'm going out now,' he said, on the landing, before heading downstairs.

She turned her head to listen, closed her eyes to be sure. And when she heard all the front door locks click and slide and clunk shut, Robin leaped into action, across the carpet, down to the ground floor – she swung round the bannister and went up the hall. Although she was rushing, she tried to act normal for the cameras, so it looked like she was maybe just getting herself a drink. In the kitchen, out of sight, she did as she had planned, dragging a chair across the tiles and pushing it against the tall inner door. Old-fashioned, made from planks of wood painted white, it reminded her of a door on a boat, or on a beach

153

house. The bottom slider was easy – she crouched and pulled it open. With the top lock though, she had to stand on the chair, place her knee on the kitchen counter and reach up. She lifted the bolt, gripped it and, *clack*, slid it left.

Down on the tiles again, she moved the chair aside, stepped forwards and grabbed the handle. Even though she was alone, she still opened it as silently as possible. With her palm flat on the wood, she pushed, poking her head through the gap and, gradually, the rest of her body.

Inside, she found probably the messiest room she had ever seen. It was gloomy and smelled a bit like the loft at home. Like old clothes and cold air. Like the radiator had been turned off. And it was, she realised, a bedroom, maybe for an elderly person as it was downstairs. Plus, there was an antique lamp with seashells glued around the base on the cabinet beneath the window.

The window. She tiptoed through the clutter, towards the closed curtains, holding a shelf for balance and stretching her feet out like a gymnast.

All the crosses, the paintings, the strange religious objects she'd seen in the living room had been thrown in here – out of sight. Robin was, as she had hoped, less scared of it all this time around. Still, she tried to avoid the worst pictures. Particularly the one on the bed, perched upright between the pillows – it was a beast of some kind, an animal with horns. Maybe it was the Devil. Either way, it was something she didn't want in her mind, so she made a special effort to look elsewhere. Although she didn't get frightened very easily, there were some things – like a video on YouTube which made you jump with a loud noise and a monkey's face – that stopped her from sleeping. Her night light at home helped. But occasionally she would have to tuck her feet in extra tight and pull the cover up right over her ears, which would protect her – although she wasn't quite sure how.

Robin arrived at the window. She reached over an empty washing basket, held her breath as she pulled one of the curtains aside to reveal— She sighed. More bars.

OK. She turned. What else? There was no phone, but maybe there was a computer. She could send an email home. Nothing of the sort on any of the shelves, or in any of the boxes, just candles and dusty crosses. A cabinet on the left caught her attention – it was full of old books. Robin picked one of them up: *Modern Demonology*. The cover had a painting of a woman wearing a white dress, sprawled out on her back with a strange creature squatting on her stomach. And dark in the background, there was a black horse with bulging eyes.

It had been well read and opened all by itself when she held the spine and—

A bookmark fell out and landed on the carpet, near her foot. Robin reached down. It was a photograph. A photograph of *her*, at home, sitting with Mum, Dad and Button. Biting her lip, she didn't cry, even though seeing them made her stomach ache and her heart beat faster and faster. She sat on the edge of the bed. Held them in her palm. She missed them so much. She just wanted to see them, just for a second, just hear their voices and, and . . . *No. Don't.* She cleared her throat and rubbed each eye socket with the back of her hand. For a few moments she sat there, looked at the ceiling and took some deep breaths.

Right. Come on.

Robin folded the photo and slid it into her pocket. *Keep searching*, she thought, *don't get distracted. Be brave – brave like Ruby.*

Back on her feet, she found a wardrobe with two wooden doors – also painted white – which creaked as she pulled them open.

In here there were more crosses and candles and a tall stack of books. Bibles. Some of them were so old the thin pages had turned brown. Robin stroked the silky paper, then looked up and frowned.

Above, she found weird toys lined up on the shelf. Wait, they weren't toys, they were dolls. Five of them, made from wood and tatty cloth. They were small, no taller than a mobile phone. Like little dusty girls in little dusty dresses. All facing the wall. Even though, of course, they weren't real, Robin still felt sorry for them. Cooped up in here, all alone, like they'd been naughty. She turned them round, one by one, and creased her nose at what she saw. Their faces were black – like charcoal. *Maybe*, she thought, *I could use them to draw*. Although, again, she felt that would be mean because she would hate to have *her* face dragged across paper. The girls had arms too – the right hand of each one was lifted like it was saluting, or maybe pointing. But because they had no fingers, just small wooden stumps, it was difficult to be sure. And in their left hands they held a small stick, a bit like a match, or a torch. She rearranged the figures in a line, so they were all pointing right at her. Squinting, she shook her head.

'It's rude to point,' she whispered. 'Is that why you're in here?'

Is this what happens when you misbehave? You get locked away in the dark.

Robin glanced around the shelves, then down, behind her, to the left. On the floor there was a metal box full of tools and a set of . . . keys? She leaned and snatched them. But they weren't keys. They were lockpicks. And under them were some rubber gloves – the fingers twisted and stuck together. And wet wipes, and a syringe and—

Robin froze. And a test tube with a blue screw-on lid. Half filled with blood. She touched the bruise in the crease of her arm, then carefully picked at the tiny scab. With the dried skin gone, a single spot of red appeared, a perfect sphere – when it grew to the size of a pea, it started to drip. So she held her elbow and sucked the wound, wincing at the metal taste.

He *had* taken her blood. He *had* given her drugs. He was, then, definitely—

On the driveway. A sound. Outside. The car. His car.

Quickly, Robin stepped backwards, shut the wardrobe, then checked everything was as she had found it. For some reason she patted herself down, panicking. She turned. Rushing back into the kitchen, she closed the white door, bolted the bottom lock and—

A shadow in the round window in the front door. She dragged the chair across the tiles, tucked it under the dining table, then swooped round towards the sink. She grabbed a glass and turned on the tap as he walked up the hall behind her. She almost started humming a tune to herself, but thought that'd make her seem even more suspicious.

He didn't say anything as he placed a bag of shopping on the side. Robin tried so hard to act normal – taking a seat at the table, sipping her water.

'Are you OK?' he asked.

She pretended she was distracted. 'Mmm, yes, thank you. Are you?'

Julius didn't respond. It took a lot of effort not to look at the white door's top bolt, which was still open. Maybe he suspected she'd been doing something wrong. Maybe he could see it on her face. But, after a few seconds, he seemed to relax and, to her relief, started making dinner.

They'd been eating in silence for about ten minutes. She did *try* to start conversations, but Julius was, well, not quite shy but . . . it was as though he didn't know *how* to talk. Like a new kid at school.

Following her third attempt, he managed to ask her a question. He wanted to know whether they prayed in assembly and if she ever read the Bible.

'They taught us about Noah's Ark,' she said. 'And we went to a cathedral once, on a trip.'

'Did you like it?'

Robin shrugged. 'Yeah, I guess.'

'Would you like a Bible? I have a few.'

And, without meaning to, Robin's eyes flitted just a few centimetres to the left and looked over his shoulder at the white door. Immediately, she realised what she'd done and snapped her attention straight back to her plate.

'Uh yeah, OK,' she said. 'Sure.'

But it was too late.

Julius hesitated, opened his mouth, then slowly turned in his chair and stared at the door. Robin curled her toes and made fists on her lap.

'Did you go in there?' he asked.

'I . . . I was . . .'

'*Did you go in there?*' he yelled, spotting the top lock.

'I'm sorry, I just . . .'

Julius stood up so fast he knocked his chair over, went to the door, undid the bottom bolt and slammed it open. She couldn't see but heard him thudding around in there. She swallowed. Her legs started to jitter as she searched the kitchen, but there was nowhere to go. Nowhere to run.

'No, no, no,' he shouted. '*No.*'

There was another loud sound and he came storming back.

'I didn't touch any—'

'Why did you turn them around? *Why?*'

'I . . . They . . .'

He shoved the dining table aside, their plates and glasses smashing on the floor, then he crouched in front of her and checked her face, moved her hair, looking into her eyes.

'God, dear God.' He seemed worried now, not annoyed. 'Robin, no, no.'

Again, he dashed into the room, and came out with a small wooden cross. He pressed it against her chest.

'Hold this – *hold it.*'

Robin did as he said – her eyes wide, alarmed – watching him. But she didn't cry.

He was breathing fast, like this was an emergency.

'Stand up, stand up, stand *up.*'

She stumbled as he dragged her into the middle of the kitchen. 'I don't understand,' Robin said. 'I . . . I . . .'

From a cupboard, Julius removed a washing-up bowl. He put it in the sink and turned on the tap.

'Lord, cleanse this place,' he said, and then he started talking so quickly Robin couldn't hear the words. It was like a prayer, but he was mumbling desperately, as though he couldn't say it fast enough. He kept repeating the word 'light'.

Robin shuddered and scrunched her face as he poured the water on to her head. She gripped the wooden cross, lifted her shoulders and gasped as it ran down her back, splashing on the floor around her socks.

He drenched her with bowl after bowl, until her hair and clothes were stuck to her skin. As he recited his prayer, he dragged his hands over her head and flicked the water away.

When he'd finished, Robin stood shivering on the tiles, her teeth chattering. And, finally, she opened her eyes.

Now Julius had put all the dolls on the kitchen worktop. He laid them face down, then pulled a hammer from beneath the sink.

'What are you doing?' Robin waited, dripping wet, catching her breath, trying to calm herself. 'Don't.'

'As it was in the void of the beginning,' he said, and – *whack* – he smashed the first doll's head. 'Is now.' *Thud* – she blinked – another one. 'And, God, shall ever be.' *Bang.* Robin flinched at each impact, tiny shards of charcoal flying across the kitchen. 'A serpent.' *Crack.* 'A saviour.' *Crack.*

'Stop,' Robin whimpered. She was so cold. He was killing them.

He destroyed the last doll, bashing it over and over and over again.

There was fear – there was always fear. But, somehow, what he'd done made her, for the first time, extremely angry. Robin heard her own breath, short and sharp through her nose.

'Listen,' he said. He held her shoulder in his free hand, crouched and stared into her eyes once more. 'You are in *a lot* of danger. I can't keep you safe unless you do what I say. Please.' His grey hair was damp. His face – his scarred, broken, wrinkled face – was snarling. He looked so mad. So completely mad. 'There are very bad people in the world. Demons. *Monsters*. And they will do *very bad things to you*. Do, you, understand?'

'Have . . . have they got red eyes? Like in your comic book?'

He stood, held the hammer tight and grabbed a fistful of her T-shirt. 'Do you understand?' He shook her.

'*The All-Seeing Eye* isn't real, Julius. It's make-believe.'

'*Do you understand?*' he yelled, hitting the table.

Robin looked at her feet, at the flooded tiles, the powdered charcoal, black dust running like ink across the surface of the water. Some of it had flowed to her socks and stained them.

Then she lifted her head.

And she nodded. Oh, she understood just fine. Robin knew exactly the kind of person he was talking about.

'People,' she whispered, 'like you?'

Chapter 21

Sam came in through the automatic hospital doors, frantic and desperate. He could hardly speak at reception – he blurted words, names – a calm man pointed to a large red sign behind him. The ground was still lurching as he went down the glowing corridor – as if seasick, he felt his shoulder bounce off a wall. He steadied himself and dismissed a concerned nurse who appeared at his elbow to offer assistance.

Hallowfield General was different at night – a bright oasis, white at every turn. He made it to a place that bustled with emergency, through a long walkway lined on both sides with glass – like a motorway overpass. The windows were black, wet with rain, reflecting back at him. A holographic row of Sams, swaying down the tunnel in perfect unison.

He saw David first, standing in a doorway, tired and distraught. Marilyn was pale – blank in the face. That unique expression – loss in her eyes, the look of grief. He had seen it before when her father died. As he stepped close, she turned and hugged him, burying her forehead in his shoulder, her cheek sticky, hot with fevered thoughts. David just watched, passive in this moment. Something that had lain dormant for years was here again – something Sam and Marilyn shared, something beyond love and the petty disputes that had driven them apart. There, lying behind her, sedated in a white bed – the life that would bond them for the rest of theirs. When everything else had boiled away, he was all that mattered. This child – here, now. Freddie was asleep, countless wires and tubes flowed around his body, like medical vines crawling inside him.

Time seemed to slip forwards – haze and shock disobeying the rules of normal days. A doctor was speaking to them in a side room, beneath a glaring strip of light. It fizzed, flickering faster than Sam's eyes could see. He tried to listen.

'The good news is the injuries above his waist are superficial. There's no brain trauma,' the old doctor said, his shirtsleeves rolled up, his jowls hanging off his night shift. 'However, we'll need to operate on Freddie's right leg immediately.' There was a terrible pause. 'He's . . . he's got a long road to recovery. But, given time, he's going to be OK.'

Sam felt his own legs cave at this – he lowered himself into a chair and tried to pay attention, but he couldn't focus.

'I'm sorry,' he said, but no one was listening.

Marilyn and David were stunned, nodding at the man – asking questions about metal rods and recovery time. About Freddie's future.

The doctor then waved to a pair of uniformed officers Sam hadn't noticed – standing at his side, foggy, blurred impressions. Dark in vests, belts, cuffs catching the light. One of them had his thumbs resting in his shoulder straps. The other twisted a dial on his radio, pressed his lips together and gave Sam something between a nod and a frown. Routine. Normal day.

A paramedic then conveyed, second-hand, what she had managed to glean from Freddie's account. Two men, wearing animal masks – one maybe a horse – had attacked him in the underpass. He'd been walking home alone after five-a-side. Apparently, no threats were made – they simply embarked on their assault. One of the officers remarked that it was, indeed, the work of animals. What else would do this to a thirteen-year-old boy?

Freddie, they said, managed to escape and get out on to the open street.

'M,' Sam whispered, calling her over to the endless black windows in the corridor. They stood side by side, their reflections opposite. 'This . . . this is my fault.'

'No . . . Sam . . . it's . . .'

'The men who did this . . . There's a church, a religious sect. Something to do with Robin Clarke . . . somehow related to whatever's happened to her. There are . . . brothers.'

'Why would they . . . why would they want to hurt Freddie?'

'Because I hurt one of their sons. They have quite . . . quite a . . . a refined understanding of retaliation.'

'You . . . *Sam* . . .' She took a slow breath, holding back anger. 'Why are you . . . Why the fuck can't you just . . . why. . . *why?*'

'I'm . . . I'm sorry . . . I . . . '

There was a long silence as reason returned. Marylin was never one to dwell on what cannot be changed.

'He . . . he got away,' she said. 'It could have been a lot worse.'

'I think it was meant to be.'

Marilyn looked through the glass, past their reflections, into the night – then her eyes readjusted and centred on Sam's. 'How sure are you that it was them?'

'I'm sure.'

'Can you prove it?'

'I hope so.'

'And if not?'

Leaning on the railing, Sam turned to face her. He took her hands, slender and cold in his, her new wedding ring rotating as he squeezed. Lifting them, he pressed her palms flat on his chest – letting her feel his heartbeat. Just like she used to. Then, gradually, he slid her right hand inside his jacket, and beneath his biceps. He felt her fingers on the leather holster, on the metal grip. When she knew what it was, she moved her arm round further, to his back, and pulled herself into him. Her mouth found his ear and came as close as flesh can come without touching. Peach hairs standing, reaching what they could. Her lips sent goosebumps down his neck, down his shoulders. Warm breath. Perfume. Expensive shampoo. These smells. These familiar things.

'*Good*,' she whispered.

In the morning, after the surgery, Freddie was sitting up in bed, sipping juice from a carton that Sam held out for him. He was calm now, in relatively high spirits. But the noise he'd made when he woke up, the bewildered, understated whimper he emitted when he looked down at the cast around his leg – it was, bar none, the worst sound Sam had ever heard.

'Guess I'll try out for the academy next year instead,' Freddie said, swallowing the blackcurrant juice. He took the carton and held it himself.

Exhaling, trying to grasp his sinking heart, Sam looked at the floor.

'That was a joke,' Freddie added, with his resilient smile. 'You still got the receipt for those boots?'

Somehow, this was worse than despair. Beyond those strong eyes, one swollen into a purple squint, Freddie was still crying. This brave face was for Sam. Comfort he did not deserve.

They chatted for a while about nothing in particular – the adjustable bed, the brilliant power of morphine, the sweetener used in lieu of sugar in the blackcurrant juice. Eventually, Freddie gestured to the muted TV in the corner of his private room. The Clarkes were, as always, on the news.

'Is Robin dead?' he asked.

'I don't know.'

'If her dad really killed her, do you think he killed Ethan too?'

'I don't think so.'

'Why?' Freddie's eyes were glazed, dipping from the drugs, his conversation open and honest – even more so than usual.

'Because I know Francis Clarke, and I don't . . . there . . . there isn't enough evidence to suggest he would do something like that.'

He yawned. 'But the police think he did.'

'They do.'

'People at school say the parents have hidden Robin to make money, by selling the story. Is that possible?'

'It is. But quite unlikely.'

'Maybe she's flown away, like a bird?' Freddie lifted his hand, moving the white clip on his index finger. Then he closed his eyes.

'Maybe.'

'I think she's alive,' he whispered, beginning to fall asleep. 'I think she's in the sky, sitting on top of a cloud . . . Dad?'

'Yes?'

'Don't you have work to do?'

'I can stay as long as you want.'

'Nah. You should go . . . go and get the bad people.' This was what they used to tell him – a simplified job description, this was what Daddy did all day. 'And please, please don't be sad, OK? You should . . . you should smile.'

Sam stood, touched him on the head, then left him there sleeping, his drip feeding him peaceful dreams about clouds and birds and baseless hope.

Later, faint on drink and tears, Sam arrived at Isabelle's ground-floor flat. He clambered through the bushes, crunching on twigs and leaves, to check he was in the right place. At the window, he looked inside, past the curtains, and saw Isabelle sitting cross-legged on her sofa, in pyjamas, eating nuts from a bowl on her lap. It was odd seeing her relaxed in a domestic setting. Made her seem vulnerable – made her seem young. Real. Human. Sam had lost track of the date, the time, all these normal markers. From the sun, he supposed it was late afternoon.

Back at the front of the building, he thumbed the buzzer for her apartment. Before she answered, the door swung open and a woman, wearing a pale-green uniform and a small silver watch on her breast pocket, stepped past him. She had red paint in her hair.

'Keys again?' Isabelle's voice from the intercom.

'Uh, no . . . it's Sam.'

There was a pause, then a lock groaned.

'It's open.'

Sam went in through a dim, windowless hall, towards number thirty-three – halfway there, an automatic light flashed twice in the darkness, before finally coming on. Arms folded, Isabelle met him at her door.

'Can I come in?'

Isabelle hesitated. 'Sure.' She stepped aside.

In her living room, which smelled of burned matches and warm food, Sam took a seat at the round dining table by a kitchenette. Isabelle had been streaming YouTube on her TV – a video entitled 'North Serpent – London protest, 2014' was paused on the screen. The image was of a bald man, mid chant, his fist held high. A banner behind him read 'Take Britain Back'. It had 2,300 views and the bar along the bottom was blue with upturned thumbs clicked in support.

A shadow appeared.

'I know you're not working today . . .' Sam looked up. 'Oh.'

The person wasn't Isabelle. It was a younger girl. Perhaps a teen-ager. She was dressed in baggy jeans and a top speckled with paint. Blue, red, yellow splodges, some of which were neat handprints. Gentle brown eyes. Sister, maybe. The most notable difference was that, unlike Isabelle, her demeanour seemed unsettled – she held her arm across her chest and moved as though she was lost.

'To you . . . to you.'

Isabelle arrived behind. 'Abigail, this man is called Sam.'

The washing machine at his side was on, thrumming round and round quietly.

'To you. To you.'

'He's from work.'

'Happy— what name is he?'

'Sam.'

Abigail came close to the dining table. She peered down at the washing machine, then glanced around the kitchen top. But she never, not once, made eye contact. He felt sure, however, that she was analysing him, using every other sense to assess this unknown guest.

'To you,' she whispered, frowning as though listening to a near-silent sound.

'He's cool,' Isabelle said. '*He's a good one.*'

Thinking, Abigail made a fist and pressed her knuckles into her temple, rocking slightly, like she was fighting off a sudden head-ache. Then she leaned over and placed her hand on his shoulder, staring only at the wall. Isabelle seemed alarmed – she shoved a chair aside and strode forwards, hovering above the situation, tense and ready to intervene.

Sam sat still, unsure exactly what was going on. It was the first time he'd ever seen fear in her eyes, so assumed he ought to share some. But she simmered down when Abigail stood up straight and turned away. The washing machine changed modes – an internal mechanism clunked and the drum slowed to a stop, water draining as it prepared for a spin cycle.

A long silence. Nothing moved.

'No,' Abigail said, definitively. 'He is not a good one.' And then she left the room, humming, 'To you, to you, to you,' to herself, as the machine began to whir again.

'She usually doesn't touch people.' Isabelle sat opposite him at the dining table.

'It's fine. Is she . . . ?'

'A good judge of character?'

'Your sister?'

'Yes.'

Sam glanced over to the coffee table in the centre of the living room. On top, between the TV remote and a pair of glasses, there was a sliced cake. A single candle surrounded by thick ribbons of icing, dotted with tiny stars and crystal sugar. The curled wick was black now, but he could still smell its smoke. 'Is it her birthday?'

'No,' Isabelle said. 'It's mine.'

'Many happy returns.'

'You just missed the singing – Abigail gave it one hundred and ten per cent.' Isabelle stood and pointed at the window. 'Her carer, Mandy, who just left, she forgot as well – so I'll let you off.'

There was sadness here, in this small home. Sam felt he was behind the scenes, behind a curtain she'd rather keep closed. It occurred to him that Isabelle, alone besides her sister, had probably bought that cake herself.

'It's more for her than me,' she said, as if reading this thought. 'You'd be surprised how many times she can blow out a candle . . . Do you want a . . .' Isabelle pulled open her fridge and sighed, 'very old Belgian beer?'

'Sure.'

A click and a hiss, the cap clinking on the counter. 'I'm sorry,' she said, still facing away. 'For what happened to Freddie . . .' She placed a small green bottle on the table, opened another for herself, then returned to sit opposite him.

Sam put his hand over his mouth, holding in a wave of nausea. 'You OK?'

He shook his head.

'I thought it before.' Isabelle squinted at him. 'You're ill . . .'

Blinking, Sam cleared his throat. 'You're very observant.'

'What's wrong with you?'

'I . . .' He didn't really know how to phrase it. He'd told no one. But this was as direct as questions come. So he said, 'I'm dying.'

'We're all dying, Sam. Where's that trademark optimism gone?'

'I have a . . . tumour in my brain. Military grade. Best of the best. No more birthday candles.'

'Uh . . .' Isabelle seemed confused, as though she couldn't find the words. 'Is this a dark joke?'

'Yes. But it's also true.'

'Why didn't you say?'

'You didn't ask.'

There was a long pause. 'Are they . . . Can they operate?'

He shook his head again.

'Does Marilyn know?'

'No.'

'How does that square up with your honesty?'

Sam's expression didn't change. 'Withholding information is not the same as lying. If she asks, I'll tell her. She's a worrier anyway – it'd just rub off on Freddie.'

'Does he know?'

'I . . .' Sam half nodded. 'I want to tell him.'

'Shit, you sure? Pretty big burden.'

'I thought it might be better to keep it quiet. But who am I to decide? It's the truth. Imagine him living the rest of his life, angry that I didn't.'

'The truth . . . it's not a silver bullet.'

'Oh, but it is. Have you ever in your life heard a piece of pertinent information and felt worse off for it? Or would you rather know?'

'Yeah, but I'm an adult . . . It's a choice between possible anger and certain sadness. You shouldn't tell him. You've done the right thing.'

'No, I haven't.'

Isabelle stared for a few seconds at the bottle in her hands, her thumbnail picking at the label. 'How will it happen?'

There was something warm in these cold questions, in her absolute disregard for anything besides reality. She hadn't tilted her head, she hadn't tutted, she hadn't reached over the table and squeezed his hand and whispered, 'Oh, Sam . . .'

'Horribly,' he said. 'In a hospice bed, kept on a machine until someone has the decency to switch it off. Draining away, like most do.'

'I doubt that'll be the case.'

Sam lifted his beer. 'You know me well. I'm going to buy a little boat – I've already picked one. It's good, got a nice deck so I can see the sky. I'll take what I need to take. Drift out into the open water, out on to the shifting sea.'

Calm, slow breaths as Isabelle smiled. 'Hence the impatience.'

'Yes, this will be the last card.'

She shook her head. 'But nothing justifies what they did, OK? It's not your fault.'

'Always said I would die for my kid. Maybe better to say *should*. We need to find them.'

She turned her hands over, palms up.

'*You* need to find them,' he added.

The washing machine was spinning now, loud in this narrow space.

'And let's suppose, for argument's sake, you knew where they were, what would you do?'

Of course, she needed to ask. Even Abigail, with all her cognitive restrictions, had gone straight to the crux of the issue. She'd zeroed in on Isabelle's admirable misconception. No, she'd said, he is *not* a good one.

Sam sighed. 'Violence is appealing,' he admitted. 'But there's no logic in vengeance. I just want them arrested. I just want Freddie to be safe.'

Her placid eyes searched his face. 'Is *that* the truth?'

'I don't lie, Isabelle.'

'You were in a hospice bed a second ago.'

'That *was* a joke . . . jokes are fine.'

'He's safe,' she said. 'I promise. They'll keep officers on the ward around the clock.'

They sat for a while, listening only to the rhythmic drumming from the washing machine. In the next room, Abigail's song was no more than a whisper.

'Why did you come here?' Isabelle asked.

Business, business, business. 'I received an anonymous message this afternoon, from an email made of numbers. One of those temporary addresses.' Sam got his phone out of his pocket, unlocked it, then passed it across the table. 'There's a video attached. A video of Anna.'

Chapter 22

The snow in his mind had settled again. Big, flat flakes fell quickly without wind to make soft pillows on every imagined bench and lamp post, like carved marble – all the edges were impeccably rounded. Just like those cold months he remembered from Montreal. Francis had been able to get a repeat prescription of tramadol from his doctor for the toothache. Far stronger than the relatively tame pills Jeremy had shared. They were an afternoon flurry. This, at double doses, was the real deal. The roads were closed, weather warnings had been issued and all flights were grounded until further notice. Winter. Calm winter.

He'd had to bend the truth a little and say his back was playing up again – otherwise they would have given him anti-inflammatories and booked him in for treatment. The pain was still there, tingling when he bit down, like the metallic flavour of a battery. And he probably would need to see a dentist soon enough. But, in the short term, this cosy covering of opiates was sufficient.

They'd moved him, extending the amount of time they could keep him in custody once again. Jeremy said ninety-six hours in total. After that, they would release him or, and this was by far the most likely option, they would charge him.

'Body or no body,' Jeremy had said. 'You're not going home without Robin.'

His cell was a dismal concrete box. Its walls were plastered, painted grey and the bed was a creaking board which hung from chains – more a fold-down shelf. Previous inmates had decorated the back of the door with scratches and dents. Francis could imagine himself on the floor, desperately clawing at that steel when spring arrived to expose the grass and tarmac.

Lying on the thin mattress with his legs crossed, he folded his hands on his stomach, closed his eyes and breathed in the cool, silent air. In this state of chemical hibernation, he was able to assess his situation in a calmer, more rational way. The facts were these: the police had found Robin's blood in his car, on the driveway and wiped crudely off a screwdriver in the garage. Despite the aggressive interrogation, during which he was told to 'end the torment' and just *tell them* where the body was, Francis's recollection of the night had been entirely sincere. He'd done what Sam said he should – he'd told the truth. Sam. Honest Sam.

Francis had been woken by Anna shaking his shoulder – wide-eyed and panicked. Initially, he thought she was sleepwalking again. There was that manic distance on her face – as though no one was home. At her worst, Anna would have entire conversations with him. Her responses were curt and sometimes little more than grunts, but she appeared, at least to a casual observer, to be awake. But Francis could tell. He knew when there was life behind those eyes and when there wasn't.

In the half-light of her reading lamp, even with that concern, she looked beautiful. Standing over him, saying, 'Robin's gone, Robin's gone, Robin's gone.' Beautiful Anna. It was the best word to describe her. Francis felt 'pretty' was too feminine, 'sexy' was misleading and 'attractive' just fell short. Anna was *beautiful*. Even at 3 a.m., fresh from bed, telling him their daughter was missing.

Francis had met her back in Canada, when he was working in the IT department at MoleculeBlue, one of Montreal's lesser-known failed tech start-ups. The job had begun as a placement for his computer-science course. When the internship expired, they offered him a full-time position. It wasn't the best work, but it was still a real golden era in his youth. He was earning adult money, all the while enjoying a college lifestyle.

The first time he saw her was at the last of Jordan Weaver's 'legendary house parties' before Christmas. Anna, standing in the kitchen, sipping beer from a red plastic cup, was as clear as any of his recent memories. Unlike other faces, her features had the clarity of a photograph in his mind. Even Robin, even *Ethan* needed context to exist as anything more than an abstract idea.

Anna, nineteen years old at the time, though he'd have guessed younger, had been leaning on the kitchen counter, wearing a blue minidress with a Peter Pan collar buttoned right up to her neck – very English. Her slender arms were covered by tight sleeves, but her thighs were visible above the high boots and white cotton socks, pulled up an inch over her knees. Her blonde curls were held back with a matching blue-ribbon hairband. Large white flowers across her dress and big plastic hoop earrings hung by her cheeks to complete the 1960s look – which was, Francis realised only upon arriving, the party's theme.

And then to her face – subtle blue dusting across her eyelids, black liner flicking up at either side and her lashes naturally long, no need for fakes. She wore no lipstick. Again, not necessary, her lips were pink enough against her pale skin – she had the complexion of a redhead and he'd wondered if her hair was dyed. However, of course, it was all her. Beautiful, natural Anna.

If she'd been anyone else, and she'd been modelling those retro clothes, the photographer would have taken all day and a thousand shots before he'd get this image. But this was just how she stood. Effortless Anna.

174

Francis had stared from across the apartment – the party swinging all around him: two girls kissing to rapturous cheers and raised cups, someone on the floor drinking from a beer bong, half the room singing, clapping along to 'Runaround Sue' – 'hey, hey, whoa-ah-oh-oh-oooh' – a classic they'd later adopt, with more than a hint of irony, as 'their song'. A tall man shouldered into him and apologised as the drunken choir swayed and, arms up, warned him again to stay away from this girl. But none of it existed. Only her. Just beautiful, natural, effortless Anna. She had looked past him and closed her dusted eyes for a sultry blink. When they opened, they found his and kept them for the entire chorus.

Francis hadn't been brave enough to talk to her that first night. He'd never had much luck with girls – he was, as she would later tease him, quite 'camp', and perhaps this restricted his appeal. The jocks at school tended to go for something less nuanced, like, 'You fuck-ing faggot'. As far as he was aware, high school was the only place on earth where you could have the absolute shit beaten out of you for liking drama class more than lacrosse. He sometimes wished he could travel back there and whisper in his timid, twelve-year-old ear that existence gets better. One day, being shy won't mean getting hurt. He would tell himself that the world wasn't out to get him. No, he wouldn't say that – that would be a lie. Maybe this earlier version of Francis – the kid who'd cry alone in the bathroom and pray for some kind of escape – was right to feel that way. All these years had just fooled him otherwise. Now he was back as he should be – alone and in pain, for reasons he simply did not understand.

In short, approaching a beautiful girl at a party really wasn't an option.

However, a few weeks after that evening, maybe a month, Francis had been working late and was riding the night bus back to his apartment. His street was the final stop of the journey. Sitting at the rear, in his favourite seat, he'd been reading when another passenger climbed aboard. He paid little attention to her – she faced away, clinging on to the yellow pole near the front by the driver, swaying with the corners. She was wearing jeans, snug around narrow hips and a slim frame. On her head, she wore a knitted hat with a reindeer motif and a white bobble on top. Blonde curls at her neck were not quite familiar enough to place her as *that girl*.

They were turning out of a crossroads when, lifting his head from his book and looking to his right, Francis saw a quick flash of headlights hurtling towards them, skidding at unimaginable speed, then smashing, spinning wildly off the front end of the bus with broken glass and metal panels sparking on the tarmac below. It all happened within two seconds.

He lurched forwards, shouldering into the seat in front, bashing his head hard on the plastic handle. As for the girl, she was jolted from her feet and landed with her hands flat on the dirty floor.

The bus itself wasn't too damaged. Although the internal lights tripped off, the engine still rumbled. It had ended up in the centre of the junction, parked diagonally. Remaining traffic weaved around them.

'You guys all right?' the driver asked, leaning out with a frosting of glass powder in his hair. He was dark in the ambient glow – snow tinting the scene blue.

'Yes, fine,' she said in an English accent, clambering back to her feet. And then, hands filthy, knees wet with melted ice from winter boots, the girl in the bobble hat turned round and looked at Francis. 'Are you OK?' she asked, stepping towards him, wiping her fingers on her jeans.

When he realised it was her, her, *her* from the party, he smiled. 'I am.' He knew his face was red.

The man who'd hit the bus was drunk and travelling at almost triple the speed limit, so police attended the crash and checked them both over. Then the driver told them where to wait and when the next bus would arrive. Instead, Francis decided to walk. When he told the girl which direction he was heading, she said, 'Oh, great, me too.'

And off they went. They crunched along salted pavements, past huge white pillows shaped like parked cars, and then trudged through fresh snow, cutting across the park just down from his apartment.

'Anna, by the way,' she said, holding out her hand, now covered with a red mitten.

'Francis.'

At first, he'd assumed she didn't remember him. However, following their late introduction under an iron street lamp, as gold-leaf snowflakes landed on her woollen hat, she said, 'I was going to speak to you at the party but, I don't know, I guess I bottled it.'

'Bottled it?'

'It means I was scared.'

'*You* were scared? God, why?'

'You're tall and handsome and I bet you speak French.'

'*Juste un peu.*'

She replied fluently.

Confused, Francis laughed and shrugged. 'Clearly not as much as you,' he said. His accent sounded so sloppy next to hers.

When they arrived at his apartment, keen to seem a gentleman he said they would continue on to her destination together. He wouldn't have her walking out here alone at this hour. Anna hesitated, then said she would be fine – although she appreciated the offer.

But Francis insisted. 'No, no, it's OK, really.'

Anna, mittens and jeans, bobble hat and lips, leaned forwards and gave him a hug. 'I'm sorry, the truth is, the place I'm staying . . .' She looked around the street behind her. 'It's nowhere near here.'

Francis was flattered – she'd walked two unnecessary kilometres, in the wrong direction, in the freezing cold, just to be with him. It was the seed of their relationship. It was a conscious decision she'd made to keep them closer than fate had intended. A choice that meant there was no other option than to invite her inside and extend the offer of an inflatable mattress, which, with her sweet smile, she declined.

In the midst of that dark, gentle snow, the night of crashes and bruises, cold noses and warm tongues, Francis hadn't stopped to think about what she'd done. It was too exciting. Too incredible. One of those beautiful off-limit girls had taken an inexplicable interest in him. Why would he question it?

And yet, the reality of the gesture remained. What Anna had said on the pavement, next to the bus – that she was heading in the same direction – it was charming, it was cool, it was intensely alluring. But it was also, as well as all these things, a lie.

Nevertheless, they were officially a couple within the month.

It transpired that Anna was spending her gap year in Montreal, working as a barmaid to fund short breaks around the country – something that was, she said, far more idyllic in her imagination than it turned out to be in real life. Until, of course, she met him.

They danced together, and spent long evenings with take-out and garbage TV – her calves on his lap, her voice at his neck. Her company made all bad things good and all good things great. The best of life's offerings became fleeting glimpses of heaven. She wrote him letters, poems and showed him kindness he had never known. She said his eyes were blue pools, a tropical sea she could swim in all day, and his physique was perfect just the way it was. To say he'd loved her would be an understatement – but language was yet to develop an adequate word for how he felt about beautiful Anna Radisson.

Far too soon she was due to return to the UK, to study medicine – *that's right, smart too*, he'd thought, nodding at his mother when her eyebrows shot up in surprise. They promised they'd make a long-distance relationship work. But he feared she would drift away – of course, with all their splendour, angels can fly.

So, Francis went to a jeweller in town, bought a silver engagement ring and, on her final evening, took her out to her favourite Chinese restaurant. When they'd finished, he insisted they got the night bus back to his apartment. For old times' sake.

The driver took some convincing, but was noble enough to turn down the money Francis had offered. He remembered the night of the crash and said the idea was 'actually quite romantic'.

As Francis had hoped, they were the only passengers on the bus. Anna standing, holding on to the vertical yellow pole, just as she had done almost a year before. Francis opposite her, his hand around one of the hanging plastic loops above, the other buried in his pocket. The bus pulled slowly into the middle of that open junction and, with a hiss, came to a stop. The driver played his part perfectly. Anna frowned, pursed her lips, then turned to look out of the dark window.

And then the lights went off.

'Uh, OK. What's going on?' she asked. And when she turned back, she found Francis kneeling on the dirty floor, his trousers in damp footprints, his hands cupped around the velvet box. That baby face, looking down at him, fingers on her mouth, tears in her eyes. Saying yes.

Saying yes of course.

Beautiful Anna, looking down at him, saying wake up, wake up, Francis, wake up, Ethan's gone, Robin's gone. Yes, of course I'll marry you.

It's nowhere near here. I just said it was.

I just wanted to walk with you.

I just wanted to—

A sound made Francis's legs jerk straight. He rose from the brink of sleep, looking up at his prison cell ceiling. Everywhere was warm. The snow was melting. His cheek felt swollen, stretched and hot. He sat up and leaned over to the radiator, convinced it was on, but touched cold metal.

A thought kept coming to him. One he did not like to think.

Someone had hurt Robin, they had taken blood from her and planted it in locations that would have fingers pointed squarely at him. All while he slept. He didn't spend long wondering who might *want* to do such a thing. Instead, he wondered who *could*. There was really only one suspect. There she was, in his mind, leaning over him, looking down with that sweet face he'd loved so much.

Anna. Beautiful, natural, effortless, deceitful Anna.

His tooth ached enough to make his left eyelid twitch. Winter had ended. His body was wet greys and greens, streets lined with packed ice stained black by filth and shrinking. And even that turned to water when a voice came through his cell door.

'People like you don't fare well in places like this,' the man whispered. Whoever it was, Francis could tell he was smiling. 'They keep you separate. They keep you safe. Most of the time . . .' There was a *clink, clink, clink.* 'Know what that is?' *Clink, clink, clink.* 'That's metal.' *Clink, clink, clink.* 'A blind eye is cheap to buy, if you know what I mean . . .'

And then the voice was gone.

That afternoon, Francis demanded to see Jeremy. In their defence, the guards were generally obliging. They treated him with courtesy – he was allowed certain privileges. Although they didn't always act like it, he was innocent until proven otherwise. Still, to his horror, this was already starting to feel like home.

He met his lawyer in a small room with low foam chairs and a square wooden table. Handsome Jeremy had his briefcase on his lap. He placed it on the floor, then stood to greet him.

'You feeling OK?' he asked, his hand on Francis's upper arm.

After making sure the door was properly closed, he whispered, 'Someone came to my cell – threatened me. I'm meant to be segregated.'

'Did you see him?'

'No, he spoke through the door.'

'All right, wait here.' Jeremy left the room.

Francis sat down and rubbed his fingers – earlier they'd felt like silk from his moisturiser. Now they were clammy. He blew on them to get rid of the sweat. But the heat was in his core now; his clothes were damp. When Jeremy returned, he shut the door behind him and perched on the table.

'They say that's not possible.' He pushed his designer glasses up his nose. 'You a hundred per cent sure?'

'I didn't imagine it – Jesus.'

'No. It's just, they told me the only people who can access that gangway are guards.'

Turning his head to the ceiling, Francis breathed and felt his throat strain. 'Then I am truly fucked.'

All that stood between him and that clinking shank was this slick man, today wearing a navy waistcoat and pinstriped trousers – all slim fit, making him seem even younger. It felt slightly backwards to place all his faith in someone at least fifteen years his junior. Francis hoped Jeremy was still worth the money.

'Listen, I have something for you.' Jeremy stood, slid a laptop from his leather briefcase and placed it on the table. He tilted the screen open.

A video was ready to play. In the centre of the frame, Francis saw his wife, beautiful Anna, sitting on her hotel bed. The hidden camera he'd had planted in her room, despite Jeremy's disapproval, was bearing fruit. However, from his expression, Francis could tell it was rotten.

'You know how I feel about it,' Jeremy said. 'I didn't even want to look . . . but, it might be significant . . . You sure you want to see this?'

Francis glared at him, bit away the pain and clicked the white triangle in the bottom left-hand corner. And what he saw hurt him like nothing else ever could.

Chapter 23

Watching from a camera on the side table, deep within the plastic casing of an alarm clock, we see room twenty-one. We see Anna. Her suitcase on the floor. The closed curtains. The neat bed. She's sitting on a chair in the corner, still wearing the same clothes, still unable to settle. Frowning, she looks down into her mobile. As she reads from the screen, she pulls on the blonde curls hanging at the side of her face – three short tugs. Then she rubs her leg, which bounces up and down as though she's repeatedly pumping a pedal with her heel. Alone, these twitches are at their most severe.

There's a gentle tapping sound and she composes herself, wipes her face with her hand, then stands. She steps past, disappearing from view. We hear the door.

She returns with a man carrying a black rucksack – he places it on the bed and hugs her. His lower half fills the frame as they hold one another in silence for almost a minute.

Sniffing, gasping as she releases him, Anna descends back into her seat. The man then sits on the edge of the mattress, to her left, our right. When he glances around the room, and we see his face, we recognise him as Daniel Aiden. We see his tanned skin, his thin metal glasses, his dark hair, well-groomed – grey above the ears. He's wearing a loose, informal blue shirt and beige chinos. Although no stranger to

the screen, usually he knows he's being filmed. Today, he's not present-
ing anything beyond his private self.

'I got a message from Paula, at the foundation,' Anna says. 'She's
resigning.'

Daniel shakes his head. 'Why?'

'Apparently someone who's about to be charged with murder isn't
the best president.'

'No, I mean, why is she contacting you *about it?'*

'Courtesy I guess — she'd been considering it for a while, the issue of
the missing funds and so on.' Anna shrugs. 'She thought I should know
before they go public.'

'So that's it, the Clarke Foundation is dead?'

'There are other charities waiting in the wings — the kids we're
helping will be fine. Change of branding more than anything else.'

'Are you OK about that?'

'Why the fuck would I care?'

'No, yeah, of course.' Daniel touches her knee. 'Have you seen
Francis, since . . . ?'

'I spoke to him on the phone.'

'How is he?'

'Not well.' She tugs on her hair three times, then rubs her jeans.

'Have you . . . have you thought more about . . . ?'

Anna presses her fingertips into her forehead. 'He is many things . . .
but he's not a murderer.'

Francis watched the video in silence. The clock in the prison's
meeting room ticked, but after a while he stopped noticing. And,
although Jeremy pretended not to look, he wasn't exactly subtle.
His eyes kept passing over the floor, then towards Francis – a

strange pride and excitement in providing this footage. He'd certainly changed his tune.

It was not surprising to see Daniel offer Anna support. *A familiar shoulder was better than none at all, right?* As for the foundation – it was only a matter of time before it folded. Every part of his life was coming unravelled. There were plenty of reasons he'd prefer to keep the charity up and running, but a triviality like Paula's resignation was hardly high on his list of concerns.

They'd known Daniel Aiden for decades, long before he found his fame. Following Francis's proposal on the bus, Anna returned to the UK and, while he tied up loose ends in Canada, she got herself settled in a new place. The plan was, once her loan had come through, Francis would drop everything and move to England. Their student accommodation was cheap, and he managed to find work quite fast. Finally, his computer-science degree was paying for itself with a job he actually liked – creating websites for a toy manufacturer. Again, he found himself earning significantly more than his peers.

At first, Francis and Anna shared their narrow terraced house with another couple. But when one of them dropped out of university, the second followed suit. And, while searching for a new lodger, they crossed paths with Daniel – a journalism student looking for a place to call home.

The trio grew to be the best of friends and, although his relationships were turbulent, whenever Daniel had a partner, they would double-date. Which is not to say he was a third wheel. Francis had regarded him as an equal shareholder – as much his friend as Anna's, often more so.

His first impression was admiration. Francis considered Daniel to be, above all else, incredibly intelligent. Sharp in ways that at times made him feel inadequate. He was a prominent member of the university's debating society, took great pleasure in his intellectualism and eventually edited the campus newspaper. A second-generation immigrant with a thirst for knowledge and a bright future ahead of him. His Malaysian father worked in finance and his Welsh mother was an aerospace engineer. He was literally raised by a millionaire and a rocket scientist – hence his predisposition for academic success. Clever Daniel.

Francis remembered the three of them in a bar, clinking glasses the night before Anna's graduation and declaring that, come hell or high water, they would remain friends as they passed into adulthood. The three amigos.

However, geography and lifestyle soon eradicate such naive pledges. When Anna graduated, with a first, and took up a junior-doctor position, Daniel slipped away and into his fledgling media career. Different circles. They'd see him once, maybe twice a year. If there was an irony to Ethan's disappearance, it was the rekindling of their friendship. As though only loss could make it possible again.

It had been Anna's idea to push hard on the campaign and generate as much media coverage as possible. Even Sam agreed it would do more good than harm to let the story run. Francis was less sure, fearing it might achieve fame and little else. Although ultimately proved right on that front, he had eventually conceded.

Of all the people in their address book, Daniel Aiden – by then a well-regarded writer and documentary filmmaker – leaped out. And, of course, he was happy to oblige. Francis invited him back into their life, into baby Robin's life. Sweet Robin. Sweet Robin *loved* Daniel. Uncle Daniel. Clever Uncle Daniel with his funny stories.

We see room twenty-one. 'Last year, after the fight . . . you told me he can be controlling,' Daniel says. 'You said sometimes you feel like you don't even know him.'

Anna looks at the floor. 'But . . . but he wouldn't . . .' Hiding her face in her hands, both legs pump away on invisible pedals. 'He wouldn't.'

'Even before Ethan was born, before everything . . . you had your doubts. You mentioned that in Thailand, for goodness' sake.'

◆ ◆ ◆

Francis tensed his jaw – he felt sweat prickle up his spine and the throb pound through his skull. They went to Thailand almost twenty years ago. *Twenty fucking years.* Eight weeks travelling, island to island. It was the four of them. Francis and Anna, Daniel and his then-girlfriend Zara. They conceived Ethan on that trip. Had this been a fork in the road? Had her pregnancy closed one of these possible routes?

His memories of that day were as vivid as their first encounter – he recalled her face in high definition. She was lying on the beach, by his side. They were both flat on their backs, on packed white sand, the shallow waves drifting up and across their skin. He was holding her hand.

'The sea is so warm,' he whispered. 'If you close your eyes, it feels like it's not even there.'

The ocean crept slowly, only about an inch or two deep, up his legs, his sides, over the back of his head. Then it fell away again. They lay there for hours – Daniel and Zara were at the hostel, probably arguing about something or other.

Anna had turned on to her shoulder and faced him. He mirrored her.

'Those eyes,' she whispered, cupping his cheek in her slender fingers. Her nails were painted with pale, glossy rose varnish – chipped on her thumb. He could see it. He could see her black bikini. Beautiful Anna. Beautiful Anna who would turn heads on the beach and not even notice.

'Can you feel the water?' he asked.

'If I concentrate.'

'It's like I'm numb. I'm the same temperature. Reckon it's thirty-seven degrees?'

'Francis,' she said, her hand on his neck now, her thumb stroking his face. 'I love you.'

He smiled. 'I love you more.'

Anna rested her head on her outstretched arm. He could see the sand stuck to her bronzed skin – tiny flat flakes of stone. The water came up between them and washed away. As warm as blood, almost not there.

'How can you be sure?'

'You'll just have to trust me.'

He closed his eyes and felt the sun on his vision – hot and red. Then her lips on his – he smelled her perfume, her tanning lotion. When he looked again, the sand was blinding for a second, then dark as his retinas readjusted.

'I have something to tell you.' Warm sea. Warm sea you can hardly feel. Warm sea and beautiful Anna. 'I'm pregnant.'

Back now, in room twenty-one, where we see Daniel splaying his hands – gesturing for Anna to agree.

'Doubts about the relationship,' she says. 'Not about . . . not that he could . . .'

'I hear what you're saying, I do. You know I respect Francis. But the police must *have a good reason.*' Daniel, again, reaches out and places a palm on her knee. This slows the jittering, and finally he holds her leg still.

Anna stands. He looks up at her from the bed. 'I need a shower,' she says, walking out of view.

Orange light on the carpet. It fades away as the bathroom door closes. We hear an extractor fan, then water — a sudden rush of muffled rain.

Now alone, Daniel paces in the hotel room — he stands at the window, peers through the curtains, then sits on the bed again. He seems agitated. He rests his elbows on his knees and rubs his face.

'You can fast-forward about four minutes,' Jeremy said.

The footage arrives at a buzzing sound.

'Yeah,' Daniel says, standing and pacing, talking into his mobile. 'I'm with her now . . . Not particularly . . . Hmm . . . She says she'd rather stay here . . . I know, I know . . . Exactly . . . No, of course I haven't . . . Yeah, well, believe it or not, money isn't exactly her priority at the moment . . . If they're interested now, they'll still be interested next year . . . Just be patient . . . OK . . . All right. Yeah . . . yes. Bye.' Daniel hangs up.

'Who was that?' Anna asks, coming back into the room, wearing a white hotel robe.

'Don't worry.' There's a pause. 'It's nothing . . .'

'Was it June?'

He nods.

'Are they talking to producers? Now? Fucking now, Daniel?'

'Calm down, I told her it was too early.'

'Too early? Tell her to fuck off.'

'I know, of course.'

Anna sits on the mattress, throws her head forwards and wraps her thick, wet hair with a thick, dry towel. It appears, as she does this, that she's counting. She rubs her scalp for three seconds on one side, three seconds on the other, then repeats the process – three sets in total. And she stands, steps towards the camera, towards the alarm clock, and hangs her towel over a chair in the bottom of the frame.

When she returns to the bed and lifts her foot on to her knee, picking at something, Daniel sits on the opposite side. Back to back, they share a silence. Then, as though an idea has just come to him, he turns, crawls across the duvet, kneels directly behind her and begins to massage her shoulders. Anna doesn't react.

'I miss her,' she whispers.

'Me too.'

Daniel puts his legs either side of her hips and his arms around her stomach – like they're riding together on a motorbike. His head rests on her back.

'I just dream – fantasise about what I'd do.' She shuts her eyes and taps the air with her index finger, one, two, three imagined incisions paralysing whoever's responsible. 'But I think I'm physically incapable of being happy now. It's like I'm buried. Like I've fallen too low to ever climb out. It hurts so fucking much.'

When Daniel kisses her neck, which still glistens from the shower, Anna leans away. But he persists and, after two more tries, she relaxes. The intimacy is unmistakably familiar. We can tell, we can see that this is not the first time his mouth has touched her skin.

'You know I'd do anything for you,' he says, speaking into her white dressing-gown collar. Another kiss. 'Anything.'

'Stop.' Anna unclasps his fingers, then returns to the chair.

190

'Come stay with me. It's crazy being here, alone.'

She shakes her head. 'We can't.'

'And after the trial?'

'I . . .' She pushes the heels of her hands into her eye sockets, curls forward and begins to cry.

Francis closed the laptop. 'I think I get the picture,' he said.

'They talk a bit more,' Jeremy explained. 'Seems it hasn't been going on for very long. She says you're basically separated?'

'She's *still* my wife.'

'For now.'

'*Fuck you.*'

Jeremy held up a hand and retreated back over the line he knew he'd crossed. 'If it makes you feel better, she does go on to say she's uncomfortable about it.'

Francis noticed the clock ticking again. 'Christmas,' he said, sighing. 'I saw them together – they were too close. They made it into a joke. They were drunk, just being silly. Robin said, "Everyone wants to kiss Mummy at Christmas." We all laughed.' Then his mind clicked back into gear and he remembered where he was, and why. He turned to Jeremy. 'Daniel babysits her. He's got a key to the house. I think Sam should see this.'

'He already has.'

Later, in his cell, Francis thumbed out all six pills. *Fuck the dosage*, he thought, swallowing them without water. Then he waited for winter to arrive again, letting himself fall into an awful fever dream. The prison made strange noises. Odd bangs and buzzing and metal clunks. Gradually, they faded away. Sleeping on the drugs was like being in hell. It was as though he was trapped in a terrible state of limbo – he was aware of everything and nothing all at once.

Hours of comatose thought, jumbled together, leaping through time. Warm water, as warm as blood, chipped nail polish, the headlights hitting the bus, *yes, yes of course, yes of course I'll marry you. Stay away from that girl.* Their wedding day – Daniel's speech. *These two are made for each other.* The doo-wop playlist – a jovial soundtrack to these fractured images. *They're made for each other.* Why *do* fools fall in love? *Can you feel the water? Can you feel it?* It's the most wonderful time of the year. *Wake up. Francis, wake up. Robin's gone.*

The only clear things he kept seeing, in the midst of that night-terror storm, were all the days they'd been alone together, all the conversations they'd had, all the work Daniel had put in. All the ways he'd capitalised on this relentless tragedy. Oh Daniel. Clever, clever, clever Daniel.

Chapter 24

*Henry Marston Junior sits on a balcony in a hospital wheelchair –
everything from his waist down is rigid with plaster cast and wire.
He's alone, looking out at Hallowfield General's sprawling car park.
Windscreens below glisten in the sun, but it's shaded here, six storeys
high, on the shingled terrace. There are two large pot plants in the back
corners of this space. Henry's parked against the wall, one elbow resting
awkwardly on the long metal railing and the other on the arm of his
wheelchair. The camera looks down on him.*

*He breathes a final drag from his cigarette, then stubs it out on the
bricks and flicks it over the edge. Without a beat, he takes the packet
from his lap and lifts another to his lips. He lights it and smokes. There's
no sound so, when a nurse steps out, we do not hear what she says to
him. But she disapproves of something – perhaps his being out of bed,
perhaps the smoking, perhaps she's astonished to see either. However, he
simply does not care and looks back across the treetops and landscaped
grass surrounding the car park.*

*The nurse stays and crouches at his side. She touches his arm and
shakes her head. They talk silently for a few minutes and, during this
conversation, Henry chain-smokes. At two separate intervals, he bursts
into tears. Shoulders hunched, he searches the air, gesticulating with
his hands – angry, desperate misery clear on his face. The nurse listens.*

Although his upper half is animated, nothing beneath his waist moves. His toes do not wiggle, his knees do not sway.

Eventually, the nurse steps behind his wheelchair and pushes him back inside, to bed – where he really ought to be. Afternoon shadows grow long and now the evening light is dust-orange on the car windscreens below.

◆ ◆ ◆

Isabelle drove while Sam rode shotgun – an arrangement he preferred. She seemed prepared to humour him, to bring him along for this meeting. And it wasn't pity, or kindness, but courtesy. He'd given that video to her – an unusual birthday gift, one he could have kept to himself. Better this way. Together.

Initially, Sam assumed the press had planted the camera in Anna's hotel room. It wouldn't be the first time the family's privacy had been invaded. But he very much doubted the culprit would retain enough conscience to share it with him before they showed the rest of the world. Footage like that would be worth a staggering sum if offered to a tabloid. So then, it was not unscrupulous journalism, but something else entirely. Something he did not understand.

Isabelle doubted the revelation was a game changer, but agreed it warranted at least a conversation with Daniel Aiden. Although Sam understood the Clarkes' relationship was not the wholesome union depicted in public, more a practicality for Robin, for simplicity, he hadn't even hypothetically considered adultery to be a factor. If he'd had to put money on where dishonesty lay, if anywhere at all, he'd have placed it at Francis's feet. Anna seemed too troubled to juggle deception, let alone an affair. But there wasn't much ambiguity in that footage. It was indisputable – she and Daniel were something more than good friends.

They turned on to a narrow rural lane, diagonal light shining between the branches in fragmented columns, flashing at the side of his vision. To his right, the sun was low enough, pink enough, tamed enough by the atmosphere to stare at without causing harm. At least, not at a rate he could feel.

'How old is Abigail?' he asked, as the car came through the tunnel of trees and out amid wide open fields.

'Twenty-two.'

'Why does she live with you?'

Isabelle drove in silence for a few seconds. 'Our parents are dead, there are no other siblings, and I can't afford to have her anywhere else. I don't qualify for much help. We have an uncle in Israel, but she doesn't trust other people. She goes to a day centre during the week and they're quite flexible with shifts – they send carers out for medication. Honestly, I prefer her close.'

The satnav said they'd arrive at their destination, Daniel Aiden's house, in six minutes.

Sam looked down a long line of pylons, towards the sun's fire clouds, and saw a shifting flock of starlings. Cascading, then rising, a wave of silhouettes flexing in unison like an oversized bubble in a gentle breeze. As with a lava lamp, his mind couldn't help but see shapes, make pictures, find meaning in the birds, in the abstract haze, in anything that flew above him. Land, safety, a chance of survival should you fall and find yourself stranded and alone. *As long as the sky's not empty, it'll be OK.*

'What's wrong with her?'

'Nothing,' Isabelle said. 'She's fine. If you mean, what has she been diagnosed with – then low-functioning autism. She also suffers from epilepsy and she's partially deaf.'

Down a hill, down into the dark, and now the starlings were hidden. 'So you take care of her.' Sam blinked and looked back into the car.

'Mmm-hm.'

'If you could, would you change anything? Make her more like you?'

Isabelle considered this. 'I don't know. When we were younger, I did feel sorry for Abigail. There's so much she can't do. She'll never raise children, or have a career. She's totally dependent on me. But then, I can't fish, or hunt, or sow crops. And if I could, I still can't protect myself from people who come and take those things by force. How independent can anyone be?'

Sam nodded.

'It's a strange kind of high horse to think your accolades mean more than hers,' she said. 'I grew out of that years ago. The only difference between her gold-star sticker and an Oscar is the number of people clapping. As long as she's happy, what else matters?'

'When you strip this whole show down, we're all just busy chimps, chasing serotonin, dopamine, oxytocin.'

'Our gold-star stickers,' Isabelle said. 'She can have all of mine.'

Sam felt they were on an honest run, so he returned to a topic he knew she would rather not revisit – the unanswered question had niggled him. 'What happened, Isabelle?' he asked. 'What made you value the law more than the arts?'

She kept her calm eyes on the road, her wise posture straight, and took a slow breath in through her nose. 'Nothing.'

'Oh, you mustn't lie.'

'Sometimes it's easier.'

'In the short term, undoubtedly. But it's almost never ethical.'

'You were married. Your ex-wife never ask you if her legs look good in these jeans?'

'Well, what's the question?' Sam said. 'Is she tacitly asking for reassurance, fishing for a compliment? If so, I'd provide one. An honest one.'

'She's not, she wants to know what you think. And they look awful, by the way.'

'Then I'd tell her the truth. Would she rather deceit? Would she rather go out with me, *without* knowing that I believe most people will think the jeans look terrible? Or would she rather hear that, no, these other jeans look better?'

'How about . . . ?'

'You're hiding Jewish refugees in your bedroom,' Sam pre-empted, with a better scenario than whatever Isabelle was about to propose. 'The SS are at the door. They ask if anyone's upstairs. What do you say?'

'You lie. You say no.'

'And how often do situations like this occur? Odds are, you'll never find yourself in one. You have to go to the absolute extremes for justification. Encoded in any lie – even a white lie, *especially* a white lie – is arrogance. You are deciding what the recipient can and can't know.'

'All right. How many sexual partners have you had?'

'I'd rather not say. That's the truth.'

'What about when you say something untrue by mistake?' she asked. 'But you believe it.'

'That's fine too. A lie is when someone *wants* the honest truth, *expects* the honest truth, and you deliberately give them something else. It's liberating, Isabelle. You don't have to keep track of anything. You'll feel so free. Give it a go.'

Another breath, another hesitation. 'I used to work with a charity, providing theatre workshops abroad,' she said.

'A thespian missionary?'

'Sort of. Richard, my best friend growing up – the boy next door.' She smiled. 'He got me into it. After the last expedition, in Uganda of all places, instead of heading home, we decided to stay, trek around some national parks in the west. It was fun – we had a good time. I was always the more reserved, cautious type. I needed to know where we'd be, where we'd sleep, what we'd do. But Richard hated the beaten track. He literally threw my guidebook out the window. He thought it was so funny.' Another smile. 'Anyway, we hiked further west, crossed the border and entered the Congo. If we'd done our research, we'd have been warned that this was a bad idea. That part of the country was not doing well. But . . . you know.'

'Adventure.' Sam blinked.

'Exactly. Our guide, Sal, this local girl we'd met just a few days before, she promised to show us gorillas in the wild. She wanted to impress us. We were with her for, I don't know, maybe a week – bouncing around in this old jeep. Mostly dust tracks and long walks. And we were *miles* from the border now. God knows where. Late one afternoon, just before we stopped to camp, we drove past this group of people, maybe thirty of them. Men and women, civilians, some with guns. Others had jerry cans, machetes, ropes. They waved us down, stopped us at the side of the road and, I remember Sal's face, she was terrified. One of the men came to the window – peered inside. She showed them some papers, and they spoke for a while – they seemed upset, and kept pointing down the track, back the way we'd come. Kept saying, "You hit the boy, you hit the boy, get out, you hit the boy." They were shouting, trying to open the doors. I asked who they were and she just said, "We have to leave." They started throwing rocks, she floored it, took us down this hill. We almost hit one of them on the way out.

'They were . . . I guess you could call them a vigilante mob. Apparently, a few days earlier a ranger's jeep, that matched our description close enough, had run over a child near their village. Sal told us some horror stories she'd heard. Civilians taking matters into their own hands. Heading out in groups like that, looking for some kind of justice.

'But we got away. Set up a discreet camp. The following morning, I woke up early and she was gone. She'd taken her tent and the jeep and just fucking left us there. At the edge of the rainforest. I like to think, maybe, it was for our own good. But we were beyond lost. Richard and I agreed we should head back on foot. God, it was hot, humid. We had hardly any water left. Within a few hours we'd found one of the main tracks and followed it from memory. A mile or two along, there was this noise, this crazy buzzing sound. I can still smell that smoke. We came across the jeep and the whole place – it was swarming with flies.'

'What had happened?'

'It had crashed into a ditch, on the side of the path, all the windows were broken and one of the front wheels had been taken off. But no sign of Sal. Then we saw a trail of litter, tissues and a few empty water bottles and broken glass, leading further towards the trees. We followed it and we found her . . .'

Isabelle told this story with absolute detachment. She could have been reading a recipe. There was no sense of ceremony, no added drama. Just a straightforward recital.

'She had a . . . a half-melted tyre around her waist, and she was lying on her side on a patch of burned grass. I could explain the violence. I'd try and tell you what they must have done to her. But . . . honestly, you wouldn't believe it.'

'I can imagine.'

'No, Sam, no, you can't.'

'Was she dead?'

Isabelle nodded. 'She was still breathing, but . . . not for long. A minute or so and there was no pulse.'

'What did you do?'

'We covered her body and left her. We kept walking, got back to the park boundary and told a ranger what had happened. Richard didn't speak much after that. He'd always been, I guess you could say, a troubled guy – but I think that was something he just couldn't shake. He told me he kept dreaming about that jeep, those flies – all that noise. Back in the UK, a doctor said he had PTSD. They gave him some drugs, all sorts, I don't know what exactly. But nothing worked. He killed himself about eighteen months later.'

'Shit.'

'Just the final straw, I think. He wrote a long note. He said that . . . that if you're not scared, if you're not riddled with dread, and terror, and all-encompassing sadness about the world, then you haven't seen enough of it.'

Sam blinked. 'They ever catch them?'

'Who, the mob? No one *to* catch them. That's the point. That area had disintegrated.'

'Did she do it? Run over the boy?'

'It doesn't matter. But no . . . I didn't come away disillusioned like Richard. But he was right – we *should* be scared. It's easy to blame the mineral trade, poverty, drugs, money, corruption, ideology – whatever. I think the reality, the bedrock, is that people will hurt each other. That was just what humanity looks like in places the police don't go. Where you call for help and no one comes. Most people have no idea how fragile all this is. Civilisation falls to pieces given half a chance. Stability and security – it's an illusion. And it takes a lot of work to make it seem real.' Isabelle drove, her attention on the road ahead. 'The rule of law is all we have,' she said. 'And it deserves to be respected.'

Henry Marston Junior, somehow out of his bed again, sitting in a hospital wheelchair on that shingled terrace. The car park below is alive with dusk light so warm and so red, it's as though a volcano has opened up on an unseen hill to the west. The colour is eerie, hellish,

otherworldly – beautiful to anyone still able to find such things in these places.

His useless legs are rigid – but one of the casts is broken, some plaster dangles near the ground. Perhaps he's dragged himself part of the way here. When he finishes his cigarette, his hand shakes as he stubs it out and flicks it over the side. From his lap, he takes a small packet of pills. He pushes one of them into his palm and stares at it for a long while. We see him hold it in his thumb and index finger, lifting it to his face. We see him consider where it should go. And we see him decide. Like everything else, Henry throws it over the edge.

Chapter 25

Now that Robin had finished sharpening the spoon handle on the bathroom tiles, she realised something. At first, the thought scared her. She hadn't made a screwdriver, or a chisel, like she'd planned. No. Robin had made a weapon.

So, now, she had to make something else. A very important decision: should she use it?

She sat on the toilet seat, holding the spike in her hand. Gripping it like it was a knife. The point was shiny, with thousands of tiny scratches all leading up to the tip. She touched it and sighed. Could it be sharper than this? Robin didn't think so.

Then she began wondering about the sharpest object ever. If everything is made of atoms, could there be a knife that was so sharp the edge was only one single atom thick? It would slice through anything, even rocks. Even diamonds.

Even bars on a window. A knife like that, she decided, was simply impossible.

Sliding the spoon handle up her sleeve, she went back into her bedroom and, perching on the mattress, she leaned sideways and slipped it under her pillow.

Then, crawling across the bed, she went to the window. On her knees, she poked the metal bars a few times and put her hands between them – elbows on the windowsill. Even though there were wooden boards against the glass, Robin could feel the difference in temperature between each plank. Thin lines of faint light, thin lines of slow, cold air, fell across the backs of her fingers. She licked her thumb and held it at the opening, felt the chill. Closing her eyes, she placed her palm flat on the wood and wished she was out there. Wished, from the bottom of her heart, that she could push and somehow pass through these walls, these bars, these doors, like a ghost.

Today had been her saddest one so far. Because Robin had started to really doubt anyone was looking for her. It had been too long now. Robin thought about her brother. *Sometimes people do just disappear*, she thought. *Sometimes they never come home. And when everyone else gets old and has new children, eventually no one cares. No one cares about children who disappeared a hundred years ago.*

She wondered how many people cared about her. She wondered how *much* they cared. And she wondered whether it would ever even matter.

So she turned again and looked at her pillow.

And then, with sudden purpose, Robin took her sharpened spoon handle, hid it well, and slowly, in absolute silence, she left her bedroom, walked across the landing carpet and down the stairs.

There was a sound in the living room. She frowned; it was like a high-pitched rip of Sellotape.

Stepping along the tiles, creeping, Robin paused at the doorway. With the metal in her palm now, held behind her back, she leaned round the door frame and saw him.

For a long, long time she simply stared. Julius was hunched over something, in the corner, on the carpet. Facing away.

She entered the living room and, moving forwards, still slowly, still silently, like a cat, Robin approached.

He didn't notice her, even when she was at his back, standing right over him. She saw his neck, his scruffy grey hair. She heard his breath.

Robin couldn't see what he was doing but, over his shoulder, she caught a glimpse of something red in his hands.

What was it, she wondered, this sharp object in *her* hand? Could it be her way out? It was a tool, but what kind of—

He turned.

'Hey,' he said and, strangely, she was the one who flinched. 'I've got you a gift.'

She swallowed. Bit her teeth together. 'Uh . . . what . . . what is it?'

'Close your eyes.'

Maybe it would be easier to decide, she thought, *if I can't see him.* So she did as he told her.

'Here,' he said.

A sound on the coffee table, near her leg. And when she looked, she saw a large square present, wrapped in purple paper with a red ribbon tied in a perfect bow.

Julius was holding a pair of scissors. He seemed to notice her hesitation – maybe he'd realised something else was on her mind. And there was a long silence.

'It's . . . it's an art box,' he said, still on his knees on the carpet.

'Why . . . why did you wrap it if you were going to tell me what's inside?'

'I'm sorry.' He bowed his head.

And Robin pretended to smile as she slid the spoon handle into her pocket. She'd been wrong. It was just a chisel.

Chapter 26

Daniel Aiden's house was at the end of a long, winding drive, surrounded on all sides by woodland. As they pulled around the final corner, it seemed to unveil as though a green curtain of leaves was swept from left to right, presenting the home in all its glory.

The building itself was a square monolith set among the trees – white and modern. The facade, half glass with sliding doors, opened on to a well-kept garden. Up close, Sam saw the outer shell was made from shipping containers stacked together, clad in pine. One exterior side wall had been left bare, to show off the serial number stamped on the old red steel. Back again to the *Coriolis* – the hollowed metal, the blistered paint, the streaked rust tears. Wind whistling through wet handrails, lifeboats swaying on ropes, hanging in storms.

This house was industrial. It was cold.

Daniel met them on his veranda, greeting Sam with a firm handshake and a pat on the back. He held Sam's hand for a second or two longer than he normally might, tilting his head, furrowing his brow – as though they were in a state of mutual grief. Both mourning the untimely death of Robin Clarke. This morbidity, however, went unsaid. Sam could see that their visit, as far as Daniel was concerned, was a formality. No sense in dwelling on the unsavoury elephant in the room.

The interior looked like a show home, as if they'd walked right into a catalogue – pale marble, wide-open space, brand-new furniture on display. They followed him through into the kitchen. Isabelle's shoes were loud on the bamboo flooring.

'Can I get you guys a drink?' Daniel asked, his bare feet silent as he moved to his double-door fridge.

Standing by the breakfast bar, Isabelle sipped a glass of water, but Sam found himself wandering towards the living area.

On the back wall, a large shelf unit exhibited a number of unusual objects. Sam realised they were artefacts, each representing one of Daniel's films. There was a carved tribal mask from his three-part documentary on the Amazon; a scorched leather jacket, covered in sponsor logos, from his time living with a flamboyant NASCAR driver; and even a warped 7.62x39mm bullet which, he claimed, skimmed off his helmet and ended up lodged in the centre of his camera when he was covering the war in Iraq.

'Ah – you've found the good stuff,' Daniel said, arriving at his side.

He seemed to enjoy guiding them along this eclectic shrine, his hands behind his back, pointing when they came to each item.

'This,' he said, picking up a small jewellery box, 'is a pair of Elvis Presley's cufflinks.'

'You made a documentary about Elvis?' Isabelle asked.

'No,' Daniel said, turning back to the kitchen. 'It was about UFO conspiracy theories. Just so happened the guy I was with also believed the King is alive and kicking. He knew I wanted a memento, but sadly he'd misplaced his ray gun.' He laughed. 'There's a story to all of this.'

Daniel had flawless teeth – a genuine Hollywood smile. And no wrinkles. The smattering of grey in his black hair was at slight odds with his seemingly eternal youth, but it only made him look distinguished. He was the kind of handsome that gets better with motion – his expressive face, the glisten in his eyes. His skin perfect, clean and smooth, like clay. Sam wondered if he was wearing foundation. However, close up, he saw that, no, Daniel was just wearing money, a sensible diet and good genes.

Towards the end of the display, Sam discovered the awards. Shown here with greater prominence than the collection of keepsakes preceding them. Maybe his trophies mattered more than the work itself. And he'd amassed plenty over the years – Sam had reacquainted himself with this illustrious career in the car.

Daniel Aiden's documentaries were critically acclaimed – his unique brand of faux-naïf humour added broad appeal to any subject he touched. He'd started out writing political satire for some comedy shows, but soon slipped to the other side of the lens for a series of hour-long profiles on the most eccentric celebrities he could find. Later, he explored more serious themes, and took multiple trips to the Middle East, which became *Sand* – his first feature-length picture to bag him the top prizes.

Shortly after that, he started working on *The Clarkes* – the film that truly established him as a household name both in the UK and abroad. Foreign interest in the British royal family was an anomaly Sam could understand. But Britain's missing children? This was surely one of the strangest exports to gain traction overseas.

Sam was intimately familiar with this piece of work, as well as the hours of unused footage. The finished documentary was a relatively balanced exposition of the case and its coverage, although at times it did veer towards indulgence. There were long, panning shots of suburban skylines, empty playgrounds, the faint sound of children laughing, and the music often guided the most emotional scenes. Although occasionally contrived, it was effective.

They used about ten minutes of Sam's three-hour interview, peppered throughout. And the trailer featured a particularly fitting line in which he said, 'It's as though Ethan just . . . vanished.'

In one of her interviews Anna explained that, hundreds of times a day, like clockwork, she refreshes her emails, missed calls and every social-media account. Just in case. There's video of her doing this, shot between takes, with camera and lighting equipment in sight. This disregard for the fourth wall was another of Daniel's hallmarks – he captured his subjects at their most authentic, even if it meant exposing the seams.

A choir, a full orchestra and a playlist of classic pop songs provided the soundtrack. This bittersweet dissonance – upbeat music, rendered slow – allowed the tone to shift at a few points during the 89-minute runtime. Towards the end, there's a heart-warming montage set to an instrumental version of 'Runaround Sue' – said to be the track playing when the Clarkes first met.

In one scene Robin is crouched in the garden, following a line of ants back to their nest. Later, during a talking-head sequence with Anna and Francis sitting at their dining table, the living-room backdrop blurred by the shallow depth of field and studio-style lighting, Robin walks past carrying an empty shoebox. The camera zooms out, ruining the composition but creating a charming moment when a voice, Daniel's voice, asks her quietly, away from the microphone, where she's going. She replies, 'To build Bug City.'

Old footage from the Clarkes' wedding day makes an appearance. In that scene, Francis and Anna dance together, her pregnant stomach bulging beneath her white dress. At one point, the amateur camera zooms in on her bump as Francis nestles close for a kiss. Anna's eyes open halfway through the intimate moment. She spots whoever is filming, then laughs, holds her skirt and runs towards them, swinging her bouquet at the lens.

Quick edits make it seem perfect. Daniel's ability to add warmth, to find innocence and tap into the full spectrum of emotions was, Sam supposed, how he could afford to build such an impressive house.

Fortunately, the film didn't focus too much on Sam's fall from grace – his assault charge came to light during post-production. However, It closes with a 'where are they now' epilogue, during which photographs and text appear on screen. It's set to a slow piano version of one of the obscure doo-wop songs played at the wedding.

Sam's face. 'Detective Sam Maguire has since retired from service. He received two hundred hours Community Payback for ABH, following an altercation with George Hinds.'

And then George's picture, a scruffy mugshot, came on the screen. 'George Hinds received a twenty-two-month prison sentence, suspended for a year, for perverting the course of justice.'

Then Francis, Anna and Robin together on a sofa, laughing while they pose for a photo. Instead of the picture, we see this as footage. A small, close-knit family. They look happy. Resilient. Defiant. Robin squirms on Anna's lap, leaning away and frowning as her mother attempts to make her smile for the camera. Before she can, a tired, elderly dog enters and Robin slumps down to the carpet and yells, 'Button has to be in the photo too.'

The white text reads, 'The Clarkes reside in Hallowfield.'

A still of Francis's head and shoulders fades in. 'Francis Clarke continues his charity work. To date, the Clarke Foundation has helped more than seven hundred orphaned children find a home.'

After this, we're shown Anna's picture. 'Anna Clarke stood down from her consultant position, though she continues to write for medical journals, as well as lecturing on surgical practice at a number of prestigious institutions across the globe. She has donated many thousands of pounds to the Spinal Research charity.'

Then, Robin's photo. 'Robin Clarke will move up to junior school next September and looks forward to art lessons, but not maths . . . She is currently serving as mayor of Bug City.'

The last image we see is Anna sitting on their garden patio, looking down into her mobile – checking every app three times. This fades slowly to black and the final line of text comes on to the screen, without an accompanying photograph.

It simply reads, 'Ethan Clarke is still missing.'

And, with slow piano, the credits begin to roll. At the very bottom, when the music is gone, the words, 'A film by Daniel Aiden'.

Standing at the glass display, just before the awards, Sam arrived at the item Daniel had kept from *The Clarkes*. He'd made documentaries about war, murder, genocide, rape, about every shade of good and evil our species has to offer. And yet, Sam found Ethan Clarke's scout scarf somehow more distasteful than the other objects. It was the only trophy taken without the owner's permission. Even the bullet from Iraq had been fired intentionally.

'When was the last time you visited Orchard Court?' Sam asked.

'Hmm, maybe a month ago?'

'You're still quite close with Anna and Francis?' He turned away from the shelves and faced Daniel.

'Of course, we go way back. I keep telling her she's welcome here. But she won't have it.'

'Is there no other family?' Isabelle said.

'Anna's mother passed away in April and her father is in a care home. And Francis's side, they're all in Canada.'

Sam had wondered about the hotel – Anna said it just made sense. Perhaps she was worried it could look suspicious to shack up with Daniel. What might people think?

'Where were you on that Wednesday evening?'

Daniel tilted his head and frowned. 'Uh. I was . . . I was in Berlin.' Then he opened his mouth to speak, but stopped himself, glancing at Isabelle. 'Why are you asking?'

Neither of them responded.

'Are you . . . ?' Daniel laughed. 'Wow. You're at the bottom of the barrel now, buddy.'

Sam did not smile. 'Have you ever had any romantic interest in Anna?'

Again, Daniel seemed somewhat insulted. 'Um, *no*,' he said. 'We're just friends.'

This was an incredibly well-composed lie. Sam almost admired it. The slight disbelief and drop in tone implying it was unthinkable. As though this was the first time he'd ever even considered something like that. Body language, eye movement, the calculated hesitation – it was impeccable. A work of art. His alibi was almost certainly true though – too easy to check. Besides, even if he did have a hand in this, Sam very much doubted he'd use his own. Being miles away slotted neatly on to all versions of events.

'I'm sorry, but – are you suggesting I had something to do with Robin's murder?'

'You believe she's dead?'

'Wha— I . . . They've *arrested* Francis.' Again, he appealed to Isabelle. 'You've arrested him. And I understand the intention is to charge . . .'

'Who told you that?'

'Just . . . reading the room. Watching the news.'

'When was the last time you saw Robin?' Sam asked.

'Um – a few weeks ago. I was babysitting. I picked her up from school.'

'The Clarkes don't trust many people to take care of their daughter.'

'I wonder why?'

'You collected her, then what, walked back to their house?'

'Yes.'

'How did she seem?'

211

'Fine, we went through the park. She picked some flowers, played on the slide. I cooked her turkey dinosaurs in the oven. She had two blobs of ketchup, like eyes on the plate. They'd run out of peas, so I gave her sweetcorn. We sang along to the radio. Shall I go on . . . ?'

'How did you get into the house?' Isabelle wondered.

Daniel looked over to her. 'I've got a . . .' And then he stopped. Dead in his tracks. But he'd gone too far to turn back now, he had to finish this sentence. 'I have a key.'

During a second or two of silence, Daniel closed his eyes and went to speak but, again, no words came out. He sighed.

'Do you know what a crying Hecate is?' Sam showed him the picture on his phone.

Shrugging, Daniel said, 'Sure . . . it's a religious thing. About demons or something. Why?'

'Not many people know about them.'

'I know lots of things . . . Sam, seriously, what's going on?'

He didn't respond, instead he reached into his back pocket and pulled out the e-fit of the old scarred man Iris Parker had described. The narrow face, mottled flesh down the cheeks and nose and up across the forehead. Long grey hair, scraggy, digitally sketched from the new neighbour's memory.

'Do you know who this is?'

Daniel didn't look. 'Tell me, why are you asking?'

'This man was seen parked outside their house exactly a week prior to Robin's disappearance.'

'OK?'

'I think he planted digital evidence – some incriminating searches, using their router. I believe this person is somehow involved.'

'Sam, buddy, I've said it before, and I'll say it again – this case, you need to ease up. Shall we just apply Occam's razor? Whatever you're imagining, is it really the simplest explanation?'

'Answer the question, Daniel.'

He finally looked at the piece of paper. 'No,' he said, his eyes drifting slowly back up to Sam's. 'I do not know who that man is.'

Despite everything he knew about the craft – the nuance, the rhythm, the subtle tells like those he'd seen just moments ago – Sam had absolutely no idea if this was the truth, or another one of Daniel's excellent lies.

Chapter 27

A familiar living room. We see the sofa, the back of a head, the modest collection of World War II memorabilia on the left-hand wall. The crucifix shrouded in symbols – an altar, a tribute to conflict. Today the music is classical, it's Italian – instrumental, light strings, fast fingers – all wrong. The kind of sounds that serenade diners, outdoors in cobbled squares, beneath canvas parasols and late summer sun.

Gregory Marston paces up and down, up and down, in front of the large TV.

'Where is he?' Gregory checks his watch. 'Cards on the table, Henry, I am spooked.'

'He's coming.' Henry Marston Senior's half-electronic vocal cords are deep and gravelled.

A noise. The front door creaking shut. 'Thought we weren't meant to be meeting like this?' Max says, striding casually into the living room.

Passing his hand over his bald head, Gregory shows teeth. He lurches for his twin brother, grabbing the much slimmer man by the scruff of his jacket and slamming him against the wall. 'You said he was eighteen.'

Max laughs, his jacket bundled around his chin, and looks to Henry. 'I got the years mixed up,' he says with a shrug. 'Year eight, year twelve, year twenty, I don't know, fuck – I can't remember school.'

'Let him go,' Henry says, standing up.

He is by far the largest of the three men – tall and fat. Clearly though, beneath it all, he has a substantial amount of muscle. Gregory comes next on the size chart, followed by Max, who, with his long, plaited ponytail and his blood-rat eyes, looks to be the runt of the siblings.

A final shove and Gregory steps away, sits on the sofa to the right and rests his face in his hands. Like before, he wears a shirt and a loosened tie. Whereas Max is dressed in an off-white vest and baggy camouflage trousers. There's objective menace in the way he smiles, the way he moves.

'You were swinging that crowbar too,' Max says. 'And you broke protocol – we weren't meant to speak.'

'I was telling you to stop.'

'I'm still not getting what the problem is here? Aside from the fact we didn't finish the job . . .'

'Through the praise of children and infants you have established a stronghold against your enemies, to silence the foe and the avenger.'

'What?' Max says. 'That doesn't fucking mean   Don't quote that shit at me . . . Fine, OK, I'll admit it was an unpleasant thing to do. But it has to happen – we have to square it up. You can go back to your boring little life, and I'll finish it.'

'No you won't.'

'We've done worse. I mean, come on . . . Why are you so wound up about all this?'

'There's a . . . a detective, asking around for me,' Gregory mumbles at the floor. 'Some woman.'

'Well, yeah, that's how all this started.'

'Not about North Serpent,' Gregory says. 'About what you did to that . . . child.'

'We.'

'Pardon?'

'What we did.'

215

Max seems totally unfazed as he sits opposite his brother and puts his laced leather boots on the coffee table. Still standing with his back to the camera, Henry glares down at him. Max hesitates, then places his feet flat on the carpet.

We can assume then that this property – this visibly wealthy home – belongs to Henry Marston Senior, who looms high in a pale suit.

These three men, all at least forty years of age, appear to be too old for this. We see it most starkly on Gregory's face. He looks worn, as though he's been plucked from normality and dropped into this situation against his will.

The music has now moved further back in time, but up in terms of tempo. Violins. Is it Vivaldi? This shuffled playlist continues to surprise.

Well dressed like tall, suited Henry, Gregory retains some level of sophistication. It's unrepentant Max – fearless in the face of all consequences, be they mortal or otherwise – who appears the odd one out. The black sheep, least fitting of this decor, this music. The worst, as we've heard, of these siblings.

'Relax, Greg,' *Max says.* 'It was smooth. Apart from your momentary lapse, it was clean.'

'Clean? Your fucking giant pupils. I told you to be sober – what was it?'

'Ah, just a little one of my own recipes, just to take the edge off.' *Max's wide eyes mock him.* 'I'm on my way now. Brothers, I'm going to the moon. You should come along.'

'I did say we should consider alternatives,' *Henry croaks, sitting back down.*

'Diane knows,' *Gregory whispers, his voice deeper than usual. Filled with regret.*

Alarmed now, Max turns to his larger brother. 'Why? Did you tell her?'

'She still has contacts – in the force.' *Henry leans over to the coffee table and picks up a small tumbler. He drinks it in one.*

'Is she angry?'

The glass bangs back on to the wood and Henry's fingers return to his throat to speak. 'What do you think?'

'So, this woman . . . ?' Max shuffles and fidgets on the sofa. He's agitated, twitchy. 'What's going on?'

'I don't know exactly,' Gregory says. 'But Alexandra called me – said a detective came to her office, trying to track us down, asking about everyone.'

'How is that fucking horrible bitch?' Max smiles. His teeth are sharp and brown.

'Still lying for us.'

'Oh, I doubt that. Far as I can see, Greg, you're the only risk. You work in a call centre – obviously they're going to find you. Grow up.'

'This isn't a joke.'

'Then why am I laughing?'

'I have no idea.'

'How's your boy?' Max says, turning to Henry.

'Not good.' He coughs, wheezes. 'This will be difficult for him.'

'Is he going to recover?' Max asks. 'Or is he, you know, a bona-fide spastic?'

Rising, Henry snatches the glass and throws it hard at his brother – it misses, shattering on the wall behind him. 'That's my son,' he tries to shout, though it comes out raspy and seems to cause genuine pain. A gag – he grabs his own neck, swallowing, gasping for air.

'Hey, hey.' Max sits up again, having ducked for cover. 'Let's be civil.'

Henry returns to his seat, in the centre of the frame.

'Listen, it'll go like this,' Max says. 'Gregory will get called in, no comment, no comment, fuck off, la, la, la. Then all this will blow over.'

'And what about the rest?' Gregory says. 'The shit they found at the Clarkes' house? They want to speak to Diane.'

'It. Was. The. Dad,' Max yells, jutting his splayed hand at the TV.

'They're still looking for her.'

'Again, relax. Diane'll be fine. Even if they track her down, what are they gonna do? Anyway, it's as good as over. You should watch the news. Maybe that shifty fucker read something Diane posted online? Maybe he wants to lock swords with the darkness.' Max puts on a low, comedic voice, lifting his hands above his head like a zealous preacher. 'Command the Lord's bright light – drive the fiends back from whence they came. Who cares?'

'It doesn't make sense,' Gregory says. 'He wouldn't have the doll pointed at his own house.'

'OK, someone else put it there.'

'Who?'

'I don't know – this has nothing to do with me.'

'But what if it does?'

Max flexes his face, scrunches his eyes – moves his hand fast as he speaks. 'OK, OK, OK, not that it matters. But what's the alternative? Come on, come on.' He clicks his fingers. 'You're thinking someone from the church? Who? And-and-and fucking why?'

Henry clears his throat, a guttural roar of a cough. Max creases his nose in disgust – he's becoming more and more animated. Speeding up.

'There's an artist's impression that Diane's contact has kindly shared,' Henry whispers, as he pulls his mobile from his inside pocket. 'A suspect. Someone they want to speak to about Robin Clarke.'

'Oh yeah? Yeah? Does it look like the dad?'

'No.'

'Why haven't they released it – hmm? Hmm? Riddle me this.'

'I don't know, maybe, like you, they've got their sights set on Francis Clarke.'

'Hmm, yes. Oh yeah. Yes.' Max is now bouncing in his seat. 'That's been my theory all along. I said it. Do you remember?'

They ignore him.

The camera can't see Henry's phone screen – but when he shows it to his brothers it's clear they recognise the man.

'Well . . .' Max lifts his eyebrows, does an almost camp double take. 'That is interesting.'

'Think if we give them a name, they'll leave us alone?' Gregory asks. 'Great minds.'

'Oh, boys,' Max says. 'This is good. Like a game of chess. I feel, in my heart, an enormous sense of peace. Here. In my heart. Is that God?'

'No,' Gregory shakes his head. 'That's drugs.'

And Max smiles. 'Sorry I was so blasé about everything.'

'It's OK.' Gregory sighs. 'As you say, hardly the worst thing we've done.'

'It's just, I find it fascinating. You guys – you still think you're going to heaven.' Max's smile is open and he's emitting a high-pitched sound. 'But,' he waggles his index finger, 'it's too late for that.' And now he's standing, shouting, 'It's too late for that.'

The music is carrying him – he's matching the rhythm. The strings taking us fast towards some climax – towards the end of winter.

'Sit down.'

'A serpent, a saviour – a black land beyond.' He sings, ballroom dancing with an invisible partner – sidestepping, turning, turning. 'All that is righteous and all that is fond, to your heart, sing, sing, my little frogs, sing.'

'Max.'

'Shall we pray? Dear Lord, let us pray.' And, with immediate purpose, Max stops, relaxes and sits back down. He crosses his legs and strokes his chin. 'This will sound sentimental – maybe even outright gay – but you guys are my favourite people. And I'm glad we're together. Honestly, I have missed you two.'

His brothers just stare at him.

'Ah, no.' Max points. 'I know what the feeling is. Here, in my heart. This isn't God. It's love.'

Chapter 28

On the afternoon of the following day, Isabelle came to Sam's flat. Unlike before, he didn't rush to meet her outside to guide her gaze away from the chaos inside. It wasn't just that he was past shame, he also felt Isabelle deserved him at his most transparent – his most open self. And what better place can one learn such details about another than in the untouched privacy of their home.

Robin had been missing for almost a week. Six days of questions and silence. On the scale of decades, however, or the scale of Ethan Clarke, this was no time at all. A millisecond rolling from zero to nine. And yet, in this blip, Sam had grown fond of Isabelle. Her tired eyes, half dipped, serene but glassy, and bloodshot at the edges. The bone almost visible on the bridge of her nose. Her stately shoulders, the wisdom she exuded with nothing more than her spine and a moment's thought before every word she spoke. These were all well and good. But, above allure, he respected her – therefore, attraction was impossible. What did this paradox say about his self-esteem? That the instant he cared about someone they were no longer eligible for affection.

A sudden memory, Marilyn sitting on the kitchen floor, against the fridge, crying.

'You're gone, Sam,' she'd said. 'I know you loved me once. But there's nothing left to burn.'

They saw it happening – they stood by and watched as the signs appeared, as it fell apart, as all derelict things do. The only difference was that he recognised the inevitability. Marilyn mistook this candour for apathy. But Sam was just self-aware. He knew that, like the momentum of a wheel, the faster he went, the more stable he was – anything besides total devotion to a single goal was tantamount to stopping. And Sam had believed nothing hurt more than that.

Although now, the collateral damage – flesh to bait the truth from its nest – was becoming equally intolerable. A marriage, a career, even his own health – they had all been on the menu.

But Freddie, having to take his first steps a second time. Not between sofas, not between the open arms of his cheering parents, but in a hospital gym, holding railings, telling a nurse that he can do it himself. This was a price Sam had not been willing to pay. Here was the limit.

Maybe the tumour too. Maybe this malignant growth, the rogue tissue, wasn't a random turn of fate as the doctor had said, but these flaws manifesting physically – literal obsession and failure, his body trying to make abstract things concrete. Unaware of just how dangerous they were.

And this hopeless, final instalment was beginning to throb. It ached in his skull – a completely new pain. A sharp pain. He'd felt something similar lingering over the last six months or so, but nothing this persistent. Usually, he could blink away the shorter stabs. But not even scrunching his eyes shut and pressing his temples was affecting it now. He suspected he would feel this way, or worse, until he went to sea.

Funny, Marilyn had once whispered, from a midnight doorway, beyond the glow of his study lamp, 'Ethan Clarke will be the death of you.'

Perhaps the truth lay behind this curtain. Perhaps it wanted everything.

Isabelle came into the hallway, placed her keys on his breakfast bar, then turned towards the rest of his apartment. If she was shocked by what she saw, she hid it well. Her eyes passed over Sam's noticeboard, his stacks of boxes, folders, all piled up in his small, lonely home. Yet more remnants of failure.

Some paperwork was brand new. Sam had spent the night trawling through everything he could find on Daniel Aiden. He'd replayed that moment – Daniel, barefoot, standing in his cold living room next to his memento shelves, looking at the e-fit. There had been a flicker, a micro shift in his face. Although for less than a tenth of a second, and contaminated by the repetition and diminishing returns of memory, it was starting to look like recognition.

'I've been speaking to an associate of the Marstons,' Isabelle said. 'An ex-girlfriend. Quietly disgruntled. And I've got an address for Diane.' She handed him a Post-it note.

'Is this an invitation?'

'No. I just thought you should know that I'm making progress. You seen the news?'

'Bits and pieces.'

Tomorrow morning, first thing, time would run out. They would have to release Francis or charge him with murder. Sam could imagine the coverage was, as always, redefining sensationalism. A surreal idea – what if he pleaded guilty? What if he'd killed Ethan too? Daniel had suggested Occam's razor. The public consensus cut a similar line. Simple explanations.

'They'll go to the wire,' Isabelle said. 'But . . . unless we find something within the next sixteen hours, they'll charge him. It doesn't mean it's over.'

'Come on. Can you see a jury ruling anything else? They've already made up their minds.'

'Hell of a trial.'

'Expensive theatre. I'm guessing they're finished at Orchard Court?' Sam asked. 'Is Anna going home?'

But before Isabelle could respond, her pocket lit up. She stepped into his kitchen to answer her phone.

'Hello?' She paused, her face changing, her eyes widening. Looking quickly at Sam, she pointed to her mobile, then put it on loudspeaker. 'Diane,' she mouthed, placing it on the breakfast bar, next to a framed photo of Freddie, proud in his football gear.

'Is this Detective Constable Isabelle Lewin, of thirty-three Westfield Drive?'

'It is.'

'I understand you are hoping to speak to me regarding Robin Clarke,' Diane said – her accent was unusual, well spoken, slow and deliberate. A far cry from the mad, enthusiastic preaching Sam had seen in her sermon videos online. 'As you are probably aware, I no longer have ties with North Serpent. My quiet life is something I'd like to conserve if possible. Perhaps we can come to a civil arrangement?'

'I'm listening,' Isabelle said.

'Through means of no concern to you, I have seen an artist's impression of a gentleman with distinctive facial scars.'

Sam and Isabelle eyed each other, but neither of them reacted.

'Call me paranoid, but I prefer to have meaningful conversations away from the telephone. I will text you an address and a time. Please, come alone. And I'll know if you report this to anyone in your department.'

'Come where?'

'A discreet location.'

'Why do I have to come alone?'

Diane hummed – a curious moment's thought. 'Are you concerned that I mean to lure a police officer to a secluded place in order to harm her?' she asked. 'Does this sound like the behaviour of someone pursuing a peaceful existence?'

'I suppose not.'

'In exchange for you respecting my family's privacy, I will identify your suspect.'

'I . . . I can't control what the entire police force does,' Isabelle said.

'But you can control what *you* do. And, although no doubt to a lesser extent, you can control what Mr Maguire does. How are you, Samuel?'

Blinking, Sam turned to his kitchen window. Rooftops, empty streets, black telegraph wires. No birds. 'Bit of a headache, but I'll live.' Isabelle tilted her hand and pouted. 'Figuratively speaking,' Sam added.

'It is possible you are dehydrated,' Diane said. 'You must remember to drink water.'

'That is good advice.'

'Now, I understand how intrigue works. You may think, as I value my deliberate isolation, that I have something to hide.'

'Do you?' Sam asked.

'Of course. But nothing pertinent to your investigation. Security is important. It is an issue of safety. There are forces conspiring against me.'

'Why?' Isabelle said.

'You don't spend your life accusing powerful people of demonic practice without accruing a few enemies along the way. As an agent of the establishment, I am afraid I must consider you potentially hostile.'

'And what about your brothers?' Isabelle said.

'If you have any evidence that suggests they've committed a crime, it would be remiss of me to recommend anything other than your duty. May the Lord bless and protect you.'

And then the line went dead.

Isabelle and Sam stood in silence, both still staring down at the mobile.

'What should I do?' she eventually asked.

Thinking for a moment, Sam nodded. 'Easy to obscure motives,' he said. 'What if we take it on face value? What if the doll wasn't left there to bewilder, but put there by someone who actually believes this stuff?'

'Then . . .'

'Then Diane is serious,' Sam said. 'She wouldn't volunteer herself into this position unless she was telling the truth. She knows who the old man is, and she's going to tell you.'

'But why?'

'She told you why. She wants us to fuck off.'

'Obviously not a close friend . . .'

'A member of the church?' Sam said. 'All loyalty has its limits.'

Isabelle took a calculated breath and touched the back of her neck. 'I don't want to go there alone . . . Another option is plan A – bring her in properly. We know where she is.'

'Do you believe her – that she'll know if you report it?'

'She saw the e-fit.' Isabelle winced. 'That's not been released.'

'Play it straight. Do exactly what she asks. Anything else risks silence.'

The text arrived. Sam put the postcode into his laptop and brought up a map. They zoomed in on the satellite image – a square building, a long dirt track, surrounded by fields, at least half a mile from any tarmac.

'Some old barn? This doesn't feel good.'

'I'll come with you,' he said. 'We'll go a couple of hours early – I'll find somewhere to hide.'

'And if they do anything, you'll what? Be a witness?'

No more secrets. He reached into his jumper and pulled out the Glock 17. It sounded heavy when he placed it on the counter, between the laptop, the phone, the framed photograph. He tried to blink away his headache. Dull pressure, just like brain-freeze.

Isabelle turned her face, like a child refusing food, as though even looking at it was a crime. He could tell every fibre of her being wanted to seize it and arrest him. Go back to the book, stop this flagrant disregard for the law he embraced so openly. And yet, the promise – the chance that *just one more* tentative step down this path might yield results. What if trouble wasn't its only offering? What if she would play this dangerous game?

'The second it's over, you're handing that in,' she said, corrupted, polluted by the decision.

'Of course.'

'And, Sam, look at me. You're not going to do anything stupid, are you?'

'Isabelle, I don't intend to shoot anyone,' he said.

She exhaled.

'You know I can't lie.'

He had no real yearning for violence. The Marston brothers would face consequences. But not today. Not at his hand. They'd traded far too much already. Further escalation wouldn't benefit anyone – it'd be a cheap pill, a short buzz, a temporary distraction at best. The top prize was worth so much more. Sam wasn't hoping for anything less than the truth.

'And what about Freddie?'

'Be honest,' he said. His solution was effortless, elegant, simple. The truth is such a powerful animal if only we respect it. Just touch its warm skin, feel its fur, and you'll see it's like silk when stroked head to haunch, a coarse brush stroked any other way. 'Odds are, they won't even bring that up – why incriminate themselves?'

Isabelle retrieved her keys from the breakfast bar and, staring at Sam, she sighed again. 'Let's go.'

Chapter 29

Francis sat on the floor, knees up, fists clenched. It felt as though every time he closed his eyes his cell would begin to shrink. He'd look and catch it in the act and reality would put things right again. For now at least. The clock was running down. Indignant Francis did not have long left.

It ached so much to know it really was all her fault. Anna. Beautiful Anna. Lying to him again and again. He'd looked into her soul all those years ago, all those fucking years ago, and she'd looked right back through him as he asked if anything was going on.

'Between me . . . me and Daniel? Are you serious?'

He heard himself growl, the sound dull and close against the concrete. As though he could scare these falling thoughts away. Keep these crushing walls at bay.

She had promised. Anna looked him in the eye and promised. Later, when drunk, Francis had asked her to swear on Ethan's life. Anna shouted at him for even saying something like that. How could he? How *could* he?

In the morning, sorry, sober Francis had apologised.

He was right though. Francis had always been right to punish her. Every cold shoulder, every short answer, every fucking moment he'd felt insecure and small. It was all justified. Everything was completely fucking justified.

But he had always known this. Even before the proof. He had known.

Above all the anger and fear he felt there was a delicate vindication. Because nothing he had seen or learned had surprised him. It was all right there. How could he? How *could he* allow himself to forget what she was?

The tooth slid, fractured and cracked as he bit down. He tasted blood.

◆ ◆ ◆

Francis resting his face in his hands. We see his head rise from time to time. A series of images. Maybe a frame a second. It passes in silence. His head bowed. Then lifting. Bowed. Then up and looking at the door.

His head down again. An hour passes. His slight movements flicker. Low-resolution photographs with white pixeled text telling us the date, the time, the seconds rolling off the clock.

And like a ghost, he disappears between the darkness of these frames and he's at the door. His arm up. Banging at the metal.

We can only imagine the noise. We have to assume he is shouting. Eventually the door slides open and guards in full riot gear fill the entrance.

Francis stepping backwards. Francis in the middle of the room. Francis in the middle of the room, side on. Ready. His mattress on the floor. Francis against his table. Francis reeling. Francis on the ground, tripped by his chair. Francis on his feet, that chair a blur in the air, a smudge against a guard's helmet.

The actual encounter is fast, over within four of our short frames.

As he's dragged, subdued and hurt, from the cell in silence, in the absolute stillness of these images, we see him. The guards at his spread-eagled arms. We see his wild eyes. The red around his teeth.

And in his face, twisted like a death scream, we see fury so pure, so livid, it shares a border with joy. Beneath all that fire and blood, there are surely glimmers of euphoria. Glistening there on the cathartic kiss of wrath, streaming from his lips.

Chapter 30

They arrived almost three hours in advance. The meeting place was at the top of a gradual slope, about fifteen minutes' drive from the Hallowfield border. Around here, it was agriculture and woodland as far as Sam could see. All capped with clear sky, covered with clear sun – weather in high definition. They ascended at the edge of a wide, empty field – seeding grass, tall daisies, purple bellflowers all swaying gently in the wind, and a dusty, gravel track which led up to the old building.

The barn had two large doors on the front, both of which were spread open, wilting on half-buckled hinges – a rustic welcome. Isabelle parked the car on a concrete flat, between an overgrown mass of brambles and a stack of rotting logs. Sam climbed out, shut his door and took in the view. It was maybe three hundred metres to the fence at the bottom of this meadow, then patchwork crops, faded hills and rural lanes beyond. A wood pigeon sang somewhere nearby, above a hedgerow on the other side of the brown path. Its recurrent calls for a mate went unanswered.

Inside the barn, Sam turned full circle, looking up at the hand-carved rafters. The air smelled of dead plants, warm wood. Two rusted chains hung from an internal balcony and, next to a pile of empty pallets, an abandoned tractor sat on wheels bent inwards, as though it had fallen from the sky. A large hole in the roof, scabbed around the jagged rim with lichen and moss, made that seem possible. And, on the right-hand side, dry briars crawled through knot-holes in the planked walls.

Nature, with all its spikes and berries, had breached this place. As had her mother, the sun itself, which beamed in through cracks, laddered limelight for the wasps buzzing overhead. Along with a cricket, they were the only things making any noise in here. The birdsong outside was gone.

Clambering across some rubble and bricks, Sam held the tractor's bumper for balance. 'Look,' he said. 'There's a hatch here.'

They moved a few tyres off the trapdoor, then he kicked the rusted handle with his heel until it sprung free. It was rough, cold on his fingers as he lifted it open – creaking hinges, heavy timber. No treasure, only stairs – each sanded to a dull shine in the middle – leading into the gloomy earth.

Lowering himself, Sam put his full weight on one of the steps. When he realised it was sturdy, he climbed all the way down, brushing cobwebs from his cheeks.

The basement was about half the size of the barn, but narrow, propped up with whittled pillars and hammered pegs. Cool air radiated from every wall. It felt like the bowels of a galley – a shipwreck washed inland, left to bleach in the sun. Slits between the hard floorboards above were almost an inch in width – some packed with dried dirt and hay, but others clear and glowing.

This was an ideal place to hide, to eavesdrop on the meeting. And, to ensure no one would suspect Isabelle was not alone, Sam told her to close the trapdoor behind him and move a couple of tyres back on top.

They whispered to each other once or twice while they waited, but holding a conversation was difficult. They were tense, alert. On the way here, they'd spoken about Freddie, about Sam's divorce, about Abigail. About the leather bracelet Isabelle wore on her left wrist, a gift from Richard, her only memento from that lawless adventure. And, of course, they'd spoken at great length about the Clarkes.

Now though, they hardly said a word. Now, in this silence, Sam could see her sitting on top of a barrel, he looked up at her dark grey jeans and black top, her hair tied back in a ponytail.

But, from her point of view, he was just a voice in the ground.

'They're here,' Isabelle said.

It seemed the Marstons had employed similar caution, arriving thirty minutes ahead of schedule. Sam listened to the engine grumbling outside, a graunch of rubber on rocks and gravel as it parked. Then silence. A door slammed. Footsteps.

'You're early,' one of them said, as a second door thudded closed.

'As are you,' Isabelle replied, stepping away from the barrel.

The floorboards groaned and creaked, raining flecks of dirt. Two figures. Two men. As Sam leaned to his right to see more of the barn, something landed in his eye – he blinked, rubbed it away.

'You came alone?' This voice was quieter, strained – it belonged to someone who'd had throat surgery, maybe a laryngectomy. Only partial though. Half digital, half human. A coarse whisper.

'Can I ask who you are?' Isabelle said.

'Sorry, where are my manners? This is Henry, I'm Gregory.'

The large man directly above him was Henry Marston Senior. Moving lower, craning his neck, Sam saw the underside of his stomach. He was wearing suit trousers, a pale-blue shirt and braces.

'I understood Diane was coming?' Isabelle added.

'Does it matter?' Gregory said, standing at the front of the barn, almost a silhouette from Sam's perspective – his backdrop bright sky, wispy clouds, a summer haze. He was wearing jeans, a plain white T-shirt and seemed, and this was an unusual thought, like a normal person. A bald, middle-aged man, in the supermarket queue, on the pavement – there was nothing overtly threatening about either of them. However, donning horse masks and swinging crowbars, Sam imagined these brothers carried suitable malice – especially in the wet eyes of a helpless child.

'Understand the terms?' Gregory asked.

'You identify this man,' Isabelle said, holding up the piece of paper.

'Then you leave us alone,' Henry croaked.

'And what about Freddie Maguire?'

Gregory stared at her – his face blank. 'I have no idea who that is,' he said.

This was one of those textbook lies, lazy, half-hearted – essentially a confession. Although Sam's doubt had been negligible, now it was all gone. Now he knew these men were responsible. He held the pistol low and indulged himself a silent moment of violent fantasy. But no. No sense in that. Like any parent would, Sam felt the need for vengeance, but knew it was a hollow promise. It was an urge to dismiss, like all primal drives at odds with human decency. Retribution was not, irrespective of his heart's relentless claims, a remedy for rage.

'Do we have a deal?' Gregory said. 'This whole thing ends.'

'If you're telling the truth then, of course, we will stop investigating you.'

Good answer, Sam thought – *she could have lied.*

'I need your word. Promise, once we tell you who that is, it's over.'

'I promise.'

Gregory strode forwards, out from the rectangle of warm sky framing him, and further into the shadow, into the barn. 'OK,' he said, taking the piece of paper, looking down into the electronic sketch of that scarred face, the man at the centre of it all. 'The person you're after is called Ju—'

The sudden jingle of a loud ringtone interrupted him. Henry Marston Senior held up a finger and apologised. As he answered his phone, he turned his back on Isabelle and Gregory and took a few steps across the floorboards – now standing to Sam's left, near the slumped tractor. He repositioned himself to be directly below.

'Max,' Henry said, his fingers pressed to his throat for the gift of speech. And then he started to breathe heavily. Deep, seething gasps, air drawn into his lungs – hoarse and slow through the remains of his voice box.

Sam's mobile also came alive – a faint, single buzz on his thigh. Shielding the screen with his right hand, still holding the pistol, he rested it at his hip and read a text message from Lei R.

Big scene unfolding at Hallowfield General, it said. *Apparently Henry Junior's just flung himself off the roof.*

Carefully exhaling, Sam slid his phone back into his pocket. Here it was again. Modest information – changing his body, raising his pulse.

'God, dear God.' Henry was hissing above. 'My boy. My . . . my boy.'

Alarmed, as she should be, Isabelle's attention went to the floorboards. But she could not find Sam.

'No, no,' Henry breathed into his phone. 'Wait for me. I want to be there, I want to do it myself . . . Sharp tools . . . and a tooth for a tooth.' He hung up. 'Deal's off, bitch,' he whispered, turning back to Isabelle. 'My son is dead . . . You tell that fucking piece of shit—'

Sam, moving silently now in this fresh, fateful certainty, did not hear the rest of that sentence as he took a step backwards. Through a long gap in the boards above, he saw Isabelle's sad eyes.

They seemed to close all by themselves.

With his right hand on the grip, his left cupped beneath, Sam lifted the gun and aimed it at the ceiling. He squeezed the trigger and fired six shots in rapid succession – splinters and dust and smoke – the cracks booming in the tight space as voices roared and meat fell.

Fast now, through a curtain of warm rain and to the stairs. Up and up and Sam rammed through the trapdoor, sending the tyres bouncing, one of them rolling across the concrete, out of the barn, spinning like a huge black coin in the sun. Over the rubble, he saw Henry Marston dead on the floorboards – blood flowing from exit wounds on his legs and his ragged shirt, pouring into the wood. Furious wasps swarmed, strobing in new light.

Isabelle was down too, writhing on the ground next to the barrels, clutching her shin. A stray ricochet maybe. Impossible to know. She shouted something.

But Sam was running, outside, into the day, past the cars, looking down the grassy hill. Gregory Marston fleeing, sprinting as fast as he could, checking over his shoulder – panicked and glaring. His white T-shirt no larger than a postage stamp in Sam's sights. Leaning in, he fired twice, the pistol kicking in his hands. Two quick puffs of powder spat up behind his target. Another pair of shots and weeds flinched at his side – cut stalks, falling flowers, empty shells bouncing on the concrete.

Still, Gregory ran, stumbled, tried to zigzag – desperate flight – towards the hedge now, on to the gravel track. But not quick enough. Five more fast rounds echoed in the valley, the fourth producing a harsh spray – denim fibre. He spun, slamming hard into the ground, skidding flat amid rising dust.

When Sam arrived, Gregory was crawling on to the long grass, flattening it, dragging his lower half. 'I'm sorry, I didn't know he was . . .' He coughed, then rolled on to his back and held up a red hand. 'I didn't know he was a kid.'

'Give me the name.'

'Wait . . . I . . .'

'Now.'

'I . . .'

'It's someone from the church, isn't it? It's someone you know.'

'You're gonna . . . you're gonna shoot me anyway.'

'Five seconds.'

'Fuck , , . fuck you . . .'

Sam aimed.

'I thought your kid was older. *I thought he was eighteen.* I wouldn't— no wait, please—'

The final bullet made his whole body tense as turf exploded behind his head. Limp now, both arms spread wide at his sides.

Sam blinked. It was remarkably quiet. Still. Calm. No bugs. No singing birds. He felt suddenly alone, like when you turn the television off late at night.

But then a sound, pounding footsteps behind him. He turned to see a black shape, a shoulder, then thud – he was rattled, winded, face down on the ground.

Isabelle was on him, his right wrist tugged up his back – her grip solid on his thumb. Pure technique negating his strength. 'Ah, fuck,' he groaned into the grass.

'I am arresting you on suspicion of murder,' she said.

'*Suspicion?*'

'You do not have to say anything,' she went on. 'But it may harm your defence if you do not mention, when questioned, something which you later rely on in court.'

'Isabelle.'

'Anything you do say may be given in evidence.'

'Stop.'

'Do you understand?' she yelled.

There was a gristly clunk inside him. Sam grunted in pain, struggling to break free. But she pushed – he knew one more ounce of pressure and his shoulder would dislocate.

'Let me go.' He stayed still, stopped resisting. When he took a breath, he tasted the earth at his cheek. 'There's . . . ah, Jesus . . . there's still one of them left. Two if you count Diane.'

'*One of them left?* Where do you think you are? You just *killed* those men. Did they deserve to die? Do *you* get to decide that?'

'You know what they were going to do.'

'That's *not* how it works.' Another squeeze and he gritted his teeth. 'Isabelle, listen. *Listen* to me. These feuds . . . they only go one way.'

'It doesn't have to get any worse.'

'You've seen what they are – it's tit for tat – this is a zero-sum game. Got a hell of a debt now.'

'Freddie can be moved,' she said. 'We'll keep him safe. We'll keep *you* safe.'

Sam could feel his heart, flat on the ground, punching his ribs. Behind, Isabelle was panting. He sniffed and waited a moment.

'Think it through,' he said. Calm. Slow. 'These men . . . these *dead* men . . . They didn't come here to meet *me* . . .' He felt her sit a little lower, now on the small of his back, as she considered this critical fact. 'They know where you live . . . Abigail was right. I'm not a good one. Just let me go, and I'll fix this.'

'I can't, Sam . . . I can't.'

'You have to . . .'

'If . . . if I do anything other than arrest you, I'm complicit.'

'You're not . . . You just need to loosen your grip. Just let go,' he whispered. 'Just . . . let go.'

With a quick shift of his weight, Sam whipped his hand free and scrabbled out. He turned, Isabelle had the pistol. She kept it pointed at him as they rose together, back to their feet.

'On the ground,' she said. Formal now – this was work.

'You keep count of those shots?'

She nodded. 'One left.'

'Do you want to gamble? Do you think you can keep her safe? Is there an expiry date for this? How long?' Sam stepped closer. 'Give it to me.'

She took a pace back, uneasy as she considered her options. But she understood. He could see that. She knew the stakes.

'Dead brothers,' Sam said. 'Dead *siblings*. They take it *literally*. Eye for an eye. Think about what that might mean.' He gestured towards Gregory's corpse, then to the barn at the top of the hill. 'What *this* means. Just give me the gun.'

'If I do that . . . you, *honest Sam*, what are you going to say? When they arrest you, you'll say what, exactly? That I just let you go, sent you on your merry fucking way?'

'If that happens, then . . .' Sam sighed. 'Then, I'll lie.'

She lifted her aim – jutting the barrel towards him – tears in her eyes.

'If you don't believe me, then I'm lying *now*,' he said, showing his palms, shaking his head. 'Either way, you've seen I can do it.'

And then, finally, Isabelle stopped fighting. She didn't react as he carefully pressed her hands down and took the pistol. All his values, for all of hers. It was a good deal, a fair trade.

Every bit of that tranquillity, that balance – the way she moved as though she'd discovered a fundamental secret about the world, about how to live at peace – it all seemed to drain away. Isabelle faced the valley, down the hill, past the swaying daisies, past the butterflies, past the death. And, with glassy, bloodshot eyes and one of those calm breaths, she sat on the grass.

'If I see you again . . .' she said, without looking up.

'I know.'

Sam left her there and walked back to the barn. He took the keys from the floor, next to Henry's body, then climbed into his shiny black Mercedes. The dashboard lit up with some beeps and a whispering radio as the conditioner blew out cool air. Adjusting the mirror, Sam saw the murder costume he was wearing. It was smeared on his cheeks, his hair, sticky red drips dried halfway down his face. He searched around inside the car and found a bottle of water in the passenger footwell. After a couple of swigs, he poured the remainder on to a T-shirt from the back seat. When he'd wiped himself as best he could, scrubbing his neck and hands, he swapped his jumper for Henry's blazer. It was a poor fit, but at least it was clean.

As he pulled away, the wheels crunched on the gravel, then dropped in and out of potholes along the track.

Again, turning through the opening in the trees, Sam glanced up at the rear-view mirror and saw Isabelle, slouched in the same position, knees together on the ground. Her head was bowed, her arms in her lap. A perfectly still, dark figure, surrounded by greenery and meadow flowers. If it wasn't for the wisps of her fringe moving in the breeze, she could have been a painting. A picture of a lost soul, alone in this empty place with two dead men and a plume of dust from the car tyres, following him down the track, rising and drifting across the grass like smoke.

PART THREE
ANNA CLARKE

Chapter 31

Although many of the TV vans had gone, Orchard Court was still a festival of media activity. Anna stayed low on the back seat as Barney, the police family-liaison officer, pulled in through the gate.

'You got everything?' he asked, holding the steering wheel, leaning round. 'Straight to the door, all right, don't stop, don't listen.'

Anna collected her things, then put her jacket over her head and rushed across the drive, ignoring yelled questions and cameras flashing between the black iron fence bars behind her.

Inside, after she had put her bag down, Barney offered her tea. 'I'm fine,' she said.

'Is there anyone you'd like me to contact?'

Anna told him she wanted to be alone. Trained in such matters, he didn't protest much and left the house around five minutes later, having depleted all attempts at small talk.

The standard questions they asked had been updated, although the classics were familiar. And have you had any suicidal thoughts? That one was still on the list. She'd shaken her head as Barney took notes in biro. It was half true – there had been plenty of bleak day-dreams where she'd imagined how peaceful it must have felt before she was born. She suspected death was probably like that – just nothing. But it wasn't an option. What if they came home and she wasn't here waiting for them? This situation was actually worse than hopeless – Anna couldn't even kill herself.

The blinds in the kitchen were closed, so she sat at the dining table, in the dark. It was cold and quiet here. Triple glazing, all plugs turned off, and no voices in the empty house. The kind of awful silence most people can't afford. It was tidy too – the crime-scene cleaners had done a good job. Other than the faint, lingering smell of bleach products, she'd only found one sign they'd been here – a torn strip of yellow police tape on the front-door frame. It was thin, like cheap lametta tinsel. She picked it off with her fingernail, rolled it into a ball and stuck it on the inside of the new bin bag in the kitchen.

The police hadn't been quite so thorough with Ethan because, unlike Robin, there had been no blood at the house. There were no signs of injury and his bed was made. These were the only differences.

Anna took her phone out and realised it wasn't connected to the Wi-Fi. It demanded she re-enter the password. Even her mobile had forgotten. She typed it in – 'Button123' appearing as nine asterisks. Emails. She refreshed the list three times with her thumb, her ring tapping the silicone phone cover while she waited. As always, nothing important. Just the standard abuse and anonymous cruelty. But every so often, something kinder. A stranger would offer support. There was never any comfort in the unfounded claim that, one day, it'd be all right. Still, she read every single word – good and bad.

After around fifteen minutes, she pushed back the white dining chair and stood. Sniffing her tears away, Anna began her pointless ritual. She went upstairs, stepped across the thick new carpet, along the staircase railing and towards her daughter's bedroom. Dim now with no night light. The door was ajar, as it always is, and she pressed it open with a finger, as she always did. Silent, expensive hinges – wood brushing wool. The art box. The closed curtains. The row of stuffed toys on the shelf – none of their eyes glistening.

And an empty bed.

One.

Quietly crying, she turned round and went back downstairs.

Downstairs, whimpering in the hall, she sighed and turned round.

Anna went upstairs, stepped across the thick new carpet, along the staircase railing and towards her daughter's bedroom. Dim now with no night light. The door was ajar, as it always is, and she pressed it open with a finger, as she always did. Silent, expensive hinges – wood brushing wool. The art box. The closed curtains. The row of stuffed toys on the shelf – none of their eyes glistening.

And an empty bed.

Two.

Downstairs again.

Anna went upstairs, stepped across the thick new carpet, along the staircase railing and towards her daughter's bedroom. Dim now with no night light. The door was ajar, as it always is, and she pressed it open with a finger, as she always did. Silent, expensive hinges – wood brushing wool. The art box. The closed curtains. The row of stuffed toys on the shelf – none of their eyes glistening.

Anna's eyes were closed. She took a breath and looked a final time at Robin's empty bed.

Three.

One more set. Stairs, stairs, carpet, door, toys, bed. Stairs, stairs, carpet, door, toys, bed. Stairs, stairs, carpet, door, toys . . . bed. Another set. Stairs, bed, stairs, bed, stairs, bed.

Again.

We see old home-movie footage, shot on a mobile phone. The screen is small, pixelated – the size of a matchbox.

'ONE . . .' a child yells, sitting by a sofa, hiding his face. He is maybe three years old, wearing a red T-shirt beneath dungarees.

'Just . . . just go through all the numbers,' Francis is saying from behind the camera. He's giggling. Laughter has taken his breath. 'He's waiting . . . Anna, Anna, this is pure gold.'

We move out of the living room and into the hallway. Behind a door, Anna is crouched with a towel over her head. In the background, we hear slow piano and hushed violins. We know then that this recording is used in The Clarkes *– edited, scored by a full orchestra, quiet now. A sombre scene.*

'He kind of gets the concept,' Francis whispers, 'but hasn't quite grasped—'

'You'll give my position away,' Anna says, waving her hand past the door. 'Piss off.'

'TWO,' Ethan screams from the living room.

Francis sniggering. 'Aw, aw my God,' he says, crying now. 'Listen, listen, he'll wait . . . he'll wait about fifteen seconds . . . He must *be counting in his head . . . Aw, man, it's always perfectly timed. Wait for it . . .'*

'THREE – coming, ready or not.'

We move away from Anna, further down the hall in the Clarkes' home.

'Oh, hello, Daddy,' Ethan says, looking up, past the camera. Ignoring the lens, focusing on Francis. 'Mummy where?'

'I don't know, little man,' Francis whispers, his nostrils hissing with stifled laughter.

Ethan stomps around some discarded shoes. He pulls open the cupboard under the stairs. 'Mummy's hiding,' he says, glancing over his shoulder. Then he turns his attention back to Francis, toddles past him and into the kitchen. After a quick search, he returns.

When he arrives at the downstairs bathroom door, held open against the wall, he stops. Stern in his tiny face, curious and unsure, he pulls it slowly away to reveal a shadow, a shape. Anna throws the towel from her head – 'Rah!' – and Ethan flinches, erupting into laughter as he declares he's found her.

'You did *– you found me,' Anna says, standing. And, with the effortless strength of a mother, she picks him up and holds him at her hip. 'Shall we say silly Daddy?' she adds, bouncing her arm and walking towards the camera – pointing at us. 'We know how to count.'*

'One, two, three,*' Ethan says, stretching out his clumsy, chubby fingers, then cheering with Anna.*

'Those are the only numbers we need. We'll just count them slower, yeah?' She presses her forehead gently into his fair hair.

'My turn,' he says, writhing free. Anna sets him down and he disappears, running fast into the living room. 'Count,' he shouts. 'I'm hiding.'

Hands covering her eyes, Anna says, 'One,' then she waits fifteen seconds and calls out, 'two,' and finally, clocking half a minute with those three easy numbers, she yells, 'three. Coming, ready or not.'

The microphone rustles as the camera tilts, points at the wall, the ceiling, then back at Francis's face. He looks down into his phone. 'Neither of them can count. These guys are nuts.'

Back now to the living room – Ethan clearly visible behind the long curtain. A bulge and two tiny red socks beneath the glowing white fabric.

'Where is he?' Anna says. 'I just can't find him anywhere.'

Audible giggling from the moving curtain.

'Daddy, have you *seen Ethan?'*

'Nope.'

And when Ethan's head pokes out and he balls his fists in excitement, stepping from foot to foot, Anna sweeps in to grab him. Again, holding him at her hip, she speaks to the camera. But their voices fall silent, replaced by music, rising strings – long, swaying notes – a grand tragedy, loud now, loud and absolute.

Anna was still doing her rounds, although by this point she was exhausted and crawling on her hands and knees, up and down the stairs. One, two, three. Her legs and shoulders ached and her palms were raw. Eventually, she collapsed on the final step and rested her cheek flat on the second-floor carpet.

These habits start slow – she'd noticed them creeping in years ago. Simple things, like checking a door, or the hob, or even making sure she had logged out of her emails on her work computer. It didn't matter that she knew there was no need to check these things more than once.

Because, of course, memories are far from reliable.

When she was a child, these rituals were attached to abstract punishment. If, for example, she hadn't finished washing her hands before the toilet cistern filled up, then maybe she would get head lice. If her felt tips weren't all facing the same way in her pencil case, then she wouldn't win the affection of her latest crush. A particularly bizarre routine was alternating where she sat on the school bus. Window seat one day, aisle seat the next. If the pattern wasn't maintained, then maybe her mother would die in her sleep.

But as her mind and body grew, these delusions disappeared, to make way for logic and reason. The threes came later and started with locked doors. Although it was still absurd if she ever gave it real thought, Anna's consequence modelling became a little more sophisticated. It wasn't so much an impossible, unrelated penalty, but more a forecast into the future. Let's say that one day she *didn't* check the gate three times, then – Sod's Law – that would be the night Button escaped. All this played out in a second or two and soon condensed into a single, wordless urge to check things three times. Thinking one, two, three, as Ethan did.

His childhood counting became a long-standing joke in the family. Everything lasted three seconds – only sometimes there were long gaps between the numbers. It had merit – you could technically chart a minute, an hour, or even a year. But it only worked if you knew, in advance, the length of time you were measuring. One at the beginning, two in the middle and three at the end. It was useless for anything without a conclusion – any timeline that faded to a blur.

But even this hadn't been a real issue. She would count in her head, triple check doors, brush her teeth, sip drinks, everything in strict rhythms – most in sets of three. If she was rushing or distracted, and she missed one, she could survive – she might not even notice. However, since 12 August 2010, when Ethan disappeared, the urges had become overwhelming.

Anna worked hard to shelter her daughter from the media coverage and all these insecurities but, somewhere along the line, the rituals had bonded themselves to Robin.

'When you've lost one,' Dr Hunt said, 'the attachment you have to your remaining children is ripe for disorder. It's a relatively simple fix. A short course of cognitive behavioural therapy.'

But Anna did not want to be 'cured'. Even when they were involuntary, these compulsions were still a choice. She wasn't stupid. She knew the universe wouldn't change because she washed her left hand for five seconds and her right for ten. It was true that sometimes she wasn't 'in control', whatever that meant. Occasionally she would watch her body, like a passenger, as it walked into the kitchen and checked the oven dial three times. She would even say, in her head, 'Come on, this is ridiculous. Just leave it.'

But let's say she *did* just leave it and overcame the need to check. Well, then she just applied her inevitable forecast. If something happened, even coincidentally, it would destroy any remaining control she had left. It would justify the irrationality. And once you have that thought, you're locked into the commitment. Once you consider, even though it's infinitely unlikely, that you might have such agency in the world, then diligence really is your only option.

Therefore, it was, she decided, safer *and* more logical to simply obey. To check one, two, three.

Eventually, the hypothetical consequence of *not* checking became 'Robin'. Anna had to check everything *for* her daughter. She couldn't recall putting it into a conscious thought, like she had done as a child. But she understood what the feeling meant – if she did not check things three times, Robin would disappear, just like Ethan.

There was no solace in the fact that, despite her conformity, it still happened. This proved nothing, because Anna wasn't perfect. She probably *had* missed something. Even with all grounded, rational efforts, she still managed to blame herself.

And if this wasn't the case, then she was mad to believe it. Those were the only options she had – she was either guilty, or crazy. Probably somewhere between the two, she concluded.

Hours later, on the stairs, she woke up and looked across the long, pale carpet – the fibres closest to her face were out of focus, fading to clarity at the end of the hall, near Robin's bedroom. The door was ajar, as it always is. Anna climbed to her feet and wandered aimlessly through the quiet house.

In the kitchen, she hugged her thick cardigan into herself and stepped across the tiles. She stopped at Button's water bowl. It was empty, a light dusting of chalky limescale in the bottom. He was still at Daniel's, and Anna wanted to keep it that way for as long as possible.

'Call me as soon as you're allowed home,' Daniel had said.

But if she did that, he would rush round immediately. His heart was in the right place, but she was not in the mood for guests.

Turning, she stroked her fingers along the kitchen counter, over the chopping board and towards the knife set she'd bought Francis for Christmas. He did most of the cooking. In fact, he did most of everything. It was true, he could be controlling, but this wasn't always a criticism. Francis was a pretty good chef and Anna was happy to let him clean the house *his* way. Fortunately, they had similar taste in television, so his dominion over the remote was also tolerable.

The Shun-Karyi knives had cost more than a grand. Each was made from thirty-two layers of Damascus steel with strong cores cast in some obscure metal Anna had never heard of, and, crucially, they *looked* expensive. They were set on five small oak plinths above a square marble base – the ergonomic pakkawood handles stuck vertically from the top.

Anna clicked the four-inch chopping blade from the magnetised holder. Finding the handle's balance, feeling all that money, she turned it sideways. Then, with a quick flick of her wrist, she tapped the knife on the hard counter. One. Tap, the metal vibrating like a tuning fork. Two. Tap, a low sound. And three. Tap, ringing in the air. The notes were short – the blade was rigid.

Something new had started to worry Anna in the last few days. It made her give serious consideration to that therapist Dr Hunt had mentioned. The daydream about finding the person responsible for all this pain, and turning them into a catatonic lump of conscious meat with three fast, well-placed incisions at intervals along their spinal column. Anna knew, from countless hours of tense surgery, the delicate strands that you must not damage. Why? Because the consequences are catastrophic for the patient.

It wasn't that this fantasy was so vivid and appealing – that, she felt, was quite reasonable. What troubled her was how much pleasure she found here. Now it bordered on eroticism. In fact, it was the only source of warmth in her imagination. Even more alluring – and she winced and cried at this thought – than being reunited with her lost children.

Sliding down to the floor, Anna pushed her back against the fridge and put the knife on the Paris grey porcelain tiles between her legs. She knew why the image of them coming home no longer offered any joy. The reason was simple and it was awful. It was because truly, in her heart, Anna didn't believe it would happen.

She rubbed her eyes and frowned at her sore hands – they felt burned. Her knees too were tender. Strange, she had been home for hours and, somehow, she hadn't checked Robin's room yet. She rose from the kitchen tiles and went upstairs.

Anna arrived on the second floor, stepped across the thick new carpet, along the staircase railing and towards the dim warmth of her daughter's bedroom. The door was ajar, as it always is, and she pressed it open with a finger, as she always did. Silent, expensive hinges – wood brushing wool. The art box. The closed curtains. The row of stuffed toys on the shelf – all their eyes glistening.

And when she looked at the bed, she had a sudden, sobering thought. Like an optical illusion had just revealed itself and, now, she couldn't see it any other way. Calmly and in her mind, she whispered to herself, 'Oh, Anna . . . you're insane.'

Chapter 32

Anna stared through the kitchen window, through her reflection, through the black holes of her face. Someone was walking up the garden, towards the house. A dusk shadow. It was a man. Daniel. He must have seen the news.

She counted to three. One, two, three tugs on her hair and she turned, headed to the back door.

As he arrived on the patio, she grabbed the handle and pulled it open, throwing the kitchen's cold white light on to the stone slabs below.

'You didn't call,' he said, looking up.

'No. I didn't.'

'Can I come in?'

She sighed, then stepped back inside.

'Are you OK?' he asked, closing the door behind him and removing his jacket.

'Never better.'

They stood at the counter, Anna's left hand flat on the surface.

And he came close, into her space. But she cringed away from his hug.

'I'm sorry,' he said. 'At the hotel . . . I shouldn't have.'

For a while, they just looked at each other.

'Speak to me,' Daniel whispered.

Anna pressed her eyes into the crease of her elbow and leaned on the kitchen worktop. 'I . . . I don't know what to say.'

'Sit down. Please. I'll make you something to eat.'

She felt his grip on her shoulders as she stood upright again. He guided her to the table.

'Fine,' she whispered, taking a seat.

Hunched over, she felt small, like a child, as he prepared her food. They didn't say a word.

Eventually, he set a plate down in front of her. A sandwich cut into triangles. Anna felt sick just looking at it.

'I . . . I haven't slept,' she said, fingers on her temple. 'I don't even know what day it is.'

'It's fine. Eat.'

'Why are you here?'

'Because you shouldn't be alone . . . I promise, I'm not going to do anything.' Daniel pulled a chair out and dragged it close. Perched at her knees, he said, 'Yesterday . . . Sam came to see me.'

Anna just watched him.

'He was asking questions. About Robin. About that . . . thing in the tree.' He rubbed his eye. 'About me and you.'

'What did you tell him?'

'Nothing.'

'You lied.'

'Of course I lied,' he said.

'You should have come clean. Just said it.'

'To what end? What would that achieve?'

'It's—'

'This was *your* idea.'

'*What?*'

'Nothing,' he said. 'It's nothing.'

'No, go on.'

'I've been lying for *years*. Because you told me to.'

'Daniel.'

'You should have left him. But you wanted to keep pretending.' He laughed. 'All for . . .'

'For what? Say it. Fucking say it.' There was a long silence.

'For Ethan.'

'What do you want me to say?' Anna shrugged.

'*No*, what do you want *me* to say?' Daniel stabbed a finger into his chest.

'I don't even want you to *be here*. These years.' She grabbed her hair. 'All these years.' Anna rocked, banging her elbows on the wood.

'Stop. Stop it. Look, I'm sorry. It just gets to me. If we'd made different decisions.'

'What does that mean?'

'Francis . . . he's . . . I mean, Anna, what if it's fucking true?'

'So it's my fault?'

'No . . . if anything it's mine. I shouldn't have agreed.'

They'd met for dinner. They were just kids back then. It was so formal. A fancy restaurant with fancy candles. Such a strange memory. Anna had thought she was being mature.

'Whatever you decide,' Daniel had said. 'I'll respect it. Just tell me what to do.'

She'd looked at her lap. 'We have to stop.'

The tears in Daniel's eyes had the salt rock candlelight burning in them. But Anna had been sure. It was the right thing to do. She was engaged. This kind of behaviour was not normal for her.

'You can live with it?' he'd asked. 'I don't think you realise how corrosive a lie like that can be.'

'Nothing happened,' Anna said. 'Nothing.'

Young Daniel, so slim back then, nodded. 'OK.'

They had even toasted with their glasses of red wine. A clink to officially declare whatever it was they had was over.

Now, two decades on and Daniel had the cheek – the audacity – to suggest some alternative might have changed things.

'I'd like you to leave,' Anna said, sliding the sandwich away from her.

'If that's what you want. Just, please, give it some thought. They're going to charge him in the morning. It's real. It's happening.'

'Why?' She shook her head. 'Why would he do this? He's . . . he's not a bad father.'

'I'm so, so sorry, Anna . . .' Daniel touched her wrist. 'But I think he is.'

On her feet, she swept the plate off the table, smashing it on the floor – the bread bouncing amid the broken china. The food now deadly.

'Get out.'

'I wonder how Sam knew,' he said, standing. 'Why he asked about us?'

Anna strode towards him, Daniel stepped backwards, stopping at the kitchen counter.

'Maybe someone is watching,' she whispered, pointing at the ceiling. She then placed her index finger on her lips. 'Shhh.'

He turned his head away, as though a strange thought, an alien concept, had just passed through his mind. And he frowned at her with . . . suspicion? Or perhaps the beginnings of outrage. He exhaled, stifled a laugh. 'Strange, isn't it?' he said. 'That everyone suspects he's to blame. Everyone can see it. Everyone . . . apart from *you*.'

'Leave.'

'Don't you wonder? Aren't you curious? Something very dark is happening, Anna . . . what else have you lied about?'

It happened in a blink – she slammed an open hand into Daniel's face, driving the back of his skull hard, harder than she had meant to, into the corner of the glassware cupboard. He grabbed his head, stumbled and fell to one knee.

There was blood on his hand. Shaking, he gasped, breathed, touched his nose. 'Fuck.'

'I told you to leave.'

'God.' Daniel sniffed, clambered upright again. 'You really hurt me there.' He tried to catch his breath.

And once more, they stood opposite one another and shared a moment of silence.

'I remember, years ago, when we were at uni,' he said, his face scrunched and wincing, his palm on his scalp. 'You'd been drinking vodka. You lay on the sofa. I put a blanket over your legs. Left you. Early in the morning, I got up for a lecture. And you were standing right in the hall. Just standing there. Staring. Staring at me, staring *through* me, just like you are now. You were . . . you were sleepwalking. Honestly, it was the creepiest thing I had ever seen. I looked into your eyes, your pupils, they were huge. And it was like there was nothing there, like   like no one was looking back. As if something fundamental, something vital was . . . was missing.'

'Get. Out.'

'I believe in a soul, Anna . . . and I haven't seen yours for a very, very long time.'

Chapter 33

We see a modest community centre, lit jaundice yellow by old strip bulbs — their plastic casings, littered with dried insects, speckle odd shadows throughout the room. At the front of the hall is a small scuffed stage, opposite that a crowd of maybe twenty people on brown seats — like school chairs, half of which are empty. We film from the rear — and see the backs of heads, most are men, most are old. All are listening intently.

On the raised stage, Diane Marston is speaking at a lectern. Her black hair, short and thin, has a side parting. Without make-up, the bones in her face are well defined. But, at a glance, it would be easy to miss these feminine shapes. And a closer look would find felinity first. Above her wide cheeks, she's wearing large reading glasses, tinted yellow, like the rest of the room. Behind the left lens, a marbled cataract, a gloss of blue fog flooding her iris.

But none of this distracts from the passion, the showmanship, the charisma and rhythm in her voice. Diane Marston performs with conviction. Undoubtedly, she believes what she says. And, on the bare wooden walls in this dated hall, these words arrive as a chorus of echoes.

'And when they came to the crowd,' she says, not reading but reciting, 'a man came up to him and, kneeling before him, said, "Lord, have mercy on my son, for he is an epileptic and he suffers terribly. For

often he falls into the fire, and often into the water. And I brought him to your disciples, and they could not heal him."' She raises a finger. 'And Jesus answered, "Oh, oh faithless and twisted generation, how long am I to be with you? How long am I to bear with you? Bring him here to me."' Diane is animated – speaking fast. She flows across the stage, sleek, fluid and low, moving like the cat we might have seen in her. 'And Jesus rebuked the demon, and it came out of him, and the boy was healed instantly. Then the disciples came to Jesus privately and said, "Why, why could we not cast it out?" He said to them, "Because of your little faith. For truly, I say to you, if you have faith like a grain of mustard seed, you will say to this mountain, 'Move from here to there,' and it will move, and nothing will be impossible for you."'

Diane returns to the lectern, removes her glasses and cleans them with a square of beige cloth. This pause is considered, composed here for effect. It's impossible to know if the audience shares her piety but, clearly, they are captivated. The sermon is compelling – not because of its content but rather her delivery. She could sell any commodity – and today, she trades in ideas.

'We must remember the Devil's primary hallmark is deception,' she says. 'Most do not believe demonic forces exist, let alone roam free in our society. And without faith in this reality, we stand no chance of defeating them. They play among us – in government, in corporations large and small, in our own homes and hearts – in serpent, in swine, in men and in women. The sodomites, the whores, the child molesters and fiends – they will continue to thrive unless we stand, with the light at our side, and accept first and foremost that the fight is real. Make no mistake.' She juts the glasses forwards, stabbing a stem at the congregation. 'We, the Lord's children, are at war. And, in times of war, there is no weapon too nefarious. Not with stakes as high as these. Mercy will be bestowed on those who take up arms in this battle. To sin with such cause is no sin at all. And, if you look in yourself, and at your brothers and sisters, and find peace – do not take comfort. Passive onlookers, like non-believers, will see no redemption. If it's salvation we seek, first we must ask what our role has been in this fight – for He will surely wonder the same when the raging fires of judgement day take the earth by storm.'

At the end of this long, emphatic sermon, Diane thanks a few people in the crowd, shaking hands as they shuffle single file out of the community centre. The final man queueing at the exit is wearing a shiny, green polyester jacket and a pair of jeans, torn at the knees. His trainers, once white, are now stained damp brown. And his hair, a fluffed mass of grey, has been cut with little concern for style.

Hunched and timid, this short man steps towards the door. His meek hands, held at his chest, pick at themselves as Diane arrives by his side. She smiles and places her palm on the top of his head. He seems too shy to maintain eye contact, addressing the floor instead of the blessing. But when she whispers something in his ear, his chin lifts, his shoulders drop and, for a brief moment, these recreant mannerisms fade away – banished by a few reassuring words only they can hear. Diane is taken aback when he leans in for a hug, but she returns it nonetheless. Stroking his back, she nods – because it's OK, it really is OK.

When this exchange is over, the old man begins to leave again. And, in the gloomy doorway, he turns back towards the camera. We see it for perhaps half a second but, below his messy grey hair, rough, pink skin covers much of his face. A terrible injury from long ago, complete with a strip of wafer-thin scar tissue bridging his nose to his scaled cheek.

This video, like much of Diane's work, is online. Although it's a few years old, it is not hard to find. It might buffer with a spinning circle, or turn into tiny squares from time to time, but still we stream it with ease.

And, at the end of the recording, on the other side of the edit, when the hall is filled with empty chairs and the electric hiss of the camera's cheap microphone, only we can see Diane strolling back towards the stage. She seems calm as she collects her things and buttons up her coat. Maybe she thinks she's alone. Maybe she hasn't noticed, in the doorway, a shape is still watching her. A figure. A man who never left. His pixel eyes shine yellow, like grains of mustard seed, and his scars are hidden now, healed by the shadow.

Chapter 34

Robin was on her knees in her bedroom, searching through the art box. There were all kinds of different paints, pencils and brushes, which clattered around inside. In a folder, clipped to the underside of the lid, she found a plastic booklet. When she lifted it out, stencils came tumbling on to the floor. *Ah*, she thought, *that explains the spray paint.* She unwrapped one of the small cans and shook it, hearing the hard ball bearing clink and bounce around inside the metal. She liked the sound it made. As a test, she squirted a quick streak on to her open sketchbook – creating a faint leaf. It went over the edges, so it was a good job the carpet in this corner had been lined with old newspaper.

For a while, she sat cross-legged on the floor, tilting the can left, then right – *dink-dink, dink-dink.* It smelled nice, and could be a lot of fun, but the sketchbook was only A4 – she wanted a larger surface. What she *really* needed was a . . .

And Robin smiled.

She stood, shook the spray paint and went to the wall. Holding the stencil flat with her thumb, she streaked it with a short squirt of black. It felt naughty, like doing graffiti. But Julius *had* said she was allowed to decorate her room however she wanted.

'Even the walls?' she'd asked.

'*Especially* the walls.'

There were lots of stencils in the art box, but the animals were the best. She spent ages filling the side wall, all around the bathroom door, with falling leaves and hedgehogs and eagles and more. They looked really good – there was no way she could paint them this well all by herself.

Even though he'd said it was fine, when Julius arrived in the main doorway, Robin stood upright and turned round, hiding the spray can and stencil behind her. She hummed a little song and walked across the carpet, pretending she had nothing to do with the pictures. Julius seemed to like this – obviously it was a joke, he had caught her red-handed. Or, rather – she looked down at her fingers – black-handed.

'Wait there,' he said.

A few minutes later he returned and shuffled sideways into the room, carrying . . . a stepladder? He pitched it in the centre of the carpet and held it steady.

'Are you sure?' she asked.

'I'm sure the ceiling is boring,' he said.

Her tongue poked from her mouth as she shook the tin again and climbed, squeezing his hand at one point for balance.

Together they painted at least a hundred birds above her bed, over the open door and the television. They all seemed to fly from the very first one she'd sprayed, down on the wall, near the art box. A brilliant eruption of silhouettes spread across the ceiling. The problem was, when using stencils, sometimes the paint went around the edges. This meant lots of the pictures had slight borders. At first, Robin didn't like that. She even tried to colour them in with a white pen. But now it looked OK – like the frames were done on purpose. Little birds in little squares.

'It would be cool if it glowed,' she said when they'd finished, turning full circle, looking up at their creations. 'Do they do glow-in-the-dark spray paint?'

'Probably, but you leave the lamp on all night.'

She turned to him. 'Otherwise it's too dark.'

Julius left the room again and came back with a hand drill. He knelt on her bed, then removed the screws from the planks of wood covering her window, pulling them carefully between the bars and throwing them down on to the floor. The last one clattered on top of the pile and Robin smelled sawdust in the air.

'And then there was light,' Julius announced, brushing splinters off her duvet.

She could tell he wanted her to look out the window and appreciate the view. But Robin couldn't take her eyes away from that drill – it might work on the metal bars. Her plan had not changed. Although she didn't want to upset Julius, she would still escape when she got the chance. She watched as he left, and then listened to him downstairs – trying to imagine which room he was in. Where was he putting the drill? The kitchen. But then she heard the back door.

With the boards gone, she could now sit on her bed, put her elbows on the windowsill and look outside – it was sunny today. She saw him walk down the garden, to a shed at the end. If only she could get out there – she could easily climb over that fence. But where would she go? It seemed they were in the woods, very far away from any other houses. Robin could see none – it was just trees. *This makes sense*, she thought – if she were going to build a prison, she would do it somewhere secret. Maybe no one even knew this place existed. It was just her and Julius. Sometimes she felt like they were the only people in the whole world.

At the back of the garden, by an overgrown bush, Robin saw a low mound. And, near the top of it, there was a wooden cross sticking out of the grass.

It looked like a small grave.

Maybe he'd had a pet that died? Mum said that, one day, Button would pass away because he was so old. And when he did, they would bury him in their garden, just like her hamster – Pillow. Robin had called him that because he was soft and white; although she was only four at the time, she now thought the name was kind of silly. But when she'd found dead beetles, or spiders, or even ants, Mum said she shouldn't bury them. Only mammals get funerals. Although, Emma's brother had a lizard, and they'd buried her. *She* was a reptile. Maybe it depended on how big you were.

The grave in Julius's garden looked about the size of a fairly large dog. There was something etched into the wooden cross – probably a name – but she couldn't read it from up here. Robin decided not to ask him about this – in case it made him sad.

Over the past few days, he had been extra nice to her and seemed happy most of the time. But it wasn't all fun games and painting. As well as the art box, he had bought a stack of textbooks. He said they were all the proper ones, so he could teach her everything she would be learning in her normal lessons. Robin never, ever thought it would be possible but, she had to admit, she kind of missed school. Not as much as she missed her parents and Button though. She'd lost count of the days – she guessed she'd been here for about a week. But it felt so much longer.

Robin had been staring at clouds above the trees for around ten minutes or so, imagining they were faces and frogs and mountains, when she noticed something out of the corner of her eye.

'Well, hi there,' she whispered.

A caterpillar was crawling calmly across the windowsill, near her elbow. He was green and furry, with small black spots, and wriggled a bit like a worm. She watched the wave of his body – he lifted his front legs, then his tummy, then finally his tiny feet right at the back, moving forwards a little bit at a time.

265

'Why are you indoors?' she asked, letting him walk over her finger, which she held perfectly still. 'I wish I had a butterfly stencil. Then I could show you what you'll be soon. Are you excited? Can you hear me?' She leaned in closer. 'Do you even *have* ears?'

'So,' Julius said, coming into the room behind her, 'art is done – we need to do maths and then maybe . . . What have you got?'

'This is . . . Patty,' she said, holding him delicately in her hand. 'Say hello.'

'Hello.'

'To him, not to me.'

'Oh.' He looked down. 'Hello.'

'I think he wants to go outside.'

'I'll put him in the garden.' Julius extended his hand.

But Robin pulled Patty closer to her chest. 'Please may I come?'

'Maybe you can look out your window – and point to where he should live?'

'OK,' Robin said, hiding her disappointment. She rested her little finger on Julius's hand and let Patty climb across. 'Be careful.'

Julius walked slowly down the stairs and she watched him through her window, her face against the cold metal. Near a bush at the far end, to the right of the grave, he turned and looked back to her. She gave him a thumbs up. Then he crouched and put the tiny green caterpillar on the grass. *That's a good place for Patty*, Robin thought.

'You should plant some flowers for him,' she said, when Julius returned. 'He will be a butterfly soon.'

'Maybe *you* can.'

'I would love that. Please can we do it?'

'Of course.'

'Now?'

'One day.'

Robin sighed. That was *always* his answer. One day. Earlier, when he was reading to her about adjectives (describing) and verbs (doing words), she interrupted him. She knew going home wasn't an option, but she'd wondered if she could at least *speak* to her mum on the phone. And what did he say? That's right. One day. Always *one day*.

Robin knew why he was uncomfortable with this subject – because he was breaking the law. He was not a policeman, or a doctor, so keeping her prisoner was illegal. She hadn't been brave enough to tell him that though.

However, yesterday, she had plucked up the courage to question him a little bit. They had been speaking about her parents – Julius wanted to know what they were like. She told him the truth – that they loved her very much and would be missing her.

'Are they nice to you?' he asked.

'Yes. Mostly. They sometimes shout if I've been naughty. But not often.'

'Surely you're never naughty?'

Robin smiled – she had felt relaxed. 'Julius?' she'd said.

'Yes.'

'Can I ask you a question?'

'Of course.'

'Why do I have to live here?'

He said it was the best place for her and that he would keep her safe. She didn't really understand this – there *must* be a proper reason. Something he wasn't telling her.

In a way, she felt sorry for him. Sometimes, when he was reading from textbooks, he would get to a word he didn't know and ask her to read it for him. But some of the words weren't even hard. Maybe, Robin joked, *she* should be teaching *him*. He seemed upset when she said that – and she apologised straight away.

After their maths lesson, Robin lay on her bed and doodled some pictures. She drew Patty as he was now – a tiny green thing, like twenty peas with legs, all joined together in a row. Next to that, she sketched what he would look like when he transformed. She clattered the pencil in her mouth, then went for a brand-new packet of fluorescent felt tips. The wrapping crinkled as she dropped it on the floor.

When he changed, she imagined he would have dark-brown wings, with red stripes around the edges and little specks of blue that would shimmer like the inside of a muscle shell on the beach. And so, that's what she drew.

◆　◆　◆

We see the living room – all cleaned up now. No more pictures of beasts with hooves and forks and fire roaring beneath them. No more crosses. No more dolls. No more photos of the Clarkes. Aside from the bars on the windows, this could be any rural home. Julius has done a good job of making it more accommodating for his guest. He enters, holding a cup of tea in one hand and a small plate with a single biscuit in the other. Under his elbow, he carries a book. He steps towards the coffee table, keeping the mug level, lowering it carefully so he doesn't spill a drop.

Now he's seated, the book's title comes into view, English Grammar: A Pocket Guide.

Julius lifts the plate beneath his mouth and, just as he's about to take a bite, his phone rings – buzz-buzz, buzz-buzz *– on the sofa by his thigh. He places the plate back down and hesitates – alarmed at the intrusion. Finally, he picks his mobile up and answers. But he does not speak.*

After a few seconds, a female voice says, 'Hello? Julius? Are you there?'

'Diane?'

'Yes.'

'Did you get my message?' he says.

'I did.'

'And? Can I come and see you?'

'I'm afraid not.'

There's a pause. 'So,' he asks, 'why are you calling?'

'I wanted to let you know that the police may make contact.'

His hand goes over his mouth. 'Why?'

'They are looking for Robin Clarke.'

A tear runs down his cheek, and then another. But he does not make a sound. Julius can cry in absolute silence. 'Oh. I see.'

'Do you know anything about that?'

'No,' he lies.

'Well then, you have nothing to fear.'

Julius stands and goes to the window, moving the curtain aside. 'Will . . . will they come to the house?'

'I suspect so, yes.'

He lowers the phone. His hands shake – he doesn't know what to do with them. Stretched in dismay, his lips begin to tremble – but, still, not a peep. Then he brings the mobile back to his ear. 'Do . . . do you remember the story, about the shepherd and the wolf?' he says.

'Yes.'

'The shepherd sacrifices his most precious lamb, to save it from being eaten . . . Did . . . did the lamb go to heaven?'

'What do you think?'

'I think she did . . . Tell me again, tell me what heaven is like?'

'Oh, Julius, it is the most beautiful place you can imagine. It is paradise.'

Nestling himself into the corner of the room, he shields his mouth with his free hand, cupping the mouthpiece. 'I . . . I don't think God loves me any more,' he whispers, as if to keep this worry secret.

269

'The Lord loves all his children.'

'Will He forgive me, if I have to sin?'

'All men are sinners, Julius . . .'

'Can I see you again, please?'

'One day,' she says, and the call comes to an end.

He looks at his mobile. But he's weak and it falls from his grasp, bouncing on to the carpet. Back to the sofa, he pulls his knees to his chest and leans away from everything, his face pressed down, hands over his head, arms in his ears. Hysterical, desperate, he rocks and groans and cries. Then he kneels on the floor and whimpers, hitting himself again and again with clenched fingers.

'No, no, no,' he says, on every strike.

He tugs at his grey hair with both hands, then they turn to fists – he pushes them into his eye sockets. Finally, his palms come together.

'I am so, so sorry,' he whispers, tilting his head to the ceiling – or perhaps beyond, to the most beautiful place he can imagine. 'Forgive me.'

And then fast, Julius goes to his kitchen, moving from camera to camera. He takes a knife from a drawer, walks with purpose down the hall and stands at the bottom of the stairs.

'No, no,' he says, hitting himself again, this time with the knife handle.

Back to the kitchen, he puts the knife away.

'She was happy,' he whispers to himself. 'She wasn't scared. She just goes to sleep.'

He removes a first aid box from under the sink. Inside, there's medical equipment, syringes, drugs in small glass vials, latex gloves and pipettes and tubes and other things he should not have. His hands are jittery as he pokes one of the needles into a bottle and draws his thumb up, filling the entire chamber with transparent liquid. But then, once more, he hesitates. He places the items on a tray and covers them with a tea towel.

And to the freezer, where he pulls out a tub of ice cream. He puts three large scoops into a bowl. From the first aid box, he takes a pot of pills. He pours two, no, three, on to the kitchen counter and reaches up to a cupboard. Then, with the bottom of a tumbler, he presses and twists – crushing the tablets into a fine powder. He sweeps it all into the bowl and brushes white dust from his palm. To hide the drugs, he squirts a spiral of whipped cream and drizzles chocolate sauce over the top. For the final touch, a sprinkling of chopped nuts.

Then, bowl in hand, he ascends the stairs. Outside Robin's door, he wipes away his tears, takes a breath, and – tap-tap-tap *– three gentle knocks. It's barely a whisper. But she tells him he can come in.*

Chapter 35

Robin had just put the last line on her drawing when she heard a knock at the door. As Julius entered, she spun the sketchbook around to show him.

'That's brilliant,' he said, looking down at the picture.

'I didn't have quite the right colours – I think his wings will be lovely. Maybe so lovely you couldn't even draw them.'

Smiling, Julius held out his hand. 'Here.'

A mountain of blue-and-white ice cream in a bowl. He'd even added squirty cream and chocolate sauce. She would prefer it without the nuts but, as he had put so much effort into making it look nice, she decided not to mention that.

'For me?' Robin asked.

And Julius nodded.

'Thank you.'

He sat down next to her on the bed.

She pulled her feet up on to the mattress and rested the cold bowl in her lap. The metal handle clinked on the china and reminded her of her own spoon, still hidden beneath her pillow. She lifted a large mouthful and giggled, crossing her eyes as she turned to him – looking at a dot of cream on the end of her nose.

Julius smiled again and wiped it away. While she ate, he flicked through her sketchbook and she explained each picture.

'Is this Button?' he asked, pointing at a dog.

'Mmm-hm.'

'Are those wrinkles?'

'In dog years he's ten thousand years old,' she said, covering her mouth to swallow. A piece of nut was stuck in her teeth. She dug it out with her tongue and winced – it tasted bitter.

'You're not scared of creepy-crawlies, are you?' He was on a page with some beetles and a long millipede going from corner to corner.

'Nope. Not really. Although . . .' Robin remembered the sleepover at Emma's house a couple of weeks ago. They had all been tucked up in their sleeping bags when a big spider scurried across the floorboards. Everyone screamed and panicked and said it was disgusting. In the end, Emma's dad came upstairs with a glass and a postcard to get rid of it. Robin had wanted to do it herself – she wasn't frightened. She liked all animals, even insects – even arachnids. But she had pretended to be scared, just like they were. It was silly. Now, she knew, if she ever saw a spider again when they were around, she would have to act terrified. Otherwise they would realise she had lied.

'Although . . . ?'

'Sometimes I pretend to be.'

'Why?'

'Because everyone else is.'

'Why would you want to be like everyone else?'

'That's what Mum always says.'

He closed the sketchbook and placed it on the bed cover.

'Do you believe in heaven?' he asked.

Robin had sat through many conversations like this. Most evenings, he would read stories to her from the Bible. At the end, he asked if she understood what they meant. Most of the time, she would shrug and say, 'Kind of.'

But did she believe in heaven?

'I don't know,' she said, scooping some chocolate from the edge of the bowl. 'Maybe.'

'Do you know what heaven *is*?'

'It's where you go when you die, if you're good.'

'That's right.'

Distracted, Robin put some ice cream, sauce and nuts on the spoon – creating a perfect mouthful. Then she held it up for Julius.

'I'm OK, thank you,' he said.

'It's really nice.'

'Bubblegum and cookie dough.'

'Double yums.'

'And what about hell? Do you know what that is?'

Nodding, she chewed. 'Mmm. The opposite, where bad people go.' And she pointed at the floor – her fingers still black from the spray paint.

'Where would you rather go, heaven or hell?'

'Well, heaven.'

'And what would it look like?'

'I don't know . . . clouds?'

'It's the most beautiful place *you* can imagine – your very own heaven.'

'Then, I guess it would . . .' Robin put the bowl in her lap and stared at the wall, at one of her stencilled leaves. And she smiled. 'It would be just like home,' she said.

Julius touched her knee – he seemed happy with her answer. 'You've been so well behaved. Tomorrow, there will be no more rules.'

'None at all?' Robin eyed him cautiously.

'No locked doors, no bars. You can go wherever you want.'

'Really?' she said, turning. 'Anywhere?'

'Anywhere.'

'Thank you.' She knelt on the mattress and hugged him. He squeezed her, then patted her back.

'Tonight, you can watch cartoons and stay up as late as you like. And, in the morning, when the sun comes up, the world is yours.'

Robin sat back on the bed. Her eyes stung and she felt the beginning of tears, but blinked and they went away.

'Where will you go?'

Biting her thumbnail, she looked across the room, then lifted an eyebrow. 'Home?'

'So be it.'

'Oh, that's just . . . You can meet Button, I can show you my house, we have loads of flowers in the garden because we have a gardener – word of advice, don't pick them because—' Robin stopped and frowned at him. 'Why are you crying?' she asked.

'Because . . . I'll miss you.' Julius sniffed and turned his head away, so she hid her joy. It seemed mean to be so excited if he was sad.

'We can still be friends?' she said.

But he didn't respond.

After her bath, she got dry and put on her thick pyjamas. Even though she could stay up late, all she wanted to do was go straight to bed. Maybe it was because she was looking forward to tomorrow – either way, she was really sleepy.

She took the bowl downstairs and put it in the kitchen sink. It was evening now – the sun was like a big orange and the clouds were thin and long, so there were no faces in the sky. For a moment she thought she was dreaming, because there was a breeze in the kitchen. Robin stepped sideways and looked at the back door.

It was open. And it felt like she was alone.

Without even thinking, she crept towards the chilled air, then outside on to a stone patio.

'Are you tired?' Julius asked from behind.

Robin jumped and spun – all her muscles tensed. 'Sorry, I . . .'

'It's fine. You can go outside. Say goodnight to Patty.'

So that's what she did, she walked out into the garden. The grass was dry but cool on her bare feet. Even when she'd been poorly, she'd never stayed indoors for *this* long. Everywhere smelled so incredible and fresh. It was like the wind was cleaning cobwebs off her skin.

There were a few early stars twinkling in the sky above the shed roof. She looked lower and stared at the back fence – her heart began to beat faster when she considered it. There was nothing stopping her. She checked over her shoulder and saw Julius in the kitchen window, washing up. He seemed distracted. Turning to the fence again, she took another step forwards. But a yawn arrived. She tried to stop it, her jaw rigid and her eyes watery, but it still came through.

No. She was being silly. It was getting dark. She was in her pyjamas. She wasn't even wearing shoes. And when she glanced down at her feet, she realised she was standing near the grave. Curious, she leaned to the left and her shadow moved off the wooden cross.

There was no name, no date, just a single letter, 'E.'

'Don't be out there too long,' Julius called. He was on the patio, holding a tea towel and her ice-cream bowl. 'You'll get cold.'

Robin left the stars, the grass and the gentle breeze and went back indoors.

Despite being exhausted, she ran to her bed, sat on the pillow, then slid her legs halfway under the cover. She flung it up and snuggled in quickly as it fell down on top of her, letting out a fake shiver. 'Brrrr.'

'Did you say goodbye to him?' Julius turned off the main light. The window glowed faint grey, but the lamp on the carpet filled the room with red warmth.

'No – I think he was hiding,' she said. 'But it doesn't matter. Even if he's transformed, he won't forget me.'

'Yeah?'

Robin remembered what she'd read about them – and it was amazing. Scientists did an experiment where they ring a bell and poke a caterpillar to make it really stressed. After that, every time they ring the bell, it squirms because it doesn't like the sound. Then it goes into its cocoon, where its whole body, even its brain, melts down into a sort of bug soup. This then turns into a butterfly. And, when it comes out and they ring the bell again, it gets stressed because it doesn't like the sound.

'Yeah – they remember,' she whispered, resting her head on her pillow. 'Butterflies remember being caterpillars.'

'Sweet dreams, Robin,' he said, and the door creaked shut.

She pulled the cover right up to her chin, rolled to her side and wiggled her toes – now snug in fluffy socks.

Tomorrow morning, she would get to see Mum again – she was going to give her a big kiss on the cheek. She'd see Dad, and Button too. Her heart was fluttering like a hummingbird's – not from fear this time, but from happiness.

Finally, she pushed some of the duvet between her knees and closed her eyes. She thought of all the names for Julius's dog. Elizabeth, Emma, Eve. Or maybe for a boy dog, Edward, Ellis, Elliott. There weren't that many names that started with E. But she was too excited to think about sad things like that.

Robin tried to remember a time when she'd been this smiley. Not even Christmas, or Disneyland tickets, or winning the art contest at school – beating people much older than her. Nothing compared to how fantastic tomorrow was going to be. Home again.

She hardly ever thought about her brother – but for some reason he popped into her mind. Of course, she had been a baby when he'd disappeared so she couldn't remember him. And, although no one knew where he was, she sometimes imagined that, if Ethan had died, he might have gone to . . .

Her eyes were open now. The flutter in her chest sunk down, low, low into her stomach when she thought of that grass mound in the garden. A small grave. The letter E.

Julius really *would* miss her, because she was going tomorrow. Going home. Home to heaven. Determined, Robin reached under her pillow and rolled on to her back. Beneath the covers, she held the sharpened spoon handle at her chest like the dagger it always was, and decided that, no matter what, no matter how tired she got, she would *not* fall asleep.

For hours she lay there, perfectly still and awake, wondering if she too could wrap herself tightly enough to transform into something small and delicate. Something which would remember all the things that *truly* scared her. She didn't even care what colour she would be, as long as she had wings.

Chapter 36

The camera sees water. A fast river rushing over smooth egg pebbles and rocks, passing under a fallen tree which bridges bank to bank. Near the edge, a deer leans down and lowers its face to drink – the river is glaring and drips gold and fractured white in the low sun. The scene seems idyllic, composed well with a mill wheel in the background, the gentle silt slopes and the woodland behind teeming, hissing with wildlife.

And, curious now, the deer lifts its head, turns its neck to listen. Ears fanned on alert. It blinks. And then it bolts, darts along the path, splashes through a shallow golden crossing and disappears from sight. Leaves shiver. Like the fleeing birds, it heard the man approaching.

Sam, with Isabelle's Post-it note still in his pocket, parked the black Mercedes about two hundred metres from Diane Marston's home. Then he travelled on foot up the village river which, according to the map on his mobile, ran along the rear of the property. He moved fast, running, then jogging – it would be a matter of minutes before police arrived on her doorstep to tell her that, they regretted to say, two of her brothers were dead. Henry Senior cut down by inexplicable fire that rose up through the ground at his feet, as though from hell. And Gregory, executed at point-blank range amid swaying petals and futile repentance. Though Sam doubted they'd add his embellishments.

This would come in the fresh wake of her nephew's suicide. Sam pictured Henry Junior's second fall – wheeling to the terrace railing at Hallowfield General Hospital, ignoring the pain. Then, using only his upper body, pulling himself high like a gymnast, tilting over the edge and rolling, falling, spinning limp and fast and smashing into the tarmac – a sudden blur, a shadow, then crack. Onlookers would have screamed. It was a bad day for the Marston family.

Halfway down the river, Sam passed an old shack with a wooden mill wheel propped on the side. The slats along the bottom were all broken so, instead of turning, it rested in the water and welcomed crawling plant life. Nearby, up the sandy bank, there was a chain-link fence between him and an electrical substation – humming wire and steel, and weeds in the cracked concrete – a jarring throng of metal in this otherwise unspoiled countryside. And, on the corner of the closest outbuilding, Sam noticed a security camera filming across the river. He looked directly into the lens. This footage of him stained, dishevelled, here, now, reborn, heading towards Diane Marston's house – it would be evidence. Perhaps shown to a jury, or narrated by a coroner. Invariably, Sam would not be there to hear the charges.

He knew that to pass judgement on the coming events, you would first need to understand, in the haze of all this chaos, that the Marstons and the Clarkes were connected in some way. And there – the inner slice of a Venn diagram Sam did not yet understand, in which the disparate lives of these two families crossed over – was where he needed to be. That was where the truth was hiding, coiled and snug in its nest.

Sam had to beat the police. Today, and tomorrow. The deadline was approaching. They could only hold Francis for a few more hours. First thing in the morning, they'd charge him. A stark, official symbol of Sam's defeat, hanging above like a hammer – falling now to drive the final nail into Robin's coffin.

A strike to end it all. These inevitable, fragile, familiar things.

Hallowfield General would be busier than usual – all sorts of activity could go unwitnessed. He had called Lei on the way here, and asked about the officers by Freddie's bed. Perhaps, he suggested, there should be a few more. To keep him safe, just in case. To protect him from the creatures Sam lied about when, years ago, Freddie would wake in the night, convinced something was breathing cold air outside his window, nesting in his wardrobe or scurrying beneath the floorboards. *They don't exist, kid – these monsters aren't real. Go back to sleep.*

But Sam had seen them – he'd seen the work of beings best killed with lies. And he felt compassion for most – even for premeditation, even for perpetrators reasonably classed as evil. Could these people have changed their course? If the universe rewound and they found themselves in the same position again, atom for atom, is there any reason to think they could have done things differently?

Somehow, he even applied this cold determinism to the Marston brothers. He didn't hate them for what they did to Freddie, or what they might yet wish to do. It was raw necessity driving him that afternoon, not anger, not the retributive glee he had tasted when he strode, mouth open, through that warm shower of black blood. He was as much a victim of this violence as they were.

Really, nothing had changed. All this had done was add yet more urgency to Sam's seemingly limitless supply of desperation. The goal remained the same. He was heading in precisely the same direction he had been for all these years, just faster now with the unique momentum of death at his sails.

The river took a turn to the right and washed down some rocky steps – froth and bubbles spun in the top pool before gravity dragged it all over the edge. Below, it splashed and rumbled like thunder. Sam felt it in his chest. One small tributary, a shallow golden gloss over sand, led the way. Sam followed it up to a mossy, damp wall at the rear of Diane's property. The water bled from a clay hole, leaving green streaked algae down the bricks. He placed the gun on top, then hoisted himself up.

Standing now at the foot of her garden, Sam looked at the mansion ahead. The grounds were tidy and preened – the turf fit for a golf course. An expensive croquet lawn with perfect borders, warm in the sunlight. He went across the grass, trespassing, stalking towards the house. Instead of a plan, he had focused only on results. All he knew was that he would be leaving this place with Freddie's and Abigail's guaranteed safety, and the scarred man's identity too. Exactly how he was going to achieve this was still unclear.

Now against the building, he ran, bent at the waist, past a trellis, along the plain rendered walls. The rough surface brushed the shoulder padding on Henry's blazer as Sam rounded a corner, ducking out of the late-afternoon sun. At the back door, he reached up, pulled the handle down and eased it open.

Gun low, he crept in through a porch area, along a row of hooks, past waxed coats and boots, stepping heel first, keeping his torso steady, as though moving on tracks. An open door. He saw a kitchen. Rural in design, like a farmhouse. Blue-and-white porcelain on a shelf, terracotta tiling and a bunch of garlic bulbs hanging over the windowsill. Smelled like mud, and steam.

A kettle began to whistle on the hob as Sam took a single stride towards the doorway, then froze.

'Give 'em another call.' A voice, now a person. A slim man with Gregory's features walked across the kitchen. Max Marston, the final brother, faced the window. He was wearing combat trousers, laced leather boots and a white vest. A long rat-tail at the top of his spine was plaited so tight it reminded Sam of a dressage mane – glossy bulges, packed hair woven into a black rope. Aside from the scalp feeding this, Max was bald. The pale skin on his shoulders and neck was laden with a collage of dark tattoos – lines of scripture, a snake fighting a lion, triple six below the horsehair and, running above his ear, the words 'Trust no bitch' in a calligraphic font. Most notable, however, was his physique. Max Marston was extremely underweight – his clothes just rags, his flesh little more than bone.

'I said, I *said* I should have gone,' he shouted.

'You're a liability,' a female voice called back from another room.

Shaking his head, Max took a mug from the cupboard and pulled a handle below the worktop – the cutlery drawer slid to the end of its runners. He stopped. Reflected in the chrome kettle, Sam saw a pointed beard, flicked moustache and eyes that narrowed, suspecting something wasn't quite right.

As the whistling continued to rise, Max turned and looked Sam directly in the eye.

'If you'd gone you'd have ended up doing something really . . . *stupid*,' Diane whispered the last word, appearing in a doorway.

She seemed suitably alarmed by the pistol in Sam's hand. But Max was nonchalant, leaning now on the kitchen worktop, tapping a cigarette packet.

'Easy . . .' Diane said, showing her palms.

Max lit a match, then mumbled, the filter tip bouncing in his mouth as he spoke. 'How's your kid?' He took a drag, stoking the ember, then shook the flame out. 'See, me . . .' he pointed with two fingers, laughing through smoke '. . . I'd be mad about that. Hopping mad.'

Without even looking, Sam lifted his arm and fired the gun. There was a harsh thudding sound, a hollow thump, followed by

Max falling sideways across the open cutlery drawer, snapping it, sending knives and forks clattering, spinning across the tiles. He grabbed his shoulder and gasped, trying to get to his knees.

Diane was reaching for something.

'*No*,' Sam said, drawing his aim back to her. She held her hands up.

'What is it you want?' she asked, removing her yellow-tinted glasses, folding the stems and sliding them into her top pocket.

The million-dollar question. 'Give, me, the, name,' Sam said. 'I want this to end. I want no more violence.'

'Ah, fucking hell. You're going about it in a funny way.' Max shuffled to a sitting position on the ground and retrieved his cigarette. He smoked with his uninjured arm. The tattoos on his biceps were glazed now with blood.

Frowning, Diane seemed to realise something. 'Where are Henry and Gregory?' she asked, eyeing the blazer.

'I'm sorry. Your brothers are dead.'

She sighed.

But Max dropped the cigarette and clambered back to his feet, slipping once, holding the counter for balance. His eyes were lined with tears. His hand firm on the wound. The three of them stood and stared – all taking stock of the situation. Of what it meant. Of what would happen next.

'Stop,' Diane said, glancing between them. The peacekeeper. 'No one else needs to get hurt.'

'Is that true?' Sam asked, looking at Max.

He turned to his sister, who appealed to him for caution, diplomacy, maybe even deception. But Max just smiled and shook his head.

'No,' he said, speaking only to Sam. There was common ground here. An unspoken understanding. 'I'm afraid not.'

Crossing herself, Diane began a murmured prayer – a panicked, quick appeal to anyone who might be listening. 'In the name of the Father, and the Son . . .' she whispered. 'As it was in the beginning, is now, and shall ever be . . .'

'Thank you,' Sam said. *See*, he thought, *honesty always guides the way.* Even complicated problems have simple solutions when cast in radiant, glorious truth. Here, on Max's face, was every justification he needed.

Sam aimed the pistol at his head. Max, still smiling, closed his eyes. There was a liberating sense of letting go. Sam thought about that night he'd wandered alone to the roadworks, to the half-built shopping mall, up and up the spiralled ramp, down and down this troublesome path. Drunk on corrosive frustration, on empty mystery and impending defeat. The unfortunate inevitability of all this mayhem, this senseless journey – it all led here.

Sam, falling now, finally embraced the rising void. And, as the kettle hissed and screamed and rattled, as steam rolled and curled on the ceiling, as the mumbled prayer came to an end, he squeezed the trigger.

Click.

There was an awkward pause. Max looking down, his brow lifting in excitement, his eyes wide.

The gun had jammed.

'Uh-oh,' he said, gripping a knife from the counter, coming forwards.

Wrestling with the slide, clearing the lodged round, Sam stepped away, stopping against a wall. Max lunging, stabbing. The bullet pinged free, spinning, and they grabbed each other's wrists. Pinned now, Sam felt a knee come up and, as he blocked it, heard a loud sound to his right. Spray. Something wet on his face, blinding him with quick heat – his eyes burning, yelling in agony. It was in his nose, his sinuses – sudden fire. He blinked – took a look at the room, a snapshot. Max moving to the left. The gun went off – a crack. Another photo. Max gone. More mace. A long, direct spray across his ear, his hands – turning, he took a lungful and spun, fired again. Coughing, wheezing, dark and desperate as something hit his leg. One more picture – the last he could take – and the pepper spray caught his open eyes. Somehow disarmed, Sam was shoved to the ground on all fours. A hard strike smashed his teeth together, filled his mouth with the tang of iron and sent him flat on his front. The kettle whistled, howling above him.

'They say it leaves the whole world blind,' Max said, as he pressed a knee into Sam's back and drove something sharp down into his shoulder. He shouted as the knife tip touched the tiles below him.

And then helpless, dazed and lost, Sam felt a tug on his hair. His head lifted, pulled back, exposing his neck.

Cold steel on his throat and—

'Stop,' Diane said. 'Don't do it in here.'

'Why not?'

Sam rolled, bucking the weight off his body. Then he crawled, his hands slipping, squeaking on the floor.

'The police will arrive soon. They will talk to us. Clean this up.'

'Where shall we take him?'

'Take him home.'

Sam's eyes were scrunched shut as he patted the ground. He only felt cutlery, forks, knives, scraping metal.

'Not even close,' Max said.

A final thud, the kettle whispered silence and Sam's remaining senses fell away.

Chapter 37

Shortly after Sam's eighth birthday, his father seemed to lose the knack for successful grant applications. Marine research was never an easy sell but, during the 1970s, when money was tight across the board, counting fish and seabirds became an academic luxury few organisations were willing to fund. They sailed back to the UK, and stepped off the *Coriolis* for the final time. Sam remembered that day clearly. It was foggy, cold – gulls just shadows circling in the mist. He stood on the stone harbour wall and waved to the ship he'd called home for so many years – a farewell to the very ground that held his first memory. His life began, just as it would end, at sea.

Following their parents, he and his brother turned and walked across the port car park, to start their new days on dry land. A normal school, static and dull, awaited them. No more dark nights, no more infinite skies, no more nocturnal adventures to the stern railing to see endless stars above and below.

Later, when he was well into his twenties, he asked his father whatever happened to that big red hunk of floating metal.

The *Coriolis* had begun its life as a cargo ship. It was an old vessel, well past its best and had always been destined for scrap. Their time aboard was borrowed. So, it was retired, and docked for months, rusting and abandoned. In the end, it fell into the Navy's hands. A tugboat dragged it out to sea, and left it at a suitable range for weapons testing. Sam had pictured an operations room. He'd seen the image as old footage – men, naval officers in uniform, standing in a line at a console of buttons, levers and spinning radar lines. Ahead of them, through the glass, perhaps a mile away, a maroon ship, small and vulnerable, out on the open water. They'd have watched through binoculars. A radio would crackle with voices. And then a roar of fire nearby, a long plume of arched smoke and, a few seconds later, a silent grey explosion on the starboard side, rocking the target – white spray raining as the sound arrived. The stern sinking, tilting the whole thing on a flooded axis. Within two minutes, waves and bubbles and nothing.

The *Coriolis* was deep underwater, resting on the sand – somewhere without light. Full of new life now. Sam imagined it caked in coral, marine algae and seagrass. Perhaps lit from time to time by curious undiscovered creatures that glow and swim through the narrow metal corridors, darting for plankton around his old bedroom, sending shadows lurching up the brown walls.

He remembered the free-diving nomads they saw in the Andaman Sea. The Moken people. They'd lived on the ocean for countless generations. They could hold their breath for minutes at a time, descend to the depths, and help themselves to all the fish they'd ever need. Sam, perhaps five years old, had played with the children on a beach, somewhere in the Mergui Archipelago. White sand, hot enough to hurt your feet, sting your eyes. He'd swapped a bottle cap for a perfect, spiked shell the size of his fist. He had thought it was a good deal, until he saw hundreds of similar shells littered all over the rocks nearby. But he didn't care. Another man's treasure.

His father told him the Moken tribes have always had unlimited food beneath them. Their lifestyle had been so successful, for so many years, that, in their language, they did not have a word for 'worry'.

Sam dreamed of one of those tanned children, lying in his rusted bedroom, underwater, flicking that bottle cap with his thumb and watching it spin and sink down into his hand, dancing like an autumn leaf.

They have no word for worry, he thought, as he felt the need for air. *He* was holding the bottle cap now, swimming, kicking for the surface, desperately hoping he'd make it up in time.

No word for worry.

And he was awake.

The first thing Sam noticed was the taste of blood around his back teeth. He explored the damage with his tongue, and found at least three molars were missing. Grunting, he realised his jaw was broken too.

Finally, he opened his right eye, then pressed his palm into his left, wiping his sticky lashes clean. He flinched at the tender bruising around his socket. Although blurred and sore, his vision was working without too much pain. So, he reasoned, many hours had passed since he'd been pepper-sprayed.

Hanging above, he saw a human hand – it had lost all its colour. Grey flesh, trapped in cuffs, connected to a thick radiator. When he moved and the metal clattered, he discovered it belonged to him. Only one hand was cuffed though. But his other arm, thanks to his stabbed shoulder, felt virtually useless. It would go no higher than his head.

Cold stone – he was lying on the ground. Sitting up, grimacing through his injuries, his free hand lay limp across his lap as he looked around the room. He did not recognise this place.

It had a high ceiling, wooden beams bridged by cobwebs, sagged with dust. A single light bulb, without a shade, hung from a wire and lit the space. Shelves filled with clutter – tools, a car battery, a blue crate of old electronics. Three Hecate dolls faced the brick wall as though they'd misbehaved. To his right, directly opposite the radiator, he saw a pipe organ, half covered by a faded sheet. Near that, stained-glass windows, stacked up against the wall. Cardboard boxes – 'candles', 'cushions', 'plates' written on the sides in black marker – piled high between a desk and a long pew. Two grey lumps of granite, a broken headstone, had been slotted together to make a carved cross on the floor. These looked like rescued items from a derelict church, stored here by someone who'd rather not see them crumble.

'We used to raise so much hell in this house.' The voice made Sam twitch and turn. It was Diane, sitting on a foldable chair right behind him. 'When we were children, they called us the Four Horsemen of the Apocalypse.' She laughed, then sighed. Craning his neck, he shuffled round to face her. 'I would say, but Mother, I am a girl. And she would say, no, no Diane, *you* are Famine.'

Sam tugged on the handcuffs, inspecting the lock. Urgent now – he really was trapped.

'Funny, actually, to think about that,' Diane added. 'Henry and Gregory – young. Alive.'

Exhaling, Sam realised his struggle was pointless. He slouched against the radiator, his left arm hung at shoulder height. 'I'm sorry this had to happen,' he said, frowning at the dull ache in his ear.

'*Had* to happen?'

'Your brothers, they . . . they would have hurt my son again.'

'And that would have been unjust?'

Sam didn't respond. Instead, he checked his pockets and felt wild anxiety when he couldn't find his phone.

'It was a genuine offer, wasn't it?' he asked. 'You know who that man is.'

'I do.'

Rattling his wrist, Sam said, 'No harm in telling me now.'

One last brush with the truth.

He looked up at her as she pressed her hands into her knees, stood and stepped past him. 'Are you familiar with demonology?'

Sam rested his head on the cold metal. 'Diane, please.'

'It's all quite clear, should you read the text, Samuel.'

He laughed and coughed.

'What, might I ask, is your issue with piety?'

'I've got no problem with religion,' Sam said, watching her as she paced in front of him. 'You can wear the clothes, sing the hymns – maybe everyone *should* come together once a week, community is important. We're social beings after all. Lovely buildings. Beautiful music. Art. And Christmas, well, it was always a hit in my house. These stories, they're fine with me, Diane. I'll go all the way with you. Right up until you say it's true.'

Now she sniggered. 'I don't think you quite understand how faith works.'

'You ever watch cartoons with a kid? It's no less fun to know they're just . . . moving pictures. No less joy, no less value.'

'Here you are, solving humanity's greatest follies,' Diane said. 'I suppose you believe removing truth would negate all the ugly things you blame on doctrine? One simple adjustment – tweak the dial. Consider it fiction.'

'It'd certainly help.'

'But something powerful brought you to my home. Something related to conviction. What is it that drives you?'

Sam thought of hunger, survival, the existence bias that curses every living thing. Had the simple animal call to protect his own child, perpetuate his genes, drawn him to this situation? There aren't many obligations that so reliably unveil the dormant feral creature prepared to bite fingers and claw eyes. Or was it something above primal biology – was it:

'The truth?' he said.

'OK. Well, the *truth* is, yes, I do know him.' Diane spoke softly, flowed with grace, fluid, her limbs in constant motion – for her, this was a performance. 'The man is called Julius Jacob. You can tell, from the scars on his face, that he has seen hell in his time.'

She picked up one of the dolls, turned and came back. Holding it for Sam to see, she touched the charcoal, stroked the frayed cloth dress.

'It was Julius. It was his idea to burn their faces.' Diane inspected the hand-carved figure. 'Do you see? Like him, they have witnessed hell. Oh, they've looked into the fire . . .'

'He came to your sermons? He's a member of North Serpent?'

'No, no Samuel. No. He is a friend. More. He's like family.'

'Where is he?'

'Like me, he values privacy. He lives in . . . in a secluded place.'

'Where?'

She thought for a moment, then inhaled. 'You're right. What's the harm? Do you know Wrenwood Common?'

Sam nodded.

'Do you know who owns it?'

'You?'

'Yes.' She smiled. 'Western track, before the first sign, only house, you can't miss it. I used to live there myself.'

'You sold it to him?'

'I *gave* it to him.'

'Why?'

'Because I'm kind.'

'Kind enough to take these cuffs off?' Sam asked.

Diane crouched, the doll still in her fist. Close now, he saw her left eye was missing, replaced with what looked like a marble. No, it was a cataract – bleached blue. Her short black hair, parted to the side, reminded him of a headmaster. Strict. Formal. And her glasses, tinted yellow, were meant for a man – too big for her face.

'I would, but that may upset Max. He is exceptionally traumatised by what you've done. He loved his brothers.'

'This man, Julius, he might have something to do with Robin Clarke,' Sam said, deliberate, slow – as though explaining something to a child. 'A little girl.'

'*The Clarkes.*' Diane glanced to the ceiling and groaned. 'Everyone is obsessed. What is it about that family you people find so engrossing? Photogenic children? Is it that simple? I'm not an avid follower of such lowbrow news, but I recall seeing a picture of Mrs Clarke, then *Miss*, of course, on her wedding day. Big and pregnant. Perhaps it is God's will that their bastard son should disappear.'

'And their daughter?'

'Sinners are punished, Samuel. Who are we to question judgement? Have you thought that what happened to the Clarkes says more about Francis and Anna than it does about Ethan and Robin?'

Sam blinked. The headache was overshadowed by damage elsewhere in his body. Now he was aware of the hole in his shoulder – the stab wound sealed shut with a rolled bandage and duct tape. It was a crude dressing that pulled on his chest hair when he moved, but it worked – he had not bled to death. Sadly, he doubted the efforts to keep him alive were symptoms of compassion.

Diane stared at him. 'It drives you crazy, doesn't it? You'd give anything to know what happened to those children. Maybe you were close to an answer.'

'Do you know where they are?'

'If I did, do you think I would tell you?'

'I think you'd take pleasure in *not* telling me.'

'Quite possible. But unfortunately . . . I have no idea.' He believed her. Julius, then.

'Just . . .' He held his hand up. If he thought it would have helped, he might well have begged. 'You need to speak to the police.'

'I already have.'

She told him that, while he was unconscious, she and Max had given statements. They had been released without charge – they were, after all, relatives of murder victims. Officially, nothing more.

'Did you tell them about Julius?'

'No – you spoiled that deal, remember?'

Sam closed his eyes and let out something between a sigh and a whimper.

'Henry and Gregory were good men,' Diane said. 'Henry Junior was a good man. Me, I am a good woman. I have no doubt that we will be reunited in the kingdom of heaven. But Max? We've always had trouble with Max. In his youth, he would hurt our neighbours' pets. He would go for long walks and return with the ears and eyes of cats and horses and cows, sticky and wet in his pocket. Our parents thought he was a psychopath. But Max possesses a great deal of empathy, making him capable of cruelty you could scarcely imagine. And . . .' she tilted her head and tutted '. . . you've made him very, very angry.'

Diane stood – Sam checked the radiator, the brackets and bolts. 'And you're OK with this?' he asked. 'Will you be forgiven?'

'As you well know, the forces of hell have an advantage the righteous lack,' she said. 'Evil does not discriminate. Darkness corrupts darkness with just as much zeal as it corrupts light. As we ask of soldiers, to travel to distant lands and commit the gravest of sins. Why? For all we deem *good*. To sin, and condemn yourself.' She turned away. 'There can be no greater sacrifice than this.'

'If it helps you sleep . . .'

'People think, with all the suffering in the world, God must be unwilling, or unable, to intervene,' she said, walking to the shelves, her hands clasped behind her, the doll gripped at her waist. 'But it's so much worse than that, Samuel. The divinity that holds power here isn't apathetic, or inept, but hostile. *That* is the truth no one is brave enough to accept. But maybe you are.' Diane carefully placed the figure on a shelf, then rotated it so the finger was pointing at him. She turned back. 'Maybe that's why you chose the Devil. Maybe it seemed like the safest bet . . .'

And then she left, and Sam was alone.

This, Sam realised, was a garage. He turned and saw, behind him, through some shelves and boxes, that the back wall was a tall shutter door. A padlock bolted into the concrete floor kept it sealed shut, and faint, cold air whistled through the gap and crept along the ground. He felt it on his legs.

Opposite that, to his left, an open doorway. When he leaned out, away from the radiator, he could see a short flight of wooden stairs leading up to the main part of the house. It was difficult to judge the time. However, a narrow window high on the wall above the desk was blocked by something black enough to be night. Early morning, perhaps 2 a.m.

Crucially, this wasn't where he'd come yesterday. That much was obvious. This meant they had moved him while he was unconscious. Like the vague invasion you feel after anaesthesia, he did not like the idea of Max and Diane touching him, lifting him, dragging him into this place.

Sam thought again of Isabelle, and her warnings. She must have realised he'd encountered trouble. But when the remaining Marstons insisted they hadn't seen him, as he was sure they had, what conclusion would she draw? That he had changed his mind? Impossible to know. At any rate, he found little hope when he considered the world outside these walls.

He had another look at the handcuffs, turning his wrist, pulling on the chain. Then he twisted his body round, placed his feet flat on the bricks and drove back as hard as he could, yanking at the radiator. A deep metal clunk and groan above him – the plumbing aware of his plight as he went limp from exertion and pain.

'Fuck,' Sam whispered.

Footsteps. On the stairs. Max came down into the garage carrying a plastic bag – his arm in a sling, his shoulder dressed with better care than Sam's. At the desk, he spent a few minutes preparing a school-style chemistry set – a Bunsen burner, beakers with blackened bottoms, test tubes and various bottles of transparent liquid and white powder. When he moved, his long, plaited hair danced like a tail. Next, he took a large hunting knife, a wood saw and a hammer from the bag. Then he uncoiled a wire and plugged in a soldering iron. Sam could smell the heat, hear the electric squeal.

'You ever had a psychedelic experience?' Max asked, turning from the desk, swirling a small cup. He sniffed it, then shuddered.

Sam didn't respond.

'I heard you never lie.'

Again, Sam stayed quiet.

'What would you do, if I unlocked those cuffs?' Max reached into his back pocket and pulled out a set of keys.

'I'd rather not answer.'

'Something bad I bet.' Max pointed at him, waiting.

He couldn't disrespect the truth, not now. 'I'd probably kill you,' Sam whispered.

Smiling, Max came towards him, across the flat concrete, under the single, uncovered light bulb. His shadow, shrinking behind, passed beneath his feet, then stretched out long again, over Sam's lower half. Backlit now, he loomed tall – skeletal eye holes, loose cloth and laughter. There was something in his hand. A brown clump of matted fur.

'I believe you,' he said. 'And if we're being honest, I should probably explain what all this is. I'm a bit of an amateur chemist and I've . . . invented . . . is that the word? I've made, mixed, created this . . . stuff. Basically, it starts with LSD – just off the street. Pretty strong. Then there's some uppers to get your heart rate going, and a sort of mellow punch in the middle to keep you ultra-sensitive. I've tried a tiny micro-dose and I can tell you, fuck, it was *not* very nice. It's going to be a hell of a ride . . .' Max squatted and turned into the light. 'You ever read about witches?'

The object he was clutching, Sam saw, was a dead rat. With a quick slice, he made a hole in its belly fur and poured blood on to his hand. Max then wiped his nose, sniffed and rubbed the liquid into his face, ensuring it went in his mouth and eyes. Alarmed and frowning, Sam stayed silent.

'The sort of shit they did to people possessed by demons – Diane loves all that,' he said, waving the limp rodent as he spoke. Heavy raindrops fell on Sam's trousers – grey innards dangling out like a bundle of newborn worms. 'It's fucking weird, right. They drowned them and burned them and shoved things, you know, up them.' Max lifted his index finger and curled his lip. 'But there's some shit they did in Europe in, I don't know, the past. A long time ago. It's all based on hooves and claws.' He shuffled, crouched closer – his cheekbones glistening whenever the yellow bulb caught the rat blood on his skin. Max spoke fast, fidgety, and Sam suspected he was not sober. 'Works like this,' he said, flinging the small corpse away. 'They'd put tourniquets on your legs and arms, then remove your hands and feet. Then, from about here . . .' he touched his own chin, in the centre of his pointed beard 'to about *here* . . .' and pressed his fingers into the back of his head, near his plait 'they'd peel all the skin. Chop off the hooves, the claws, then unmask the beast. Symbolic. You get it, right?'

Sam searched around the floor nearby, his heart gaining pace. Nothing in reach.

'No eyelids at this point, so the eyes would get pretty sore,' Max went on. 'But they got rid of them too. Pop. Pop. Ah, oh no. You're thinking – without eyes, they wouldn't be able to see. Remember the drugs though – *extremely* vivid hallucinations. You will see plenty. Then they'd do some old-fashioned stuff – bit of boiling water, funnels, pliers – the usual.' He reached out, placed his hand on Sam's knee and sighed. 'But, after all that, I'm sorry to say . . . it got really, really nasty.'

Max pushed himself upright and wandered over to the organ.

'Look at all this. Diane actually collects this shit,' he said, pulling the sheet off. He pressed a key – the note was loud. 'Any requests?'

Sam ignored him.

After a bit more chemistry, Max took his phone from his pocket and propped it on the desk, ensuring the lens was facing across the garage.

'Do you mind if I film this?' he asked. 'I promise I won't share it. Private use only.'

Then, turning on his foot, Max strolled back. In his right hand he held the knife and, in his left, a ball of cotton wool. Sam's attention was on the blade – he considered his range and the odds of success if he tried to snatch it. If that opportunity arose, he'd only have one attempt. But he could barely lift his free arm.

Again, Max squatted next to him and threw his long plait over his shoulder. 'And I want you to think hard, when you're here, blind, bleeding, tripping your fucking tits off, about all your regrets . . . Now. Open your mouth.'

When Sam leaned away, Max tutted, pinned Sam's free hand on the ground with a knee and put the point of the knife against the bridge of his nose, just below his eye.

'OK, if you—'

He thumbed the wet cotton wool into Sam's mouth. Although he kept his jaw clamped, Sam tasted the rat, and the salt, as the harsh, cold chemicals rubbed his cheek lining, seeping between his teeth.

'Ah, ah, there— Jesus, hold still.'

Grunting, Sam tried again to pull away, but felt the metal slide up, now touching his lower eyelashes. He looked down, only the handle was in focus – the rest was a silver blur.

'There we go, yummy medicine.'

After about thirty seconds, Max released his grip and stood. Choking on the wet fibres, Sam used his tongue to push it to the front of his mouth. It slapped on to the concrete when he spat. But it was obviously too late.

'Should be feeling something within twenty minutes, half an hour,' Max said. 'Then we'll crack on.'

The drugs were like cleaning fluid – the vapour rough on his throat. Sam swallowed and gagged as something tickled his cheek – he wiped a sticky tear and saw that his fingers were red.

'Can . . . can I have some water?' he croaked.

'This isn't a hotel.' Max turned away. 'Or, yes, maybe not a bad idea.' He spun back and pointed. 'Stay hydrated. Good thinking.'

In the corner of the garage, he emptied a glass jar, pouring out nails and screws. Then he filled it with water at a filthy sink. The plumbing clanked again. The jar was dripping when he returned.

'I've always had this ache, here,' Max said, touching his chest, handing Sam the drink. 'The only time it ever eased was when I was with my brothers. I . . . well . . .' And then he began to breathe faster and faster, and finally started to cry, cupping his face – his tears cleaning the blood away. 'I don't think I can handle it . . . When you see them, can you . . . tell them I'm sorry? And that I love them.'

'Doing this won't make you feel better.'

'Oh dear . . . Sam.' He sniffed, composed himself. 'Oh dear. You don't know me at all.'

Max left the room, his feet heavy on the wooden stairs.

The jar felt greasy – an old label half torn off, leaving a layer of furred paper and black glue. Sam's hand was shaking, spilling the murky liquid as he sipped. Somehow, he managed to finish it.

For a few seconds he sat in silence and considered the coming hours of his life. *No*, he thought, blinking – whatever happened, however this played out, his role would not be passive. He would reclaim control. And there was only one way.

Sam held the jar by the base and tapped it against the concrete. It cracked. A second try shattered it into four big shards and countless hairline splinters. He took the largest triangle of glass, which had a thick, curved rim as a handle, and passed it up to his cuffed fingers. Holding it carefully, he lifted himself to a seated position.

Then he turned his free arm over and exposed his wrist. This was it. The shock and pain and adrenaline leaving him with no other choice but quick, decisive action. *Don't hesitate*, he thought – *don't let doubt seep in and trick you. Just stop. Stop falling for it – stop believing that existing is always preferable to not. Fuck these biochemical lies – fuck the disapproving rage of every single one of your billion ancestors who, from microbe to ape, survived to give you this infinitely unlikely gift, this inevitable curse. Grand thoughts for grand decisions.*

A few junkie slaps with his trapped hand got the tubes bulging. He found a large blue vein beneath his skin. *The* large blue vein. *No word for worry*, he thought, as he pressed the glass into his flesh. He took a deep breath, which juddered at the end.

As he drained, Sam lay on his side, turned his wrist to the floor and saw the pool spread and spread. It was so still – no ripples, just a perfect circle expanding on the concrete. A red mirror. An eye. The uncovered bulb above buzzing in the centre, like an iris made of fire, the reflected glare from some great thing he did not believe in, watching him, judging him.

Now, all he had to do was wait.

Chapter 38

We see the man, lying on the ground, handcuffed and resting. Peaceful now. His eyes are closed. The shard he used to cut himself set at the edge of a large red puddle. Max's phone films the garage, shows us this bleak picture. And everything is still.

We hear slow footsteps and gentle humming. But then silence.

'Ah, shit,' Max says, walking into view. 'Diane,' he yells. While he waits, he moves towards the camera – there's clattering as he leans over the lens and, when he steps away, he's lighting a cigarette.

Diane appears on the right-hand side of the frame, in the doorway, and sees what we see. She seems genuinely surprised.

'Gave him some water . . . glass jar. I'm too nice.'

'I must say, I never had him down as a coward.'

'I don't know.' Max sighs. 'I probably would have done the same in his shoes.' He goes to the back of the room, squats next to the man and holds a hand above his mouth. Then, looking over his shoulder, he gestures around the floor. 'Good few pints here.' Max stands and kicks the body. The head is limp as it lolls. 'This fucker's dead.'

'Clean it up then,' Diane says.

Holding the filter tip with his thumb and middle finger, Max takes a final drag from his cigarette, then drops it on to the man's chest. It burns on his T-shirt.

'Were you . . . ?' Diane squints right at the camera. 'Were you filming *this? For goodness' sake, Max.'*

'Go get some sponges and a bucket,' he says, as he returns to the desk. Keys jingle in his hand. 'And be more.'

The tobacco ember smoulders – a thin wisp of smoke rising and curling from the man's sternum, like steam from a winter bullet wound.

Diane's feet thud on the five wooden steps leading up into the house, and she's gone.

'I'm disappointed, Sam,' Max says, strolling towards the radiator, beneath the uncovered light bulb – his shadow long and short and long again. 'You just couldn't resist, could you?'

Avoiding the blood, he kneels and slides the cuffs to one side – they clack along the thick metal. He puts the key in the lock. But, before he turns it, Max hesitates. He throws his long ponytail over his shoulder and moves two fingers on to the man's throat, to check for a pulse. Better safe, he's probably thinking, than sorry.

Sam, young and serene aboard the *Coriolis*. He watched as fire roared in the centre of the deck – distorted groans and agony from the hot steel. But he stood on the bridge and, instead of pain, allowed himself to enjoy the late-night horizon beyond the flames – where lightning flashed stark and vivid across the sudden skyline, orbs of midday sun, diamonds in the sea spray. And out there he saw an island, black rock peaks jutting out of the still water – somewhere unearthly, uncharted land made of stone and mist and hope.

Robin had bled. Whether she was taken, murdered, used as a pawn in a complex scheme to frame an innocent man – the reality was, that precious liquid had changed fates. Sam was still quite sure Francis was no murderer, and yet – those microscopic specks had convinced the world otherwise. Blood is a powerful thing to see.

The incision he'd made in his wrist was a puncture rather than a slit. It allowed him to drain approximately three pints – however, he'd timed it slightly wrong and cut a little too deep, so guessed it was closer to four. These clocks were ticking. His plan hinged on perception – it had to look like he'd lost a fatal amount of himself. As for the bottom of the jar, the crown of deadly shards, he'd kept that hidden beneath his right knee. Holding his breath like those worriless free-divers was no issue, nor was his tolerance for fire, but if Max decided to check his heart before undoing the cuffs, Sam would have to adapt. He would have to innovate.

'*Are* you dead?' the voice whispered in the darkness, from the horizon, and two warm fingers arrived on his neck.

The flames still burned as Sam returned to the room. And, when he took his first breath, he looked up to see a startled face – the purest shock, eyes wide and white. Always best to be honest.

'Yes,' he said.

Then, in one swift motion, he swung his free hand from beneath his knee and smashed that crown of glass hard into Max's throat. Clawing for the wound, spraying when he coughed, he turned and choked as Sam reached out, grabbed his hair and pulled him back through their blood. Still one-handed, he tried to strike the lodged glass, to finish the job, but Max sprawled and rolled away. Stretching, Sam threw a kick, and fell short, hearing the cuffs clatter on the radiator pipe. *The key*. It was still in the lock.

Manic, mad, dying, but moving, Max went to his knees, slipped and fell forwards.

Halfway to the desk, to the tools, beneath the light bulb. And rising now, swaying in the corner of Sam's vision, shouldering against a shelf unit, knocking things off. Fumbling with the key, Sam looked left, right, left, right – to the lock, to Max. At the desk, Max turning back – in one hand he held his neck and in the other a hammer.

The cuffs clicked open and released him. Up and three clumsy strides across the wet concrete as Max swung – forearm lifting to block, cracking and falling. Now on his knees, dizzy – Sam tried to stand, he tilted sideways, his shoulder going through the stack of stained-glass windows. Trying again, he reeled and saw a blur – a shadow disappearing through the doorway.

Floorboards creaked as Sam clambered to his feet and took stock of the damage – his left arm was broken. His right arm in no better state, still dripping. He held it above his head, then crushed the packet of cigarettes. With his thumb, he snapped off a couple of filters and pressed them into the wound. Then he grabbed a greasy rag and some duct tape. Using his teeth, Sam worked quickly, holding his wrist out and wrapping it up, staggering through the pain.

He checked the desk for a weapon, for anything, for—

The knife. Reaching for it, Sam stumbled again, crashing on to his front across the clutter, sweeping items from the table.

When he searched himself for strength, he found nothing but rapid nausea – an alien sense, something well beyond doom. He covered his mouth, gagged and tried to breathe. But the fractured stained glass on the floor was shifting in his peripheral vision – reds and yellows and blues swimming like living paint. Confronting the sight, staring it down, just made the colours boil and spit. And behind his eyelids, he discovered only horror – he saw himself back at the radiator, trapped in the cuffs. He looked again. An ambient throb to the world, to his skin. Darkness and he felt his memories recalled at once with total clarity. As clear as any present moment. As real as now.

This new power worked both ways – he could roll the dial forwards as well as backwards. He could close his eyes and shift, like a phantom, an ethereal hologram of himself – returning to the set past or venturing into the equally immutable future.

Max would have the gun by now.

Looking again, Sam was on the desk, smashing the glass out of the narrow black window with the knife handle. He hoisted himself up and rested his stomach on the frame. Face down, he placed his hands on the bricks and shuffled through, falling head first on to the grass outside.

Crawling prone, he winced on his elbows – his shoulder filled with gristle, his jaw and arm aching. Swollen, hot. He was quite sure his ulna was shattered. But his hand wasn't wilting, which meant his radius was intact. Detached from his injuries now – the confusion seemed to come in waves, each growing taller and fiercer. *Drugs. Fuck. Were there drugs?*

Sam was boxed in by a small courtyard. The only way out was through the building. Back inside.

On his feet, he jogged down the side of the Marston family home, round to the courtyard patio. It was dark – late at night or early morning. And he could hear a sound, like an air-raid siren, coming from the woods. But the echo was all wrong – it was real, but not real *now*. Perhaps it was something bleeding back down the timeline a warning from the future. A dread call from the chaos. He turned his eyes to the stars and saw a crackling howl – fast raindrops in headlights.

Curious about the outcome, he ventured forwards and watched himself grab the patio door handle, slide it open on its runners and—

'Let me out,' a female voice yelled. Sam rolled around the wall and stood outside.

Diane was muffled, locked somewhere. Hidden away safely while her noble brother dealt with the monster in the garage. But it was in the courtyard garden now, coming through the side entrance.

Inside again. An open-plan living room. It was like a building site – ongoing renovations, fluttering plastic on some of the windows, holes in half the walls. Mostly, Sam was astonished by the sheer scale of the place – it was easily a mile in width, stretched to the impossible proportions of an early dream.

There, a hundred feet tall, Max was in the kitchen, walking with purpose across the tiles. In one hand he held Sam's pistol and in the other a red-stained towel, pressed into his neck. Flat on the ground, ducking behind the sofa, Sam peered over the arm. The fabric pattern thrummed on his fingertips – gravity pushing the shapes down an infinite fractal descent, somewhere he could easily fall if he were to slip.

He went quick and quiet into the kitchen, staying low against the counter, held there by the swelling tides and storm waves now splashing at the black windows, throwing him left and right, up and down and in unthinkable directions. New dimensions defying the confines of mere vibration and language.

Lost again in a memory. Gone and searching and the siren was a fire alarm. It made sense. Red bulbs were spinning somewhere on a wall. Confused, he touched a man's chest and found the blaze – now just a small burn in cotton, a white blister beneath. A body. He centred himself into it. And the room was still. And the man was moving again through the hall, towards the garage staircase.

Waiting there, facing away, something like Max Marston was armed – his tail curled like a windswept ribbon. If Sam approached slowly, he would turn and get a clear shot. And if Sam approached quickly, he would turn and get a poor shot.

No further consideration needed, Sam took a breath and went sprinting, diving knife first towards the creature, which spun and made two cracking sounds. Sparks flew from his hip as they both fell down the narrow stairwell, thudding back into that red garage.

The knife and gun bounced and skidded across the concrete. Crawling, Max arrived at the pipe organ, clambered up on to his knees and rested on the stool. Then, dazed, he leaned down for the blade.

But it was gone.

Strong and calm, Sam coiled the rat-tail once around his own hand and twice around Max's neck. Panicked, struggling for air, Max drove back to his feet and, somehow, managed to grab Sam's forearm, sending an electric shock of sharp pain through his entire body. Sam let go, slid to one knee.

But, as Max turned, Sam rose again, seized him by his wet throat and pinned him against the organ – creating a long, lingering rendition of every note. Feeble fingers slipped off Sam's face as he squeezed, showing teeth, holding eye contact, yelling now.

'St . . .' Max groaned. 'St . . . st . . . op.'

A revelation. For reasons he didn't understand, Sam obeyed. He loosened his grip and placed his left hand gently on Max's chest to feel his glowing heart. Both panting, both injured, they shared a peaceful moment – an unspoken truce. There was the most incredible sense of connection, as though their lives transcended time and petty disputes, and all there was, and would ever be, was this light, this love. This intimate, tranquil camaraderie. Two sentient beings here, now, forever.

He cupped Max's cheek and smiled.

Without a doubt, it was the most beautiful thing he had ever seen.

'Goodbye, Max,' he whispered.

And then, with abattoir efficiency, Sam slammed the knife through his temple.

Like dropped rags, Max slumped down, on to the organ's keyboard – the dead weight producing a sudden jarring sound – a toddler's symphony, echoing through the entire house.

Cleansed now, rich and fine, Sam turned, stumbled and ascended the wooden steps, gliding up with the noise, lifted by the bold cathedral song. Upstairs, he passed through the gigantic open-plan kitchen and to a carpeted staircase, following the *thud, thud, thud* of another heart aboard this sinking ship.

At the far end of the second-floor corridor, Sam found a closed door. The runner rug at his feet was perfectly black, a digital streak, devoid of all texture. His boots were silent. All he could feel was that yelling from behind the wood.

'Let me out, Max, let me out, let me out, let me out.'

But Max is dead, Sam thought.

'What?'

He touched his mouth. *I stabbed him. Listen. We can hear his music.*

Diane carried on shouting as Sam knelt and breathed. He found some more clarity by squeezing his arm and looking at his long, shimmering hand – it was being sucked away. This madness had to stop. Who were these poor people? What possible justification could there be for all this carnage and senseless death? *You can hear him. He's trying to save your soul, Samuel. Listen to what he says. The answer will guide you.*

Just kill her.

Sighing, Sam lifted the gun, pressed it against the door and fired two shots into the wood.

Diane was spread out on the floor when he entered the room.

'This is not a battle I can win,' she said. 'I know that.'

Without looking, he sent three more rounds into the tiles, but it kept talking. Accusing him. Nothing it said was unreasonable. Something that came crawling out of the earth – a foul perversion of all moral balance.

Stepping over the rambling flesh, he found a medicine cupboard. Pulsing, swaying, singing pills – *pass out, pass out* – he squinted at the packet. The air-raid organ still coming from the walls. Found the letters b, e, n, z, *orange* and pushed three, four, into his red hand and threw them into his broken mouth.

He turned and fell back down that red graphic, blue, black, bitter and harsh and calling out and sputtering, now it covered every piece of the house. The kitchen. There he bit the lid off a bottle of vodka and poured half of it down his open throat. It stung his cheek, some of it dribbling. The voice told him to pass out, he thought, as he tried again. He coughed and threw it away into the water. His skin buzzed as all his hearts thumped in the bricks of his body and neck and his flesh became the eternal, wordless void.

Then, the ground gave way and he splashed into cold liquid. He swam to a piece of floating debris – a fragmented lump of wrecked ship. It was hard to get his leg on to it, but once he did he knew he was safe. Stranded out there, Sam spent more than a thousand years lost at sea – he went with the tides, passing around the globe. Relative to the spinning planet, he was totally still. All motion passed beneath him. And the clawing beasts, horned and tailed and fire-eyed, lurched from any shadow. But every single one scurried away in terror whenever he approached.

Of all those endless centuries, alone on that hopeless craft, he could only remember a single dream. It was about a woman called Isabelle. She told him she could take him wherever he wanted to go. But, when he answered, his voice was silent – no matter how loud he screamed.

Chapter 39

Somewhere in the story, there was a lake. Sam could hear it. The first thing he saw was the silt and packed rocks, rippling beneath the clear, shallow water. A single blot of red, like ink from a dropper bottle, fell down – a quiet plop. It flowed deeper, turning to a long wisp of colour as it dissolved. An inverted mushroom cloud. Seeping from the duct-tape dressing on his forearm, which hung straight beneath him, he watched a clean track of blood read his palm – it spiralled round his index finger, then grouped on the tip for intermittent drip . . . drip . . . drips, like a leaking tap.

He was lying on his front, on a jetty, on the lake – old timber as worn as driftwood. Rolling over, he looked up at the empty sky. It was dawn. With a great deal of effort, Sam clambered to his feet and stood at the edge. Below, a half-sunken boat, still tied, bumped every now and then against the vertical beam. And ahead, fog and trees around the borders, inversed in the fresh water – perfect mimics of themselves shimmering, as cold and grey as the morning above.

Sam shivered and hugged himself. 'Ah.' He twitched.

His left arm shook uncontrollably, like a crippled dog's leg, buckled, locked in place against his chest. Vibrations aside, he realised he couldn't move it. And his hip – he used his other thumb to pull his belt aside as—

Fresh warmth pumped from a hole and poured quickly down his thigh, running through the heavy planks at his feet. He gagged and tightened the buckle another notch. When he flexed his jaw, he realised he was deaf in his left ear. It felt permanent. Some wounds he could remember, others were a mystery – hangover bumps best left forgotten. But, as always, if he traced the blame he found himself, hands sticky with regret.

Bound for land, he limped along the jetty, swaying, stepping cautiously over missing slats. To his right, at the end of a wide mudflat, he saw a craggy cliff. A zigzag slope led down the rocks from the woodland above and a few sheets of corrugated iron and scaffold boards made a walkway to what looked like a cave. On the stone face, over the shaded entrance, soot stains from a campfire. The nook was impossible to access from the beach. Concealed. Discreet. A familiar thing.

Sam frowned and took a few paces across the sand, framing the jetty, the shoreline and a bare tree in his vision. Pale, twisted branches had been cut away, the remaining limbs left to resemble a crucifix. Although now new twigs sprouted from the ends, and the whole thing leaned towards the water. He had seen this image before. A photograph used as a banner on North Serpent's website. This all belonged to Diane Marston. No, it belonged to her next of kin.

He pushed on through some mulch woodland and up a steep footpath. At the top, he passed his legs over a fence, tripped and fell into the grass. Whimpering, he felt the morning dew seep through his clothes. Damp, and on his knees, he vomited – his spine arching, coughing out nothing but hot saliva. It took him almost a minute to get upright again.

Finally, following vague intuition through unpopulated countryside, he arrived at a house with a large garage on the front. The

Marston family home was silent now and filled, wall to wall, with cold hell.

It was, by some margin, the worst crime scene Sam had ever encountered. Max still slumped on the organ keyboard, his head bowed – around him, the concrete was painted, smeared, wet. And opposite, the rat seemed to claim Sam's blood. At the radiator, he unlocked the handcuffs and put them in his pocket. Upstairs, Diane was sitting in her bed, wrapped in blankets, equally lifeless. The disparity between what he could recall and what he saw was irrelevant – they were dead and he was alive – it was not his job to ask how or why. Where would you even begin?

On the living-room coffee table, he found his personal effects – all lined up. Like leaving a cell, he retrieved each item in turn. Mobile. Wallet. Pistol. A handful of change. Someone else's car keys. In the bathroom, he cleaned himself and strapped his broken arm with a makeshift sling. There was a long raincoat over the back of a chair in the kitchen. He put it on, and let the left sleeve dangle empty.

Outside again, on the driveway, Sam pressed the key fob and one of the cars – a blue saloon – blinked its lights at him. Before he started the engine, he used Max's phone to make a call.

'Nine-nine-nine emergency, which service do you require?'

'Police,' he said, and threw the mobile out of the car window. It bounced and landed face down on the shingle.

Generally, Sam was a rational man. When it came to the conflict between heart and mind, he typically dealt with the latter. But today, as every part of him that made sense screamed, yelled, begged him to go to hospital, he listened only to the ache caged in his ribs. *Go to Wrenwood Common. Go to Julius Jacob. Go to – God, anyone, please – the truth.*

The car was, thankfully, an automatic. But still he swerved, and lurched, and gripped the steering wheel like a lifeline at sea.

He leaned against the door, his head on the glass, nestled and tense. And somehow, Sam managed to drive.

As he did, he put his phone on loudspeaker and called Marilyn. He asked if Freddie was OK and she said he was fine – still sleeping. There were plenty of reasons to cry, but when she asked for his, he couldn't answer. Instead, he heard himself apologising, saying bold, incredible things – the nostalgia and sorrow of a man on his deathbed.

We see a petrol-station forecourt. A blue car arrives. The man climbs out, takes the pump and rests his head against the vehicle's roof while he fills the tank. Then he steps away, tries to hang it back up, but can't, so drops it on the ground. Fuel trickles out. He stumbles towards the door. Inside, store CCTV captures him shouldering shelf to shelf down an aisle, reaching into one for balance, sweeping crisps and nuts to the floor. At the fridge, he grabs a bottle of water, two energy drinks and slides them into his raincoat pocket.

'Are you all right, mate?' the clerk asks.

The man waves a hand and heads for the exit.

'Uh, you need to pay for that.'

Tripping again, he pulls his wallet out and simply drops it on the floor. 'Sorry.'

The door beeps as he leaves.

Driving now, Sam poured electrolytes and calories into himself – trying to draw another hour from this body. Despite the car's heating, he could not get warm. After a long, swerving journey, he turned into the western lane of Wrenwood Common, beneath dark evergreen trees – tall and straight with their own shaded climates. The track was tarmacked but covered in potholes, twigs and seeds. Not a council priority, he supposed, serving just one house. And that house – a trembling mirage in this shock, surreal and soft. Hardly there at all.

Pulling up, Sam switched the engine off and tilted sideways for his phone, to make his third call of the morning. He told Isabelle not to talk while he explained all the things he'd learned, all the things he'd killed, since he left her in that meadow. Could he still spin the dial and go back there? See the flowers. Smell the grass. Hear their deal. All his values for all of hers.

'Wait for us,' she said. 'Please.'

Looking through the car window, he sighed. 'Sorry,' he said. 'I just . . . I just can't.'

'Sam—'

But he hung up, opened the door and fell out on to the road. Back to his feet, he limped towards the house. The garden was overgrown, and Sam, almost at the front step now, found acute fear in the empty silence. A strange, dreadful certainty that he was in the wrong place. And it was too late.

The camera looks down on Julius in his security room, with his wall of monitors. He's asleep at the desk – forehead on his elbow. But, a sound, something bumps him awake. Leaning into the central screen, he sees that, like him, Robin has closed her eyes. And he stands.

She's snug, peaceful in her bed. When Julius enters and places a small tray on the carpet, she doesn't stir. He picks up a syringe and sits down on the mattress, by her side. And still, she sleeps. We see her rosy cheeks, flushed and warm, as he strokes a blonde curl from her face.

Tender, Julius takes her arm and pulls it on to his lap. He lifts the syringe and flicks it a few times to clear the bubbles.

Asking once more for forgiveness, he hopes aloud that she will be welcomed into the kingdom. Even if he himself has renounced such mercy. He tells us his soul is a small sacrifice to pay for hers.

'I am sorry,' he says.

Then he gently slips the needle into the crease of her elbow and whispers a sweet farewell. With his thumb on the plunger, he begins to press down. But, as though he's triggered it himself, time coalesces. A noise chiming from the walls and turning his head. It sounds like a doorbell. And it just won't stop ringing.

Sam, on the front step, noticed a camera on the doorframe. Reaching up, he used his thumb to carefully press a single print of blood over the lens. He checked his watch and tried the doorbell again and again. Still nothing. He retreated, looked up at the second-storey windows, which, like the others, were covered with metal bars. Strong enough to keep an intruder out, or a prisoner in. Certain he didn't have the strength to kick through the door, he pulled the pistol from his belt, rested against the frame and placed the barrel on the lock. But a shadow arrived. And the door opened.

The moment he saw that face, those scars, Sam stood straight and pointed the gun. A dim flash of adrenaline – his remaining blood doing its best.

'Turn around,' he said. 'Do it. Now.'

Julius did as he was told as Sam pressed the Glock into his back and walked him inside.

'Where is she?'

Tilting his head, Julius glanced upstairs.

So, Sam seized his collar, holding both the fabric and the gun's grip with his good hand, and pushed him forwards. 'Up,' he yelled. 'Go.'

Again, he forced Julius to walk – this time all the way to the second floor.

On the landing, Sam put him against the wall.

'Stay there, don't move. Don't you fucking move.'

To his left, a door with a latch lock. Stepping backwards, he kept the pistol on his target, who took a quick peep over his shoulder.

'No, face the wall.'

Sam leaned down and used his broken elbow to lift the small hook.

The door creaked open.

Julius stirred. 'She'll just . . . drift off . . . '

Slowly blinking, dreamy and real, Sam turned towards the room.

A sleepy child, standing in her pyjamas, was staring up at him.

For a moment, he couldn't speak. Robin eyed his wounds, the gun, the sheer state of him – her chin dimpled and quivered. Tears began to flow.

'Hey,' Sam said. 'It's OK.'

'Go back to bed – he's a bad man, don't—'

'Shut up – *face the wall.* Listen to me, Robin, listen. Run. Run downstairs and outside. Run down the road. Don't stop running until you see a police car.'

'I'm . . . I'm sorry,' she whispered. 'I . . .'

'It's fine, it's fine, it's all fine. Just, please, do what I say.'

'I . . . I . . .' She gestured to Julius, concerned about his well-being.

'*Do it,*' Sam yelled, loud enough to scare her.

She flinched, and something fell from her sleeve. A short, straight, silver object. Hesitating just once more, she went down the stairs, through the open door and disappeared.

'Get on the floor,' he said, after she was clear. 'On the fucking floor.' Shaking, Julius complied and sank to his knees. 'Hands.'

'You don't understand.'

In Robin's room, Sam saw a small tray poking out from under the bed. Two glass bottles, syringes, a needle.

'What were you doing? *What were you doing?*'

'You're making a mistake.'

'*Show me your hands.*'

Gradually, Julius passed both hands behind his back. Sam holstered the gun in his belt, then took the handcuffs from the raincoat pocket. He closed one ring around Julius's right wrist, pulled it towards the other and—

An elbow swung back into Sam's hip. It happened quickly – in one clean motion, Julius ducked, scrabbled across the floor and grabbed whatever Robin had dropped. It was sharp, like an ice pick. Sam reached for the pistol again as a clenched fist came up hard into the centre of his chest. Winded, he thought he'd been punched. But gasping, glaring, he looked down and staggered. The metal skewer had gone in deep through the cigarette burn – a bullseye.

'What *is* that?' Sam wondered, oddly calm in fresh shock, his good arm slack at his side. The pistol fell heavy on to the landing carpet between them.

They stood, face to face, and both seemed surprised. Before he could flee, Sam grasped Julius by the wrist.

'Get off me.'

But Sam wouldn't. He couldn't. Instead, he walked backwards, through the doorway – holding him the whole time. Now they were in the dark, gloomy room. It was warm in here. Smelled of fabric softener. Smelled like Robin.

Somewhere along the line, Julius had obtained the gun – he was pointing it at Sam's navel as their feet jostled. 'Get. Off. Me,' he said.

317

Staring into his eyes, Sam pulled them even closer together, into the raincoat, and used the last of his strength. A quiet clatter and then *click-click-click* – the remaining cuff ring closed on his own wrist. Now, they were connected. Now, neither of them was going anywhere.

'Your move,' Sam said.

'Get off, let me go, get off,' Julius screamed, yanking, tugging Sam's arm straight, firing again and again into his torso at point-blank range, driving him further into the room.

Sam fell backwards, on to the bed – dead weight coming easy. He could see a haze of brick dust from the bullet holes in the wall above his head. A broken window whistled, like breeze on a bottle rim.

Hysterical now, Julius yelled, threw the gun away and snatched the spike from Sam's chest – stabbing him five, six, seven times, shouting, 'You don't know what you've done,' over and over.

But Sam barely reacted to this ferocity, this violence – as he'd said to Robin, it was fine. It was all fine. As long as she had a good head start. *Only the children matter*, he thought. *Nothing else.*

After a while, the noise seemed to fall silent. He just watched as his arm was stretched up into the air, but Julius wasn't strong enough to lift him from the mattress. The image reminded him of Freddie, pulling him by the hand – come and play, come and play. But he couldn't. He was too tired. It'd been a long night.

Now a rag doll, his body useless, Sam relaxed as Julius searched each pocket. He grabbed his hip and rolled him on to his side; fingers rifled but found nothing.

Sam blinked. He saw something on the carpet – he was able to tilt his head to read: *The All-Seeing Eye*. And he remembered. Julius Jacob was the main character. The hero. JJ. A familiar name.

'It was his favourite book,' Sam whispered.

Tugged again, flat on his back, he stared up at the desperate man, at his scars and silvered hair.

'Grey . . . Iris . . . she . . . she said you were middle-aged. You dye it that colour, don't you?'

'Where are the keys?' He collapsed on to the floor, rested at Sam's knee – pleading.

'You know,' he said. 'In this light, you . . . you don't look a day older than eighteen.'

Here he was, disguised, disfigured – Ethan Clarke, all grown up.

'Oh, kid,' Sam whispered, liquid streaming from his mouth. 'I've been looking for you.'

Again, he tried to raise his head for another glimpse of that face – those eyes, these *familiar things*. It would be good to see them just one more time. But he couldn't get even an inch off the bed. Sighing, Sam went limp.

'Wow. Look at that,' he said – cold goosebumps on numb flesh. 'Look, Ethan. Can you see them?'

A thousand birds flocked above him – shifting left, then right, speckled at the edges, like stencilled graffiti. For a while, Sam wondered if they were real. Was the ceiling actually alive with wings and feathers? He felt his eyelids dip. When they opened again, he followed the pictures down the wall, to the corner of the room. On top of a chest of drawers, he saw a tin. Spray paint. Oh, it was true. The birds really were here. And, as he took his last lungful of this air, Sam squeezed Ethan's hand, closed his eyes and smiled.

Chapter 40

A dark TV studio. Producers, runners, silhouetted figures move amid the shadows. Beyond this bustle, Francis and Anna, starkly lit beneath countless bulbs, are seated on a semi-circle sofa.

'Sixty seconds.'

There are two large cameras in view – one wheels to the left, passing around a cable taped on the concrete floor. It's busy behind the lights – people wearing headphones, holding clipboards, adjusting equipment, pointing. Someone fiddles with a teleprompter and the show's director claps them away.

'Come on, move.'

The backdrop is an artificial city skyline, a Gaussian blur softens rooftops and clouds. Above this the wall turns industrial grey and, even higher, metal warehouse girders. But, when we move forwards, the chaos behind the scenes, on the left, the right, the top and bottom of the frame, it all shrinks, until a final picture emerges. Spotless carpet, plain sofa, gloss and lights. A contrived set – the product of design.

Dead centre in this limelight oasis – the people we're here to see. They're well dressed. Their faces clean and smooth with foundation. Once again, the Clarkes are ready for the cameras.

◆ ◆ ◆

The voice whispered in the muted chill of a most graceful winter. A *tap-tap* on his cell door. Francis had thought: *this is it*. A murder charge awaited. The time had come. But, in fact, there was a call for him. It was Jeremy.

No greeting, no hello, no phatic pleasantries to warm him up. Just three sublime words.

'They found her.'

Francis didn't smile – rather he opened his mouth and turned his head to the ceiling, as though catching snowflakes.

Formalities wrapped themselves up quite fast – he went from killer to victim at the flick of a switch.

When Jeremy – cool, suave, *handsome Jeremy* – arrived, Francis held out his hands and shrugged.

'I never doubted it,' Jeremy said.

'Come here.' Francis strode forwards, grabbed him by the neck and planted a firm kiss on his cheek.

They left through a fire exit in the prison's east wing. Jeremy carried Francis's bag, his own briefcase, and walked ahead. He clunked the door bar, pushed it open and let delicate daylight fall into the drab corridor. Breathing, Francis stepped outside a free man. Innocent, exonerated Francis.

Across the parking lot, they stopped beneath a swaying birch tree – its speckled bone branches, still thick with summer green, began to rattle. And, as though a gift from Mother Nature herself, the breeze plucked a single leaf. It fell, spinning, and caressed the air near his hand. Autumn. Francis knew what followed these amber days.

'How's the tooth?' Jeremy asked, opening the boot, placing the bags inside.

'Feels much better,' Francis said – his blood still soft.

He climbed into the back seat, rubbed his dry hands with moisturiser, then checked the time on his phone. A little under three hours until his next pills. Today he was celebrating, so he'd call it two hours and a double dose. Perhaps he was hooked on these chemical distractions – but, then again, *so what? Addiction is only a problem with diminished supplies. Hunger only a concern for the poor.* Francis would be able to indulge himself with every sensory delight the world had to offer. *All the things that make life worth living surely hinge on freedom.*

And yet, amid this triumph and relief, Francis still felt the weight of guilt in his stomach. As he had done as a child. Relentless persecution takes its toll. *It was*, he thought, *the logical destination for victims of any injustice.* Because when you're attacked with sufficient frequency, sufficient severity, sooner or later you'll start to wonder if – in some way – you deserve it.

But, despite countless hours spent crying alone, in a cell, in his bed, in a high-school toilet, racking his brain, asking this very question, he was unable to find a single reason why that might be so.

This made today's absolution feel hollow, maybe even temporary.

However, with a firm nod to himself, Francis decided there and then that it *was* over. Never again would he allow himself to think like that. He did *not* deserve this cruelty. And he *would* reclaim the happiness and joy the world owed him.

Jeremy drove out through the side gate and, turning down the road, had no choice but to pass along the front of the building – mere metres from the press. There were hundreds of cameras – the car strobing as they picked up speed. With a smile, Francis bid farewell to that sprawling complex of walls and wire.

'Tell me about these people,' he said.

'North Serpent is a . . . like a hardcore Christian Identity group. It's all quite sketchy at the moment, but they're saying it's somehow connected.'

'Strange.'

'Very. Set up by a woman called Diane Marston,' Jeremy said, approaching a corner, checking his mirrors.

'They arrested her?'

'Well, they would.' He indicated to turn, looked both ways. 'But she's dead. Whole family killed yesterday. Pretty much a massacre.'

'I see.'

Of course, Francis was curious, but he was in no rush for these answers. All that mattered was that Robin was safe and he was vindicated. The elaborate schemes to tarnish him had, for whatever reason, failed. And quite right too.

'The detective, Isabelle Lewin.' Jeremy stopped at traffic lights, catching his eye in the mirror again. 'She's looking into it. Links to the Clarke Foundation?'

'Still seems unlikely,' Francis said. 'But she's welcome to try.'

They were able to use a staff entrance at Hallowfield General Hospital. Still, two photographers with long lenses had it covered. Francis pretended not to notice as they clicked away.

Inside, he saw Anna from behind, standing at the foot of Robin's bed – she was clutching the frame, her knuckles clenched white. As she turned, she covered her mouth and began to cry hysterically. He held her against his shoulder and stroked her hair, weaving his fingers through the curls.

Sweet Robin was asleep.

'I'm so sorry,' Anna mumbled into his collar.

'It's OK. It's over.'

Francis touched her neck, feeling the skin Daniel had kissed. Gently, he placed his lips on the exact spot and, in his imagination, smelled him on her. Now was not the time to bring it up. Maybe it would be something he never mentioned. Admitting that he knew was, in turn, confessing to his own distrust – although, as he'd suspected at the time, the ends justified the breach in privacy. Her grip was strong – beautiful Anna clawed at his clothes, desperately bundling herself into his chest, as though she couldn't get close enough. It wasn't just anguish. It was remorse. This crazed affection would disappear if he asked her about Daniel now. Forgetting what he'd seen was not an option, but perhaps he could pretend to forgive her. Like he had done so many times before.

'I knew,' she whispered. 'I knew it wasn't true.'

Smiling, Francis nodded. 'Of course.'

Over Anna's shoulder, he looked at his daughter, sleeping soundly in the hospital bed. Her eyelids flickered with a dream – Francis hoped it was a nice one. Sweet little dreams for sweet little Robin.

'How is she?' he asked.

'They've sedated her, but she's fine.'

Rolling news now. Nothing better than a drip-fed story. Something they can talk about for hours on end. All day, all night. Boundless speculation.

'As details continue to emerge, we're joined in the studio by Detective Chief Inspector Phil Webber, who led the investigation into Robin Clarke's disappearance.' The reporter turns at the desk as the camera zooms out to reveal his guest. 'I suppose now the question has to be: how did you get it so wrong?'

'The investigation is still ongoing but, yes, it is clear mistakes were made.'

'And the suspect, Julius Jacob, what is known about him?' The screen cuts to that e-fit, and we see how poor it really is – capturing the scars, the hair, but little else.

'Not a great deal at present.' Phil clears his throat. 'The operation at the property, where it is understood Robin was kept, may take some days.'

We see footage of the house, set in tall trees along Wrenwood Common's western track. It's a soot ruin now, flanked by white tents. The second floor is partially collapsed – brick walls are all that remain – fire has torn everything else to ash. Everything besides the metal bars – some of which have survived and protrude from the scorched frame like curved fence spikes, claws warped in the heat. The blaze has singed surrounding plant life, creating a black clearing in the woods. 'I'm afraid it is too early to formally identify the remains inside.'

'And the connections to so-called North Serpent?'

'Again, the investigation is complex and we're working with colleagues to establish the sequence of events that led to the Marston killings.'

'What about the speculation that this is related, at least in some way, to the disappearance of their son, almost a decade ago? Part of the justification for arresting Mr Clarke was, as I understand, built on the assumption that lightning does not strike twice.'

'As I say, we . . . we're looking into every possibility. No stone is being left unturned. The reality is Robin is home, safe, and all charges against Mr Clarke have been dropped.'

'We'll have to leave it there.' The camera pans away from Phil and centres on the reporter again. 'And, of course, later in the programme we will bring you that exclusive interview with Anna and Francis Clarke.'

◆ ◆ ◆

For the second time, Francis met Isabelle Lewin at the Hallowfield Criminal Investigation Department. She took him into a quiet office and offered him a drink. He asked for water. It was cold and he squeezed the flimsy plastic cup, reminiscing about the dismal hours he'd spent in situations like this, unable to leave. Now, should he feel the urge, he could stand up and walk out. He hoped never again to enter a room without such liberty at his disposal. It had been a humbling way to learn that his worst fear was not shame, or pain, or even death – but the confines of a cage.

Isabelle wore a tight-fitting black top and charcoal jeans. Her slender hands were feminine despite her solid, defined forearms and sturdy collarbone. Dark, worn eyes. The kind of smoky make-up some women spent hours brushing on to their eyelids – she achieved the look with nothing but exhaustion. Tired Isabelle.

There was a stern formality in the way she spoke and moved. But, every now and then, when she turned her gaze to the wall between her calm blinks, Francis discovered an intense vulnerability. This weary dejection had aged her – added lines to her face, depth to her eyes. Still, it was undeniably attractive.

'I thought I should tell you in person,' she said, stepping around the desk. 'The remains at the house do not belong to Jacob.'

Francis sighed, because he knew what that meant. Sitting opposite, she confirmed it with a nod. This was unfortunate. Robin had described her saviour simply as 'the man who came'. Amid the trauma, she didn't quite appreciate the gravity of her rescue. Sweet Robin might never understand. And maybe that was for the best.

'I hope he found peace,' Francis said. 'He was one of the good ones.'

Isabelle exhaled, then sat up straight. 'Sam killed four people.'

'Protecting his son? Saving my daughter? Adults keep children safe, that is our job. In his position, would you have done any different?' There it was – that shimmer of instability – a diffident hesitation. 'What's wrong?'

'I let him do it,' she said.

'How do you mean?'

'I had the chance to stop him.' Unsettled, sorry Isabelle. 'And I didn't.'

'Good – imagine the alternative . . . Do your colleagues know?'

There was a pause and she shook her head.

'And in the inquiry, what will you say?'

'I'm . . .' Isabelle took a deep breath. 'I'm going to tell the truth.'

'Well, I think he would have liked that.'

She got back on track and ran through the other things they'd found at the house.

'What about the garden?' Francis asked.

'Nothing. Dog bones. Collar reads "Eli" – Diane Marston's old number on the back.'

'And your gut – what does it say? You think Jacob took Ethan as well?'

Isabelle just shrugged. Then she showed him a series of photos. Diane, Max, Gregory and Henry Marston. Francis did not recognise any of them.

As she slid the pictures back into a folder, she said, almost in passing, 'I wanted to ask you about the Clarke Foundation.'

'Go ahead.'

'It's had financial . . . difficulties?'

'Yes, some.'

A piece of paper arrived on the desk. Isabelle pointed to charts and numbers. 'Over the past few years, the foundation's made some unusual payments, which seem like grants.'

Francis nodded. 'Could be grants.'

'But they're not – the trail goes dead. Look at this. Offshore accounts. Funds are concealed.' She spread more sheets out in front of him. 'And these?'

He glanced down at the figures. 'You think it's been stolen?'

'I don't know. But someone went through a lot of trouble to frame you. It would be nice to know who and why. These paths often lead to money.'

One document had members of staff and stakeholders listed next to their respective roles. He tapped it. 'Daniel Aiden is a founder, he's a senior trustee . . . and, as we know, the sneaky fucker's not averse to lying . . .'

Isabelle took this point, turning her head to show him that she too had considered it. 'Have you spoken to him, since your release?'

'Briefly.'

'And . . . ?'

'This isn't my area of expertise, Isabelle, but there's a motive – he's the only person who could access the house, he knows the Wi-Fi password. He's smart.'

'It's a leap.'

'Who else has benefited so much from Ethan's disappearance? *The Clarkes* did wonders for his career.'

'What did he say, when you spoke to him?'

'He was kind, supportive. Although he did ask us for an interview. Can't resist the airtime.'

'Did you agree?'

'No. It's the last thing Anna wants.'

Isabelle thought for a few seconds. 'Do it,' she said.

'Why?'

'You still haven't confronted either of them?'

'About the affair? No.'

'Daniel's spent his whole career making films,' she said. 'Proving that, if you let people talk, they expose themselves. He just gives them enough rope.'

Francis had to admit he did very much like the idea of beating him at his own game. But could clever Daniel ever be clumsy Daniel? Foolish Daniel. Backed-into-a-corner Daniel.

The fake studio skyline, the plain sofa, the Clarkes waiting for the camera to roll. Francis has his hand on top of Anna's – he holds it

*at his left thigh. Dressed in beige chinos and a pale-blue linen shirt,
Daniel Aiden moves into the frame and sits opposite the couple. He
adjusts a microphone clipped by his chest as someone says, 'Thirty
seconds.'*

*Everyone who shouldn't be seen scatters away into the shadows, like
roaches under light. And then, with a final countdown, we are live.*

*Daniel doesn't reference notes, or the scrolling text on the tele-
prompter. Because he knows this story. He's told it before.*

*'On August the twelfth, two thousand and ten, a ten-year-old boy
disappeared from his home,' he says, speaking directly into the lens with
his trademark delivery. His voice is open, sincere – an authority to every
word. 'Since that day, his mother and father have lived in a state of
limbo, not knowing the fate of their first-born child. His name is Ethan
Clarke . . . Believing there could be no greater pain, an all-too-familiar
tragedy struck the family again earlier this month, with their daughter
declared missing in almost identical circumstances. Now, Robin Clarke
is home and the family is, once more, attempting to rebuild their life.
Today, the parents in the eye of this storm have been brave enough to
share their side of this extraordinary tale. Francis, Anna, thank you for
taking the time.'*

*Anna's eyes wander to the floor – she is uncomfortable. It is obvi-
ous she does not want to be here. But Francis remains engaged as they
discuss the recent weeks – he answers every question, considers each
response.*

*'For you, perhaps more than anyone,' Daniel says, shaking his
head in awe, 'this . . . this must have been like some kind of living
nightmare?'*

'It's not been an easy ride, no.'

*'What passes through your mind? What keeps you going through
something like that?'*

*'Honestly, Daniel – hope.' Francis leans forward and maintains
eye contact. These two men look as though they're speaking only to*

each other. We see the intensity, the stand-off, the tension in the air. Anna, between them in the frame, simply listens. 'A long time ago,' Francis says, 'an old friend told me something I'll always remember. He said the truth is a kind of prey – a creature that has to be pursued and dragged into the light. But I think of it more as a predator. I think, given time, the truth will take up the hunt itself. All we have to do is wait – because, Daniel, sooner or later, it will come and find you . . .'

◆ ◆ ◆

The following day, Francis was seated at the dining table, rewatching the interview on his phone. Scrolling back and forth through the video, he studied him for any chinks. But he was impenetrable. Total composure throughout.

He was so engrossed he didn't even notice Anna behind him, until she reached down and put her arm around his neck.

'Why are you watching that?' she asked.

'Dad, do you like it?' Robin said. She'd been drawing at the kitchen table and was now presenting a picture of a felt-tip butterfly.

'Very good, lovely – Mummy will put it on the fridge.'

Still holding his mobile, Francis stood and went to the bathroom. He placed the phone on the shelf below the mirror and looked at his face. Both the real him – wrinkled, fatigued – and the television version – well lit, made-up.

However, just as the final comments arrived, the video disappeared – wiped clean off the screen by an incoming call. Black glass. White text. Number withheld.

Francis clicked the hands-free button on the earphone wire to answer. He did not recognise the voice but, when it spoke, he realised who was talking. And the earth shook, every word drummed with midsummer heat, shock and thunder. A hollow squeeze replaced his heart as he held eye contact with himself and tried to find some breath amid the adrenal hurricane. But, like this moment, it was impossible.

'Dear God,' he whispered. 'Ethan?'

Chapter 41

Francis did exactly what Ethan said and told no one about the call. Instead, he travelled alone, as instructed, and left his car where he always used to – in the top right-hand corner of the forest visitor centre parking lot.

Those arduous hikes, the scout-badge expeditions – years ago now but all so familiar. These woods hadn't changed and still stirred colourful, happy memories from the moving branches – the leaves like brush bristles, painting murals as he passed. Despite the hypnotic landscape, Francis felt his armpits had dampened his shirt, not from exertion, but nerves – sheer confusion about the unruly future waiting for him at the end of the long, winding track.

As he walked, he followed Ethan – small, running ahead, throwing sticks for Button and finding trees to climb. A revenant in his imagination, smiling in columns of sun that cut down through the canopy, lighting the thick air, dense with wildlife. Insects, butterflies, occasional rabbits that loiter in the undergrowth and seem bold – as indifferent to his presence as the projections themselves. 'This way?' the picture asked. But there was no answer. Francis simply could not see himself in these memories.

He arrived at their meeting place ten minutes later than scheduled, having forgotten just how far it was from any roads or registered footpaths. Twigs crunched beneath his trekking boots as he clambered down the slope and over the protruding roots. Around the rocks, resting his hand on the rough surface for balance, he saw the secluded spot for the first time in almost a decade.

The hazel tree had grown – now a giant shroud of golden leaves dominated the area. Backlit in the sun, it gave the space an eerie glow – the saturation tweaked up a few notches, brightness just a touch above reality. Subtle enough to believe. Different enough to know something fundamental had changed.

Before he found anyone, past or present, he noticed a pile of dry mud – a spade stuck in the top, like a single candle on a birthday cake. Someone had dug a hole and, all around it, fallen leaves on the ground created a soft, golden carpet. But, at odds with the heat and the grave, this illusion dissipated as he crept further through the outlying trees, into the unveiling scene.

And Francis stopped. A full-grown man stepped into view and stood over the fresh pit – hunched shoulders, a green coat, scraggy, grey hair. Even when he turned, Francis could not believe the bounding ghost he'd imagined on the way here had appeared. Surely this was something else.

The scarring was worse in the flesh than in the digital gradients – the composite artist had sketched him from a memory of a shaded glimpse and, as such, omitted most of the damage. For someone who knew that face so well, reality's effort was a work of pure horror. Perplexity came first, followed by a feeling Francis rarely encountered. It had all the physical tells of fear.

'Fucking hell,' he whispered. 'Is . . . is that you?' But as he moved in for a closer look, the stranger reached behind and drew a black object from beneath his coat. It was a handgun. 'Hey.' Francis stood still, his arms slightly raised. 'Where . . . where did you get that?'

'From a man.' The broken voice – a deep impersonation of Ethan's – even more harrowing than on the phone. Having missed the transition, the low-pitched words boomed straight from the uncanny valley – a sound that was, in every conceivable sense, absolutely wrong.

Ethan. Strange, ruined, ugly Ethan.

'What . . . Where . . . where have you been?'

'I was hiding.'

'You . . . ?' In the early days, they had considered this an option – Ethan's bed was made, some things were missing. Although, even if he *had* run away, it would have been short-lived. Engineering his own disappearance, for any longer than a week, was incompatible with survival. And yet. 'Why?'

Snarling with what was left of his lips, Ethan aimed the pistol. 'You know why.'

Again, Francis opened his posture, showed his palms. 'I'm . . . I'm sorry,' he said, lowering his head for eye contact. 'But no, really, I don't.'

They shared a short silence, until Ethan looked away and asked, 'Did you touch her?'

'Calm down.'

'*Did you touch her?*'

'Who?'

'You *know* who.' He came forwards, gun high. 'Robin.'

'I . . . Of course, hundreds of times a day. I kiss her goodnight. Ethan, please.'

'That's not what I mean. Did you do . . . did you do to her . . .' he closed his eyes '. . . what you did to me?'

'*Pardon?*' Francis took a long, slow breath, lifted his finger and glared. He was pleased to see it still worked – the child cowered, visibly shrinking, right on cue. 'What, are, the, rules?'

'I'm . . . I'm not allowed to say it.'

'And I won't warn you again.'

Bolstered by some new courage Francis had never seen before, Ethan composed himself. 'Answer the question.' But he couldn't look at Francis. Too frightened. A puppy that knows it's been very, very naughty.

'How can I answer the question, when I don't know what you're talking about? Now, if you'd like to ask me something specific, I'm sure I—'

The pistol cracked – dirt and leaves spat into the air near Francis's boot. Canopies erupted – birds taking flight.

'Put, it, down.'

'Just tell me.' He raised the barrel. The next bullet would kill.

Francis opened his mouth to speak, but stopped, sighed and smiled. 'I . . .' He laughed. But there was uncertainty here – it was possible he might not wield dominance any more. Wild volatility and a loaded gun. His options were limited. And, clearly, he didn't have long to pick one. 'Honestly,' he said. 'No.'

With the seal broken, the forbidden topic was now fair game, dead centre on the table. 'Why?'

'Look, let's not do this,' Francis said. 'Just relax, please—'

'Is she not pretty enough? Too old? Surely not too *young*?'

One more stab at the warning – the rage and wrath that makes most of them tremble. But armed Ethan was now immune. Francis heard his own heavy breath and swallowed. This situation was not in his control – and it scared him beyond measure.

Ethan turned, gestured up at the trees. 'Do you remember bringing me here?'

'Stop.'

'You were so cruel.'

'Is . . . is that why you've done all this? Tried to destroy my life?'

'You started when I was her age. I can't let you hurt her.'

'I . . . I won't.'

'You're sadistic. That's where you find pleasure. It's not just power – you like to punish.'

Hopeless, startled Francis. He just stared back at him. It was unnerving to hear a deranged teenager summarise what should take many therapist hours – and so concisely too.

'There are others, aren't there?'

Once again, it felt as though Ethan was delving right inside him. Reading thoughts Francis was yet to have.

'Fuck . . . I . . .' He had to smile.

And Ethan did not like it – he stormed forwards, gun up, now just a couple of metres between them. *Answer me.*

'All right.' He flinched. 'Fine. Yes. There have been . . . there have been others.'

'The Clarke Foundation?'

Hands out, shaking, Francis saw lies fall off his short list of options. So, he bowed his head, and nodded.

'Is it like a dream?' Ethan whispered. More curious than angry. Perhaps even fascinated. 'Hundreds of them. Are you spoiled for choice? How many children has the charity helped? How many orphans, how many private hospital wards? How many quiet voices? Can you come and go as you please? So famous, so kind. All this generosity. Who could even suggest it wasn't real?'

Francis's tooth throbbed out a quick pulse, as though the injury had heard its name. It felt like that size-three Converse trainer, emblazoned on the heel with cartoon penguins, had kicked up hard into his face all over again, splitting the root of his lower left molar. A vibrant redhead – he should have known she'd come with a side of fire. But a slight toothache and his snowballing affinity for prescription painkillers were well worth the cost – both hurt far less than the itch of unsated desire.

Still, reality seemed to flood him – his lungs filling with the truth as he began to suffocate in these unthinkable things *that never even happened*. Except, of course, they did.

He thought of Isabelle and her perusing the foundation's books, peppered as they were with the other occupational hazard – the bravest companions and their tall tales about Mr Clarke's unusual games. *Silence was ever so expensive.* Again, he told himself that he must not worry, everything was neat, orderly, loose ends tied up well – none of those avenues led anywhere worth going. All still under control. The only genuine risk was right here, backlit from the dead in yellow and gold, holding him at gunpoint.

'Look, Ethan,' he whispered   gentle voice now. A different strategy – let the beast sleep. 'What can I do to make this better?'

'Get in.'

'No, please.'

Ethan lunged, grabbed him by his jacket collar, dragged and shoved and Francis stumbled and fell into the hole. He turned, his back against the mud wall. Dirty fingers up. Trembling.

The barrel was aimed at his head as the scarred creature stalked round to the top of the grave.

'I'm sorry – God, please, I am sorry.' Francis pleaded with his empty hands.

The face was distressing when it smiled. The scar tissue like flayed flesh, raw, exposed muscle fibres that might start bleeding at any moment. Difficult to read, but it seemed Ethan was trying to offer comfort.

'I forgive you,' he said, looking down at him. Tender compassion – a superior reassurance. 'It's not your fault.'

'No . . . I . . .'

'You don't even realise – that's what's so scary about them.'

'Them?'

'You have a demon inside you.'

Fuck, Francis thought, now certain he was dealing with madness. But he nodded and stood upright in the ground, the leaves at his elbows. 'Yes.'

'They taught me how it works.'

'Who?' *Keep talking, keep him talking.* 'The church? North Serpent?'

'She doesn't like that name any more.'

'Diane?'

'Yes.'

'Is that where you went, to live with her?'

'Eventually. When I was bigger.'

'Did . . . did she know who you were? Tell me what happened. Tell me.'

'No. I . . . I had to lie. I had . . .' Ethan blinked and sniffed – one wet eye formed a tear. It fell before he could wipe it away.

'Who did that to your face?' The question seemed obvious – and silence answered for him. 'You did it to yourself . . .'

'My photo was everywhere.'

'But . . . what did you eat, where did you sleep?'

'Lots of places. I used my survival skills. Diane, she owns land. Woods. A cave. A lake. I found her website when I researched the Devil. He is everywhere.'

'You hid the doll in the tree? Pointed it at the house? Her torch exposes evil, doesn't it?'

'The internet said it would fix you. But it didn't. You were still possessed.'

'Do you really believe that?'

'*You changed.*' He showed teeth as he jutted the gun. 'It was instant. I remember when you became cruel. You took me to the shops, we had milkshakes. I had a doctor's appointment. And then the way you looked at me was never the same again. That was the day it happened.'

'If it's true then I don't deserve . . . no one should die like this.'

'It's the only way to be sure. I've tried everything else.' Standing above him, Ethan lifted the barrel once more. Took aim. Then averted his eyes. This was it.

'No, don't. Look. *Look at me*. Ethan. Please.'

'I just can't let you do it . . . not to her.'

'I won't,' desperate Francis screamed. 'I promise. I promise. I promise I won't.'

Again, Ethan seemed to refill with strength to shout, 'You hurt me, countless other children but not Robin? Give me one good reason to believe that.'

'It's . . . I . . .'

'Go on.'

'I would never hurt Robin . . . I would never hurt Robin . . . because she . . . she is *my daughter*.'

'And I'm your son,' Ethan's voice rose at the end – a screech of despair.

But Francis tilted his head, felt his eyebrow move mere millimetres. Just enough to seed doubt.

And in that very moment, Ethan's faith, his certainty, his mad theories and juvenile confusion began to collapse.

There was no need to actually say it. In fact, Francis realised, he never even had. But perhaps this terrestrial explanation might be his ticket out of this grave.

'No, Ethan,' he whispered. 'You're not.'

'Stop . . .' Crumbling Ethan tried to maintain his aim. But he was weak. 'Stop lying.'

'The doctor's appointment . . . you remember.' Nod him back there. 'They swabbed your cheek.'

'I . . .'

'They took your saliva.'

The DNA test had seemed like a moment of fleeting insanity, something Francis expected to feel ridiculous about when recalled. How had he been so paranoid? Anna's dishonesty, her fucking treachery was all in his head. Surely it was all in his head. Just like she promised.

But when he saw the results it was like every wretched, nasty, spiteful thing anyone had ever said to him was suddenly true. A laughing stock. The fucking lies. That stupid fucking whore and this disgusting little shit he'd been raising as his own.

The entire ordeal seemed to unleash something within him. A delicate, delightful blend. Some beautiful, endlessly cathartic middle ground between lust and hate.

'Who . . . who is . . . ?'

Again, Francis let answers dance alone in the silence.

'Daniel?'

'He and your mother . . . they . . .'

'Does she know?'

'No one knows.'

'You *were* punishing me. Does it help – passing on the pain? Giving it to someone else?'

A full, honest confession. Is this what it was going to take? 'When you disappeared . . . Daniel came back . . . It's . . . it's a coping mechanism. It's that simple. I'm selfish. I am precisely what you say I am. I am a monster. But Ethan, you're not . . . You can't kill me. If you do this, then you're as bad as they are.' Yes. It was working. He was deflating. 'I'll turn myself in. Come on, let's go home. Mummy and Button have missed you.'

There was a pathetic glint of excitement. As though, with a face like that, normality was possible. Francis had him though, so he didn't break character.

'I need help,' he said as he moved to the edge, hands always in sight. 'You can help me.'

'You'll tell the truth.'

'Yes. *Of course.*' Slowly, carefully, Francis climbed out. 'You're good.' Kneeling. 'You're a good person.' On one knee. 'I can see that.'

Ethan stepped back, hesitating, his grip slack now as Francis gradually rose to his feet, advancing at a steady pace.

'You . . .'

'That's it . . . calm down.' Side on, like approaching an animal. 'Let's put all this behind us.'

'I . . .'

'Easy. Just . . .'

And he sniffed, breathed and finally lowered the gun.

Quickly, but not *too* quickly, Francis leaned down and eased it from his fingers.

'Did you dig this all by yourself?' He put the pistol in his jacket pocket.

'I did.'

'Come here.' Just like the feeble embrace from his mother, he came forwards, into open arms, and cried on Francis's shoulder. 'Hey, hey, it's OK.' He grabbed the back of Ethan's head. 'It's over now. It's over.'

'I wanted . . .' Ethan whimpered. 'I wanted them to know you were bad. I wanted to keep Robin safe. I was trying to be clever.'

'And you *were*. Planting blood. Picking locks. Leaving no other evidence. And you hid all this time. You are so smart – much smarter than me, that's for sure. You've certainly got your father's genes there.' He hugged him close, held him tight – his mouth at the rubbery ear. 'Who shall we tell? Huh? Who shall we tell?'

Lifting his head, Ethan paused for a moment – their cheeks just touching. 'Everyone,' he whispered.

'Good boy.' Now it was a single-armed hug. A proud hug. 'What say we clean all this up and head back to the car, hey?'

'Yes . . . I would like that.'

Francis should have done this years ago.

'But, on the other hand.' He looked past Ethan, through the trees through the golden leaves falling in the sunlight. 'As I always say . . . it'd be a real shame to waste such a lovely hole.'

Teeth together, he drove the pistol into Ethan's chest, pointed up and pulled the trigger twice. The sound was drier than he expected – like a baseball bat hitting a sandbag, a muffled thud. Ethan slumped, heavy on his shoulder, and Francis shoved him off. Falling backwards, he flopped against the side of the grave, rolling down, his arms limp, dragging some loose earth on top of his clothes.

Francis wiped the gun clean and threw it into the ground, along with Ethan's jumper, bunched up at the base of a nearby tree. The dirt didn't take long to shovel – he swept a lot of it straight off the pile. When it was all filled in, he brushed the ground with his foot and picked up a handful of leaves, twigs and dried mulch, which he spread over the low mound. You could hardly see it.

Then he checked the area, but felt confident that necessary precautions had already been made. Ethan wouldn't have lured him here without a clear plan of action. Even as a child, he was remarkably intelligent – sometimes worryingly so. He would have tidied the scene and prepared it well for murder. The grave too was sufficient in depth, the trees provided good cover and the ground would erode all footprints within the day.

As for the spade – the last thing left, Francis rubbed it down and, on the long walk back to the car, javelined it over the quarry fence. A distant splash – like a perfect full stop.

He took a couple more pills, then, after the three-mile hike, washed and creamed his hands in the visitor-centre toilets. Even before the drugs entered his bloodstream, he felt wonderful.

At some of his lower moments, Francis had been concerned his habits might come to light. Not from Ethan – evidently, he would sooner push his own face into flames than tell another soul – but by some other means. Something for which he couldn't account. He'd hoped for the simpler of the two scenarios – that Ethan was dead. It had niggled at him – never to the extent of Anna's obsession, but the not knowing had become a low-level anxiety Francis couldn't shake. Like the pay-outs, the legal fees, the odd kick to the jaw and a manageable dependency on opiates, it was just another thing he had to cost. But now even that was gone.

Although jubilant, he was not made of stone, and there could well be fear in him if he were to go searching. However, it was overshadowed by immense satisfaction and closure.

Along with the hard work and sacrifice of good old honest Sam Maguire – Ethan had inadvertently orchestrated what might just be an ideal scenario. An attentive wife, riddled with fitting repentance, Daniel's cuckoo genes cleansed from the earth and, perhaps most incredible of all, Francis was now the mainstream media's very own darling. Ethan Clarke. The gift that keeps on giving.

Back in his car, Francis checked the mirror and cleaned his face. He licked the edge of a tissue, dabbed a small streak of mud from his temple, then looked at himself for a while. More than once he had been told his pale eyes – blue, if a colour at all – resembled those of an Arctic dog. Maybe a husky. But no. Francis was a wolf. Only now, thanks to fate's kind hand, he was dressed head-to-toe in exquisite, priceless wool. And it felt so fucking good on his skin.

Chapter 42

' . . . because she still lived at the castle,' Francis read quietly – a bedtime-story whisper. He held the picture book on his lap, looking at Robin from time to time. 'And every night, when the drawbridge was up and the shutters were down, she would tiptoe to the stables.' He acted this out with two fingers, which he turned into legs – he walked them down the cover and she smiled. 'Down and down the stone staircase, round and round the spiral column, through and through the secret tunnel. At the front of the castle, she sat in her saddle and looked to the mountains. "Where have they gone?" asked Ruby. "Are the giants coming back?" "No," said Emerald, her hooves clip-clopping on the cobbles. "They're in their caves now."' He turned a page. '"What are they doing?" "Why, my darling diamond, they're sleeping."' And Francis gently closed the book and placed it on the carpet by his feet.

Robin stared up at him, holding her one-eyed teddy which, having previously outgrown, she returned to now for comfort. Passing her fingers over the bear's limp ear, she held her hand near her mouth. Francis could tell she was tempted to suck her thumb, but she resisted the urge.

'How tall is a giant?' she asked.

'Very. Even bigger than me.'

He bent down and placed a kiss on her warm cheek. Like the last few nights, she wrapped her small arm around his neck and held him for a couple more seconds than normal.

Flat on the mattress again, she sighed and glanced across her bedroom. 'Julius was a bad man, wasn't he?'

'He was.'

'But, when I was there, he was mostly kind.'

'He was just pretending. You don't need to worry about him any more.'

'He said he would keep me safe.'

'Sadly, sweetheart, he was lying.'

This was idle, tired chatter – she was just thinking aloud.

'Will you keep me safe?' Robin asked.

'Of course,' Francis said, tapping her nose. 'But only if you promise to do exactly what I say.'

Head on pillow, eyes shut, she smiled again. 'I promise.'

'Good girl.' Her knee was protruding from the covers – Francis slid it back into the warmth. Then he stroked her hair, pulled the duvet up over her shoulders and tucked her in. 'As snug as a bug in a rug.'

He clicked her night light on, pulled her door to and, humming quietly to himself, went to his own room.

Later, in their en suite, still humming, he took his trousers off then washed his face. Anna was already there, brushing her teeth at the right-hand sink. Three scrubs, change angle, three scrubs, change angle. Rinse the bristles, then three knocks on the china to flick off excess water. Like clockwork.

'You're in a good mood,' she said, holding back her fringe, spitting a mouthful of white dribble. Anna turned on the tap and leaned over – three quick slurps.

'Don't rinse,' Francis said. He hung his towel on the hook. 'I read that it's better for your teeth to leave some toothpaste behind. And better for your breath.'

Tiny little sparkles of pain on her face – delicious. He lived for those glimmers. The subtle ones were, by far, the best.

Her punishment required nuance and guile. This was a marathon, not a sprint. A war of attrition. Not that there was any sport in it nowadays. Anna was still a gibbering wreck most of the time – her routines hadn't improved since Robin's return. If anything, they'd been exacerbated. Perhaps the trauma was permanent. But, as with her shame, this only made his life easier.

A curious reverie arrived as he flicked on the bedside lamp and unclasped his watch. Perhaps he was emboldened by this new level of violence – as though it had stirred another dormant impulse. He imagined killing Daniel. And Francis knew now, without question, that he was capable – should such a thing become necessary, or sufficiently enticing. There's a word for the man who decides who lives and who dies.

Anna was already lying down, facing his side of the room. Her thick curls were in a bun and she was wearing her silk dressing gown over a top and her pyjama bottoms.

'You shouldn't wear it in bed.'

'I just get so cold recently.'

Francis waited. And then it happened. Anna tutted, sat up and removed the expensive lilac gown. It landed in a pile on the floor and he stomached his disgust. Of all the absurdities found in obsessive compulsions, Anna still managed to neglect tidiness and order. She couldn't even do mental illness properly.

He climbed into bed, showing her his back.

Unlocking his mobile, he felt the mattress creak as she nestled into him, kissing his neck once – for affection and probably warmth too. She would get none.

With sufficient body heat stolen, Anna moved to her side of the bed and took her phone. *The futile ritual continues*, Francis thought. Refresh every means of communication three times.

When she had finished, she faced him again.

'Do you remember the beach?' he said, sliding his phone under his pillow. He rolled on to his back and let Anna rest her head on his biceps.

'The beach?' she asked, rubbing his shoulder.

'Yeah, when you told me you were pregnant.' Warm sea. So warm you can hardly feel it. The same temperature as blood. Warm sea and beautiful Anna.

'Of course.'

'That was one of the best moments of my life.'

'Yeah?'

'Yeah.' Francis squeezed her hand.

'Me too. I thought about our family . . . I thought we would be . . .' She sighed. 'It was so nearly perfect.'

A flawless circle – the happiest day of their lives all the way round to now. Glorious, cold Ethan.

'You know . . . Isabelle was asking about Daniel the other day. She seemed to think you guys might . . . well.'

'Oh, Francis. We don't need to retread all that.'

'No, no . . . I . . . I wanted to say . . . you always told me I had to let it go. I feel like, now, I really can. I trust you, Anna. I should have been able to say this a long time ago. Nothing could come between us. I know you'd never, ever do anything like that. I shouldn't have accused you. It's like all that ugliness in the past is gone. Buried. I'm so, so sorry I ever doubted our relationship.'

He reached up and turned his lamp off – the room was dark, lit by the faint strip of Robin's night light coming through their door, open just an inch or so. They'd spent thousands on new home security, but Anna still refused to let him close it. But that was fair enough. Who knows what terrors might be lurking out there?

If Francis could have his quirks, Anna could have hers.

'We'll be OK,' she said

'Yeah,' he whispered, with all the glee she'd never see. 'We're going to be fine.'

Chapter 43

Back to that image at the side of the river, now the golden water is overcast grey – flowing away in stop-motion increments. Low resolution, low-frame rate. It is clear we have shifted back in time – the mill wheel turns, the fallen tree is old, but now it stands on the bank. And, from the bottom of the frame, we see a child. A small boy, with his hood up over his head and a rucksack strapped to his back. He follows the water that, miles from here, feeds a lake, overlooked by a cave we've seen before. In the eyes of a child trying to hide, it could be considered ideal.

Previous footage like this, the snippets of him on camera, hood up, head down, iconic features covered with bandages, scars, shade, has all been short, blurred, unreliable. The feral teen who comes from the woods and steals from the bins – he's an urban legend.

It continues, flickering forwards on a scale we rarely grasp – days pass first with sweeping shadows, arching suns, tracer stars, pinwheel nights. Weeks make months as seasons shake the trees, kill the leaves, fell that wooden bridge across the water. Time colours the view brown and white and green and back again, slowing finally on our eighth rotation.

◆　◆　◆

And blinking to another place, here he is, older, transformed, looking right at us. A close-up of all that remains of the missing child's face.

Ethan Clarke fills the entire screen and addresses the camera directly. He tells us a story.

'A sad story.'

It's about a boy who runs away from home and stays hidden until fire and age have sufficiently disguised him. He tells us about Diane Marston, who took him in, taught him how to combat the demonic forces that prowl among the good and feast on innocence. They have agents on every street, in every town, in every country on earth. Chances are, he whispers, they're nesting closer than you'd dare to think. Diane was the only person who understood.

With her guidance, her answers, it all started to make sense. At fifteen, he lived with her – the Marstons became his new family. They were all kind, he says, and he shakes his head and smiles.

'Even Max.'

But they did not, he insists, know his true identity and – despite what the news might say – they were good people. North Serpent is not the hateful group depicted in the media. Their motives, like his, are righteous.

He tells us that, in order to expose the depths of actual malevolence, he must once again employ the Devil's greatest trick.

'Deception.'

Perhaps, had he been brave enough, he could have achieved this sooner. And for that, he is truly sorry. He is sorry all this chaos and death and sin have rippled through so many lives. The two families – three if you count Sam's – utterly destroyed by a single host of this omnipotent darkness. Such is their power. All of it avoidable. If only he'd answered honestly when adults had asked the simplest of questions.

'I'm fine,' young Ethan would lie. He had feared the truth and its consequences.

But he doesn't blame himself and can't, not even under the watchful gaze of the Lord, regret his actions. The results will justify these devious tactics. All that matters, all that has ever mattered, is that Robin escapes unscathed. His own redemption is simply irrelevant.

Ethan talks about this sacrifice. He speaks of the books that make an impression on us when we're small and searching for meaning. When our minds are young. He appreciated the unique value of cameras and the depravity they so often illuminate long before these timeless fables confirmed his suspicions.

He'd sought solutions in these stories. But Hecate's torch, her pointing finger, had failed him. It seems these dark arts are not an exact science. Perhaps he was childish to think they were.

Cameras, however . . . they always work.

Towards the end, he tells us it might be difficult to watch the following film. The file will transmit in real time to another location. And, if it goes according to plan, there is a very good chance he won't be around to stop the footage.

So, there will be some delay. But, once the battery has died, it will publish automatically online. The public domain, a memetic theatre previously filled with a vacuum of half-truths and conspiracy, seems the best place for this video, whatever it unveils.

And he says a prayer

'Ultimately, we will lose the fight,' he adds. 'You can't defeat them. But you can shine the light. You can show the world.'

Once it's all laid out, he steps away from the lens, exposing a backdrop of woodland. We watch from a camera, lodged in between a thick branch and the trunk of this hazel tree. Another one of Ethan's all-seeing eyes. Like him, a lot of effort has gone into ensuring it stays hidden.

There is a clearing. The ground is soft, covered in broken twigs and a shallow layer of yellow leaves. Birds sing in the canopies, flutter down through the sun, through the golden flakes and breeze.

Everything is in place now.

He walks across the dirt, over the fallen leaves and checks his watch. He picks up a spade.

And then, in clear, high-definition clarity, Ethan Clarke begins to dig a grave.

◆ ◆ ◆

It was 11 a.m. and the house was quiet. Anna sat at the kitchen table and, having read the emails, absorbed the usual cruelty and kindness, the hollow messages that meant nothing, she had clicked on a link.

A few short, momentous minutes later, she pushed back her chair, stood and walked across the kitchen tiles, her fingertip stroked along the counter. She stopped, turned to her right – the double doors spread open, the glass gold, heaven's rays shining. A gentle domestic sound – the wooden wind chimes clattered without rhythm.

Francis was standing outside on the patio, in the morning sunlight, sipping his coffee and looking out towards the fields at the end of their long, wide garden. Beyond him, beyond the fences, harvest tractors were making stripes in the dry crops, adding dust and depth to the view.

'It's a lovely day,' he said, still facing away, swigging from his mug.

Anna agreed – it was spectacular. Better than she had ever envisaged. There was another sound, a whisper in the distance, were they sirens?

'What were you watching in there?' he asked.

'A video.'

Her phone buzzed inside, sliding along the kitchen table. The landline too began to ring.

Francis's mobile vibrated in his pocket. He took it out. 'It's Jeremy,' he said, turning, frowning at the inexplicable orchestra of tones and bells.

'Answer it.'

But when he lifted it to his ear, faced the end of the garden again and heard those words, Francis was unable to speak.

The webcam at the top of Anna's laptop. Behind the vacant chair, we see the kitchen counter, the Shun-Karyi knife set that cost more than a grand – a gift for Christmas, a gift for Francis. Ergonomic pakkawood handles sticking vertically from the top, each blade set on a small oak plinth above a square marble base. One of the slots is empty.

Tilting her head, embracing the sky, Anna felt her eyes sting. But there was no reason to cry, no sense in anger. No need for any of this drama. It was a straightforward matter. Calm and nodding to herself, she breathed it all in. This déjà vu – surreal in its clarity. As though, somehow, rehearsed so many times, it had already happened. It was, she realised, simply another routine. One, two, three. Just as she had seen.

Ethan said it was a sad story. *But it can't be,* she thought. Because, if that were true, then how come she was smiling?

For the first time in these long years, Anna felt the gentle touch of peace. This moment, like every moment, was the end of something else. *Because what is now,* she thought, *if not the very sharpest edge of then?*

Anna remembered medical school – that first surgical demonstration, those precious, irretrievably delicate spinal nerves. So vital they appear to glow in her vision, even through uncut flesh. She knew exactly what she must *never do*. And, even with the approaching storm, those sirens on the horizon, she had plenty of time to do it. One, two, three. Her steady hands.

He was right there on the patio, as he always is, and she took three steps towards him, as she always did. She felt the handle on her cardigan sleeve, wood brushing wool. The garden, swaying in the background, the grass alive with morning dew. Every blade was glistening.

Fantasies rarely retain their promise. But today, it was precisely as she'd imagined. It was just so effortlessly familiar.

After all, she'd had this dream before.

Chapter 44

Ten years pass.

We see an eighteen-year-old girl sitting alone at the back of a coffee shop, wearing a dark woollen hat that presses her blonde hair flat against her head – a few strands curl at the brim. Robin Clarke drawing in her sketchbook.

As she finishes her tea, she checks her watch and turns her attention towards the door. And a person enters. Initially, we can't see his face but, when he approaches the table, he's unmistakable. The last decade has altered Daniel Aiden in a number of ways. He has gained some weight – broader shoulders, wrists and neck – and now he fills his clothes. His hair is entirely silver and his face distinguished with new creases – dark eyes remember every smile. Middle age suits him well.

They greet one another with a kiss on the cheek and a short hug.

He sets his bag on the ground and unravels his scarf. As he removes his smart, double-breasted jacket, a waitress takes their order. After her departure, we hear that, when they last met, Robin was sixteen years old. She's taller now, he says, and looks so much like her mother.

'Honestly,' he whispers, staring at her like she's some kind of hallucination, something impossible. 'It's arresting.'

The drinks arrive as Robin and Daniel continue to reacquaint themselves – they fill the time between them with compliments, idle commentary about their respective lives and the early spring weather.

But there are odd silences in this exchange – a vague reluctance to engage on her part. Though careful not to seem rude, she keeps her syllables low and her questions rare.

'College good?' he asks.

'Almost finished now.'

'University?'

She nods, holding her mug with both hands.

'Art?'

'And design.'

'Good for you,' he says. 'Really.'

Robin places her drink on its saucer and looks out of the window.

'Anyway.' Daniel shuffles in his chair. 'As discussed – all green-lit and ready to go.' He pulls a folder from his bag. Having removed a few sheets of paper, he puts his reading glasses on and takes a breath. 'The hard part is over – now we've just got to make the thing.'

'The producer who called – is she coming?'

'I thought it would be best to discuss it with you myself.'

She turns her head back and faces him again. 'Am I the star of the show?'

A smile – Daniel's eyes are warm. 'It'll be a comprehensive film – but, yes, a lot will focus on you. Is that OK?'

Shrugging, she sighs. 'I guess.'

'I think it'll be illuminating. There's so much people don't know. We shot a couple of snippets last autumn, they're online if you want to see. To get the tone.'

'I'll have a look.'

'We even spoke to Freddie Maguire. Gives quite an insight. Funny, he's so shy when he's talking about his football career. But he'll talk for hours about his father. Sam was . . . well . . . you know.'

She nods. 'I know.'

Daniel clears his throat. 'Where are you . . . where are you living now?'

356

'Still at Tom's.'

'Tom is your . . . boyfriend?'

'We haven't said it in those terms, but . . .' Another shrug.

'Would he be comfortable to answer some questions – straightforward, talking-head scenes?'

'I'd rather keep him out of it.'

'That's cool, absolutely fine.'

Daniel passes a piece of paper to her, she reads a few sentences. 'How long will it take?'

'We'll probably shoot a month with you – on and off.' He unlocks his phone. 'I'm away this weekend, but we're doing some filming around town next Friday – are you free? Down on the bench, near the memorial. We can send a car.'

'I'll meet you there – it's not far.'

'Great – two p.m. And, Robin.' He reaches across the table, but doesn't quite touch her hand. 'I am grateful for your involvement – I know it's hard. But you really are the only good thing in all this.'

'As you said – ten years, seems a milestone.'

Robin was surprised by the nerves and doubt. Filming wouldn't be much fun – they would use some of *that* footage. Plus, although he hadn't said so, Daniel might want to get shots of her talking to her parents – something she rarely did nowadays.

Speaking with her mother was a challenge – they had grown apart through her early teens, while Robin lived with Daniel, and things had never been quite the same. There was something cold about her. A distance she did not like. Robin could stare into her eyes and it would be as though no one was looking back – like a face on the television. Clear as day, but not really there.

In some strange way, despite everything, she found conversations with her dad more straightforward. He might be vilified – guilty of crimes most consider worse than monstrous. But he had never hurt her and he was still, whether she liked it or not, her father. People were horrified to hear that – as though she had any say in the matter. Robin couldn't choose her family, or the compassion she'd developed in spite of them.

On their first date, Tom asked how she could even speak to her dad after everything he'd done.

She knew what he meant, but decided instead to answer the question in practical terms. Maybe she ought to feel guilty for quite liking the simplicity of their relationship. The silence. The tubes. The accordion that breathed for him.

'It's actually pretty easy,' she'd said. 'One blink for yes, two blinks for no.'

◆ ◆ ◆

The light was ideal, and Robin spent the rest of that afternoon at home, painting. Having finished a new piece, she took her finest brush, filled a lid with black and dipped the end to a wet point. She rolled her hair over her ear and, near the root of a tree, stroked her first initial. She would sign her work 'R. Clarke' and always, without fail, she would sigh.

Although she would never tell Tom, she often imagined their wedding day. Of course, she was getting ahead of herself – she knew these thoughts were ridiculous and, frankly, embarrassing. But, still, she yearned to smell the ink – to see the words flow from her hands. Clarke meant nothing to her now – certainly nothing good. She wanted his love. She wanted his surname.

Tom was kind – he didn't mind her filling his apartment with all her work. She'd commandeered his spare room – an open-plan studio with plenty of space for plenty of mess. It really was perfect. The roof was flat and had a lantern window in the centre which glowed with natural light. Although, now, some of the terrace ivy had spread on to the glass, so dappled grey leaves drifted across the floorboards throughout the day. Robin would chart their journey as she painted and knew that, when the shapes arrived at the desk, there was less than an hour of sun left – depending on the season. And, often, the whole place would flicker with everything flying overhead.

◆ ◆ ◆

We see the bench, from a CCTV camera on the corner of an adjacent building. The timestamp ticks, Robin has come early. She sits and waits for Daniel Aiden and his crew, for the documentary filming to commence. This camera has a set pattern – on the left of its axis, it captures the wooden seat and half of the war memorial behind. Then it turns slowly away and looks down the high street. A busy market, tarp canopies flex and ripple, steel stall supports rattle in the breeze – in digital, monochrome silence.

It stops here for a few seconds, filming the road and, at the very end, the barrier to the beach. And, in reverse, the camera sees it all again and returns to Robin. Now she's biting her thumbnail and holding her phone. She looks over her shoulder. Her knee bounces. Swivelling once more – towards the beach and kites and pixel windsurfers cutting white lines across the water.

And, with our final glance, it is 1.50 p.m. and the bench is empty. Robin Clarke, like so many things, is gone.

We can't see her. We can't hear her telling Daniel she'd made a mistake, that she's spent long enough in front of a lens, in the thoughts and conversations of strangers. Nor can we watch her painting alone in that perfect room, beneath that lantern window, lost in the shadow of all the birds above.

ABOUT THE AUTHOR

Photo © 2019 Kayt Webster-Brown

Martyn Ford is a journalist and author from the UK. His debut middle-grade children's book, *The Imagination Box*, was published by Faber & Faber in 2015 to critical acclaim and went on to become a trilogy. This was followed by 2019's standalone title, *Chester Parsons is Not a Gorilla*. This is his first novel for adult readers.

Printed in Great Britain
by Amazon

46052602R00218